MRS. SLAPMAN AT HOME.—(Book First, Chap. IX.)

ROUND THE BLOCK.

An American Novel.

WITH ILLUSTRATIONS.

NEW YORK:
D. APPLETON AND COMPANY,
443 & 445 BROADWAY.
LONDON: 16 LITTLE BRITAIN.
1864.

CONTENTS.

BOOK FIRST.

NEW YEAR'S DAY.

BOOK SECOND.

POLISHING.

BOOK THIRD.

THE TRAIL OF THE SERPENT.

BOOK FOURTH.

CHILDREN OF THE WORLD.

BOOK FIFTH.

MANŒUVRES.

BOOK SIXTH.

MYSTERIES OF THE NIGHT.

BOOK SEVENTH.

JOURNEYINGS AGAINST FATE.

BOOK EIGHTH.

A DRAMATIC INTERLUDE.

BOOK NINTH.

THE INQUEST.

BOOK TENTH.

DONE ON BOTH SIDES.

BOOK ELEVENTH.

DISCOVERIES.

BOOK TWELFTH.

SPECULATIONS—PECUNIARY AND MATRIMONIAL.

BOOK THIRTEENTH.

THE STRANGE LADY.

BOOK FOURTEENTH.

HAPPY DAYS.

BOOK FIRST.

NEW YEAR'S DAY.

CHAPTER I.

THE BLOCK.

On the east side of the block were four brown-stone houses, wide, tall, and roomy. Seen from the street, they had the appearance of not being inhabited. In the upper stories, all the curtains or blinds were closely drawn. In the lower story, the heavy lace that hung in carefully careless folds on each side of the window, seemed never to have been disturbed since it left the upholsterer's hands. Whatever life and motion there might have been in the basement, were sheltered from observation by conical firs or square-clipped box borders, set out on strictly geometrical principles in each of the four front yards. The doors were ponderous and tight fitting, as if they were never meant to be opened; and the vivid polish of their surfaces showed no trace of human handling. No marks of feet could be detected on the smooth, heavy flagstones which led up from the sidewalk, or on the great steps flanked by massive balustrades. The four mansions, in their new, lofty, and apparently tenantless state, looked like the occasional residences of people for some purpose of ceremony, rather than the dear homes of the small, loving, domestic circles that really lived there.

Such was the outer view of the east side of the block, and

it is the only view that the reader of this book will get; for it is the author's intention profoundly to respect the select seclusion of the occupants.

Now, the west side of the block was in all respects, exactly opposite to the east side. The houses were built of bricks, dingy with the whirling dust of twenty years. Two of the three stories swarmed with women and children, always visible at all seasons; and the lower story was devoted to some kind of cheap trade. Wholesale business is gregarious in its ways; but it is the habit of retail business to scatter, so as to present, in the same neighborhood, no two people in exactly the same line. Thus it happened that, on the west side of the block, there was only one drygoods dealer, whose shop front and awning posts were festooned with calicoes and other fabrics, ticketed with ingeniously deformed figures, and bearing some attractive adjective, expressing the owner's private and conscientious opinion of their excellence. There was one bootmaker, who strung up his products in long branches, like onions; and, although his business was not at all flourishing, solaced himself with the reflection that he had a monopoly of it on the block. There was one apothecary, between whose flashing red and yellow lights and those of his nearest rival there was a desirable distance. A solitary coffinmaker, a butcher, a baker, a newspaper vender, a barber, a confectioner, a hardware merchant, a hatter, and a tailor, each encroaching rather extensively on the sidewalk with the emblems of his trade, rejoiced in their exemption from a ruinous competition. The only people on the block whose interests appeared to clash, were the grocers, who flanked either corner, and made a large and delusive show of boxes, barrels, and tea chests; and it was strongly suspected that they were identical in interests, under different names, and maintained a secret league to catch all the custom of the vicinity.

The south side was a gradation of buildings, from the two-story brick grocery on the west corner to the grandest of the stone mansions on the east. With the exception of two or three houses built in the early history of the block, and occupied by obstinate old proprietors, it presented such a regularly ascending line of roofs, that a giant could have walked up stairs from one end to the other. Although each house was built upon a plan peculiar to itself, and supposed to reflect the long-cherished views of the original owner, there were certain resemblances among them. This was sometimes the effect of a jealous rivalry; sometimes of imitation. In one dozen houses there was a costly struggle for supremacy in window curtains. In another dozen, the harmless contest pertained to Grecian urns crowned with flowers, or dry dolphins, tritons, or naiads, rising from the bosoms of little gravel beds in miniature front yards. In a third dozen, there was a perspective of broad iron balconies elegantly constructed for show, and sometimes put to hazardous use, on warm summer nights, by venturesome gentlemen with cigars, or ladies with fans.

About the middle of the block was a colony of doctors, who had increased, in five years, from two to ten. Their march was eastward, and it could be calculated to a nicety how long it would be before the small black, gilt-lettered signs of their profession would press hard upon the great house at the corner. Why they thus congregated together, unless with the friendly purpose of relieving each other's patients in each other's absence, and so saving humanity from sudden suffering and death, was a mystery to everybody but themselves.

The north side lacked variety. One part of it, comprising twenty lots, had been built up on speculation by an enterprising landowner. The houses were precisely alike, from coal cellar to chimney top, with front railings of exactly the same pattern, crowned with iron pineapples from the same mould, encompassing little plots of ground laid out in walks similar to the fraction of a hair; the sole ornaments of which were four little spruce trees, planted at equal distances apart.

This row of houses was very distracting even to the occupants, with whom it was a feat of arithmetic to identify their homes in the daytime, and much more so at night, when the landmarks were shadowy and indistinguishable. Occasionally, well-meaning tenants found themselves pulling at wrong door-bells; and there was one man who got tipsy every Saturday night, and rang himself quite through the row before he tumbled in on his own hall carpet. It was in counting the spruce trees, he said, which had a perplexing way of doubling, that he invariably lost the track.

In nearly every house on this block there was a piano. The piano was the great equalizer of the block. And, though in the loftier houses the pianos might have been larger and costlier, and unquestionably noisier, it did not follow that they were better played or pleasanter to hear than the humbler instruments which served to swell the tumultuous chorus in hours of morning practice. With regard to these pianos, it may here be observed, that a gentleman with a passion for statistics, who chanced to be well acquainted through the block, made the remarkable discovery that the players were usually unmarried ladies; and that, when they acquired husbands (as they occasionally did on that block), they put aside the piano as something quite incapable of contributing to their new-found happiness.

CHAPTER II.

THREE BACHELORS.

Near the centre of the north side of the block stood a house in which three men, who have much to do in this story, were whiling away an hour before dinner, at the edge of evening, in the month of December, 185–. The house had strange stones let in over the windows and door, and was broad and sturdy, and was entered by steps slightly worn, and was shaded by a tall and old chestnut tree, and showed many signs of age. It was because of these evidences of antiquity, although the house was in good preservation and vastly comfortable, that it had been picked out and rented by the three men, two weeks previously.

Yet the three men exhibited no marks of age, past or coming, upon them. The oldest, Mr. Marcus Wilkeson, looked no more than thirty-two; but frankly owned to thirty-six. Being six feet and two inches high, having a slim figure, round face, smooth brow, gentle eyes, perfect teeth to the utmost extent of his laugh, and a head of hair free from the plague-spot of incipient baldness which haunts the young men of this generation, his appearance, now that he was confessedly a man, was very much like that of an overgrown boy. On the contrary, when he was really a boy, his extraordinary height (six feet at sixteen years) had given him the outward semblance of a premature man. Probably his long legs and arms, which were exceedingly supple, and were always swinging about with a certain juvenile awkwardness, contributed much to the youthfulness of his appearance.

At the time of his introduction here, his legs were as quiet as in their nature they could be, having been elevated, for the greater comfort of the owner, to the top of a pianoforte, and presenting an inclination of forty-five degrees to Mr. Wilkeson's body, reposing calmly and smoking an antique pipe in his favorite chair below. One of his long arms was hanging listlessly by his side, and the other made a sharp projecting elbow, and terminated in the interior of his vest. This was the attitude which, of all possible adjustments of the human anatomy, Mr. Wilkeson preferred; and he always assumed it and his pipe the moment he had put on his dressing gown and Turkey slippers. He was well aware that popular treatises on the "Art of Behavior" and the "Code of Politeness" were extremely hard upon this disposition of the legs. His half-sister, Philomela Wilkeson, who was high authority, had often visited his legs with the severest censure, when, upon suddenly entering the room where he was seated, she found the offending members confronting her from the top of the piano, or the table, or a chair, or sometimes from the mantelpiece. While Marcus Wilkeson admitted the full force of her strictures as applied to legs in general, he claimed an exception for his legs, which were always in his own or other people's way when they rested on the floor, or were crossed after the many fashions popular with the short-legged part of mankind.

Marcus Wilkeson's heretical opinion concerning legs was part of a system of independent views which he entertained of life generally. He had given up a profitable broker's shop in Wall street, a year before, because he had made a fortune ten times larger than he would ever spend. Having fulfilled the object for which he started in business, and for which he had toiled like a slave ten years, he conceived that nothing could be more sensible than to retire from it, make room for other deserving men, and enjoy his ample earnings in the ways which pleased him most, before an old age of money getting had deadened his five senses, his intellect, and his heart.

Persons who knew Marcus Wilkeson well were aware that he was a shy, self-distrustful fellow, amiable, generous, and that the only faults which could possibly be alleged against him were an excessive fondness for old books, old cigars, and profitless meditations, and a catlike affection for quiet corners. And when his half-sister Philomela—who had no hypocritical concealment about her, thank heaven! and always told people what she thought of them—pronounced the first of those luxuries "trash," the second "disgusting," and the other two "idiotic," he met her candid criticisms with a pleasant laugh, and said that, at any rate, they hurt nobody but himself.

To which Philomela invariably retorted: "But suppose every strapping fellow, at your time of life, should take to novel-reading, and such fooleries, what would become of the world, I would like to know?"

And her brother, puffing out a long stream of smoke, would respond: "Suppose, my dear sister, every woman was destined to be an old maid, as you are, what would become of the world, *I* would like to know?"

The conversation always terminated at this point, by Philomela declaring that coarse personality was the refuge of weak-minded people when they could not answer arguments, and that, for her part, she would never take the trouble to say another plain, straightforward word for his good; whereupon there would be a truce, lasting sometimes a whole day.

Fayette Overtop, the second of the three young men—the one looking out of the window, drumming idly on the glass, and continually tossing back his head to clear the long black hair from his brow, over which it hung in an incurable cowlick—was a short, compact, nervous person, twenty-five years old. Mr. Overtop had been educated for the law, but, finding the profession uncomfortably crowded when he came into it, had not yet achieved those brilliant triumphs which he once fondly imagined within his reach. For three years he had been in regular attendance at his office from nine A. M. to three P. M. (as per written card on the door), except in term time, when he was a patient frequenter of the courts. During these three years he had picked up something less than enough to pay his half of the rent of two small, dimly lighted, but expensive rooms on the fourth floor of a labyrinth in the lower part of the city.

Mr. Overtop, when asked to explain this state of things, about which he made no concealment, always attributed it to a "lack of clients."

If he had clients enough, and of the right kind, he felt confident that he could make a figure in the profession. Having few clients, and those in insignificant cases only, of course he had no opportunities for distinction. He could not stand in the street and beg for clients, or drag men forcibly into his chambers and compel them to be clients; and he would not degrade the dignity of his calling by advertising for clients, or taking any means whatever to get them, except by establishing a reputation for professional learning and integrity. The only inducement which he ever put in the way of clients, was a series of signs, outside the street door, on the first flight of stairs, at the head of the first landing, on the second flight of stairs, at the head of the second landing, and so on to the fourth floor, where the firm name of "Overtop & Maltboy" confronted the panting climber for the eighth and last time, painted in large gold letters on black tin, nailed to the office door.

Mr. Overtop was willing to give clients every facility for finding him, when they had once started at the bottom of the building; and would, as it were, lead them gently on, by successive signs; but good luck and a good name, slowly but surely acquired, must do the rest.

A snug property, of which Mr. Overtop spent less than the income, fortunately enabled him to indulge in these novel views, and to regard clients, much as they were desired, as by no means indispensable to his existence. In his unprofessional hours, Mr. Overtop was everything but a lawyer. He was chiefly a philosopher, a discoverer, a searcher after truth, a turner-up of undeveloped beauties in every-day things, which, he said, were rich in instruction when intelligently examined. He could trace out lines of beauty in a gridiron, and detect the subtle charm that lurks in the bootjack.

As not unfrequently happens, in partnerships of business and of other descriptions, Matthew Maltboy—the young man standing before the blazing coal fire, and critically surveying his own person—was quite the opposite of Fayette Overtop. Maltboy was fat and calm. Portraits were in existence showing Maltboy as a young lad in a jacket and turn-down collar, having a slim, graceful figure, a delicate face, and a sad but interesting promise of early decay upon him. Other portraits, of the same original, taken at later periods of the photographic art, represented a gradual squaring out of the shoulders, a progressive puffiness in the cheeks, lips, and hands, incipient folds in the chin, and a prevalent swollen appearance over all of Matthew Maltboy that the artist permitted the sun to copy.

Portraits of Maltboy for a series of years would have proved a valuable contribution to human knowledge, as showing the steady and remarkable changes through which a man who is doomed to be fat passes onward to his destiny. But Maltboy stopped sitting for portraits when he reached the age of twenty, deciding, as many another public character has done, to transmit only the earlier and more ethereal representations of himself to posterity.

By some compensating law of Nature, there were given to Maltboy a light and cheerful heart, a tendency to laugh on the smallest provocation, and a nice susceptibility to the beautiful. Not the beautiful in rivers, forests, skies, and other inanimate things, but the beautiful in woman. And as Overtop was gifted to discover charms in material objects which were plain in other eyes, so Maltboy possessed the wonderful faculty of seeing beauty in female faces, where other people saw, perhaps, only a bad nose, dull eyes, and a pinched-up mouth. This mental endowment might have been a priceless gift to a portrait painter, who was desirous of gratifying his sitters; but it was for Matthew Maltboy a fatal possession. It had led him to love too many women too much at first sight, and to shift his admiration from one dear object to another with a suddenness and rapidity destructive to a well-ordered state of society.

Though these multiplied transfers of affection occasionally caused some disappointment among the victims of Mr. Maltboy's inconstancy, it was wisely ordained that he should be the principal sufferer—that every new passion should involve him in new difficulties, and subject him to a degree of mental distress which would have reduced the flesh of any man not hopelessly predisposed to fatness. As Mr. Matthew Maltboy stood by the fire, he was not taking the profitable retrospective view of his life which he should have taken, but was glancing with an expression of concern at the circumference of a showy vest pattern which cut off the view of his legs.

The apartment in which the three bachelors were keeping a meditative silence, was large, square, high, on the first floor back, commanding an ample prospect of neglected rear yards, and all the strange things that are usually huddled into those strictly private domains. The furniture of the room was rich and substantial, but not too good to be used. The chairs were none of those frail, slippery structures of horsehair and mahogany so inhospitably cold to the touch; but they were oak, high backed, deep, long armed, softly but stoutly cushioned with leather, and yawned to receive nodding tenants and send them comfortably to sleep amid the fragrant clouds of the after-dinner pipe or cigar.

At one end of the room was Marcus Wilkeson's library, consisting of about five hundred volumes, of poems, novels, travels by land and sea, histories, and biographies, which the owner dogmatically held to be all the books in the world worth reading. The admission of a new book to this select company of standard worthies, Mr. Wilkeson was vain enough to regard as a high compliment to the author, and as a final settlement of any disputes which might have been abroad as to its merits.

On another side of the room was a grand piano, open, and covered with the latest music, and sometimes played on in a surprisingly graceful manner by the fat fingers of Matthew Maltboy. On the walls hung some pictures, that were not unpleasant to look at. There were two portraits of danseuses, with little gauzy wings, and wands tipped with magic stars; one large, full-faced likeness of a pet actress, taken in just the right attitude to show the rounding shoulders, the lightly poised head, and the heavy hair, to the best advantage; some charming French prints, among them "Niobe and her Daughters" and "Di Vernon;" and a half dozen pictures of the fine old English stage-coach days. Over the fireplace were suspended several pairs of boxing gloves, garnishing the picture of a tall fellow in fighting attitude, whose prodigious muscles were only a little smaller than those of all the saints and angels of all the accredited masterpieces of ancient art. A pair of foils and masks, neatly arranged over each corner of the mantelpiece, completed the decorations of the room.

The three bachelors had gone into housekeeping by way of experiment, as a relief from the tedium and oppression of hotels and boarding houses, and as an escape from female society, which was beginning to pall even upon the huge appetite of Matthew Maltboy.

But two weeks of this self-imposed exile—with no female society but Miss Philomela Wilkeson, and Mash, the cook—proved rather too much for Matthew's fortitude. He yawned audibly.

"I understand you," said Marcus; "you are sick of this."

"Well—hum—it's a little prosy at times." Maltboy yawned again.

"Incorrigible monster!" cried Marcus. "What shall we do with him, Top?"

The person addressed swung back the rebellious cowlick from his forehead, as if to clear his thinking faculties from a load while he considered the grave question. "Do with him? Do with him? Oh! I'll tell you." Here the speaker's eyes flashed with the light of a great discovery. "Tether him like a horse, with a certain limited area to feed in. D'ye see? D'ye see?"

"A horse? Can't say that I do," returned Mr. Marcus Wilkeson.

"And I can't say that *I* do, either," added Mr. Matthew Maltboy. "A horse! Why not say a donkey? I should see it quite as well."

"As you please," resumed the impetuous Overtop. "A donkey, then. Perhaps the metaphor will be better. What I mean—what you two are so dull as not to see—is to put this unreliable Maltboy on a moderate allowance of flirtation; to keep him, for example, within the limits of this block. D'ye see? D'ye catch the idea?"

"It begins to dawn on me," said Wilkeson.

"And I catch a ray or two of it," added Maltboy. "But——"

"Excuse me," interrupted Overtop, stepping between his two companions, and gesticulating wildly at each of them in turn, as if he would dart conviction into them like electricity from the tips of his fingers. "Here is a block full of people.

Their houses are joined together, or nearly so, all the way round. The inhabitants hear each other's pianos playing and each other's babies squalling all day long. If a fire breaks out in the block, it may be all burned down together. If the measles makes its appearance on the block, it probably runs through it. Is there not, therefore, a community of dangers among us; and if of dangers, why not of pleasures? Why should not the inhabitants of a block be regarded as a distinct settlement, or tribe, whose members owe kindness and good-will to each other before the rest of the world? Looking at it in the light of humanity, is it not our duty to know our neighbors?"

"And Matt would say, To love them too—that is, the young and pretty ones," observed Wilkeson.

"Precisely," said Maltboy.

"Excuse me," continued Overtop, deprecating further interruption with both hands. "That is the point I was just coming to. Since Maltboy *must* have female society, and cannot be kept out of it by main force, why not give him the range of this block? Catch the idea, eh?—in its full force and bearings?"

Wilkeson and Maltboy implied, by nods, that they caught it.

"And—ahem—I think I'll take the same range too," added Overtop. "Not because I care a pin about female society, but just to test my new theory."

Cries of "Oh! oh!" from Marcus Wilkeson.

Overtop laughed. "You'll be a convert to it yet, my good fellow."

"Never," said Marcus, inflexibly, "so long as books and tobacco hold out."

"We'll see," replied Overtop. "But let me think how we are to begin." He rubbed his nose with a forefinger, then tossed back the cowlick, and said, impetuously: "I have it—I have it! We know Quigg, the grocer, at the corner below, for we are customers of his. Of course, he has an immense number of customers on the block, and will make New Year's calls on all of them, in the way of business. Why can't he take us in tow? It's as plain as daylight."

"Plain enough, I admit," said Marcus Wilkeson; "but what will Quigg's customers say?"

"Poor fellow!" returned Overtop. "How feebly you hermits reason about society! If you had knocked round town on New Year's days, as Matt and I have often done, you would know that visitors are valued only because they swell the number of calls, and that it is entirely immaterial who they are, or who introduces them. The militia general, the banker, the judge, the D. D., the butcher, the drygoods clerk, are units of equal value on that day, each adding one more to the score which is privately kept behind the door. We shall be welcome; never fear for that. You must come with us, and see for yourself."

"I thank you," said Marcus Wilkeson, laughing. "No such fooleries at my time of life."

"Very well," said Overtop. "Matt and I will try to represent the new firm of bachelor housekeepers creditably. Matt will look after the pretty girls, and I after the sensible ones—that is, if there happen to be any on this block."

"Agreed," observed Matthew Maltboy, catching a view of himself in a glass over the fireplace, and not wholly displeased with his appearance.

"Another thought strikes me," said Overtop, explosively. "It's nearly half an hour to sunset. I am impatient to begin my acquaintance with our fellow citizens—our future friends, if I may so call them. Let us look out of the windows, and see what the excellent people are doing. Perhaps it may interest even a recluse and bookworm like you."

"Nonsense," rejoined Marcus Wilkeson. "There's no curiosity in my composition."

And yet, when his two companions stood at the window of the little back parlor, pressing their noses against the glass, and looking out, he could not resist the temptation to join them, although he thought proper to punch them in the ribs, and call them a pair of inquisitive puppies, by way of showing how much he was superior to the great human infirmity.

CHAPTER III.

PEEPS.

THE uniform row of houses on the other side of a dead waste of snow, to which the attention of the three friends was ardently directed, promised, at first sight, a poor return of instruction and entertainment. The rear view presented one dull stretch of bricks irregularly set even in those houses which displayed imposing fronts of brown stone. The blinds were of a faded green color, and broken. The stoops, the doors opening on them, and the steps leading down to the dirty, sodden snow, had a generic look of cheapness and frailty. Whatever the censorious critic might say of the front, he could not charge the rear with false pretences; for there was apparent, all over it, an utter indifference to the opinions of mankind. Perhaps because the owners of the houses did not expect mankind to study their property from that point of view.

"Say!" was Mr. Fayette Overtop's first remark, after a moment's observation; "do not those rustic fences on the roofs remind you of the sweet, fresh country in summer time?" Mr. Overtop alluded to the barriers which are erected to keep people from getting into each other's houses, and which are scaled not without difficulty even by cats.

Neither of his friends answering this remark except by a quiet, incredulous smile, Overtop continued, a little pettishly:

"And you really mean to tell me that that pastoral object, happily introduced on the roofs of houses, does not recall the green fields, daisies, babbling brooks, and cloudless skies of early boyhood? Humbug!" The speaker flattened his nose still more against the glass by way of emphasis.

"You look for beauties among the chimney pots, while I

search for them in back-parlor windows," said Matthew Maltboy. "Observe where I throw my eye now."

Mr. Maltboy threw his eye toward a house near the middle of the block. His companions followed it, and saw a tall girl with prodigious skirts standing at a window, and looking, as they thought, at them. The view which she obtained was evidently not satisfactory, for with her handkerchief she wiped off the moisture from several of the panes; and, when the glass was clear to her liking, shook out the folds of her dress, and peered forth again, this time more decidedly, at the window occupied by the three friends. Her use of the handkerchief was not lost upon Maltboy, who straightway pulled out his extensive cambric, and polished up their window too. This improvement of the medium of vision on both sides, enabled the three friends to form some idea of the tall girl's personal charms. Her figure was straight; her hair was black; her eyes were brilliant; her complexion was healthy; she exhibited jewelry in her ears, on her neck, her bosom, her wrists, and her fingers; her dress gave her a great deal of trouble, as she leaned forward to look out.

"Charming, is she not?" said Maltboy.

"Hard to say, at this distance," returned Overtop, who, feeling neglected in the matter of the rustic fence, was controversially disposed.

"You may find it so," said Maltboy; "but as for me, the flash of her eyes—there, now, for instance!—is convincing enough."

"Perhaps you have seen her before," remarked Marcus Wilkeson.

"*Per*haps," was that gentleman's answer, implying, by his accent and accompanying wink, that he had seen her repeatedly.

"And said nothing about her to us, you inveterate humbug," added Marcus.

Mr. Maltboy felt the compliment conveyed in the word "humbug"—as most people do when that accusation of shrewdness and deep dissembling is brought against them—and smiled.

"I confess," he replied, as he polished the window simultaneously with the performance of that process across the way, "I confess I have noticed her several times; but what was the use of mentioning it to a pair of woman haters like you?"

His two companions laughed pleasantly, thereby expressing their gratification at the return compliment involved in the phrase "woman haters."

"You are such dull fellows now," continued Maltboy, "that perhaps you will say this fair stranger is not looking at us; that she does not desire to be seen by us—that is, by me; and that her rubbing of the window with a handkerchief is not a signal which she expects to be answered."

"We say nothing," replied the disputatious Overtop. "We only wait for proof. It is easy to find out whether a signal is meant or not. Rub the window now."

Maltboy did so, concluding the act with an unmistakable flourish of the handkerchief. Whereupon the tall girl averted her face, pulled down the curtain, and eclipsed herself.

Wilkeson and Overtop laughed, and, with a common impulse, punched Maltboy triumphantly in the ribs—a friendly salute that was always vastly amusing to that gentleman.

"Be it understood, at this stage of affairs," said Marcus, solemnly, "that I reject the Overtop theory, and wash my hands of all responsibility for Maltboy's misdeeds.—Hallo! There he is again."

"Who? Where?" exclaimed his two friends.

"In the house nearly opposite—the one with the grape arbor. Isn't he a fine old fellow?"

Overtop and Maltboy looked, and there saw, sitting at a window, and placidly gazing out of it, an old gentleman with long and thick white hair, a ruddy face, a white neckcloth, and a large projecting shirt frill—which were all the peculiarities of person and dress that could be distinctly made out. He was smoking a long pipe, and placidly rocking himself to and fro. His appearance, through the two windows, was that of a finely preserved relic of a past generation.

"He always has a long pipe in his mouth, and looks benignantly into the open air," said Wilkeson.

"So even *you* are not wholly devoid of curiosity, and do take some interest in the people on our block," remarked Matthew Maltboy.

"I have noticed the old gentleman often, when I have been reading near the window; and own that I should like to know him. I think, too, from certain signs, that he would not object to knowing me. Unless I am much mistaken, he has bowed to me several times. But fearing that the supposed bow might have been nothing more than a sleepy nod, I have never ventured to answer it. Step back a moment, and see if he observes me."

Maltboy and Overtop retired a few paces. A moment afterward, the old gentleman looked over to Wilkeson, and made a bow at him about which there could be no mistake.

"Answer him." "Answer him," said his two friends. Acting upon this advice, Marcus Wilkeson, blushing, returned a courtly salute, which was immediately reciprocated by a still lower bow, and a pleasant smile from the old gentleman. Wilkeson bowed again, and added a smile. The old gentleman did the same; and this odd exchange of civilities was beginning to get awkward for Wilkeson, when the old gentleman's attention was suddenly called off.

A slender young man, whose broad black mustache contrasted unpleasantly with the sallow whiteness of his face, dressed in the jauntiest costume of the period, and bearing in one hand a black cane with a large ivory handle, which looked, even in the distance, like a human leg, stood by the old gentleman's side. The old gentleman put down his pipe, seized the young man's disengaged hand, and gazed affectionately at him (so the three observers thought). Some conversation then took place between them, during which the old

2

gentleman repeatedly pressed the young man's hand, and sometimes reached up and softly patted him on the shoulder. The young man appeared to receive the words and caresses of the old gentleman with a sullen indifference. Several times he pettishly drew his hand away, and at last shook his head fiercely, folded his arms, and seemed (though the spectators could only conjecture that) to stamp the floor with his foot. At this, the old gentleman bowed his head in his hands. The young man held his defiant attitude unmoved, until, glancing out of the window, he saw for the first time that he was watched. With a jerk, he pulled down the curtain, and cut off a scene which the three observers had begun to find profoundly interesting.

"Well," said Marcus Wilkeson, "though I have given up making calls as a business, I shall certainly take the New-Year's privilege of dropping in on the venerable unknown over the way."

"Two things are plain," said Fayette Overtop. "One is, that the pale, rascally looking young man is the old man's son. Now, I don't suppose either of you will dispute that?" (Overtop paused a moment to receive and dispose of objections, but none were made.) "The other is, that the old fellow is immensely rich—worth a million or two, maybe. Perhaps you *would* like to argue that point." Overtop smiled, as if nothing would give him greater pleasure than to annihilate a few dozen opinions to the contrary.

"To save argument, as usual, we admit everything," responded Wilkeson. "But, pray condescend to tell us how you know this fine old boy to be superlatively rich."

Overtop smiled upon his ignorant friends, and answered:

"Because he wears a white cravat. The man isn't a clergyman, is he? Do clergymen smoke pipes? He isn't a Quaker, is he? Do Quakers, or those of them who indulge in white cravats, wear their coat collars turned down? Consult your own experience, now, and tell me whether you ever saw anybody but a very rich man (with the exceptions already stated) wearing a white cravat. I leave it to your candor."

Wilkeson and Maltboy nodded their heads, as if stricken dumb with conviction.

Overtop, gratified with this ready acquiescence, modestly went on to say that he would not undertake to explain the phenomenon; that task he left to some more philosophical mind. He contented himself with making a humble record of facts.

"And now that each of you have made a discovery in the row of houses, let me try my luck." Overtop rubbed the window, looked out, and carefully surveyed the row from end to end, and back again. "Ah, I have it!" he said. "A real mystery, too. Look at that four-story house near the western end of the block, the one a trifle shabbier than its neighbors. Do you see, in the open window, a man with a pale, intellectual face, gray hair, and arms bare to the elbows, filing away at something held in a vise before him? Now he stops to examine a paper—a plan, probably—which he holds in his hand. Now he wipes the perspiration from his forehead. Can't you see him?"

"Distinctly," was the joint reply.

"What do you suppose he is doing?" asked Overtop.

"No idea," said Wilkeson. "Perhaps mending a tea-kettle."

"Or repairing an umbrella," suggested Maltboy.

Overtop smiled, and said:

"A person with the slightest powers of observation, would see that that man has genius in his face; that his thin arm is not used to hard mechanical labor; that his brain is so heated with great ideas, that he tries to cool it by opening the window. The tinkering of an umbrella or teakettle would not make a man sweat in midwinter. You won't deny the force of that suggestion."

As he spoke, a young girl advanced from the back part of the room, and stood by the pale workman's side. She wore a bonnet, and a shawl tightly wrapped around her. Though the features of her face could not be distinguished in the distance, it was not hard to detect a pleasant expression in her eyes, a smile on her lips, and a high color on her cheeks, as if she had just come in from the street. She held up a little basket for the workman's inspection.

He paused in his labor, took the girl's head between his hands, and kissed her fondly on the brow. Then he opened the little basket, and drew from it a loaf of bread and a piece of cheese, which he began eating hurriedly. He also seemed, by signs, to press the girl to eat; but she shook her head, smiled more than before, and looked up affectionately into his face. Having bolted a few mouthfuls, the workman placed the remains of the repast on the bench or table before him, kissed the young girl, and resumed his work. She watched every motion of his hand with eager eyes. Once she moved as if to close the window, but he shook his head, and again wiped the sweat from his brow.

He had consulted the paper, and attacked his task with fresh energy for the third or fourth time, when his eyes happened to rest upon the window full of scrutinizing faces. His lips moved in some sudden exclamation, and then he shut the window with vehemence, and drew the curtain which obscured the lower half of it.

"Not a very kind reception of your theory, so far," said Marcus.

"Prejudice—nothing more," said Overtop. "When they see that we have no wish to pry into their private affairs, but are animated with a neighborly regard for them, they will not repel our advances. It isn't human nature."

CHAPTER IV.

QUIGG.

During the following two weeks, up to New Year's day, the three friends made little progress in their observations. The tall girl in the immense skirts appeared rarely to reward Matthew Maltboy's ardent gaze, and even then seemed to look down at the dingy snow beneath, or the clouds overhead, or to something or somebody across the way, but never to the fluttering Maltboy.

Nothing more was seen of the pale and grayhaired workman; for he kept the lower curtain of his window jealously drawn. But at night his shadow, strongly projected on the curtain, was in incessant motion; and far into the morning hours a gigantic head and arms shifted and blended upon it in grotesque forms. At the other window of the workman's apartment the young girl often sat, book in hand, and moved her lips as if she were reading aloud. Her eyes were never seen to wander to the outer world with those longings for freedom and fresh air which are natural to the youthful heart, but were always fixed upon the book, or upon some object within the room. She was entirely unconscious of the distant and imperfect scrutiny to which her form and movements were subjected by Marcus Wilkeson, who had begun to take a strange interest in her, and in the shadow on the curtain, since the healthy and amiable old gentleman directly opposite had ceased to smoke his pipe and indulge in his tranquil meditation daily.

Twice only had he shown himself, and then, after a grave bow to Marcus Wilkeson, who returned it with more than the usual inclination of head, the old gentleman had taken a few whiffs at his pipe, looked out of the window with a troubled air, and vanished from the sight of his sympathizing observer, as if the quiet old sitting place had lost its charm for him. The young man—the disturbing element of the old gentleman's life, as Marcus Wilkeson regarded him—was not again seen in the room where he had made his first appearance, but was discovered, several days after that event, sitting at a table near a window in the second story, and writing industriously. His labors were evidently not disagreeable; for, after an hour's engagement with his pen, he would sit back in his chair, laugh, take a long drink from a black bottle which stood at his elbow, and light a fresh cigar. Whatever his occupation, he was completely absorbed in it, and did not notice the pair of keen eyes peering at him from behind a book in the house opposite. Every afternoon, about three o'clock, the young man sat at the table with his bottle, cigars, and writing materials, and pursued his pleasant labors.

Marcus Wilkeson would never have pretended that it was not highly improper to watch one's neighbors. He would have denounced it as deserving of the severest reprobation. But he would have said, that if, while he was sitting, according to his invariable custom, at his own window, for the sole purpose of reading a book, people chose to bring themselves within the range of his vision, he was not therefore under obligations to vacate his seat. He would have insisted that any glances which he might have directed at his neighbors, were so levelled in fits of mental abstraction, or in the exercise of a friendly regard for them. The Overtop theory he discarded as fallacious, and likely to get its talented founder into trouble.

That founder and his only follower, Maltboy, were determined, however, to put the new social system into practice on New Year's day, and had secured the ready services of Quigg, the grocer, as originally proposed by the sagacious Overtop. Marcus Wilkeson obstinately refused to participate in this projected grand tour; which refusal was too bad, said Overtop, because the fourth seat in the double sleigh that had been hired for the occasion would be left vacant.

At last came New Year's day; and the sky was cloudless, and the sun was bright, and the weather was just cold enough to make the blood tingle pleasantly, and the snow was a foot deep, and well beaten down in the side streets. The elements themselves had conspired to give the Overtop theory every chance of success.

J. M. Quigg, grocer, was elaborately attiring himself in the snug sleeping room behind his store, at ten o'clock on the morning of the eventful day. He little knew the tremendous importance of the part which he was about to perform. He looked upon Overtop and Maltboy, not as the expounders of a new social philosophy, but as cash customers to a considerable extent, and as partners in defraying the heavy expenses of a large double team. Mr. Quigg exercised the virtue of prudence even in his dissipations, and derived pleasure from the reflection that he would make his annual round of complimentary calls in an elegant turnout at a moderate cost.

Therefore Mr. Quigg hummed pleasantly as he dressed himself, by the aid of a large mirror which he had taken for a bad debt, and which was the only ornament of the plainly furnished little room. Mr. Quigg was a man of business, and never fretted with cravats, nor made himself unhappy on the subject of hair. Three turns and a pull adjusted the former; and a half dozen well-directed dabs with a stiff brush regulated the latter. Fifteen minutes after he began his toilet, he took a comprehensive view of himself in the large mirror, and mentally expressed the conviction that, for a man of thirty-seven, he was not bad looking.

Quigg was right; and his just opinion of himself was shared by the young widows and unmarried ladies of his acquaintance. He was about six feet high, with a graceful figure, and the head of a statesman. A more intellectual face, and a broader or more massive brow, assisted, perhaps, in its general effect, by a slight baldness, were rarely if ever seen. A distinguished professor of phrenology had picked out Quigg's head from among half an acre of heads at a lecture upon that subject in the city, and had pronounced it the "model head," greatly to the disgust of all the other large-skulled men in the hall. The professor had also assured Quigg, upon learning who and what he was, that it was a solemn duty he owed to society to abandon the grocery business, and devote himself to "philosophical culture, the development of the humanities, and the true expansion of his interior individuality." Notwithstanding this flattering opinion, Quigg still sanded his sugar, and reduced his whiskey, and found his delight as well as his profit in those gross material pursuits.

The interior Quigg, of whom the professor had spoken so hopefully, was still undeveloped. The professor's views of Quigg's head had, however, made a deep impression upon the owner of it, and had given to Quigg's ordinary observations on the weather, the state of his health, and the other familiar topics to which his remarks were principally addressed, an oracular importance in his own opinion. Such were the deceptive effects produced by his large, polished brow, and slow, imposing speech, that he always seemed to be on the point of uttering vital truths. But the listener's ear ached in vain for them.

Quigg put on his overcoat, took a small glass of bitters from a bottle kept behind the large mirror, locked up the store, proceeded to the nearest restaurant, hastily despatched a lean, unsatisfactory chop and a cup of weak tea, gave a half dime to the waiter who bade him, in a loud and significant voice, "Happy New Year, sir," and then returning found the double sleigh punctual to appointment.

It was a swan-shaped vehicle, brightly painted, thickly covered with buffalo robes, and drawn by two high-stepping horses, which tossed their heads and shook their bells merrily as if they shared in the prevailing jovialty of the day.

On the front seat, and nearly filling up the whole width of the sleigh, sat the driver. His shoulders were broad enough for two men; his legs and arms were of twice the common size, and he had two well-defined chins. He seemed to be double in all his dimensions, like the sleigh.

"Hallo, Quigg!" said the driver, in a voice of double strength, snapping his whip playfully at that gentleman as he approached.

"Hallo to *you*, Cap," returned Quigg, pleasantly. "It is a very fine day. I guess there will be a great many calls made" Quigg uttered these words slowly, as if they were precious, and he hated to part with them.

"Shouldn't wonder," answered Cap, which was a short name for Captain (nobody knew of what), and added, without any apparent sequence of ideas: "I s'pose you're goin' to take some brandy along, old fellow? It's hardly fair for me to be sittin' into the cold outside, with nothin' to drink, while you chaps are drinkin' your champagne punch before a warm fire."

Mr. Quigg reflected a moment, as one who reckons up profit and loss. He then said:

"A good idea, Cap. Brandy is not a bad thing on a cold day." He spoke with impressive solemnity.

"Or any other day," added the driver. "Partickley 'lection day. Leastways, such was the 'pinion of the voters into my ward, last December, when I run for School Inspector, you know. Unfortinitly, I didn't know the ropes then; and thought, when I got the nomination, I was sure to be 'lected. My 'ponent issued tickets for free drinks at all the rum mills into the ward. I didn't find out his game till about two o'clock in the arternoon, and then I tried it myself. But I was too late. He had six hours' start of me, and beat me by five hundred drinks—I mean votes."

Mr. Quigg nodded, and said, "Of course," as if he had often heard of such instances, and there was nothing surprising in them. He then abruptly cut off the Captain's political reminiscences, by unlocking the store and entering it. After a few minutes' absence, he returned with a half-gallon jug and a tin dipper.

"A nice, fat little feller," rapturously exclaimed Captain Tonkins, taking the proffered jug. Placing it in the bottom of the sleigh, where such of the public as were stirring in that vicinity could not see the operation, he half filled the tin dipper, and, raising it suddenly to his mouth, drank the contents with a double gulp. "Prime stuff, that," said the Captain, smacking his lips. "A hogshead of it would make a school commissioner, an alderman, mebbe a mayor of you, Quigg."

"I dare say," said Quigg. "But what would a dull, practical fellow like me be good for in public life?" This was Quigg's habitual way of depreciating himself, and it always impressed the hearer with a sense of Quigg's eminent ability.

Quigg then drew a pair of yellow gloves on his large, hairy hands, slightly ripping the two thumbs and most of the fingers in the operation, took a seat in the double sleigh, and proclaimed himself ready to start.

CHAPTER V.

PLEASURE AS BUSINESS.

Captain Tonkins cracked his whip with professional sonority over the heads of his lively horses, and they started off at a slapping pace, which brought them to the house of the three friends before the bells had fairly begun to jingle in unison. The door was instantly opened, and Overtop and Maltboy presented themselves, dressed in the most elaborate and captivating style. Marcus Wilkeson appeared just behind them, in his dressing gown and slippers, calmly smoking his well-browned Meerschaum.

After the salutations of the day, both Overtop and Maltboy addressed a last appeal to Marcus to give up his ridiculous prejudices, and join the party; but he obstinately refused, saying that he should make only one call, and that was upon the old gentleman over the way.

The arrangements for the day had already been made. The party were to call on a few dozen of Quigg's customers (selected from a carefully prepared list of one hundred) within range of a mile or two; also on a few friends of Overtop and Maltboy, who could not well be slighted, and then come back to the block.

Quigg looked upon the day as one of business, and not of

pleasure, and had methodized a system of callmaking, which was submitted to his companions, and highly approved by them. The order of exercises was as follows: First, a jerk at the doorbell; second, precipitate entrance, hat in hand; third, "Happy New Year," remark on fine weather, and introduction of friends; fourth, a second remark on fine weather, or any other one remark which might occur to friends on inspiration of moment; fifth, acceptance of one sip of wine, and one bite of cake, if any offered, with compliments on excellence of both; sixth, reference to list in hand, observation on the necessity of retiring, and regret for the same; seventh, precipitate retreat.

The system did not work smoothly at first, in consequence of Overtop's and Maltboy's strained, excessive efforts to make themselves agreeable. It happened that, at the first two or three houses visited, Maltboy discovered charming young ladies, and could not resist the temptation to linger beyond the prescribed minutes, and talk trifles to them. It also fell out, that Overtop found a number of those sensible women for whom his heart ever longed, and whose starving souls, as he called them, were not to be satisfied with the dry crust of ordinary compliment. To them, therefore, he addressed observations on the inner or spiritual significance of the New Year's call; on the reminiscences of childhood suggested by sleigh bells; on the typical meaning of snow as the shroud of death, and, at the same time, the warming garment of coming life; on wine or lemonade (as the case might be), as an emblem of hospitality; and on many other little things as expressive of the loftiest truths.

It was only after earnest remonstrances from Quigg, that the discursive Overtop brought himself down to the rules of the day. In deference to Quigg, Mr. Maltboy also steeled his too susceptible heart against the attractions which he was perpetually encountering, and kept strictly to the weather. He, as well as Overtop, was surprised to find that the single stereotyped observation, "It's a fine day," was, after all, more acceptable than a longer and more strikingly original remark· for it imposed no tax upon the conversational resources of the ladies, and left them unfatigued to succeeding scores of visitors.

About this time, it was observed of Captain Tonkins that he began to show signs of fatigue, rocking heavily in his seat with every oscillation of the sleigh, and talking thick like a jaded man. These phenomena seeming to require some explanation, the Captain stated that he had been up late the past three nights, and could keep himself awake only by taking occasional draughts of Quigg's brandy. The Captain then proceeded to indulge in random recollections of his political career, and withering denunciations of one Larry Mulcahy, his successful rival for the office of School Inspector, whom the Captain did not hesitate to brand as a jailbird.

When the party returned to the block where the Overtop theory was to be tested, Mr. Quigg's services were found invaluable. He had not only been the principal grocer in the vicinity for five years, but he had served on Ward Committees for the relief of the poor at other people's expense, and had participated largely in those admirable institutions for the promotion of matrimony known as Sociables. Therefore, Quigg knew about everybody on the block worth knowing. There were a few persons in that old house near the corner, who sent in for herrings, cheap butter, and pounds of flour, and whom, of course, he did not know. There was a queer old Dutchman in that square, old-fashioned house in the middle of the block, whom neither he nor anybody else knew.

They went through half of the sorth side of the block, and found only plain and commonplace people. Overtop and Maltboy began to be weary. The former was gradually discovering that his theory was a bore. The latter wondered whether Quigg knew the tall girl, concerning the identity of the front part of whose residence Maltboy was at fault, although he knew every brick of the rear.

"In this 'ere house," said Quigg, "I shall be treated

rudely, because they owe me fifty dollars for groceries. It's a curious fact, but I have noticed that debtors always act kind o' cold to creditors, as if it was the creditors that owed the money."

Mr. Quigg spoke with an important air, as if he had made an original discovery in human nature.

CHAPTER VI.

SOMETHING HIDDEN.

WHILE this exploring party were going through the block, Mr. Marcus Wilkeson dressed himself with more than usual care, preparatory to a call upon the unknown old gentleman over the way, who that very morning had appeared at his window, the first time in three days, and tendered the compliments of the season in two low bows and a smile. Having carefully adjusted his necktie, and smoothed the creases of his gloves, Mr. Wilkeson grasped his old friend, a hickory cane, by its sturdy elbow, and marched forth to make his solitary visit.

As he turned the corner of the street upon which the unknown old gentleman's residence was situated, thinking of the oddity of the call he was about to make, and half inclined to abandon it, he saw, in a doorway a few yards in front of him, a little girl who bore a striking resemblance to the patient creature that he had often noticed sitting at a window in the room of the pale mechanic. A single glance at the cracked and dirty front of the building established its connection with the weather-stained and shaky rear premises in which the worker toiled at his strange task from morning to night, and far into the morning again.

The little girl was earnestly talking with a rough, hungry-looking fellow in a greasy cap and tattered blue overalls. As Marcus approached, he heard the following fragment of conversation :

"Yer can't fool this child again, now, I tell yer. Why don't he pay me? *that's* what I want to know. I *will* go up." The man stepped forward, as if to ascend the stairs.

"Please don't, Mr. Gilsum," said the girl, in a sweet, pleading tone, laying a red and toilworn little hand softly on his arm. "Papa will pay you next week. He will, believe me, sir."

"So you told me last week," growled Mr. Gilsum, "and the week before that. It's all humbug. Why don't he pay me now? *that's* what I want to know." Again he put a foot forward, and was again restrained by the hand of the little girl.

"I have tried very hard to earn money, Mr. Gilsum," said the musical and plaintive voice, "but have been disappointed. Next week I am sure I will have some for you."

"Pshaw!" ejaculated the man, pulling the greasy cap over his eyes in a spirit of savage determination. "I can't waste time talking. I *will* find out why he don't pay me now."

The inexorable Mr. Gilsum pushed aside the feeble hand of the little girl, and was about to go up the stairs in good earnest, when Marcus Wilkeson, who had lingered near the door to catch the exact purport of the conversation, called out to him:

"Hallo, my friend! what's the row?"

Mr. Gilsum stopped, and, turning, said snappishly:

"None of yer business. Unless," he prudently added, "yer a friend of the comical old chap up stairs, and want to pay his debts."

"I am a friend, and I will pay them," rejoined Marcus, speaking from the impulse of the moment. Since he had become rich, and could afford the luxury, he frequently spoke and acted upon impulse, without regard to consequences.

Mr. Gilsum's face suddenly changed from an aspect of moroseness to one of bewitching amiability. He stood in the doorway, and said:

"It's only a matter of ten shillings, sir, for brass and

screws, and little odds and ends from my shop—the locksmith's shop over in the next street—you may remember it, sir. I'm sure I don't want to be hard on the gentleman."

To cut short explanations, which he hated, Marcus paid the locksmith his ten shillings, and suggested that he need not wait longer. The locksmith, having received the money, thought it incumbent upon him to apologize and explain still further, till Marcus took hold of the door, as if to close it, when he accepted the hint, and departed, mumbling an apology as he went.

The young girl, who had looked on in amazement, turned a pair of soft blue eyes toward the face of the stranger, and said:

"Papa will thank you very much, sir."

Marcus now had an opportunity to observe her more closely. Her figure was slightly formed, and undersized for her apparent age of seventeen years. Her face would have been plain, but for one peculiarity which made it charming, in his practised judgment. This rare excellence was her complexion, which showed a perfect pink and white, without roughness, spot, or blemish, under the strong light of a noonday sun, made more dazzling by its reflection from the snow. Marcus had never seen but one such complexion, and that was many years ago. He looked at it in silent wonder, until the delicate bloom in the centre of her cheeks began to invade the neighboring white, and the large blue eyes drooped in confusion.

"Pardon me, my child," said Marcus, in a gentle, reassuring voice.

She looked up, much embarrassed, and said:

"Will you be so good as to walk up and see my poor father, sir? He will be delighted to meet a friend, for he is very much in want of one, sir."

"I do not know him, my child; but I should be happy to make his acquaintance."

The girl was surprised to learn that her father's benefactor was a stranger to him, and looked doubtingly at him for a moment—but only a moment—and then ran briskly up the stairs, asking him to follow.

The stairs were uncarpeted, and had little feet-worn hollows in the middle of them. The banisters were rickety, and had been notched by the knives of reckless tenants. The first and second floors were occupied by different families (so Marcus inferred from the distinct set of baby cries issuing from each), and the halls were dirty, and flavored with a decided odor of washing day. But on the third story he saw a clean, white floor, and drew breaths of pure air from an open rear window, and heard no noise save the dull sound of filing.

The little girl paused a second at a door bearing the inscription, "Private," asked the visitor to please wait, and opened the door just wide enough to admit her body, and entered, nearly closing it behind her. In the one glance which Marcus then obtained of the interior of the room, he saw the pale mechanic hastily rise from a jumble of cog wheels before him, and put up a screen to shelter his work from observation, after which he stepped forward, or rather sprang, to meet his child.

Mr. Wilkeson heard a few words of hurried conversation between the father and daughter, and then the door was thrown wide open, and the mechanic stood in full view. He was a man of medium height, of a spare build, and attired in faded, seedy black. His head seemed altogether too large for his body; and his almost livid complexion, hollow cheeks, and gleaming eyes, told a story of constant and consuming thought. The strange, fixed glitter of his eyes was unpleasant to behold. Marcus had noticed the same thing in insane persons.

"My name is Minford," said the mechanic, in a deep and solemn voice, "and I thank you for saving me from the annoying visits of that impertinent fellow. I beg, sir, that you will give me your address, and assure you that the sum shall positively be repaid to you next week."

"Never mind the repayment," said Marcus, kindly. "The sum was a trifle for me."

The mechanic's eyes flashed with new fire, and his lower lip curved with pride, as he answered:

"But I shall insist on returning it, sir. We are temporarily poor, sir; but we are not beggars yet. I trust that, some day, we shall be in a position to confer benefits, instead of receiving them."

Marcus knew that the man was turning over in his mind the troublesome question of "MOTIVE," with which so many people like to make themselves unhappy; and he therefore said:

"I took the liberty of assisting you, sir, because I am a neighbor of yours, living on the other side of the block, in a house which can be plainly seen from your window; and I think it is the duty of neighbors to be neighborly, on New Year's day at least. My name is Marcus Wilkeson."

The mechanic's face assumed a pleasanter expression. "Perhaps," said he, "you are the gentleman that I have sometimes seen sitting with a book, in a window covered with grape vines?"

"I am," returned Marcus.

"As a scholar, then—as one who is superior to mean motives and vulgar curiosity—you are welcome to my poor home. Pray, walk in, sir. Pet, give the gentleman a chair."

The girl, whose face had been clouded during the first part of this conversation, brightened up at its close, and obeyed her father with alacrity, brushing the clean chair with her handkerchief, to make it the more acceptable to their visitor. She also took his hat and cane, and placed them carefully away.

The room was simply but neatly furnished, and very clean. The hand of taste and order was everywhere visible. Snow-white curtains festooned the two small windows, and concealed all of a turn-up bedstead but two of its legs. A small array of white crockery shone from an open closet; and a squat-looking stove, which made the apartment agreeably warm, was smartly polished, and was evaporating cheerful music out of a bright teakettle. Through a door partly ajar could be seen another room, covered with a rag carpet, and the companion of the first in simplicity and neatness.

Marcus had not intended to look at the mechanic's corner, which was almost completely screened from view, being desirous to justify the high opinion which Mr. Minford had expressed of him; but his eyes were irresistibly attracted to the mysterious spot, and obtained a clearer glimpse, through an open space between the two screens, of a something composed of cogwheels, springs, bands, and levers. His host, observing this casual glance, much to the guest's mortification, rose, and placed the screens close together at right angles, thus shutting out a view of the corner.

Mr. Minford opened his lips as if to offer some explanation of the act, but did not offer it. A moment afterward, he said:

"I have not always been a poor man, Mr. Wilkeson. Six years ago I possessed a handsome fortune, which enabled me to pursue certain philosophical experiments, in which I had taken great interest, at leisure. An unfortunate speculation in real estate, year before last, nearly ruined me. I converted the remains of my property into cash, and went on with my experiments, undiscouraged. Like all laborers in the cause of science—which is the cause of humanity—I have met with many obstacles. Several times, when I have been on the point of perfecting my great invention, some small, unforeseen difficulty has occurred, compelling me to reconstruct large portions of the machinery. Eighteen months passed away, and I found myself penniless. I tried to borrow money, but without success. Now, who do you suppose has supported us the last three months?"

"Some benevolent relative, perhaps," said Mr. Wilkeson, hazarding a wild guess.

"You are right, sir. And a near and dear relative it is—no other than my little Pet here." Mr. Minford placed his right hand fondly on the shining head of the young girl, who sat on a low stool by his side, looking into his face.

She blushed deeply, and said:

"You forget the unknown good friend who sent the letters with money to you, papa."

"No, no, I don't, Pet," continued Mr. Minford, patting her playfully on the cheeks; "but you were the dearest and sweetest of my guardian angels. You know you were, you rogue. Why, sir, you will hardly believe it, but this little creature, when she knew our money was nearly gone, taught herself the art of embroidery, with the aid of some illustrations from an old magazine, and in less than a fortnight could work so beautifully, that she was able to earn from three to four dollars a week. When she first told me that she was going out to look for work, I opposed it fiercely; but the obstinate little Pet would have her way. She was lucky enough to get a job from a milliner, and pleased her employer so well, that steady work was given to her, until last week, when the kind-hearted lady died, and now little Pet has nothing to do. Some people think, because she is young——"

"Please don't talk about me any more, papa," said Pet, who had been blushing deeply, and looking very beautiful in the visitor's eyes. "You forget what the postman used to bring you every Saturday."

"No, I don't, you little, troublesome, impertinent Pet. I was just about to speak of it, when you interrupted me. You must know, Mr. Wilkeson, that every Saturday the postman, on his first morning round, delivered to me a letter, marked "New York City," containing two dollars, without a word of writing inside, and addressed to me in large capitals, each nearly half an inch long. The object of this singular style of address was either to make it so plain that the postman could not mistake, or to disguise some handwriting which otherwise I might recognize. Now, as I have no relatives living, and no friends that I know of, who would lend me a dollar except on the best security, I am greatly puzzled, as you may suppose, to guess the name of my unknown benefactor. Generous man! For aught I know, he may now be dead, or himself reduced to poverty; for, last Saturday, the regular weekly remittance failed to come."

"Then I see that I am just in season to help you," said Marcus Wilkeson, who, during the recital of this brief history, had decided upon his course of action.

"I thank you most gratefully," returned Mr. Minford, "and fully appreciate the noble motives of your conduct. Your appearance convinces me that you are entirely disinterested. But I should feel ashamed to take money from you, without giving some security for its repayment. I shall therefore insist upon making over to you a certain interest in the invention, the most valuable of modern times, which lies almost finished behind those screens. Let me give you some idea of it, and you can then decide how much money you will advance, merely as a matter of business. I cannot consent to put our negotiations upon any other ground. The invention, then, is——" The speaker looked at the corner as he spoke, and paused.

Marcus Wilkeson knew that the inventor was about to part with his secret unwillingly, and that he would regret it forever after. To save him from unpleasant feelings on that score, and to maintain friendly relations between them for the future, Marcus put a stop to the reluctant disclosure. He said:

"Never mind it, Mr. Minford. I know nothing of mechanical matters, and take no interest in them. Your explanation would only be wasted on me. Besides, it is entirely uncalled for, as I am willing to take your own opinion of the invention, and will pay you five hundred dollars for a one-tenth interest in it, if those terms will suit." Marcus took a keen delight in acting upon this singular impulse, and was sorry he had not said a "thousand," when he saw the glow of happiness that irradiated the sweet face of Pet, still sitting on the stool by her father's side.

"Heaven bless you, sir!" said Mr. Minford. "You will be the means not only of relieving me and my dear child, but also of conferring the boon of a great discovery upon mankind.

THE BOY BOG.

But your terms are too liberal, sir. I shall insist upon assigning one fifth of my right to you, which, mark my prediction, will prove of itself a fortune. Furthermore, I feel that I ought, if only to show my complete confidence in you, to tell you what it is. It is——" Mr. Minford hesitated for a word.

"Now I beg, as a particular favor, that you won't tell me," said Marcus, goodhumoredly. "If you bore me with any of those dull details, I'll—I'll take back my offer. As to the proportion of the invention which I am to have, I will accept one fifth, since you insist on it, not because I want it, but that we may not say another word about the matter."

"As you please, sir. But how shall I sufficiently thank you?"

Marcus, who was already overcome with the gratitude which shone from the large, soft eyes of the young girl, answered, with a laugh and a blush (he had not outgrown the habit of reddening on occasions):

"By changing the subject."

Mr. Minford was about to protest against this extraordinary method of thanking a benefactor, when a rap was heard at the door.

CHAPTER VII.

THE BOY BOG.

In reply to the invitation, "Come in," a tall boy opened the door, and started back on seeing a stranger.

"Do come in, Bog," said Mr. Minford. "I have good news to tell you. This is a friend of ours, Mr. Wilkeson. What with his running of errands, and doing little jobs for us, we really couldn't get along without him. Oh, walk in, Bog; you're always welcome here."

"Now *do* come in, Bog," added the little girl, in a winning tone, rising from her stool, stepping to the door, and placing a hand on his shoulder.

The new comer, after a few shuffles on the threshold, and an unintelligible murmur of words, walked in with painful awkwardness, and took a seat upon a corner of the chair which Pet offered him, as if the whole chair were more of a favor than he could conscientiously accept. He was a bony, strongly built stripling, with a record of anywhere from seventeen to nineteen years written in his red, resolute, honest face. He wore a coarse but neat suit of boy's clothes, one inch too small in every dimension, a white turn-down collar, and a black neckerchief fastidiously tied; and carried a slouched cloth cap in his hand, with which he slapped his knees alternately, after he had taken a seat, and continued to do so without cessation.

"Well, Bog," said Mr. Minford, kindly, but condescendingly, "you are just in time to hear good news. This gentleman has taken a partnership in my invention (Mr. Minford thought it best to state the case that way), and, with his assistance, I shall be able to complete it and bring it before the public immediately."

"Glad to hear it, sir," answered the boy Bog, blushing hard, lifting his eyes from the floor long enough to glance at Mr. Minford and his daughter, and all the while slapping his knees vigorously.

"He is in the bill-posting business," said Mr. Minford to Marcus. "You may have seen him at the head of his company of walking advertisers. Ha! ha!"

Marcus remembered having seen that honest face, that thick head of hair, and that identical cap, sticking out of the top of a portable wooden frame covered with placards, setting forth the virtues of quack medicines, the excellencies of dry goods, or the unequalled attractions of concert saloons. He also remembered that this wooden frame was much taller than any of the long procession of frames which followed it, and that, from a hole in the right side thereof, protruded a fist about the size of the boy Bog's, clutching a broomstick, with which the inmate kept a semblance of order among the wilful and eccentric occupants of the frames behind him. "Oh, yes; I have seen you very often, Bog. How do you like the business?" said Marcus, pleasantly.

"Very well, sir, thank you," replied Bog, with his eyes still on the floor, "'cept when the boys poke fun at us; 'cos we can't run after 'em in them boxes, and wollop 'em. 'S rather hard, that." Bog caught Miss Minford's eye as he concluded these remarks, and blushed till he perspired, to think that he should have dropped such a brutal observation in presence of that young lady.

Mr. Minford noticed the confusion of his young friend, and unintentionally added to it, by saying:

"Bog is a good boy. By his industry, he earns eight or ten dollars a week, not only supporting himself, but his aunt."

"Not this week, nor last week neither, Mr. Minford," said Bog, mopping the modest sweat from his brow with the sleeve of his coat. "The adv'tisin' line a'n't as good as't used to be. I only got three jobs with my company the last fortnight, and nary cent of pay from any of 'em. Of course, all my boys had to be paid just the same."

"And you paid them?" asked Marcus.

"Certainly," said Bog.

"Then be good enough to accept five dollars from me, as a reward for your honesty," said Marcus, acting upon another of his impulses.

"No, thank you, sir. No, thank you," returned Bog, quickly, to prevent Marcus from pulling the money out of his pocket. "I sha'n't take it, sir; I won't have it anyway. I'm goin' into the reg'lar bill-postin' business, as Jack Fink's assistant, to-morrow, and can earn all I want." Bog blushed, but this time with honest pride, though he was flustered to look up and see that Miss Minford nodded in approval of his independent spirit.

Bog then slapped each knee about a dozen times with his cap, and betrayed many symptoms of fever heat and great mental distress. After which, he said that he had only called to see if he could do anything for them.

"Now do you mean to tell us that it is not a regular New Year's call," said Mr. Minford, playfully, "and that you have not a dozen more to make?"

Bog looked guilty of an enormous fraud, dropped his cap, in his confusion, twice, murmured something inaudible, rose to his feet, and backed out of the room, making one comprehensive bow to everybody, and saying "Good-night" before it was two P. M.

As Bog shut the door, everybody laughed, but not so loud as to be heard by the boy; and, under the cover of the general good humor, Marcus rose, and said that he must go. He was afraid he had made his visit too long for a first one. He would call again on the following day, if agreeable, and complete the proposed arrangement. In conclusion, he placed his card in Mr. Minford's hand, with the names of a few references pencilled on the margin.

Mr. Minford was very sorry that their pleasant acquaintance should take his leave so abruptly, and hoped that they would enjoy many visits from him, not merely as a business partner (Mr. Minford laid emphasis on this), but as a friend.

Pet repeated her father's regrets and hopes in the more impressive language of her sweet eyes, and, for the twentieth time that day, conjured up, in the memory of Marcus Wilkeson, a vague reminiscence of the distant past.

CHAPTER VIII.

MALTBOY'S TWENTIETH AFFAIR.

THE house which had elicited Quigg's last sagacious remark, was a three-story brown-stone front, and was one of the finest looking on the south side. The heavy mahogany door was opened by a slovenly girl, who ushered the callers into the front parlor, which was carefully darkened, according to the custom of the day. The only objects plainly visible were two female figures, each seated near a front window, under the rosy shade of damask curtains artfully disposed. One of the ladies, whom Matthew Maltboy was not slow to recognize, looked like a fountain of pink silk, gushing out with great vehemence in high, curving jets on every side; from which fountain a slim, graceful figure had risen as far as the waist, like a modern Arethusa. The gleam of a shapely neck, of a pearl necklace and diamond cross, of diamond earrings, of an enormous gold brooch, of golden gyves an inch broad on each wrist, as the rose-tinted rays fell on those natural and artificial charms, produced a dazzling effect in the shady corner. On plainer persons, this display might have seemed, in Maltboy's eyes, a glaring instance of bad taste. But, looking at that small, oval face, those large, flashing black eyes, complexion of red and white, so beautifully blended that it hardly seemed a work of nature, pouting lips, even, white teeth, and heavily braided hair, Maltboy thought that no decorations could be too gaudy for a creature of such radiant loveliness.

At the same instant (as their feet passed the parlor threshold) that Maltboy made these comprehensive observations, the quick eyes of Fayette Overtop were scanning the lady that basked in the subdued light of the other window. She rose from a smaller fountain of silk to a less height than her companion. She was fat to such a degree, that the bodice of her dress seemed ready to burst with the excessive pressure beneath, immediately suggesting to every beholder the obvious humanity of enlarging it, by taking only a small portion from the superfluous silk below. She was quite pretty, and very healthy, and had a smile lurking on her lips, and in the corners of her small blue eyes, and in the dimples of her round, red ckeeks, and in the curved crease which was beginning to show under her apple of a chin. She wore plain colors, and exhibited no ornaments save a large brooch with braided hair in it. The lean Overtop immediately felt a tender inclination toward this fat young lady.

Mr. Quigg paid the compliments of the season in his neat,

settled style, to Miss Whedell—the tall young lady—who received them with marked coldness, and then begged leave to introduce Messrs. Overtop and Maltboy, to whom she smiled graciously, rising slightly from her chair, and sinking back again, without disturbing the symmetrical flow of the silken fountain. With a wave of her jewelled right hand she performed the ceremony of introduction between the three callers and Mrs. Frump—the fat young lady—who also carefully raised herself about two inches from her chair, and lowered herself again, without disarranging a ripple.

In compliance with an invitation from Miss Whedell, the three callers sat down. Mr. Maltboy gravitated by a natural instinct to the side of his charmer. Mr. Overtop was drawn by an irresistible impulse into the vicinity of Mrs. Frump, having detected in her general appearance certain indications of what he called "a sensible woman." Mr. Quigg, feeling that he was one too many, took a seat equally removed from the two ladies, and commenced playing soft tunes on his hat, and looking vacantly about the room.

"I had begun to wonder, Mr. Maltboy," said Miss Whedell, "what makes our friends so backward to-day. I do declare, we have not had a caller for more than—how long is it, Gusty, since Colonel Bigford dropped in?"

Maltboy thought her voice had a sweet, metallic ring.

"About half an hour," replied Mrs. Frump, after a brief mental calculation.

"Why, Gusty!" exclaimed Miss Whedell; "how can you sit there and tell such stories? You know it is not five minutes."

"Just as you please, dear," said Mrs. Frump, leaving on the minds of her hearers the impression that her estimate was the correct one.

"I never saw anything so slow," pursued Miss Whedell. "Would you believe it, Mr. Maltboy—here are two hours gone, and we have not had more than—how many callers have we had, Gusty? You keep account of them."

Mrs. Frump drew out a little memorandum book from one of her pockets, and consulted. "Exactly eleven, Clemmy," said she.

"Gusty Frump," returned Miss Whedell, with some warmth, "you ought to be ashamed of yourself! We have had fifty callers, to my certain knowledge."

"I presume you are right," said Mrs. Frump, with a smile that irradiated the whole of her fat face, and again imparted the idea that Miss Whedell was wrong.

"For one," said Matthew Maltboy, improving the opportunity to put in a word, "I should not be surprised to learn that you had a hundred."

Miss Whedell appreciated the delicate compliment, and beamed fascination upon him.

"It has been a horrid, dreary winter, has it not, Mr. Maltboy?" said she, in a tone that invited sympathy and confidence.

Mr. Maltboy, supposing that she alluded to the prevalent snow and ice of the season, said that it certainly had.

"No balls, no opera—or none to speak of—no parties, no anything. You will hardly believe it, Mr. Maltboy, but I declare I haven't been to twenty parties this winter—have I, Gusty?"

"To only two that I know of," responded Mrs. Frump, in a winning voice.

"You provoking creature," said Miss Whedell, "to talk so, when you know that I have been to at least eighteen parties!" Miss Whedell scowled charmingly as she spoke, and then added, with a pleasant smile, for the benefit of Mr Maltboy: "She's a gay young widow; and you know what widows are."

Mr. Maltboy's knowledge of that species of the human family was extensive and exact. He nodded, to signify that he knew something of them, and felt forearmed, from that moment, against the charms of Mrs. Frump.

Mrs. Frump told Miss Whedell that she thanked her very

much for the compliment, and laughed so prettily, that Fayette Overtop determined to apply some of his grand tests for the discovery of sensible women.

Abandoning the vein of commonplace conversation which he had worked during the five minutes since his arrival, he remarked:

"It really makes us feel young again—does it not, Mrs. Frump?—to renew this charming custom of receiving and making calls."

Mr. Overtop spoke in general terms, like a philosopher; whereas Mrs. Frump made a personal application of the remark to herself, and replied, rather coldly: "I have no doubt that it makes *old* persons feel younger," and then she looked at Matthew Maltboy, and seemed to be listening to the conversation between him and Miss Whedell.

Mr. Overtop paused a moment, and tried again: "Is it not pleasant, though sad, Mrs. Frump, to think of the friends whom we knew many, many years ago, who no longer live to greet us on this festal day?" The speaker alluded to mankind at large.

Mrs. Frump responded tartly, that she could not speak from experience, of course, but she presumed that Mr. Overtop's opinion was correct. And again she glanced at Maltboy.

Mr. Overtop briefly rested, and then remarked:

"It may be merely a poetical conceit of mine, but it seems to me that the horses prance higher, and shake their bells more merrily on New Year's than any other day, as if they partook in our enjoyment of the occasion. May not the horse, by some mysterious instinct, know that it is the beginning of the year?"

Mrs. Frump smiled, and answered: "Not being a horse, of course I can't say. But I would suggest, whether ostlers do not give their animals an extra quantity of oats on New Year's day, to make their action more stylish?"

Mr. Overtop marked a quizzical expression in the widow's left eye, and was disgusted.

For the third time she looked intently at Matthew Maltboy, who was putting in a few words with great animation; and then turned her face toward Mr. Quigg, who was taking his third mental inventory of the furniture, and executing "Hail Columbia," with variations, on his hat.

"It's a finer New Year's day than the last one, is it not, Mr. Quigg?"

Mr. Quigg, who had an astonishing memory for dates and conditions of the weather, replied, after a second's reflection:

"It is a much finer day, Mrs. Frump. It rained last New Year's. Perhaps you may remember my leaving an umbrella at the house where you were then stopping, in Sixteenth street, and my calling for it again, on which occasion you said I reminded you of Paul Pry, in the play, who was always forgetting his umbrella."

The widow laughed, and said that she distinctly remembered the circumstances.

Mr. Quigg, thus encouraged, went on:

"New Year's days differ very much. The one before the last was very snowy in the forenoon, with hail in the afternoon; and the one before that was so mild, that I found an overcoat really uncomfortable. The one before——"

"Excuse me for the interruption," said Mrs. Frump, suddenly, "but I can't help saying how much Mr. Maltboy looks like Dr. Warts. Doesn't he, Clemmy?"

"Like Dr. Warts!" exclaimed Miss Whedell. "Who's he?"

"Why, don't you remember, Clemmy, the doctor that you consulted about your hair?" The widow looked the picture of guilelessness as she asked the question.

Miss Whedell turned slightly red in parts of her face that were not red before, and involuntarily raised her hands to two heavy braids of hair which fronted each ear, and adjusted them. Then she said, sarcastically:

"Mr. Maltboy must feel much flattered at being compared with a notorious quack."

Mrs. Frump, with a laugh spreading all over her gentle face, replied:

"Oh! of course you call him a quack, because he could not save your——"

"You are rude, madam," said Miss Whedell, with emotion.

"And you are silly, miss," retorted Mrs. Frump, still smiling, "to take offence at nothing."

"You ought to be ashamed of yourself, madam."

Greatly to the relief of the three callers, who were seized with a desire to laugh aloud during this short, snapping dia logue, a bell rang, and a new figure entered upon the scene. The two ladies rose about three inches, and greeted him as Mr. Chiffield. Mr. Chiffield bowed stiffly, smiled mechanically, and cast a sweeping glance at the three men present. This glance, and the looks with which it was met, called up a singular train of associations.

Maltboy remembered the new comer as a fellow who had trod on his corns getting into an Amity street stage. Overtop remembered him as an eccentric individual, who always carried, without the slightest reference to existing weather, an umbrella under his arm, with the point rearward, and held at just the angle to pierce the eye of a person walking incautiously after him. Overtop had frequently felt a strong inclination to pull the umbrella out from behind, and ask the bearer to carry it in a less threatening manner.

Mr. Chiffield, on the other hand, readily recalled Matthew Maltboy as a suspicious person whom he had seen hanging around an up-town hotel, about a year and a half before (when Maltboy was paying his ineffectual addresses to a cruel Cuban beauty who passed the summer months at that house). Mr. Chiffield had always supposed him to be a confidence man of superior abilities.

Of Overtop, Mr. Chiffield was vaguely reminiscent. Unless he was mistaken, that person was the one who wore an entire suit of pepper and salt, including a felt hat, necktie, and gaiters, two summers before.

Mr. Quigg was a novelty in Mr. Chiffield's eyes; but Mr. Chiffield was well known by sight to Mr. Quigg, who also remembered to have heard that he was a partner in the great drygoods house of Upjack, Chiffield & Co.

Mr. Chiffield was about forty years of age, and had a bald head, a square, heavy face, scanty whiskers, small, shrewd eyes, and a bilious complexion. He dressed in profound black, wore his necktie negligently, exhibited neither ring nor breastpin nor gold chain, spoke as if he were always thinking inwardly of his private business, and never laughed. These peculiarities indicated, beyond any doubt, that Mr. Chiffield was a wealthy man; though it might be difficult to trace the exact processes of reasoning by which this conclusion was reached. Any unprejudiced stranger, seeing Mr. Chiffield, and being told that he was a partner in a large drygoods house, would instantly think, "That drygoods house will stand in the midst of fires, earthquakes, and financial revulsions."

With that fine instinct peculiar to lovers, Matthew Maltboy immediately recognized in Mr. Chiffield a rival—and a dangerous one. Having seen much of society, Maltboy was well aware that Mr. Chiffield's mature age, his grim appearance, his sparse whiskers, and even the bald spot on the top of his head, were eminent advantages with which youth and bloom, and a full head of hair could not cope—unless with the aid of that fascination which Matthew flattered himself that he possessed, and which, he thought, he had used to some purpose during his hurried conversation with his twentieth enslaver, Miss Whedell. The usages of New Year's day, as well as frequent impatient nods from Quigg, and suggestive coughs from Overtop, would not permit of his staying longer. He therefore rose to take his leave, his fellow pilgrims doing likewise, when Miss Whedell remarked that they were in a great hurry, and regretted that they could not remain a few minutes more.

The captivated Maltboy toyed with his hat in an uncertain way, and was half disposed to sit down again, when Quigg hastily produced his visiting list, and said, with his best business smile·

"We should certainly be very happy, Miss Whedell; but we have seventy-five calls still to make, and it is now (consulting his watch) two o'clock."

As the three visitors withdrew (declining, at every step, a pressing invitation to taste the refreshments which were piled in mountainous form on a table in an adjoining alcove), Maltboy exchanged a look of deep, sentimental meaning with Miss Whedell, who rose at least six inches from her chair, and followed it with a slight hostile glare at Mr. Chiffield, upon whose equable face it fell harmless. Overtop bowed coldly to everybody, as if he were disappointed in the human species; and Quigg gave a parting grin at the room in general, and at nobody or nothing in particular.

"We're all right, Top," whispered Maltboy, as they descended the steps to the sidewalk. "She smiled slightly when I mentioned having seen her from our back parlor window. I have obtained permission to call again."

"You'll have to do it without me, my dear fellow," returned Overtop, tossing back his head from force of habit, the offensive cowlick being then suppressed by his hat. "Nothing on earth could induce me to speak to that dull widow again."

"She doesn't live there," said Quigg. "She is some connection, I believe, of the queer old Dutchman that I spoke of, and is probably only helping Miss Whedell to receive callers. I should think, from the way they abuse each other, that they were old and dear friends."

CHAPTER IX.

MRS. SLAPMAN AT HOME.

Full of new and pleasant thoughts, Marcus Wilkeson walked on toward the half-antique house which contained the strange old gentleman. Just as he was about to swing back the iron gate of the front yard, he saw, at a distance, the two friends of his bosom and Mr. Quigg descending a flight of steps to the sidewalk. They saw him at the same time; and both Overtop and Maltboy violently beckoned him to approach. Mr. Quigg added his solicitations in a calmer and more dignified manner, moving his arm like an automaton three times from the elbow. Even the driver, Captain Tonkins, in the spirit of invitation peculiar to his mental state, steadied himself on the seat, poked his right arm and his long whip toward Marcus, and said: "Hu-hullo there—come along!" Having done this, Captain Tonkins furtively poured a gill of brandy into the tin cup, and drank it under cover of the buffalo robe.

In compliance with this general request, Marcus forbore to open the gate of the old gentleman's house, and joined his friends.

"How many people have you called on, you old humbug?" asked Overtop, as Marcus drew near.

Marcus was on the point of alluding to the chance acquaintances that he had made that morning; but a moment's reflection stopped him.

"I told you," said he, "that my only visit was to be to our odd old neighbor. I was at his gate, when you called. And now, what do you want?"

"I want to tell you," said Matthew Maltboy, "that Miss Whedell—the Juno-like young lady with the handkerchief, you know—is——"

"All your fancy painted her," interrupted Marcus.

"She's lovely—she's divine," said Maltboy, rapturously finishing the quotation. "I have made an impression. Congratulate me, old boy!"

"I do," said Marcus, laughing, "and only hope that you will find it as easy getting out of the scrape as into it. And what have you discovered, Top?"

"That there isn't a sensible woman or an original idea, so far, on the block. I wouldn't budge an inch farther, but for Quigg's promise to introduce me to a young widow who lives next door—a regular prodigy of science and art, according to his story. I think you said she was a widow, Quigg?"

"I suppose so," said Quigg, "as I never saw nor heard of her husband; and she's lived on this block five years last May."

The three besieged Marcus to lay aside his scruples for once, and join them in visiting this accomplished lady. Marcus fought them until his patience was exhausted, and then gave in.

The door to which they climbed, bore, on a large and shining plate, the name "Slapman." This door was opened to them by a tall negro in livery, which, like the wearer, had a borrowed appearance. As they entered, they saw a little wiry man, with a pale face full of wrinkles and crowsfeet, bounding up the first flight of stairs, two steps at a time. When the little man reached the first landing he looked back, and directed a strange, suspicious glance at the callers.

The opening of the parlor door discovered a room full of men, who were sipping wine, eating cold fowl and confections, talking and laughing loudly with each other, or exchanging repartees with a lady who stood in the centre of the apartment and shed her light upon all. This lady was Mrs. Grazella Jigbee Slapman.

Previous to her marriage, she had been not altogether unknown to the corners of several weekly newspapers, under the name of "Grazella." She had also cultivated a natural talent for painting, so assiduously, that a little cabinet piece of hers, representing a cat, a lobster, and a plate of fruit, was considered good enough to exhibit in the window of a Broadway print shop, in which her uncle was a silent partner, and was approvingly paragraphed in a paper partly owned by her first cousin. To gifts capable of producing results like these, she added a great aptitude for music; although an incurable indolence, she gracefully said, had always prevented her from learning the piano. While yet sustaining the name of Jigbee, she had achieved a high reputation in private circles as a merciless judge of music. But her conversation had been, from earliest girlhood, her chief attraction. She possessed the extraordinary faculty of talking with a dozen persons upon a dozen different subjects at the same time.

Unlike many people similarly endowed, she did not exercise this wonderful gift for the brutal purpose of putting down feebler intellects, but only to elicit TRUTH, which she often declared to be the sole object of her existence. When, by her alliance with Mr. Slapman, a thrifty speculator in real estate, she was installed as mistress of a fine house and furniture, and a few thousand a year, the lady naturally gathered about her a still larger circle of admirers. Her researches for TRUTH were met halfway by people that were supposed to deal in that article, abstractly considered; such as poets, painters, sculptors, reformers, inventors. Anybody with a new idea was sure to be understood and encouraged by her. Her fondness for new ideas was as keen as an entomologist's for new bugs or butterflies.

Mrs. Slapman had not made the mistake of neglecting her physical and perishable charms in deference to her intellectual and immortal nature. She was twenty-four years old, and had clear, sparkling eyes, a fresh complexion, good teeth, rich, heavy hair, and a substantial figure. The pursuit of TRUTH did not disagree with her health.

Mrs. Slapman bustled out of the little knot of persons about her, and advanced in a frank, hearty way to meet her visitors. To Mr. Quigg she nodded patronizingly, as to one whom she had long known to be guiltless of new ideas; but to the strangers who sought her society, she addressed a cordial smile.

Mr. Quigg, having performed his office, judiciously stepped aside, and left the honors and burdens of conversation with the three friends.

Matthew Maltboy, with the rashness of youth, opened the verbal engagement, by remarking that it was a fine day.

This wretched conventionalism was met by a "Very," so obviously sarcastic, that Marcus Wilkeson decided not to utter a remark which was at that moment on his lips.

At this embarrassing juncture, Fayette Overtop came to the rescue. "As we alighted from our sleigh, Mrs. Slapman, I noticed how firmly the snow at the edge of the street was pressed down by the feet of the hundreds who have called on you; and I could not but think how truly that white surface, upon which the prints of so many boots were beautifully blended, typified the purity of the motives which brought the owners of those boots to your door."

"A most original and charming remark!" said Mrs. Slap man. "I must repeat it to Chickson. The author of 'A Snowflake's Lament' will appreciate that felicitous observation. You have heard of Chickson?"

Mr. Overtop read new books, magazines, literary papers, in considerable quantities, but did not remember to have ever met with the name. Speaking upon impulse, and to avoid explanation, however, he said:

"Oh, yes—certainly, but have not the pleasure of his acquaintance."

"You should know each other," said Mrs. Slapman. "Excuse me a minute." She ran with girlish haste to the other end of the parlors, and brought back an undersized young man. When he had been introduced to Overtop, and shaken hands with him, the enthusiastic hostess quoted, somewhat imperfectly, the beautiful conceit which Overtop had just uttered, and remarked that it would be a capital subject for a poem.

Mr. Chickson turned his eyes upward to the ceiling, and then downward to the floor, as if he were committing what he had heard to memory, and then said it was very curious, but he had thought of the same theme before, and was intending to write a poem on it next week.

"Now, that's just like you, you provoking creature!" said Mrs. Slapman, tapping the poet playfully with her fan. "It's really selfish of you to keep all your poetical thoughts for your poems."

Mr. Chickson smiled pleasantly, but said nothing; and when Mrs. Slapman's attention was momentarily attracted by a passing remark from another person, the poet improved the opportunity to slip away and take another glass of champagne in the corner.

"Ah! gone, is he?" said Mrs. Slapman, remarking his disappearance. "Though one of the most promising of our young poets, he is dull enough in conversation. It may be said of him, as of Goldsmith, 'He writes like an angel, but talks like poor Poll.' You may have read his poem, 'Echoes of the Empyrean,' published in the *Weekly Lotus*."

Mr. Overtop was wicked enough to say that he had read and admired it.

"It is a curious fact in the history of the poem, that the subtle thoughts which it evolves were the topic of discussion at one of my *conversazioni;* and on that very night Chickson told me he had forty-five lines written on the subject. The knowledge of that trifling circumstance lends additional interest to the poem."

"That is, if anything could lend additional interest to it," observed Overtop.

"You are right," said Mrs. Slapman. "TRUTH, like that which animates every line of the 'Empyrean,' needs no factitious attractions. You have read the 'Empyrean?'"—turning to Wilkeson and Maltboy, who had stood hard by during this conversation, calm patterns of politeness.

Mr. Wilkeson, not understanding the question (his thoughts wandering back to the pale mechanic and his child), nodded "Yes," and was immediately put down on Mrs. Slapman's mental tablet as a quiet gentleman of good taste. But Matthew Maltboy, distinctly understanding it, was candid enough to say "No," and from that moment was as nothing in the eyes of the lady.

Overtop proceeded to deepen the favorable impression which he had made upon this charming patroness of intellect.

"Did it ever occur to you how many subjects for the highest order of poetry lie unnoticed all about us? Take that chandelier, for example, the prismatic drops of which are dull in the shade, but sparkle with all the colors of the rainbow in the gaslight. Might not those hidden splendors be compared to that genius whose brilliancy is alone evoked by Beauty's radiant smile ?"

Marcus Wilkeson squirmed, and Matthew Maltboy felt uneasy, while their friend was delivering this elaborate idea, and felt easier when he reached the end in safety. Mr. Overtop himself shared in the sensation of relief.

"Beautiful! beautiful!" cried Mrs. Slapman, in a species of rapture. "I must repeat that delicious thought to Chickson. But not now." And she looked inquiringly at Overtop, as if in expectation that he would utter another new TRUTH immediately. That gentleman not happening to have one on his tongue's end, Mrs. Slapman was kind enough to give him time for reflection.

CHAPTER X.

INFIRMITIES OF GENIUS.

"ALLOW me to point out some of my friends, Mr. Overtop. Among them are faces which you may have seen. If not, you will at least recognize several of the names."

"But I must protest that I am monopolizing too much of your time, madam," interposed Overtop, conscious that his neglected friends were looking on awkwardly, and waiting for him.

"And I protest against your protesting," said Mrs. Slapman, with a merry laugh. So saying, she motioned him to one of the front windows, and, under the shade of heavy blue and gold curtains, commenced to point out notable guests.

Mr. Overtop observed, first with regret and then with pride, that their withdrawal into a corner elicited looks of surprise and curiosity, not unmingled with envy, from the little group that hovered about the refreshment table, and drank Mrs. Slapman's fine wines, and laughed and joked together.

He was glad to see that his two friends sauntered through the parlors, examining the pictures and articles of taste which caught the eye on every side; and that Mr. Quigg was engrossed in the examination of some books on a centre table, opening them, and smoothing their fair pages with his hand as if they were ledgers.

"You see that stout man with the double chin—the one drinking champagne, to the left of the table? That is Mr. Scrymser, a gentleman who has made several aeronautic excursions, and talked about a balloon voyage to Europe last year. You may remember his portrait, and plans of his air ship, in the illustrated papers."

"I do," said Overtop; "and also that he didn't go."

"Precisely. Some trouble about the currents, I believe. You note that small man, with the sharp face—the one sipping a glass, to the right of the table? That is Mr. Boskirk, inventor of the 'Submarine Summer House,' a species of diving bell, which is to be owned and managed by a Joint-Stock Company. I have promised to take a few shares in the concern."

"Excuse the digression, madam," said Overtop, "but ought not these two gentlemen to change places in life? Is not the heavy one peculiarly adapted to the diving bell, and the light one to the balloon?"

Mrs. Slapman smiled, and looked faintly surprised, as if the remark were unworthy of her guest. "Probably you know that gentleman under the picture of a landscape, talking very earnestly to another gentleman, who seems to want to be getting away."

"The man with the long, curly, red hair? I know his face well, and, though I have no further knowledge of him, am morally certain that he is a social reformer."

"Why?" asked Mrs. Slapman.

"Because I never saw a man with long, curly, red hair, who was not a social reformer. Men with red hair—the true carrot tint, I mean—have a natural propensity for reform.

Some of them repress it, but others give rein to their inclinations, go into the reform business, and hang out their curls as a sign to all mankind. And all mankind interpret it as readily as they do the striped pole in front of a barber's shop."

"A striking thought, truly, and full of TRUTH," said Mrs. Slapman. "I will mention it to Mr. Gormit. On reflection, however, I won't. I might wound his feelings, for he is an exquisitely sensitive creature. As you have ingeniously discovered, he *is* a social reformer. At present he is only known to the public as the editor of the 'Humanitarian Harbinger;' but his select circle of friends are well aware that he is devoting his ripened genius to the production of a work called the 'Progressional Principia,' which will be in four volumes, and exhaust the whole subject of social science. This immense undertaking is a favorite subject of his ordinary conversation. He is probably, at this very moment, giving a general outline of the book to that gentleman on his right.

"That slender young man with the Vandyke beard, cutting into a cake, you may not need to be told, is Patching, the painter of those delicious interiors which have been seen every year by those who had eyes to find them, in obscure corners at the rooms of the National Academy of Design. In short, Patching is the subject of a conspiracy in which the Hanging Committee is implicated. But though professional envy may place his works in the worst possible light, and for some time cast a shadow over his prospects, an independent public taste will ultimately appreciate his genius. Mark the melancholy that overspreads his features, as he tastes that glass of sherry. Next to TRUTH, melancholy is the chief characteristic of his style. In a miniature portrait which he painted of me, last year, and which is regarded as a capital likeness, he introduced a shade of sadness, which is, at least, not habitual with me."

Mr. Overtop hastened to say, that of *that* fact he needed no assurance.

"Without giving a minute account of all my guests, I may say generally, that they include novelists, dramatists, actors, and musicians. Some you may know by sight. The acquaintance of all you may make at a future time."

At this strong hint, Mr. Overtop replied, that he should be only too happy. He had by this time come to the conclusion that there never was a more candid and delightful widow than Mrs. Slapman; and, furthermore, that she was that rarity—a sensible woman—of which he had been so long in search. Mr. Overtop mentally hugged himself.

"By the way, sir—you will pardon the impertinence of the question—but to what profession do you belong?"

"I am a lawyer, madam," said he, fearful that the announcement would not be well received. "Fayette Overtop, firm of Overtop & Maltboy."

Mrs. Slapman mused a moment, and said:

"It is a little singular, that, among my large collection—I mean circle—of friends, there shouldn't be a single lawyer."

"As I am a *single* lawyer, Mrs. Slapman, it is within my power to supply that deficiency among those who are honored with your friendship." Mr. Overtop thought, with some reason, as he finished this remark, that he had never said a better thing in his life.

Mrs. Slapman's severe taste rejected Overtop's pun, but not himself, and she was about to say that she should put him on the list for her next *conversazione*, when another awkward interruption occurred, in this wise:

Signor Mancussi was a gentleman with an Italian name and a perfect knowledge of English, who sang bass parts in a church up town, and enjoyed the reputation of having personated the chief Druid in Norma, at an early period of the New York opera. M. Bartin played one of numerous violins at the Academy of Music, and was believed to be kept down only by a powerful combination. Three months before this New Year's day, both of these gentlemen had volunteered their services, in company with many other musical people, to give a grand concert in aid of a benevolent enterprise. To M. Bartin, as a man supposed to know something of sharp management, from his connection with the opera, was intrusted the supreme control of the whole affair. It is due to M. Bartin to say, that he tried to perform his laborious duties faithfully and with perfect justice to his associates.

When, therefore, in ordering the printing of the gigantic posters which heralded the concert, he directed his own name to be placed at the head of the "eminent artists who had offered their services for the occasion," and in type half as large again as any of the rest, he only expressed a conscientious opinion of his superiority over all of them. In this opinion his associates happened to disagree with him, each one claiming that himself, and nobody else, was entitled to typographical precedence.

Most keenly was the alleged injustice felt by Signor Mancussi, who stood at the foot of the sloping list in letters less than an inch long; and he had made a solemn vow to revenge himself on M. Bartin the first time that they met after the concert. Their simultaneous appearance at Mrs. Slapman's was that time. M. Bartin had been privately informed of the Signor's intentions, and regretted that that gentleman's ridiculous vanity should get the better of his judgment. Seeing him at Mrs. Slapman's, M. Bartin avoided the Signor's presence, fearing they might come into a collision disgraceful to the time and the place. The Signor, for the same considerate reasons, kept shy of M. Bartin. After dodging each other for a long time, they were at last brought, by accident, face to face. M. Bartin was calm. Signor Mancussi tried to be tranquil, but those small, lean black letters at the foot of the list rose vividly to his mind; and, before he could check himself, he had whispered, or hissed, between his set teeth, the word,

"SCOUNDREL!"

M. Bartin was taken unawares, but had sufficient presence of mind to reply, "You're another," in a whisper, low, but freighted with meaning.

Whereupon the Signor responded, also under his breath, "You're no gentleman."

To this assertion, M. Bartin answered, with masterly irony, "And you *are* a gentleman, now, a'n't you?"

Up to this point the controversy had been pleasantly conducted in whispers, and was unnoticed by the bystanders; but M. Bartin's last insinuation had the strange effect of maddening the Signor still more. He lost his self-control, and said, in an audible voice:

"You're only a scraper of catgut, anyhow."

M. Bartin, also oblivious of the proprieties, retorted, louder still:

"And what are you but an infernal screech owl?"

Cries of "Hallo!" "What's the row?" "Hush!" and "For shame!" rose from all parts of the room, and the two musical gentlemen, conscious that they had grossly misconducted themselves, stepped back a yard from each other, and were immediately surrounded by several friends, and kindly told that they were a pair of fools.

Mrs. Slapman and Overtop rushed to the spot. The latter measured the two combatants with his eye, to see if he could safely undertake to pitch both, or either of them, out of the room, if requested so to do by the widow, and concluded that he could not.

Mrs. Slapman was much embarrassed by this painful outbreak. It was only three weeks ago that M. Bartin had dedicated a new quadrille to her; and but a fortnight since Signor Mancussi had sung four operatic airs gratuitously at one of her musical and dramatic *soirées*. But respect for herself and for her guests—especially for Mr Overtop, of whose talents she had formed an exalted opinion—pointed out her path of duty, and she followed it. She stepped between the two disputants, and cast a look of surprise and regret at each.

"I was hasty," said Signor Mancussi.

"And I was too impulsive," said M. Bartin.

"Then, gentlemen, if you would merit my continued friendship, please make up your little difference, by shaking hands."

They recoiled from the proposition a moment, but, being pushed together by their respective friends from behind, took each other's right hand, shook it once feebly, and said distinctly, with their eyes, "We shall meet again!"

"Very well done," said Mrs. Slapman, with the air of an empress, tempered by a charming smile. "And let us hope that is the end of it. Now, Mr. Overtop, allow me to offer you some refreshment."

Mrs. Slapman was in the act of handing a glass of champagne to the favored Overtop, when an unearthly shriek was heard, which startled the steadiest nerves. This shriek was repeated three times in quick succession, and seemed to come from the sidewalk in front of the house. There was a general rush to the window; but Wilkeson, Overtop, Maltboy, and Quigg ran for the street at once, surmising the source of the cry.

There stood Captain Tonkins, in the sleigh, leaning against the dashboard, holding in one hand an empty jug, and in the other his whip. Around the sleigh were a dozen men and boys, who had been convoked by the cry of "FELL' CITIZENS!" More men and more boys were seen coming in the distance.

As the four lessees of the sleigh approached him, the Captain again yelled, "FELL' CITIZENS!"

"For heaven's sake, stop, Captain!" cried Quigg.

A smile of contempt played upon the Captain's large lips, as, shaking his whip defiantly at the agitated group, he shouted:

"I—I know ye. Don' think I doknowye. You're Mulcahy men, ev' moth's sonofye; and you've come to this 'ere meet'n' to put down free-ee-dom of speech. But yer carndoit. 'Peat it, yer ca-arn-doit. I d'fy ye. I d'fy ye."

The Captain was a powerful man; and Quigg, as well as his companions, singly and collectively, shrank from trying physical persuasion on him. Besides, a crowd of people had gathered, who were greatly enjoying the scene, and desiring its continuance for an indefinite period.

"FELL' CITIZENS!" continued the Captain, "now these vile tools o' Mulca-a-hy silenced, warntellye I'm can'date School 'Spector in this ward. Fuss place, I'm only reg'l can'date. Secun' place, I feel great int'st mor'l wants of all your chi-i-ld'n. Masay they are my own child'n, Go'bless'em. Third place, my dear FELL' CIT'Z'NS, if yer'll jess step in ter Phil Rooney's 'fore ye vote, yer'll find some whi-i-sky there; and that—that's bess arg'ment, after all."

Having reached the logical end of the first and last speech ever made in public by Captain Tonkins, the Captain tumbled out of his sleigh, and sprawled upon the snow; whereat the bystanders shouted for joy, and the widow Slapman and two large windows full of guests shook with laughter.

"'S pla-at-form fall'n'?" asked the Captain.

"Yes," replied one of the citizens, humoring the idea; "the platform gave way, and you tumbled to the ground."

"I—I'no' who di't," resumed the Captain. "Them Mulca'men. They saw-awed posts." Here the Captain descried two widow Slapmans smiling on him from a window, and gallantly kissed his hand at them.

His heavy body was tumbled into the rear of the sleigh, a buffalo robe thrown over it, and Captain Tonkins was then unconsciously borne toward the bosom of his family, in Minetta lane (a friend officiating as driver), amid the cheers of his late audience.

The three bachelors were satiated with their day's experiences. They raised their hats to Mrs. Slapman, still laughing at the window, and walked smartly home. Mr. Quigg, deriving much comfort from the thought that Captain Tonkins had not been paid for his sleigh, and would not be, hastened to a neighboring stable, hired the only remaining team, and continued his round of calls, giving one minute to each.

BOOK SECOND.

POLISHING.

CHAPTER I.

THE ENIGMA.

Marcus Wilkeson's new acquaintance throve rapidly. Mr. Minford's dealings with the world had made him shy and suspicious, and he was at first disposed to keep his benevolent visitor at a safe business distance. But the heart of the thoughtful mechanic could not long resist the kind and earnest sympathy of the man who sought to be his friend.

With a caution born of experience, however, Mr. Minford, before admitting the new guest to his full confidence, called upon a number of Wall street brokers and South street merchants, to whom Marcus had referred him, and learned from them that that gentleman bore a reputation of the rarest honor and purity of character. While giving this united testimony, however, they all agreed in condemning Mr. Wilkeson's eccentricity—insanity, one broker called it—in retiring from business at the very moment when he was most successful, and had a great fortune within easy reach. The fact that he had retired with one hundred and fifty thousand dollars, instead of mitigating his offence in the eyes of those critics, increased it. "Why," said a noted bear, "with that amount of capital, and Wilkeson's first-rate talents—when he chose to use them—he might have become the king of Wall street. It's a pity so smart a fellow should make a wreck of himself." And the bear heaved a sigh of commiseration; which was by no means echoed by Mr. Minford, who gathered, from all this evidence, an increased esteem for his benefactor.

From the time when he first crossed the threshold of the house on his mission of mercy, Pet had looked upon him with the deepest reverence. She had read, in story books, of mysterious gentlemen who went about doing good merely for the pleasure of it, and who always reached the scene of distress with fairy-like certainty, when everybody and everything would have gone to ruin without them. Such a strange, supernatural embodiment of goodness seemed Marcus Wilkeson to her childish fancy. When he entered the room—and he was an every-day caller now—she looked around with great anxiety to see that all the chairs were in their proper places; that there was no dirt or dust visible anywhere; that everything was in a state of order and cleanliness worthy so exalted a guest.

She would run to take his overcoat and hat and cane, and place them as carefully in the clothes press as if they had been the robe, crown, and sceptre of a king. Then she would sit in her little chair, and take her sewing, or knitting, or embroidery, and pretend to be all absorbed in it, while she was listening eagerly to every word that Marcus addressed to her father, and occasionally looked up at the face of their guest, and thought how noble it was, and how proud she should be to call him uncle.

When he spoke to her, as he often did, and asked her about her work, or her companions, or her studies (upon the latter subject he had grown quite curious, of late), she would feel that she was blushing, and answer, with downcast eyes, and be half glad and half sorry when he ceased to question her, and would then sit and torment herself by recalling what she had said, and thinking how much it might have been improved.

A sharp-eyed observer, had such been present, accustomed to studying the human face and weighing motives, would have been puzzled to guess the exact nature of the feelings which Marcus entertained for the pretty, innocent young creature who sat there, always plying her little fingers at some useful work. The puzzle would have been a still greater one for Mr. Wilkeson himself. He felt a profound interest in Pet; and she it was, and not the pale mechanic or his novel machine, that led him daily up those three flights of rickety stairs to that humble room. He said to himself, and he would have said to anybody who was entitled to call upon him for an explanation, that he had always loved children, and that the beauty and goodness of this child had deeply interested him. If there was any other motive at the bottom of his heart, he studiously concealed it from himself, as he would have concealed it from all the world.

During these visits, Mr. Minford pursued his work without interruption. The screens, which were at first jealously closed, were now thrown open, and the inventor sat there in full sight of his visitor, laboring at his great mechanical problem. Repeatedly he had begged of Marcus the privilege of explaining to him the principles of the machine; but that gentleman had always resolutely declined, for the reasons before stated. And he had always observed that, a few moments after such refusal, the face of the inventor would brighten up, as if with joy that he had not parted with his secret even to one who held a fifth interest in it.

Of the wonderful results which the machine was sure to accomplish, Mr. Minford was never tired of talking, nor Mr. Wilkeson of hearing, although, at these times, his eyes followed the flying motions of Pet's fingers, as if they were a part of the wonder of which the inventor discoursed so glowingly.

Precisely what the machine was to effect, when completed, Marcus Wilkeson would never have known, if he had been the most attentive of listeners. Mr. Minford spoke in vague, general terms, that afforded no clue to the mystery. He talked of old philosophers and mechanicians, who had failed to discover an unnamed secret of Nature, because they had no faith in its existence. Complete faith in the existence of the thing to be discovered, as well as in the ability of the searcher to find it, he regarded as indispensable conditions of an inventor's success.

The fact that the natural law which he was trying to demonstrate had been pronounced an impossibility by professors of science, should weigh as nothing in the mind of any man who remembered how every great invention of the age had in turn been stamped "impossible" by those dogmatizers in their academical chairs, their books, and their reviews. Latterly (Mr. Minford confessed), the scientific theorists had been more tolerant toward other people's inventions (they never invent anything themselves); but with regard to the one upon which he was now engaged, they had, with complete unanimity, decided that the thing could not be done, and charitably called every man an idiot or a lunatic who attempted to do it.

"The world has at last fallen into this belief," Mr. Minford would say, bitterly, "and the few people with whom I am acquainted would all agree in echoing these scientific opinions, if they knew what I am working at. But no one shall know—excepting you, Mr. Wilkeson, to whom I should be most happy to explain everything, if you would only let me. This prejudice is too deep rooted to be readily pulled up. Even when my invention is perfected, and has entered upon its boundless career of usefulness, I know that it will be called a humbug; that people will look at it, and see it in operation, and still say it is a lie. Yet the time will come when the professors of science will feel proud to expound, by formulas, the very invention which they have shown, by formulas, to be an absolute contradiction of all the laws of Nature. As for the rabble who make up the world (the inventor's lips curled as he said this), they will be glad to atone for the mad hue-and-cry with which they will follow me at first, by giving me, at last, limitless wealth and immortal fame."

Mr. Minford's eyes flashed; and Marcus Wilkeson, looking up at them from Pet's volant fingers, saw in their sudden glare what he took to be the evidence of genius; but what, in an ordinary man, he would have called a decided symptom of insanity.

CHAPTER II.

A DELICATE PROPOSITION.

One afternoon—when Mr. Minford was in excellent humor, having made a great discovery in the course of his experiments the previous night—Marcus thought it a good opportunity to propose something that had been on his mind for a week past.

"Mr. Minford," he said, "will you excuse me for meddling a little in your household affairs?"

"Not if you offer me any more kindness," returned the inventor, smiling gratefully at his guest. "I am too much in your debt already."

"But you forget that I hold an interest in your invention, which you would make me take. I consider that more than payment in full."

"So you have confidence in my success?"

"You have begun to inspire me with it, I confess," replied Marcus, indulging in a little unavoidable flattery. "But—but it was not to *you* that I was about to offer any kindness," he continued, emphasizing the personal pronoun, and looking hard at Pet, who bent patiently over her work, and began to blush in anticipation that her name would be mentioned. Mr. Minford raised his eyes from a ratchet which he was finishing in a vice, and glanced with curiosity at the speaker.

"Do you not think, sir, that your daughter might profitably spare a few hours every day toward the completion of her education? You have told me that her studies were interrupted by a change in your circumstances, some years ago."

"Certainly she might," answered the inventor, "and I thank you for the suggestion. This machine has so completely engaged my thoughts, that I had quite lost sight of the dear girl's education. I should say, however, that I have been expecting at any moment to put the finishing touch on my invention, the very first profits of which I shall spend in employing a dozen teachers, if need be, for my little Pet. She shall be an educated lady, if money can make her so. Sha'n't you, Pet?"

The young girl's fingers twinkled faster at her work. "I hope so, father," said she.

"But, Mr. Minford, it is possible—barely possible, you know—that your invention may not be completed, nor money be realized from it, for many months; perhaps one or two years. Suppose—only suppose, of course—your triumph to be postponed for even one year; your daughter will then be one year older, and less fitted to acquire the accomplishments which you desire her to possess, than she now is. Pardon the suggestion, if it is an obtrusive one. I plead the sincere interest which I take in you and her as my only excuse."

"No apology is needed, my dear sir," replied the inventor "I know and appreciate your thoughtful kindness toward us; and I consider your advice most excellent, especially as I intend to travel in Europe, and take out patents for my invention there. It would be desirable to have my Pet learn French, and also to improve her knowledge of music. You understand the English branches pretty well, I believe, my dear. Let me see—how long is it since you left school?"

"Three years, pa."

"True! true!" said the inventor, sadly. "It was when our troubles first began, and I found it necessary to economize. But I did very wrong to take you from school at that time."

"You forget, pa," replied his daughter, in a sweet, chiding voice. "You wanted me to go on with my studies, but I said that you must save the tuition money, and let me learn to keep house. Don't you remember, pa?"

"Yes, child; I remember. And I was selfish enough to allow you to make the sacrifice. But you shall have schooling to your heart's content now, whether you will or not. I agree with our dear friend, that no time should be lost in resuming your education. I shall insist upon setting apart two hundred dollars for that purpose. Enough money will still be left to perfect my invention; and that, too, within a month, notwithstanding" (he added, playfully) "Mr. Wilkeson's discouraging remarks a moment ago."

"And I shall insist upon not taking the money, pa," said Pet, laughing, but shaking her head, and patting her feet on the floor in the most decisive manner.

"And *I* shall insist on furnishing the money," said Marcus Wilkeson, folding his arms, and looking very much in earnest. "Let us see who can be obstinate the longest."

"Then *I* shall insist on your taking another fifth interest in the invention. Upon that point I am immovable." Mr. Minford folded his arms likewise, to imply that nothing could shake his granitic determination.

"Ah, now I see some prospect of a friendly arrangement. I will pay five hundred dollars for another fifth, and esteem it a good bargain, provided your daughter consents to let one half of it be spent on her education. What do you say to that, Pet?"

"That I thank you very much for your kind offer," said the young girl, whose eyes sparkled with gratitude; "but I must not accept it. Pa will need all the money he can get to finish his work. I know it."

Marcus and the father exchanged pleasant looks, and the former said, with an ill-assumed sternness:

"Then I don't advance another cent to him. I have named my conditions, and they must be accepted. You have no idea, Pet, what a tremendously obstinate fellow I am when I'm roused."

Nobody could have gathered the idea from his intensely amiable face at that moment.

"I see, my dear, that we must yield to this determined man," said Mr. Minford, winking at Marcus. "We shall never have any peace with him until we do."

"You know best, pa," returned his daughter, who shrank timidly from any further discussion with their guest.

Marcus Wilkeson was delighted with the perfect confidence which father and child reposed in him. "Now that this little matter is happily settled," said he, "I must tell you that I have already taken the liberty of selecting a school for her."

"How can we ever repay your goodness?" said Mr. Minford.

"It is situated only two blocks away," pursued Marcus.

"Capital!" cried Mr. Minford; "for then she will never be far from home."

"And if you want me at any time, pa, you can send for me, and I can be here in a moment," said Pet. "It will be so delightful!"

"It is a private school, and, if your daughter prefers, she can be taught separately from the other pupils. Miss Pillbody, the teacher, tells me that she can give her an hour and a half in the morning, before ten o'clock, and half an hour in the afternoon, after four o'clock."

"That will suit me exactly, pa," cried Pet, clapping her hands with glee; "because then I can get your breakfast, dinner, and supper, and do all the housework, without any interruption in my studies."

"Miss Pillbody thought the arrangement would suit you. She is a perfectly competent teacher of French, Italian, the English branches, music, drawing, the dead languages, and higher mathematics—quite a prodigy, I assure you, for a lady not yet twenty-two years old." (Marcus was addressing the father.) "I have been particular in my inquiries, and all who know her speak in the highest terms of her remarkable attainments, her ability to teach others, and her goodness of heart. Your daughter will like her, without doubt."

"I know I shall," said Pet, with enthusiasm. "There are so many things that I will learn, pa. First, music——"

"She has a fine piano, and plays splendidly," remarked the guest. "I heard her."

"And French and Italian, to please you, pa—that is, if I can learn them—and everything else that the lady will teach me. I shall be so happy, sir."

The father and the guest smiled at the zeal with which this young beginner proposed to grapple with the difficulties of human knowledge. It was fortunate for her that a long series of hard and injudicious teachers had not already sickened her of learning, and that she brought a fresh and uncorrupted taste to the work.

Pet was thinking which one of her two dresses (equally faded) she should wear to school, and what bit of ribbon or trimming she could introduce in her old bonnet, to improve its general effect. Marcus Wilkeson was marvelling at the confidence which the inventor and his daughter placed in him, and at what there was about him to inspire it. Mr. Minford was congratulating himself on having met with a man so generous and sincere as this Mr. Wilkeson, and so entirely disinterested, too: "For," reasoned the inventor, "he cannot appreciate, as I do, the enormous value of my discovery, and does not dream that his portion of it will compensate him for his outlay more than a hundred times over."

The silence was broken by a sound as of heavy boots trying to move softly on the stairs, and a subsequent modest rap at the door.

CHAPTER III.

AN AUXILIARY OF MODERN CIVILIZATION.

THE boy Bog rapped, and entered. He was more neatly dressed than when Marcus saw him on the occasion of his first visit. His patched and threadbare coat was replaced by a neat roundabout jacket; his greasy, visorless cap, by a flat felt hat, of which the brim was symmetrically turned up; his tattered shoes by great cowhide boots. The boy was of that age when the human frame grows with vegetable-like rapidity; and he seemed to have increased a little all around within three weeks.

The boy looked distressingly awkward in his new articles of attire. Had he stolen them, he could not have appeared more guilty in presence of the rightful owner.

"Why, Bog!" said Mr. Minford, reproachfully; "where have you been these three weeks? Not called to see us once!"

The boy's confusion increased at this unexpected salutation, and he hung down his head at the threshold of the door. Mr. Minford partly reassured his bashful visitor, by springing forward, shaking him heartily by the hand, and saying, with earnestness, "My good lad, I am always glad to see you." Pet was also by his side in an instant, and warmly shaking the other hand. "You look real nice, Bog," said she. Mr. Wilkeson also came forward, and said, "Don't you remember me, Bog?" and clasped him by the right hand when the inventor had relinquished it.

Bog bowed and scraped and blushed, and murmured "Thank you, very well," several times, confusedly, and at last settled down into a chair which was pushed under him by Pet. Having crossed his legs, he began to feel a little more at ease.

"You've been very busy of late, haven't you, Bog?" asked Pet, charitably anticipating an excuse for the boy's long absence.

"You'd better believe it," replied Bog, not looking at her, but studying the pattern of his left boot. "The day arter I called here last, Mr. Fink he got a job to stick up bills for a new hair dye, all the way from here to Dunkirk, on the Erie Railroad. Well, he couldn't go, cos he had lots o' city posting, yo see; so he hires me to do it for ten dollars a week and expenses. The pay was good, he said, because the work was extry hard. The bills was to be posted on new whitewashed fences, new houses, and places generally where there was signs up telling people not to 'post no bills.'"

"That was a singular direction, Bog," said Mr. Minford.

"So I told Mr. Fink," replied the boy; "but he said as how them were the hair-dye man's orders. He said the idea was to make folks look at bills who wouldn't notice 'em if they was on a place all covered over with adv'tisements. They was to be posted up high and strong, so that the owner of the property couldn't tear 'em down easy. Mr. Fink thought the idea was a good one; but he owned it was a little risky."

"Perhaps that is why he didn't care to do it himself," suggested Marcus Wilkeson.

"Mebbe," said Bog; "but I didn't consider it no objection. I told him I was goin' to be a bill poster, and wanted to study every branch o' the business." At this point Bog hitched his chair nervously, uncrossed and recrossed his legs, as if he were conscious of trespassing on the patience of his auditors, and then went on: "Well, I hurried home, and saw that aunt didn't want for nothin', and then I started on my travels. I should ha' called and seen you, Mr. Minford," he added, casting a side glance at the inventor, "but I hadn't time."

"No excuse necessary, my good Bog," returned Mr. Minford, kindly. "Business before pleasure, you know. But I am anxious to hear how you got along with the job."

"Well, pooty hard," said Bog, emphatically, "though I made out to go all through the State, and stick up six thousand bills, every one on 'em on a new house, shop, or fence. Lemme see—I was chased seven times by big dogs that was set on me, shot at three times——"

"Why, poor Bog!" interrupted Pet; "you wern't hurt, I hope?"

"No, Miss Minford; I wasn't hurt," answered Bog, looking her in the face for the first time since he entered the house, "though I got one through my old cap."

"I'm *so* glad it was no worse, Bog."

These words of sympathy from the young girl flustered the poor boy for a minute. Then he rallied:

"Besides that, I was took up four times by the perlice, and was carried afore justices of the peace. When they asked what I had to say why I shouldn't be fined, I told 'em the whole truth about it, and they all laughed except one, and said it was really funny, and they hadn't no doubt the hair dye was a very good thing to take, but could tell better after they had tried some. I told 'em that the hair-dye man would send 'em a dozen bottles apiece. Mr. Fink had d'rected me to say this, if I was 'rested and brought afore a justice. The justices—that is, all of 'em but one—then said they didn't want to be hard on me; and as that was my first offence, they would let me go without any fine. And they did, after givin' me their names, and tellin' me to be sure to have the bottles sent on jest as soon as could be. Ye see, they were all as bald on the top o' their heads as punkins. But the fourth justice that I was took to, he wasn't bald, but had a crop o' hair like a picter; and when I offered to put down his name for a dozen bottles, he swore, and fined me five dollars for what he said was a insult to the dignity of justice, and five dollars for postin' up bills in places where it was agin the law. Mr. Fink had give me money from the hair-dye man to pay fines, as well as my board; so I didn't care. But—but I am talking too much."

Bog paused, because, on taking a stealthy observation around him, he suddenly become conscious that his three auditors were listening attentively to his story.

"Not at all, my dear Bog," said Mr. Minford. "I, for one, am curious to know how this ingenious plan of advertising, in defiance of the law, succeeded." Mr. Wilkeson expressed himself curious on the same point. Bog, thus encouraged, continued:

"When I come home, after havin' stuck up six thousand bills in the principal towns and villages along the route, I went right to Mr. Fink. He shook hands with me, and ses he,

'Bog, your fortun's made.' 'How's that?' said I. 'Why,' ses he, 'you're the greatest bill poster I ever heerd of. Professor Macfuddle" (that was the hair-dye man) "ses the money has begun to pour in to him like sixty, and he is buyin' up all the hair dye in the market, and puttin' his labils on it to supply the demand. He has given me ten dollars to present to you, besides the thirty for your wages.' Mr. Fink then give me forty dollars, and ses he, 'That a'n't all; for I have so much business now, I want a pardner, and I'll take you, and give you one third of the earnin's.' I rather guess I snapped at the offer; and we is goin' into pardnership to-morrer."

"Success to you," said Marcus and the inventor together. They saw, in this illustration of his bill-posting talents, only an evidence of business shrewdness that deserved encouragement. The young girl, however, viewed it in the light of a violation of law, and therefore could not conscientiously approve of it. Bog noticed her silence, and guessed the cause.

"Thank you very much," said he; "but I forgot to say I a'n't goin' to do any more business on the Erie plan. It a'n't right. Come to think it over, I was sorry I done it; and so I told Mr. Fink; and he sed it wasn't exackly reg'lar either, and he shouldn't never ask me to do it agen."

"I am glad of that," said Pet, quietly.

Bog's eyes were instantly turned toward her with an expression of pride and gratitude.

"Oh! of course, it is always best to obey the laws," observed Mr. Minford.

"And I wouldn't for a moment be thought to advise anything else," added Marcus Wilkeson; "though I never could help admiring pluck and sharpness in business affairs."

"I am going to school again, Bog," said the young girl, hastening to change the subject of conversation.

Bog looked up, surprised and pleased.

"Mr. Wilkeson," said Mr. Minford, "has taken another small share in my invention, and pays me in advance for it. With that, Pet will finish her education." The inventor would have made this disclosure of his private affairs to no other human being but Bog; for this simple boy was the only person he had ever known (excepting Marcus Wilkeson) who had not openly ridiculed his mysterious labors.

"I am very glad to hear of it, sir," said Bog, awkwardly, but with an air of profound respect. "How—how is the *ma-sheen*, sir?" Bog asked the question hurriedly, as if the machine were a sick person, whose health he had until then forgotten to inquire after.

"Getting on finely, Bog. Only two or three springs, a cog here, a ratchet here, a band at this point, and a lever up there (Mr. Minford touched portions of the machine rapidly), and then look out for a noise!"

"A noise!" repeated Bog, with juvenile earnestness.

"Not an explosion, my good fellow, but tremendous public excitement—plenty of fame, mixed with a good deal of abuse at first, and a *little* money, I hope." The inventor's eyes flashed with the fire that Bog had often seen; and when he emphasized the word "little," Bog knew that he meant to express the boundlessness of the wealth that his labors would bring to him.

"I believe it," said Bog, with sincerity pictured in every lineament of his honest face. "I've always believed it."

"So you have, my dear Bog; and your faith has often cheered me," replied the inventor, patronizingly. "By the way, how's your aunt?"

"Oh, yes; how *is* your aunt, Bog?" asked Pet. "I had quite forgotten her."

"She's pooty well, ony them rheumatics troubles her some. They're workin' their way from her left arm into her head, aunt says. Week afore last they was in her feet, and they've ben clear round her and goin' back agen since then. Queer things, them rheumatics!"

"They are very painful, Bog, you know," said Pet.

"Yes; so aunt says." Bog did not add, as he might have truly done, "A thousand times a day."

"Give her my kind regards, Bog, and say I will call and see her," continued Pet.

"My respectful regards also," added Mr. Minford.

"Thank you," said the boy; "but I guess you better not call, Miss Minford. Aunt's a good woman, but kind o' cur'us, you know. Them rheumatics has made a great change in her." Bog here referred, but made no verbal allusion, to a certain friendly call which Pet had once made upon his aunt, on which occasion that elderly lady had entertained her visitor with a monologue two hours long, giving her a complete history of the malady, from its birth in the right great toe, three years previous, through all its eccentric phenomena, to that stage of the disease which made it, as the venerable sufferer observed with some pride, the "very wust case the doctors ever heerd of."

Upon this fruitful theme, Bog's aunt could and would have discoursed for hours longer, but for the appearance of Bog, when she sought a new relief from her agonies by abusing that poor fellow, charging him with neglect and ingratitude, finding fault with the food which he brought home for her from market, and asking him when he was going to buy that soft armchair he had promised her so long. Bog laughed, and explained this outburst, by saying to Pet, "It's only aunt's rheumatics;" but the old lady rejected the explanation, and went on scolding and faultfinding with such increased fierceness, that Pet hastily put on her bonnet and shawl, and bade the rheumatic grumbler "good-by," saying (which was true) that her father would be anxious about her. Since then, the young girl had kept away from Bog's aunt.

"I've bought her a nice, soft armchair lately," continued Bog; "but it don't do her no good. The rheumatics seem to be getting wusser all the time; and the thing that makes them wussest of all is calls. So I guess it's better for aunt you should keep away, Miss Minford." Bog prided himself on his tact in putting forth the last argument.

Then the conversation turned on Pet's education; Marcus

and her father fondly discussing what it ought to be, and Bog listening, and looking stealthily at the young girl, still busy at her work; and they all sat, happy in thoughts of the future, far into the twilight.

CHAPTER IV.

MISS PILLBODY.

MISS PILLBODY'S school was unknown to the pages of the City Directory. It was never advertised in the newspapers, with a long list of "Hons." and bank presidents as unimpeachable references. The bright little plate on her door exhibited only "Pillbody," in neat script, and no hint of the existence of a school within. The school was select to such an extent, that not more than a dozen pupils were admitted to its privileges; and so private, that, outside of that number, its name was not known except among its graduates; and there were reasons why they should hesitate to spread its reputation abroad. If strictly classified among the institutions of the city, it might be termed, "A school for female adults in good circumstances, whose early education had been neglected."

The idea of this school originated with Miss Pillbody; and, like many other valuable ideas, it was hit upon quite accidentally.

Dorcas Pillbody was the only daughter of a man who had amassed a fortune in the oyster business, and had finally retired to a four-story house in Sixteenth street, near the Sixth Avenue, where he purposed to spend the balance of his days in the dignified enjoyment of his hard-earned money. To this secluded oyster dealer, as solitary and happy in the midst of his new grandeur as a bivalve in its native bed, came a plausible stockbroker, who, after a series of interviews, persuaded Mr. Pillbody to make a small investment in the "Sky Blue Ridge Pure Vein Copper Mining Company."

The small investment unfortunately turned out well. In

less than sixty days, the shares that he had bought at ten per cent. sold at seventy-five, and ultimately advanced to par Delighted with this unexpected result, Mr. Pillbody determined to stake largely (he had been a wholesale oyster dealer, and was a man of comprehensive ideas). Again his venture prospered. Mr. Pillbody, intoxicated with success, invested his entire means in the purchase of two new mines in a Southern State, whose unparalleled richness was certified to by mineralogists of great reputation.

Just as Mr. Pillbody was making arrangements to bring these mines before the public, his stockbroking friend, through whom he had effected the purchase, left for Europe, and it was then discovered that Mr. Pillbody's mines, if they existed at all, were ten feet under a swamp, on property which belonged to somebody else, the title deeds of which had been forged by the adroit operator. Mr. Pillbody could not endure his misfortune. He wrote notes bidding farewell to his wife and child, and commending them to the care of their relatives, to whom he had always been bountifully generous. Then he went to Staten Island by ferry, there took a row boat, proceeded to a celebrated oyster bed which was the scene of his youthful labors, and drowned himself.

The widow and daughter (the latter twenty years of age, healthy, and finely educated) applied to the two brothers of the deceased for assistance, and were at once kindly received into their families, and sat upon sofas and ate from tables purchased with money (never repaid) of the late Mr. Pillbody. The two brothers, upon application to the proper tribunal, were appointed executors of the estate, and were not long in discovering that it was insolvent. Mother and daughter were shifted about with almost monthly regularity from one house to the other; and, though they tried to make themselves useful in every capacity except that of a servant, they could not disguise the conviction that their departure was an event a great deal more welcome than their coming. The widow's talent for dressmaking (she had been a milliner's apprentice before marriage), though of a high order, and exerted to the utmost, failed to please. Miss Pillbody's thorough knowledge of French, and the higher branches of an elegant education, as well as her proficiency on the piano, and her sweet, simple style of ballad singing, were worse than useless acquirements in her uncles' families.

Her uncles were cold, stern, ignorant men, who had an intense hatred for the mere accomplishments of life. Each had two daughters, who, with the natural tastes of the sex, were not averse to the graces of education, in the abstract, but could not bear to see them displayed by their "stuck-up, pauper cousin," as they often termed that hapless young lady in private conversation. A kind offer, which she was imprudent enough to make, to teach them all she knew, had set them against her from the first.

The widow endured the cold looks and cutting words of her husband's relatives, and even the reproaches which they heaped upon his folly, with a widow's patience, and seemed content to remain a poor, broken-down, dependent creature. Miss Pillbody, on the contrary, was quick to discern and to resent, mentally, the uncivil treatment daily experienced by her mother and herself. Had she been alone in the world, she would have left those inhospitable roofs when the unkind hints first began to be dropped, and trusted to the cold charity of strangers; but she could not bear the thought of being separated from her mother. So she endured her wretched state of dependence as best she could, while she quietly sought for some means of employment that would yield them a living.

Profiting by the lessons she had learned from her uncles, she did not apply to any person who had known her father and received favors from him in their better days. She asked no favor from any one—only work, at a fair price. By diligent hunting, she found several opportunities. She could earn four dollars a week by embroidering (at which she was skilful, and had taken premiums); or two dollars and a half for teaching French, twice a week, in a country seminary; or her board and washing for inducting a family of four little musical prodigies into all the mysteries of the piano. But these tempting offers would still have left her mother with her uncles, and she spurned them all.

CHAPTER V.

A FRIEND IN NEED.

ONE day, as Miss Pillbody was riding up Broadway, intending to visit a Teachers' Agency for the sixteenth time, she accidentally made the acquaintance of a middle-aged lady, who talked a great deal upon the slightest provocation, trifled sadly with grammar and pronunciation, and was excessively friendly and amiable. The diamonds in her ears and on her fingers, and her overdone and gaudy style of dressing, were some indication, though not a convincing one, that she was a woman of wealth; and Miss Pillbody made bold to ask her if she knew anybody who wanted a private teacher in her family.

The lady said she did not, "unless," she added, laughing very loud at the humor of the suggestion, "you come into my family, and learn me something."

The remark was unpremeditated, but, the moment it was made, the lady seemed to be greatly struck with its force, and immediately followed it up with the question, "Do you s'pose you could learn grammar and pronunciation, and how to talk French, to a grown-up woman like me?" Miss Pillbody thought the lady with the diamonds was joking, and laughed by way of reply. "But I am ra-ally in earnest," continued the lady, thoughtfully, turning three heavy cluster rings on her little left finger. "Ye see, my early eddication was rather poor, 'cos I was poor then; but my old man made a spec' in tobacco, last year, and now I'm pooty well off, and live in good s'ciety. I kinder feel the want of grammar, French, and a few o' them things. I like your face and your manners and if you can learn me 'em, I'll give you ten dollars a week to come to my house one hour every day, and be my private schoolmistress. It'll be rather hard, I s'pose, to learn an old dog new tricks; but there is no harm a-tryin'."

Notwithstanding the oddity of the proposition, Miss Pillbody saw by the lady's face that she meant what she said. "I think I understand English grammar, and French, and the other branches usually taught at academies," she replied, "and should be very happy to accept your offer."

"Then consider the bargain closed," returned the lady. "Here is my 'dress" (handing her a card), "and you may come to-morrer mornin', at ten o'clock, if that'll suit you. I have no children, and the old man will be out at that time, and we shall be as snug as two bugs in a rug, ye see."

Miss Pillbody was delighted with the sudden prospect of an honest living thus opened to her, and she only feared that she would not be able to do enough for her money. So, after she had again thanked the lady for her kindness, she said:

"I think I could give you lessons on the piano, madam—unless you understand that instrument better than I do."

"Lor' bless me, child!" responded the lady, holding up her thick, red hands, and making the diamonds flash in the sunlight; "Lor' bless me! them fingers is too stiff to play the pianner now. I've got a splendid pianner, though, with an oleon 'tachment, three pedals, and pearl keys—cost eight hundred dollar; and a nice piece of furniture it is, you may believe. I let it be out of tune all the time. That's an excuse for not playing when anybody asks me to, ye know. I don't mind tellin' you this, because you'll be sure to find it out." And the lady laughed very loudly at the confession of this small deceit, which Miss Pillbody assured her was by no means confined to herself, but had been adopted by her ingenious sex from time immemorial.

When the middle-aged pupil and her young teacher separated, as they did on the arrival of the stage at an up-town jeweller's, where the former got out to make a few purchases,

Miss Pillbody felt as if she had known her patroness for years, and that, in that coarse, showy, good-hearted woman, she had found a true friend.

And so it turned out. However dull Mrs. Crull might be as a scholar, she was quick-witted as a friend, and was constantly bestowing unexpected kindnesses upon Miss Pillbody. Scarcely a day passed that the young teacher did not receive from her pupil some little present—at times rising to the value of a bonnet or a shawl. Mrs. Crull's all-embracing kindness would have extended to the widow Pillbody too (in whom she was much interested from the daughter's accounts of her), but for the shrewd objection which she entertained against intrusting any one with the secret of her pupilage. Miss Pillbody was often and particularly enjoined by her not to tell any one—not even her mother—of it; and she saw the advantages of carefully observing the request. Great pains were taken to keep Mr. Crull, and the housemaid, cook, and coachman, from a knowledge of the mystery.

On Miss Pillbody's arrival daily at ten A. M., she was ushered into the drawing room, where Mrs. Crull was always anxiously awaiting her. The servant was told to say to callers that "Mistress is out" (Mrs. Crull bolted at this trifling deception at first, but soon got used to it), and the lesson began.

Mrs. Crull at first thought she was competent to learn her native tongue and French together, in a series of half-hour lessons; but she soon found out that the latter language had some eccentric peculiarities quite beyond her powers of articulation, and that the spelling of a word did not afford the slightest clue to the method of pronouncing it. After floundering about heroically but hopelessly through the introductory chapter of the first French grammar, she gave up the polite tongue in despair, consoling herself with the reflection, that speaking bad French was worse than speaking no French at all.

Miss Pillbody, who did not venture to advise her pupil on her choice of studies, but left her to consult her own fancies undisturbed, heartily approved of Mrs. Crull's conclusion, though she acknowledged that New York society by no means took that view of the case, but tolerated bad French with a courtesy worthy of France itself.

Mrs. Crull's studies were thereafter confined to English spelling, grammar, and writing. She declared that she knew enough of arithmetic to count change correctly, and wanted to know no more; and that geography was of no earthly use to her. Besides, she never could remember the names of places.

It was in pronunciation that Miss Pillbody's system achieved the greatest good. Anxious to strengthen herself on that weak point, Mrs. Crull set a watch on her language, and gave every word a good look before she sent it forth. The effect of this constant introspection was most happy; but, at times, Mrs. Crull would be thrown off her guard by a rush of ideas, and all the old blunders would come out. Toward other persons, she became, to some extent, a free teacher, and would, in the most obliging manner, rectify their little errors of pronunciation, when she was sure of them, and sometimes when she was not.

Of course, Mr. Crull was taken in training by her. That gentleman, having made the discovery, early in life, that the less a man says, the more he is supposed to know, had acquired a habit of taciturnity which had become a second nature to him. His conversation consisted mainly of grunts and nods; and it was astonishing how much he could express by them. At any rate, they had "made his fortin', and he couldn't ha' done more'n that if he'd talked like a house a-fire"—which explanation, often repeated, was about the longest one ever known to be uttered by Mr. Crull. Therefore Mr. Crull did not offer a large field for the exhibition of his wife's new acquirements; but, by drawing him into conversation, and then lying in wait for him, she found opportunities to exhibit them for his good.

At first, Mr. Crull only stared and grunted. Then he

laughed (his laugh and Mrs. Crull's laugh were very similar, and were their strongest bond of union). Once he said, "Wonder what's the matter with the ole woman?" And, on a subsequent occasion, when Mrs. Crull had convicted him of three mistakes in five words, he ventured upon this protracted remark: "Guess the ole gal feels rather big since she got inter wot they call good s'ciety, eh?" This was in allusion to the recent successful speculation in tobacco, which had enabled Mr. Crull to buy the best house in Twenty-third street, and take the second best pew in a fashionable church, thereby placing Mrs. Crull at once within the charmed circle of society.

As for himself, Mr. Crull took very little interest in society, having observed that society had taken very little interest in him until that "lucky turn in terbacker." Mrs. Crull would smile, and confess that society had claims upon people, and that, when one is in Rome, one must do as the Romans do. The moral of which proverb was, that Mr. Crull ought to improve his speech. Mr. Crull replied, by asking "wot difference 'twould make a hunderd years from now?" Which observation, when Mr. Crull condescended to speak at such length, was a favorite argument with him. But he little suspected his wife's secret.

CHAPTER VI.

BRANCHING OUT.

To Miss Pillbody, this quiet little arrangement proved a fortune indeed. In two weeks after she became acquainted with her benefactress, she was rich enough to take lodgings for her mother and herself at a decent boarding house. The old lady entertained singular notions about the rights of relationship, and held that it was the duty of her husband's brothers to give them a home for the balance of their lives, and regarded her daughter s desire to cut loose from her uncles, and be independent, as a romantic and absurd notion, born of novel reading, to which Miss Pillbody was a good deal addicted.

To gratify her daughter's whim, the widow Pillbody finally consented to move into a boarding house, though she did it in the firm belief that the good luck which the young lady had fallen upon would be of brief duration, and they would be glad to come back to their relatives again—their "natteral protectors," as Mrs. P. called them.

In their new residence, Miss Pillbody was happy. The money which she earned weekly, and which was always paid to her in advance, was sufficient for her own and her mother's board. In addition to other presents, Mrs. Crull had forced small sums upon her acceptance, at different times; and Miss Pillbody began to enjoy the odd sensation of laying up money in a savings bank. Of the future she thought but little; first, because she had no head for plans; and second, because Mrs. Crull had promised to set her up in a private school; and Miss Pillbody placed a blind trust in that lady. An accident, in this wise, caused the fulfilment of the promise much sooner than was expected.

Mr. Crull, in getting out of a stage, one day, slipped on the step, and dislocated his left shoulder. At his age, careful treatment was necessary for an injury of that kind; and the family doctor peremptorily forbade him to leave the house for a month. Mr. Crull therefore stayed at home, growling like a bear in a cage, and solacing himself with the determination to bring a suit for damages against the stage company, the carelessness of whose driver (in Mr. Crull's opinion) caused the accident.

Mr. Crull, like a good husband, would have nobody to nurse him, apply his embrocations, and put on his bandages, but his wife; and Mrs. Crull, like a good wife, cheerfully and tenderly performed that duty. But this rendered necessary the abandonment of the daily lessons at her house; for she was liable to be summoned to her husband's bedside at any moment (he sent for her at every new twinge of pain); and, furthermore, it was his custom to crawl out of his couch every half hour, and wander restlessly through the house, until his wife, under the stern instructions of the family doctor, sent him back to bed again.

Mrs. Crull, though not wanting in love for her disabled consort, was loth to abandon her lessons. Having tasted of the Pierian spring, she desired to drink deeply.

As Miss Pillbody could not continue her course of instruction at Mrs. Crull's residence, without being detected in the act by the invalid lord of that mansion; and as it was clearly impracticable for Mrs. Crull to go to Miss Pillbody's boarding house, and turn the widow Pillbody out of the little room which mother and daughter jointly occupied, the generous pupil hit upon the idea of renting the ground floor of a house for her teacher, setting apart one room as a schoolroom, fitting it up for her in comfortable style, and helping her to get wealthy adult pupils enough to pay all the expenses of the establishment, and a handsome income besides.

Miss Pillbody thankfully accepted the noble offer; though she feared that she would never obtain scholars enough to repay the money which Mrs. Crull was willing to advance, and also to defray the current expenses of housekeeping.

Mrs. Crull entertained no such fears. She had great faith in the efficacy of advertising. She had personally known three quacks who made half a million apiece out of patent medicines; and one woman who had turned a common recipe for removing superfluous hair into an eligible establishment in Thirty-second street, and a country cottage, with sixteen acres under good cultivation. She believed that newspaper advertising was the shortest and surest road to fortune; and the only standing cause of quarrel between her and her husband was the latter's incredulous "Pooh! pooh!" at her theory upon this subject.

At her request, Miss Pillbody drew up this advertisement, and caused it to be inserted twice in three daily papers:

"To Ladies in Good Society who desire to Improve their Education.—A young lady who has moved in wealthy and fashionable circles, and has received the best education that New York city could afford, having met with reverses in fortune, would be happy to accept, as private pupils, a few ladies whose early cultivation was, for any reason, neglected. French, Italian, Spanish, vocal music, the piano, and all the English rudiments, taught at reasonable prices. Particular attention paid to pronunciation, spelling, and writing. Satisfactory references given and required.

"N.B.—Pupils taught separately, and at different hours.

"For further information, address 'Educatrix, New York Post Office.'"

There were many points in this advertisement to which Miss Pillbody's modesty took exception; but Mrs. Crull insisted upon them in a way that permitted no refusal. The little bit of bragging was the principal thing, she said. She had always observed that people are inclined to believe bragging advertisements, though they openly profess that they can't be taken in by them. As for the satisfactory references, she would undertake to give them, if they were required—which, of course, they would not be, as the mere offering of them invariably sufficed. If called upon, she would say that she knew a wealthy lady, the head of a family, who had derived the greatest possible benefit from the instructions of "Educatrix." If asked who she was, she could answer, that "Educatrix" would on no account allow the name to be made known, as it was a great merit of her system that she kept the names of her pupils a profound secret from each other, and from the rest of the world. The good sense of this regulation would at once be appreciated by all mature ladies who wished to repair the defects of their early education. Her own position as the mistress of an elegant mansion in Twenty-third street, would (Mrs. Crull reasoned) entitle her statement to ready belief.

The plan worked capitally. "Educatrix" received fifty

answers to her advertisement, and was busy more than a week calling at the houses of those who desired an interview with her. The ladies were all in good circumstances, and, without an exception, were the wives of men who had made sudden fortunes, after the manner common in the United States. Finding themselves elevated above the necessity of cooking their own dinners and washing their own clothes, they keenly felt the want, hitherto unknown, of an education which would fit them, in a measure, for that society whose portals were now thrown wide open to them. Miss Pillbody's gentle manners and polished ways gained for her the confidence of all; and she could have had fifty pupils daily, at two dollars a lesson (the fixed price), of one hour each, if it had been possible to teach that number.

Acting on the advice of Mrs. Crull, Miss Pillbody decided to accept only twelve pupils, for twenty-four lessons each, and devote six hours daily to them. This arrangement would give her six pupils a day; and the twelve would complete their course in about two months. Then she could take twelve more, and so on. It was plain, from the success of the first experiment, that there would never be a scarcity of pupils.

Mrs. Crull then rented the first floor and basement of a suitable house in a quiet neighborhood, furnished it nicely, hired a grand piano for the front parlor, and turned over the premises and their contents to her young teacher. Miss Pillbody brought her mother to their new home, a fair share of which had been set apart and fitted up expressly for her.

The old lady admitted, with some reluctance, that the house was not badly furnished, and that her daughter's prospects might be worse than they were. But who was this mysterious woman, that took such an interest in her daughter? What was her motive? she would like to know. And why was she so anxious to avoid her (Mrs. Pillbody)? To which questions her daughter responded, as she had done fifty times before, that her teaching was strictly private, and that none of her pupils would visit her, except under a pledge of the profoundest secrecy. Mrs. Pillbody shook her head doubtingly, and said, "We shall see," adding that she only hoped they would be as comfortable there as they were at Uncle John's and Daniel's, that was all.

The school throve. The pupils came with great punctuality at their different hours, and were unknown to each other and to the world. The secret of the school would never have got abroad, but for the incaution of a certain Mrs. Brigback (wife of a man who had been connected with the City Government for two years on a nominal salary, and retired rich). She was so delighted at the progress which she made in the English rudiments, and in the French (being able to ask for bread, or fish, or concerning a person's health, in that language), that she could not refrain from confidentially advising another lady (the wife of a street contractor, suddenly opulent) to take a few lessons from the same accomplished teacher. The street contractor's wife was perfectly indifferent to society, and had no wish to remedy the defects of her early education. She promised secrecy, and the next day told the story, at the expense of her friend, to a mutual female acquaintance, who passed it on with embellishments to a third, who amused a fourth with its narration; and so it went through a succession of confidential people, until, one day, it became the subject of conversation in a stage in which Marcus Wilkeson was riding. He could not avoid hearing it; and, although the two ladies (themselves shockingly astray in their grammar) laughed at the absurdity of the thing, Marcus Wilkeson thought it was a capital idea. A plan which he had been idly revolving in his mind for the education of Miss Minford, began to take shape. The inventor (he reasoned) would not be likely to object to a strictly private school for his daughter, if the teacher were a lady of correct principles, and highly educated.

Upon the last point, Marcus Wilkeson determined to satisfy himself. So he addressed a note, through the General Post Office, to "Miss Pillbody, New York City," requesting the privilege of an interview on business, at the residence of the lady, the exact location of which she was asked to designate.

The letter was advertised (Miss Pillbody's address being unknown to the carrier), and, about two weeks after it was written, an answer came back to Mr. Wilkeson, at his house, giving information as to the whereabouts of the lady, and appointing the time for an interview.

Mr. Wilkeson called, and in five minutes' conversation was satisfied of Miss Pillbody's moral and intellectual qualifications as teacher, and thought himself very fortunate in securing a vacancy among the pupils (caused by sudden illness) for Miss Minford. With what perfect confidence the suspicious inventor, as well as his simple-hearted daughter, accepted the frank offer of their friend and benefactor, we have already seen.

CHAPTER VII.

THE LITTLE PUPIL.

It was a pleasant winter's morning, when Mr. Minford and his daughter, and their singular friend, made a formal call on Miss Pillbody, by appointment. The inventor had overcome a difficulty in his machine, by introducing a cam movement, and was in excellent humor. As he walked along the streets, he said that the snow and the sky and his future all looked bright to him now. Of the two former objects his assertion was obviously true; and Pet enjoyed the shining scene, as youth, health, and innocence always do, without reference to the future.

A few minutes' walk brought them to Miss Pillbody's private schoolhouse. A pull at the bell summoned a stout, red-faced servant girl to the door. To the question, if Miss Pillbody was in, she said, "Yaas, sir, ef yer plaze" (Miss P. had vainly endeavored to correct her English), and ushered her visitors into the reception parlor, or schoolroom.

A pleasant place it was, and nicely warmed with a smouldering coal fire, the coziness and comfort of which were fitly reflected from the red carpet, and red curtains, and red plush covered furniture. The grand piano, hired for use, gave the room that completely furnished appearance that nothing but a piano can give. A book of instruction, open at a passage which strongly resembled a rail fence through a rolling country, showed that inexperienced hands had recently been pounding the instrument. There was no sign of a school on any side, excepting a small blackboard, which had been hastily thrust into a corner, and which bore, faintly traced in chalk, a sum in simple division.

The visitors sat down in the warm red chairs, and looked around the room but a moment, when Miss Pillbody entered by a door connecting with the rear parlor. She bowed gracefully to Mr. Wilkeson, and was by him introduced to his two companions. To the father she was profoundly respectful, and to the daughter tender and affectionate, grasping her hand closely, and smiling a welcome upon her.

Pet was instantly fascinated with her future teacher. There was something lovable not only in her intelligent face, pale with the protracted labors of her daily life, but in the infirmity of her eyes, for she was shortsighted, and could see objects distinctly only by nearly closing the lids. This peculiarity, not disagreeable in itself, won upon Pet's compassion, and made her feel more at home in the strange lady's presence than if she were conscious that a pair of full-sighted orbs were looking at her, and accurately noting her defects.

Miss Pillbody's occupation, for some weeks past, had given her a new idea of the value of time, and she proceeded at once to business, without wasting a single word upon the weather. In less than five minutes, she had, by artful inquiries and a winning voice, found out the exact range and extent of Miss Minford's acquirements, and agreed with the father that a further education in the English branches was unnecessary at that time (with the exception, perhaps, of an occasional exercise in reading), and that his daughter might devote twenty-four lessons to French and the piano, with hopes of success, provided she could study and practise several hours a day at her own home.

Mr. Minford replied, that she could study French at home to her heart's content, but he had no piano. Whereupon Mr. Wilkeson took the liberty of suggesting that it might be possible to borrow one, at a moderate rate, by the month, and set it up in their front room. Miss Pillbody applauded this idea, and it was instantly agreed to.

"For certain reasons, which I will not now mention," said Mr. Minford, "I am anxious to hurry up her education."

"By the way, what is your first name, my dear?" asked Miss Pillbody. "It is quite awkward to call you Miss Minford, you know."

The inventor answered for his daughter. "Her name is Patty, miss; and we call her Pet, for short, instead of Pat, which would be hardly appropriate."

"A pretty name," said Miss Pillbody; "and she *is* a pet, if I mistake not." The teacher looked archly at Mr. Minford, and then affectionately at the daughter, through her half-shut eyes. "I promise you she shall be a pet here, provided, always, she learns her lessons like a good girl. We always insist on that first." The teacher waved her hand with magisterial authority as she spoke, but accompanied the act with a laugh, which made Pet laugh also.

During this conversation, Mr. Minford had dwelt upon his machine in an undercurrent of thought; and an idea just then occurred to him, which he was desirous to test immediately. He therefore rose, and said that they would not detain Miss Pillbody any longer, and that his daughter would call and receive the first lesson at any time which that lady would name.

"Her hour will be from nine to ten o'clock every other morning, and from three to four on alternate afternoons," said Miss Pillbody. "It is now half past ten," she added, consulting a watch. "Mrs. Penfeather, my eleven-o'clock pupil, is out of town to-day; so Miss Minford—that is, Pet—can commence now, and I will give her until twelve o'clock. This will save time."

"Good!" remarked the inventor. "The great point is to save time. For certain reasons, as I said before, you have none to lose in educating my daughter. And, that we may not detain her a moment, Mr. Wilkeson, we will leave, if you please."

Marcus Wilkeson was glad to do this, for the conversation had already reached its natural terminus. He therefore followed Mr. Minford's motion, and grasped his hat and cane.

"You are not afraid to stay here, child?" said the inventor.

"Oh, no," replied Pet, with a happy laugh. "I already feel quite at home."

"And she shall always feel so here, I assure you, sir," added Miss Pillbody.

Mr. Minford's new idea occurred to him again with fresh force, and he hurriedly said: "Good-by, Pet. Be a good girl, now, and see how much you can learn in your first lesson." Then he kissed her, jerked a bow at Miss Pillbody, and made his exit into the hall. Marcus Wilkeson added his best wishes for the progress of the little scholar, bade her and her teacher a pleasant farewell, and followed Mr. Minford.

The child ran after them to the front door, and exchanged good-bys with them until they had turned the corner of the next street, when she entered the schoolroom, and straightway began her first lesson in the accomplishments of life.

BOOK THIRD.

THE TRAIL OF THE SERPENT.

CHAPTER I.

"ONE—TWO—THREE—FOUR."

PET studied hard, and made great progress. Her father and Marcus Wilkeson watched her developing education with equal pride, and constantly applauded and encouraged her.

The inventor did not know one word of French beyond the colloquial phrases with which everybody is familiar; but he would ask his daughter to read the crisp and tinkling tongue to him for hours at a time. He would hammer softly and file gently as she read, so that he might not lose a word of it. He would hear no news but that which she translated from the tri-weekly French paper published in the city. With correct and careful tuition at Miss Pillbody's, these constant exercises at home, ambition, and an excellent memory for languages, Pet was soon able not only to satisfy her teacher, but to make herself understood, in a small way, by a real French woman, Mdlle. Duchette, the forewoman of a candy store on the nearest business avenue.

Pet followed every lesson on the piano at Miss Pillbody's by three hours of daily practice at home. Marcus had hired for her a small piano, warranted to be just the thing for beginners. In other words, the keys and pedals were nearly worn out, and could not be much further damaged by unpractised hands and feet. This instrument was squeezed in between the bureau and the washstand, filling up the last spare place in the crowded little room. Pet wanted to have it set up in the next apartment, and practise there in the cold, alone; but neither her father nor Marcus would listen to that proposition for a moment.

Mr. Minford's nerves were extremely sensitive to sound. They vibrated to it, like an Æolian harp in the wind. He placed pianos, cats, fish peddlers, and hand organs on precisely the same footing, as nuisances. Nothing but the ruling desire to make a lady of his child, could have steeled him to the endurance, hour after hour, of her monotonous "One—two—three—four," and the discordant banging which accompanied those plaintive utterances.

The permanent discords with which the piano was afflicted, or the striking of a false note, would sometimes set his teeth on edge; but he would only hold his jaws tightly together, beat time with his head, and smile a hypocritical approval. Sometimes he would torture himself playfully, and make Pet laugh, by running a musical opposition with his three-cornered file—a small but effective instrument.

Marcus Wilkeson was equally tolerant of Pet's practice, and there was little false pretence in the patience with which he listened. Happily, he was not all alive to sounds. Screeches and harmonies were pretty much the same to him. Since he was a boy, he had been trying (privately) to sing, or whistle, "Auld Lang Syne," and had not yet mastered the first bar of it. He watched Pet's little fingers moving up and down the piano with mechanical repetition, and was truly interested in the sight—for two reasons: first, the motion was graceful; and second, she was acquiring an accomplishment which he held in the highest esteem, because Nature had put it entirely beyond his reach.

Sometimes, but not often, Bog was a listener at these rudimental concerts. Since Marcus had come to the relief of the family, Bog felt that his mission was ended. He knew that it was a piece of pure hypocrisy to call once or twice a week to see if he could be of any service, when he was aware that Mr. Minford had hired a woman, who lived on the floor below, to do all their household work, marketing, cooking, and general errands. He knew that Pet, on these occasions, asked him to go for a spool of thread, or a paper of needles, or a package of candy, merely to gratify him with the idea that he was making himself useful. When he came into the room tidily dressed, and highly polished as to his boots, he blushed even redder than he used to. It was not the acquisition of a little money by Mr. Minford that had exalted his daughter in the eyes of Bog, but the French and the music. These two accomplishments seemed to lift her into an upper air of delicacy and refinement, for which Bog felt that his miserable education and clumsy manners quite unfitted him. After Bog had performed some little invented errand for her, she would reward him with a short exercise, and Bog would sit, with open mouth and crossed legs, staring at Pet's face and hands alternately, and beating time with his large red hands on his knees.

Bog knew the negro songs of the period, and admired them. He would have liked to hear Pet play them, but feared she would think his musical taste very bad if he asked her to. Her "exercises," as she called them, he considered something perfectly wonderful, and belonging to a class of scientific music which a poor fellow like him could not be expected to enjoy. But, like many an older and more worldly-wise person, he pretended to be thrown into raptures by it, and, at every pause in the playing, would say, "Beautiful! a'n't it?" "That's prime!" or "Splendid!" or "The best I ever heerd." Sometimes, at his earnest entreaty, Pet would read a page of French to him; and he would listen with awe and reverence, as to a beautiful sibyl prophesying in an unknown tongue.

Bog always paid these visits in the afternoon. Marcus Wilkeson always called in the evening. The two had met in the house rarely since New Year's. When they accidentally met on the sidewalk, within a square or two of the house, as they sometimes did, Bog colored up as if he were guilty of something. Once Marcus Wilkeson saw Bog at a distance, turning suddenly down a side street, as if to avoid him; and Marcus wondered what could be the matter with the boy. By industry and tact, Bog made money in his new partnership, and had already laid up a snug sum in the savings bank.

Between Pet and her teacher a feeling of sisterly affection had sprung up. Miss Pillbody turned with a feeling of relief from her dull elderly pupils, stiff in manners, and firmly set in their habits, to this fresh, impressible young creature. What she did conscientiously to the others for pay, she would have done to Pet for love, had not her bills been settled in advance. Whenever Miss Pillbody had a spare hour or two, afforded by the indisposition of one of her older scholars (from excessive fatigue occasioned by a dinner party or other laborious hospitality the night before), she would send the red-headed servant to Mr. Minford's, and notify Pet, who was only too happy to go to her beloved teacher, and take an extra lesson.

Mrs. Crull could not be called a promising pupil. Her intentions were excellent. Her patience and her good nature were unbounded. She was always punctual at her lessons. Neither cold nor storm could keep her away. While she was in the schoolroom, she would resolutely deny herself the pleasure of indulging in more than a dozen episodes on the fashions and bits of scandal which she picked up in her cruise through society.

With the exception of these little wanderings, she would go through her recitations with as much correctness and docility as a sharp-witted child of twelve years. She felt a childlike pride in gaining the approval of her teacher. When she was under Miss Pillbody's instructions, and knew that every mistake would be courteously but firmly corrected on the spot (the teacher's invariable custom), she kept such a guard upon her tongue that she sometimes read or conversed in long sentences without making a single error. But when she was out of Miss Pillbody's sight, there were certain blunders which she fell into as surely as she opened her mouth.

Sometimes Mrs. Crull and Pet would meet on the door-steps of Miss Pillbody's house—the one going in and the other coming out—or on the sidewalk in the neighborhood. Mrs. Crull would catch the child by both hands, smack her heartily on the cheek (no matter how public the kiss), and then a conversation something like this would follow:

"How bright and pretty you look this mornin', my darlin!" (Mrs. Crull could not remember to pick up the "g's," except under Miss Pillbody's eye, and then not always.)

"Thank you, Mrs. Crull; I am quite well. How are you, marm?"

"Oh! smart as a trap. Haven't known not a sick day these ten years." (Mrs. Crull was weak on the double negatives.)

"How do you get along?" From motives of delicacy, Pet never added, "in your studies."

"Well, I don't mind tellin' you, as you are my confidential little friend." Here Mrs. Crull would look around cautiously, to be sure no one was listening. "The other studies isn't so hard, but grammar knocks me." (Mrs. Crull's nominatives and verbs were irreconcilable.)

Then Pet would say, telling an innocent fib:

"I don't observe anything very wrong, Mrs. Crull."

"Ha! ha! there you are flattering me, you little chick. I know, or think, I have improved a good deal with our dear Miss Pillbody; but a smart little scholar like you must see lots of mistakes in me."

At this point, Pet would blush, and murmur, "No—no!"

"Humbug!" Mrs. Crull would say. "I know my incurable faults, and I know that you know 'em. But Lor' bless you, child! there is plenty of ladies in good s'ciety" (Mrs. C. always slurred on the first syllable of that word) "who talk as bad as me. Their husbands, just like mine, got rich suddenly, you see. I tell you, I was 'stonished to find how many of 'em there was. They are thicker'n blackberries. I found out something else, too." Here Mrs. Crull would shake her head knowingly, like one who had discovered a great truth.

Pet would know what was coming, but would ask: "Pray, what is it, Mrs. Crull?"

"Why, I found out that, if you give good dinners and big parties, and keep a carriage, and have a conservatory, and rent a pew up near the altar, your little shortcomin's in grammar isn't no objection to you. 'Money makes the mare go.' However, eddication, as Miss Pillbody says, is a good thing of itself, and I shall keep on tryin' to get it."

These conversations always ended by an invitation to Pet to visit Mrs. Crull. "I'll have our carriage call for you," she would say, "at your father's house. We have no children, you know, and the old man would be very good to you; though, of course, it wouldn't do to hint about the school. But I can trust my little friend for that. Come, now, won't you?"

But Pet always modestly declined these kind invitations. She knew her father's pride, and his aversion to the patronage of rich people.

CHAPTER II.

THE FALLING BOARD.

ONE afternoon, Pet had been taking an extra lesson from Miss Pillbody, and had started homeward with a light heart, humming to herself a musical exercise which she had practised for the first time that day. A few doors from Miss Pillbody's, some workmen were repairing a wooden awning. The framework was covered with loose boards, which the carpenters were about to nail down. A feminine dread of danger would have induced Pet to make a wide detour of this awning; but her mind was so fully occupied by the musical exercise, that she walked, unheeding, right under it.

"Look out! look out!" shrieked a chorus of voices overhead, accompanied by a rattle of falling boards. Pet sprang forward just in time to escape one of them, and to catch another on her shoulder. It touched her gently, not even abrading her skin, for its fall had been stopped midway by a young man.

"Stupid!" "Silly creature!" "The girl's a blockhead!" "Where's her eyes, I wonder?" shouted the carpenters, after the manner of carmen and stage drivers, when you narrowly escape being run over by *their* carelessness, at the crossings.

"Shut up!" said the young man, savagely. "Why the d—l don't you keep your boards where they belong, instead of tumbling them down on people's heads?—I hope you are not hurt, miss?" (in a gentle voice).

"Oh, no; not at all. I am sure I thank you, sir, very much." Pet blushed, and hurried away.

The young man and the carpenters then exchanged the customary abusive epithets with each other, which might have resulted in something more serious (though such verbal encounters rarely do), but for the desire of the young man to overtake the young girl whom he had saved from a bruised shoulder, or a worse accident. Shaking his fist at the four jeering carpenters, and muttering a farewell execration between his teeth, he rapidly followed Pet, and soon came up with her.

"You are sure you are not hurt?" said he. "Those scoundrelly workmen! I'll thrash one of them yet."

Pet was confused by the second appearance of the young man at her side, though she knew that he would follow her; even her brief experience having taught her that it is not in the nature of man to do a kindness to a woman, without exacting a full acknowledgment for it.

"No, sir; I am not hurt the least bit," she replied, looking in his face no more than gratitude and civility required. Here she would have stopped, but she feared (charming simplicity of girlhood) that the young man would, some future day, get into trouble with the four carpenters. So she added, timidly: "As for the workmen, sir, they were not to blame. It was all my fault, running into the danger. I—I beg, sir, that you won't say another word to them."

This was a long speech for timid Pet to make to a stranger, and she blushed fearfully at the end of it, and wished that the young man would go away.

"They deserve a thrashing, every one of them," said he; "but, for your sake, I let them go." The young man spoke in a sweet voice, and his manner was respectful. Pet had observed, in several hasty side glances, that he was nicely dressed, and not ill-featured, in all except the eyes. But had his eyes been large and handsome, instead of small and forbidding, she would have desired his absence all the same.

"You say you are not hurt," he continued; "but you may be, without knowing it. I have heard of people receiving serious injuries, and never finding them out till they got home. Have you far to go, miss?"

"Only two blocks farther," said Pet, turning the corner.

"The very route I was going," observed the young man.

Although Pet felt that the young man's company was unnecessary and disagreeable, she did not like to tell him so. She kept silence until she reached her home, when she said, "I stop here, sir." She would have added, "Good-by, sir," or "Thank you, sir," or something equivalent, but instinct checked the expression, and she darted into the entry (the door being accidentally ajar), and shut the door after her, before the young man could say a word. Although the door was shut, he raised his hat respectfully as one often does on Broadway *after* he has passed a female acquaintance upon whom he suddenly comes—the salute being received and acknowledged with a stare by the next lady, or ladies, following after. The young man then noted the number of the house, nodded satisfactorily to himself, and strolled very leisurely along the street, as if neither business nor pleasure had urgent demands upon him.

CHAPTER III.

SNEAKING JUSTIFIED.

Neither Pet nor the young man saw the awkward figure of an overgrown boy, who had followed them at a distance, on the other side of the street, keeping the trunks of trees between them and him. This clumsy figure, upon which a suit of good clothes and a new cap looked strangely out of place, was Bog.

The boy Bog was often seen lounging about the neighborhood of Miss Pillbody's school; and if the policeman on that beat had not known him to be an honest lad from childhood, he would have watched him as a suspicious character. From whatever part of the city Bog came home after a bill-posting expedition, he invariably made a circuit past Miss Pillbody's school, keeping the other side of the street always, and never looking at the house. He walked hurriedly by, but came to a sudden stop at a grocery store halfway up the second block beyond, and there he would stand, partly covered by an awning post, and look strangely around, letting his eyes fall occasionally, and as if by accident, on that house. If his object in these singular manœuvres was to see Miss Minford, he always failed to improve the opportunity when it offered; for, as surely as Pet came out from the school, or turned into the street to go toward it, so surely did the boy Bog walk off whistling in another direction. Nobody can understand the motives of Bog's conduct, except those who have done the same thing in their youthful days.

On this eventful afternoon (eventful as a starting point in a history of sorrows), Bog had taken his usual circuitous route home from a profitable professional tour on the east side of town. Reaching the grocery store, he sheltered himself behind the friendly post, and commenced looking up and down the street, and across the way, and into the sky, always winding up his mysterious observations by a single glance at Miss

Pillbody's front door. When Pet came out, after her musical exercise, the boy Bog flushed up a little, turned upon his heels, and walked quickly away. He had not gone a dozen steps, before the shouts of the workmen and the sound of the first falling board reached his ears. He suddenly turned about, and saw a young man catching the next board that fell. His first impulse was to run to Pet's assistance; but a fatal spell chained his feet.

Poor Bog had dreamed a thousand times, by night and by day, of the ineffable bliss of rescuing Pet from a mad dog, from a runaway horse, from the assault of ruffians, from drowning, from a burning building. He had his plans all laid for doing every one of these things. He would have coveted the pleasure of whipping three times his weight of any well-dressed, white-handed young men, who should presume to insult her. In imagination, he had done it times without number; and had contrived a private method to double up a number of effeminate antagonists in succession. But, in all his reveries, he had never anticipated peril to Miss Minford from a falling board; nor had it occurred to him that the supreme felicity of saving her from death or injury would ever be the lot of anybody else.

The entire novelty of the accident and rescue struck him with amazement, and fastened him to the spot long enough to see that Pet walked away apparently unhurt. Hardly knowing what he did, or why he did it, he shifted his body behind the awning post so as continually to keep himself out of Pet's sight. Then the strong conviction came upon him that it was his duty to escort Pet home; for, although she did not seem to be hurt, she might be. This conviction was met and almost put down by the thought that Pet would know he had been watching for her; and he could not bear that. While he was halting and sweating between these two opinions, the unknown young man had finished his little colloquy with the four carpenters, and, by walking fast, had caught up with Pet.

Then the boy Bog decided that his wisest course, under all

the circumstances, would be to follow the couple at a distance, and see that no harm came to her from the young man.

"If the feller insults her," murmured Bog, "just because he was lucky enough to do her a little bit of a kindness, I'll lick him till he's blue." Besides whipping him for the insults which he might offer, Bog felt that he could give him a few good blows for his impudence in assuming Bog's exclusive prerogative of rescuing that particular young girl.

Bog looked very sheepish as he sneaked from one street corner to another, and skulked in shadows to avoid observation, though he tried to flatter himself that he was doing something highly meritorious. Two or three times, when the unknown young man inclined his head toward Pet, as if to speak to her, Bog entertained a hope that she would command him to leave her, and that he wouldn't. A single gesture from her, an impatient shrug of the shoulders, a turning away of her head, would have been all the hint that Bog needed to fly to her relief, and make up for his lost opportunity by knocking his dandy rival into the gutter.

But not even Bog's sharp eyes could detect any impudent familiarity in the young man's conduct, or any desire on the part of Pet to get rid of him. "Everything is agin' me," said Bog, wiping the perspiration from his forehead.

When Bog saw Pet part from the young man at Mr. Minford's door, his first wild idea was to call on her, quite by accident, in the course of half an hour. Perhaps she would tell him—as a piece of startling news—about her narrow escape from the board, and what the young man said to her. But Bog was unequal to the dissimulation involved in this plan, and abandoned it. Then he had a notion of following the young man, and seeing what became of him. But a sudden and very decided rising of fresh blood to Bog's cheeks and ears told him that he had played the part of spy long enough. So Bog determined—as many grown-up people in graver dilemmas do—to go home to supper.

Bog found his supper all ready for him, and it was a good

one. For his aunt, although the victim of a chronic rheumatism, had contrived to preserve a sharp appetite from the wreck of her former health, and cooked three meals for herself and two for Bog (who was never home at noon) daily. She was singularly punctual, too. Breakfast was always smoking hot on the table at 6 A. M.; and supper (and dinner combined, for Bog) was never a minute behind 5 P. M. in the winter time. Bog, who had a truly boyish idea of feminine excellencies, considered that this knack of cooking, and this amazing punctuality, were more than an offset for his aunt's little infirmities of temper, and her everlasting discourse on the rheumatics.

Though the beef hash was good, and the toast nicely browned and buttered, and the tea strong, and the fire burning brightly through the grates of the stove, and the curtains snugly drawn, and everything cheerful and comfortable in Bog's humble home, the boy was unhappy, and could not eat.

Happily, his aunt was so engrossed with her own physical troubles, that she never noticed indications of ill health in other people. She held that every other human ailment was unworthy of mention in the presence of her sovereign affliction. Whenever anybody presumed to speak of their little personal sufferings before her, she said: "You should thank Heaven you haven't got the rheumatics," and would then proceed to give a circumstantial history of her acquaintance with that disease. Therefore, on this occasion, she was quite unaware that poor Bog sat opposite to her with a pale, dejected face, playing aimlessly on his plate with his knife and fork. She thought only, and talked only, of her malady, which had been pranking in the oddest manner all day, and had settled, at last, in her "limbs." Bog's aunt had no legs that she would own to.

After supper, Bog heaved a sigh, and said that he would go round to Uncle Ith's; and asked his aunt if she had any word to send by him.

"Oh, no; nothing partickler," said she. "He don't care about me."

Uncle Ith, as everybody called him, was Bog's uncle on his mother's side. Uncle Ith and the aunt had a standing difference touching that rheumatism. Whenever they met—which was rarely—Uncle Ith would ask her, with a wink, how she was; and when she candidly told him that she was in a dreadful state, he would laugh at her, and say that half of it was "imagination." This indignity he had repeated so often, that, latterly, she scorned to complain in his presence, and bore her anguish in noble silence.

"All right," said Bog, who took no part in these family differences. He put on his cap, and left the house.

CHAPTER IV.

UP IN THE AIR.

"Uncle Ith" was one of the city bellringers, and lived at the top of a tower a hundred feet high, which vibrated with every stroke of the great bell hanging midway between his airy perch and the ground. He was sixty years of age, and had white hair, but he was as strong as younger men, and could swing the clapper against the side of the great bell with a boom that could be heard across rivers, and far into the peaceful country, on quiet nights. His eyes were so sharp, that, without the aid of a glass, he could read names on the paddle boxes of steamboats, where the unassisted vision of most persons descried nothing but a blur. He had done duty on that tower during the six years since it was built; and he knew the section of the city which lay spread out beneath him as a man knows his own garden. In the daytime, he could always guess, within a street or two, the location of any fire in his district. He knew all the smokes from a hundred factories, foundries, distilleries, and never confounded them with the fires which it was his business to detect. The presence of a new and suspicious smoke among the black stretch of roofs, caught his eye instantly; and he could tell in a moment, by its color, its speed of ascent, and the quantity of sparks accompanying it, whether it came from a carpenter's shop, a stable, a distillery, a camphene and oil store, or some other kind of building. In the nighttime, he knew the lights which mapped out the squares and the streets within his range of observation, almost as well as the astronomer knows the other lights that shine down upon the sleeping city from the heavens. He could fix the position of a fire by night rather better than by day, because he had the red reflection of the flames on well-known steeples, and high, prominent roofs to guide him.

Such were Uncle Ith's qualifications for his place; and he was so loved and trusted by the firemen of his district, that no mayor, however beset by applicants for office, had ever dreamed of removing him. In all of Uncle Ith's limited relations with the world, he was esteemed an honest man; and his word would have possessed the literal novelty of being as good as his note, had necessity ever required him to borrow money. But Uncle Ith was frugal, and made his small salary suffice for himself and a family of seven motherless children.

He had one eccentricity—a complete indifference to newspapers. He never bought nor borrowed them. "What's the use of reading 'em?" he would say. "Why not imagine the murders, suicides, political meetings, and other trash that fills 'em, and save your money for terbacker?" This did Uncle Ith, and he flattered himself that it was wisely done.

The bell tower was not far from the boy's home, and in a few minutes he stood at the foot of it, and shouted to Uncle Ith: "Hallo, there!"

Uncle Ith, always on the alert for calls, poked his head out of the window, which he left partly open for ventilation in the coldest nights, and answered, rather gruffly, "Well, what's wanted?" He never allowed his own children, nor any persons except his nephew Bog, and a few old firemen, friends of his, to visit him in the tower at night. Uncle Ith was conscientious. The presence of his children, with whom he loved to converse, or that of strangers, who would stare vacantly all over the lighted city, and ask innumerable questions, interfered with the strictness of his watch. Uncle Ith was a little eccentric, too, in his devotion to duty.

"It's me, uncle," said Bog, screaming upward.

"Glad to see you, Bog. You can come up," shouted the old man in return. He slung a latch key, fastened to a string, out of the window. It slid down the side of the tower, into Bog's hand. He unlocked the door, and the next moment the key was jerked aloft. The boy entered the base of the tower. He was so familiar with every crook and passage, that the small light of a gas jet, inside, was not necessary to show him the way. Up he ran, sometimes clearing two steps at a jump, slipping his hand lightly along the rough wooden banister. A few spiral turns brought him to the bell, which hung in an open framework of timber. He gave the huge bronze a familiar tap as he passed, and wound on and upward until he came to a trap door, which Uncle Ith held invitingly open. Then he sprang into the little room at the top of the tower, and Uncle Ith shook him by the hand.

"You look well, I see, Bog. And how is your aunt?" Uncle Ith was mindful of the usages of society, and always asked after her.

"Oh, she's smart," said Bog, totally oblivious of her rheumatism, "and sent her love to ye." Bog was a peacemaker.

"Sent her rheumatism, I guess yer mean. No doubt she wishes I had it."

Bog laughed, and his uncle laughed. And then his uncle, never forgetting duty, took a sharp look out of the eight clearly polished windows that commanded a view of the surrounding district. Discovering no sign of fire, he resumed the conversation with his nephew, asking him about his business (which he was happy to learn was prosperous), and giving him a quantity of good advice which none but a genius could remember, or an angel follow. During these exhortations, Uncle Ith paced to and fro in the little room, looking out of some window at the end of every sentence. Bog sat on a three-legged stool (the only seat except a backless chair) by the side of a miniature stove, on whose top hissed the kettle, from which Uncle Ith made his pot of coffee at midnight.

The night was cold; the little fire was warm; and Bog liked to hear advice from his uncle; but his eyes would wander to a certain window, as if, for some reason, he would derive great pleasure in opening and looking out of it. This movement of his eyes was so frequent, that Uncle Ith observed it, and said:

"Ah, I see! You want to stare out of that southeast window again. Now, I think the sight is handsomer to the west, where you can see the lights of Jersey City and Hoboken, and on the ferry boats and the shipping anchored in North River. But that's a matter o' taste. Well, look out o' the window, if you want to. I guess I can trust you for fires in that quarter."

"That you may!" answered Bog, throwing open the southeast window.

The stars above twinkled crisply in the frosty air; and the sky, with its low horizon on every side, seemed infinitely vaster than it did to Bog in the narrow and high-walled streets of the city. But Bog, though he used to puzzle over the wonders of the heavens when he was a few years younger, and had picked up a little something of astronomy from his uncle Ith (who knew something of that as of many other sciences), did not turn his gaze to them. Nor did he give more than a sweeping glance at the dotted line of lights below, stretching out in long perspectives, until the two luminous points at the end seemed blended into one. There were several parks in sight, which looked like portions of the sky let down on the earth, in all but the mathematical regularity of their mock stars. But Bog's eyes passed them by. To an inquisitive mind, there was something of interest to be seen and speculated over, in the lighted windows of houses all about him. People could be seen eating their late suppers, rocking by the fire, playing the piano, dancing, taking a rubber at whist or euchre, or diverting themselves with other recreations of winter house life. In one upper chamber, a physician was presenting a child just born to the proud father. In another, there was a mysterious spectacle, which a closer examination might have proved to be the preparing of a dead body for the morrow's burial. But Bog saw none of these sights.

His eyes sought for, and found immediately, as if by instinct, one light, which, in his opinion, was the only one worth looking at on earth or sky. It was a single bright gas jet, burning very close to a window about six hundred feet distant from him in an air line. Several tall chimneys of intervening houses rose almost between him and this light, and, perhaps, their dark, spectral shapes aided him in identifying it so readily. The lower sash of the window through which the light shone was curtained, but the upper part was uncovered; and an observer on the tower, being fifty or sixty feet above the top of the curtain, could easily look into the room. Bog rubbed his eyes, into which the cold but not biting wind had brought the tears, and gazed anxiously into Mr. Minford's apartment.

The pale inventor stood a few feet from the window, attentively examining a mass of machinery before him, upon which the light shone strongly. Only the tops of the wheels and of the more complex parts were visible; but there was one lever, or bar, connected with it, which rose above the whole, and could be seen by Bog to the extent of at least two feet. This was an addition to the strange machine as Bog had last seen it, and he contemplated it with fearful interest.

Mr. Minford stood motionless for five minutes in the presence of his creation. He was ghostlike and frightful in that fixed attitude, and Bog wished that he would move. He did so, nodding his head, and smiling, as he bent down and detached some part of the machine. All but his head and his right shoulder then disappeared from view; but Bog knew, by the vibrating motion of his shoulder blade, that he was filing upon something. Mr. Minford then stooped again, as if to put the part of the machine back into its proper place. Having done this, he stood erect once more, folded his arms, and looked intently at the Mystery for the second time.

CHAPTER V.

TONGUES OF FIRE.

BUT now Bog's attention was diverted from Mr. Minford, and his heart was made to beat more rapidly by a new sight. While he had kept both eyes closely fixed upon the inventor, he had looked with an oblique, or reflected vision, into the other window of the room. This window was uncurtained, and Bog could distinctly see the chairs, bureau, and other articles of furniture. A new light (so Bog oddly thought) was suddenly irradiated through the darker portion of the apartment by the entrance of Pet from the hall. She had no bonnet on; and Bog reasoned (if he could be said to reason in his excited state) that she had been spending a part of the evening, as was often her wont, with a poor family, rich in children, who lived on the floor below. Her father smiled upon the problem before him, as a new difficulty melted away under his burning gaze. Then he turned, and smiled at Pet. She ran toward him, and he kissed her tenderly. Bog was devouring this little episode with open mouth and eyes, when the hoarse voice of Uncle Ith broke in upon the enchantment:

"Hallo! there's a fire."

"What! Where?" shouted Bog, forgetting where he was.

"Why, you blind man!" said Uncle Ith; "straight afore ye. Don't ye see it breaking out?"

Bog cast his eyes about him wildly; and, sure enough, directly in the range of Mr. Minford's house, but four or five blocks beyond, there was an illuminated streak of smoke curling up from a roof.

"It's in my district!" cried Uncle Ith. "So here goes."

He seized the long iron lever near him, by which the enormous clapper of the bell was swung, and moved it like the handle of a pump. The second motion was followed by a hoarse sound, which shook the tower to its foundations, and started into listening attitudes a thousand firemen in their engine or hose houses, in the streets, at the theatres, or at their own homes.

"Sha'n't I help you?" asked Bog, who always proffered his services on these occasions.

"Pooh! no. It's baby play for me." By this time Uncle Ith had evoked the second gruff note from the deep throat of the imprisoned monster below. Then came a third in quicker succession, and louder, as if the bell had warmed up to the work, and then other notes, until the district had been struck; and then the bell, as if rejoicing in its strength to resist blows, murmured plaintively for a repetition of them. Long before this sad sound had died away, the deep bass of the City Hall bell, the shrill tenor of the Post Office bell, and the intermediate pitches of the bells all over the city, had taken up the chorus of alarm. There was a rattle of engines, hose carriages, and hook-and-ladder trucks through the streets. There was a frantic rush of men and boys, some with cumbrous fire-caps on their heads, and putting on their coats as they ran. How they knew the location of the fire, none could guess, for it had not yet streamed out against the sky; but know it they did; and the dove goes to its cote not more directly than they centred from all parts of the district upon the exact spot of the fire. Meanwhile, Uncle Ith lashed his mighty instrument into a sonorous fury; and all the other bells played their echo, even to the far-away tinkler on Mount Morris, which, having few fires in its own neighborhood to report, took a pleasure in telling its little world of those which were raging down town.

For the information of his uncle, and to atone in part for his previous neglect, Bog devoted only a half eye to the Minford family, and kept the rest of his optics on the fire. Just after its discovery, the smoke had loomed up dense and black, as if it were trying to suffocate the flames beneath. Then it changed rapidly to a light blue, and was chased faster upward by two tongues of fire. These tongues leaped aloft with a sudden impulse, and shed a revelation of light over acres of houses, and brought out church steeples in vivid relief against the sky, and put a new gilding on storm-beaten vanes and weathercocks. All this Bog described in his own way to his uncle; and his uncle, stooping at the lever, kept on ringing with unabated zeal; and all the other bells banged away like an orchestra of which Uncle Ith was the leader.

Then Bog saw the forms of men suddenly spring into sight, as if out of the very roof, between the two fiery tongues. The tongues licked the air about them with savage whirls; but the brave fellows dodged back, and were unhurt. Then, advancing boldly again, they released their hands from something which they had been holding, and lo! four jets of water struck at the very roots of the flames, tripped at them, and made them stagger, drove them twice into the roof, and caught them with deadly accuracy as they came out again; and, in less than five minutes, changed all their brave splendor to dull, black smoke, and set the victor's mark upon them—the column of white steam which arises from the half-quenched embers, and proclaims that the fire is put out of mischief at last.

"Nothing but a kind o' white smoke, now," said Bog.

Uncle Ith, who had just rung the last stroke of a round, relinquished the lever, and looked over the shoulder of his nephew. "The fire's out," said he. "When you see the steam comin' up that way, you may know that the water has whipped." The old man then seated himself in the backless chair, produced a short black pipe from a crossbeam overhead, and rewarded himself with a few long puffs.

When Uncle Ith had a pipe in his mouth, he became didactic, and he therefore proceeded to renew his donations of valuable advice to his nephew, who was still looking hard out of the southeast window.

Bog cocked his head on one side, to make a show of listening, and said "Yes, sir," now and then, which was all that his

6

uncle expected of him. But his whole mind, and his heart, were in the little double-windowed room, where Pet was now practising upon the piano. Through the uncurtained glass, Bog could see her hands weaving music with the keys, and almost fancy he could hear it. The inventor bent over his machine, and plied the hammer, the chisel, and the file, on various parts of it. Now and then he would pause, stand erect, and look proudly toward his child, and keep time to her music with inclinations of his head. Bog, without knowing it, would do the same thing.

While the boy was gloating over this scene, unconscious of the swift passage of time, the clock on the nearest church struck nine. Bog sighed, for he knew that that was Pet's hour for bed. Sure enough. Her little hands shut up the piano, and neatly smoothed down the cloth over it. Then she lit a candle, ran up to her father and kissed him, and in a moment was lost from Bog's sight in her chamber. As she disappeared, the boy's lips murmured "Good-night" with a fervor which made that simple colloquial phrase both a prayer and a blessing.

When Pet had gone, Bog suddenly found that the night had become cold, and that he was beginning to shiver. So he shut the southeast window, and took a seat by the fire to warm himself before going home.

BOOK FOURTH.

CHILDREN OF THE WORLD.

CHAPTER I.

MYNDERT VAN QUINTEM AND SON.

One morning, when Marcus Wilkeson returned home from a ramble, he found his half-sister Philomela violently dusting the furniture and books of the snug little back parlor. The air was full of dancing motes, which looked large and suffocating in the sunshine. Marcus had politely requested his sister, fifty times at least, *not* to molest that sanctuary of meditation oftener than once a fortnight. To which she always replied: "I suppose you great lazy fellows would like to have the cobwebs grow on you. But you sha'n't, while I am in the house." Then, with a few dexterous flourishes of her cloth, she would start the dust up in a cloud.

On this morning, Marcus Wilkeson, being in the most tolerant of moods, merely said "Whew!" and took a seat by his favorite window, the lower sash of which he threw wide open, with the vain hope that some of the dust would blow out. Miss Philomela smiled at this act so as to be seen by him. But he did not appear to notice it. Then she whisked her cloth under his very nose, as if to challenge objections. After this aggravation had been repeated three or four times, Marcus felt compelled to make a mild protest.

"Great deal of dust, sister," he said, stating what he presumed would not be contradicted.

"Is there?" replied Miss Philomela, exulting in the success of her stratagem. "*I* didn't notice it; nor would you, if you had some business to look after, like other people, instead of stopping in the house all day."

Marcus had heard that argument and triumphantly put it down so often, that he did not think it worth another word. Consequently he said nothing.

This obstinate silence galled Miss Philomela; and, after waiting full three minutes to see if Marcus would not answer, and meanwhile dusting prodigiously in his neighborhood, she said:

"Well, it's some gratification to know that you do not have the hardihood to defend yourself. You are well aware that nothing can justify a healthy, middle-aged man—I may say, a young one—in retiring from active life and society, and becoming a great lazy mope."

"I'm really too lazy to discuss it now," replied Marcus, smiling, and filling his meerschaum from the tobacco pouch which hung conveniently at the window's side.

Philomela regarded him for a moment with an expression of pity and horror. Then she heaved a sigh, and muttered something about misapplied talents.

"You had better say, 'Misapplied brooms and dusters,'" retorted her half-brother. "I should be perfectly happy now, but for this confounded dust."

"Laugh away. I know you despise my sisterly advice. But you can never say that I have not done my duty——"

"To the furniture, most assuredly," interrupted Marcus.

Miss Philomela Wilkeson heaved another sigh in the best style of martyrdom, and precipitately left the room, followed by her brother's cheerful, rattling laugh.

"A good old girl enough," said Marcus to himself, "but for her well-meaning and strictly conscientious habit of making people miserable."

Then he lighted his meerschaum, closed the window squared his chair in front of it, and looked out. His face instantly flushed with pleasure at a strange sight. The blinds of the lower parlor windows across the way, which had been shut for several weeks, were now thrown open, and the white-haired old gentleman, looking thin and pale, sat in his arm-chair in his old place, and was gazing at him. At least so Marcus thought; but he hesitated to bow until the old gentleman gave a distinct salutation. Marcus returned it two or three times with emphasis, as if to express his great pleasure at seeing his unknown neighbor and friend again. He blushed as he did so, for he was conscious of wilful neglect and cruel indifference, in not having called upon him on New Year's day, or since then, during the period of the closed blinds; and worse still, in not having thought of him a dozen times, though he had taken the trouble to pass his door on his way to or from Mr. Minford's, and had felt relieved to see no black crape on the bell-pull.

"But then," thought Marcus, pleading with and for himself, "my mind has been occupied—very much occupied—with other matters. Now, if he beckons to me again, I will go over to him without a moment's delay. My old friend looks very sick and unhappy."

Just then the old gentleman reached out his thin white hand, as if the motion required an effort, and beckoned twice. Marcus answered with two bows, and immediately rose, and laid down his pipe on the window sill, thereby implying that he would come over at once. The old gentleman smiled faintly, to express his delight.

In a few minutes Marcus Wilkeson stood at the antique mansion, and pulled the bell. It vibrated feebly as if it shared with the house and its owner the infirmities of age. The bell was answered by an old, neatly dressed female servant. She had been told to admit the caller instantly, and said, "Mr. Van Quintem will see you, sir."

He entered a wide hallway, and followed the noiseless step

of the servant, trying to remember, without success, where he had heard the name of Van Quintem.

At the end of the hall the servant opened a door, and ushered him into a room decorated at the edges of the ceiling with heavy wooden carvings, and furnished in the style of the last century. The old gentleman partly rose from his soft armchair, supported himself by one hand on it, and extended the other to his visitor.

"My name is Myndert Van Quintem, sir," said he, "and I am very glad to see you." There was a pleasant smile in the old gentleman's pale face, and a warmth in the grasp of his thin right hand, that attested the sincerity of his words.

"And my name is Marcus Wilkeson, sir; and I am truly happy to make your acquaintance," responded the visitor, in his most genial manner.

The old gentleman here showed symptoms of faintness from the exertion of standing; and Marcus, taking him by the arm, forced him gently into his easy chair, and took a seat beside him.

"I must apologize for not having called before," said Mar cus. "I——"

"Not a word, sir," interrupted the old gentleman. "It is I who must apologize for the rudeness of nodding and beckoning to a perfect stranger. But the fact was, I could not regard you as a stranger. Seeing you at your window, smoking and reading, day after day, while I was smoking and musing at mine, I gradually came to sympathize with you, and to wish that the distance across the lots was short enough to allow us to converse. I thought, perhaps, that on some subjects we might interest each other. Now, be good enough to fill that pipe and smoke it, while I tell you in few words who I am."

He pointed to a meerschaum, carved into the semblance of a Dutchman's head, which looked not unlike his own. It was fitted to a long Turkish stem, and hung against the wall by a silver chain, within reach of his hand. Five other pipes of quaint design hung near it.

Marcus protested against smoking in an invalid's presence; but the old gentleman insisted upon it, and playfully but firmly threatened to smoke the pipe himself if his guest did not. So Marcus filled the large bowl from a paper of old, mild tobacco, which hung in a pouch near it, and drew a few gentle whiffs, intending to let the pipe go out. But the old gentleman watched him.

"'Twon't do," said he. "That old pipe of mine is not used to neglect. As a particular favor, now, I beg that you'll smoke, and puff out clouds, as I have often seen you do across the way."

Marcus protested again, but the old gentleman stubbornly maintained his point; and it was not till the pungent smoke began to curl upward, that he proceeded with his personal disclosure.

"Have you ever heard my name before, Mr. Wilkeson?" said he.

Marcus bowed, and said that he had not had that pleasure.

"Of course not," returned the old gentleman, not displeased with the answer. "I have taken infinite pains to keep out of public life since I retired from business, twenty-five years ago. Even before that time, I was known only to a very few persons as a silent partner in the large iron-importing house of Sniggs, Buffet & Co. I had no relations, and few friends, in the common acceptance of that much-abused word. My only happiness was in my wife—that is her picture hanging over the mantelpiece—and this house, which my father built, and which, according to a tradition in our family, is on or near the spot where my great-great-grandfather, the fourth Myndert Van Quintem, perished by the hands of the Indians."

"Then," interrupted Marcus, "you belong to an old Dutch family?"

"To one of the oldest on record," replied Mr. Van Quintem. "My great ancestor, the genuine original Myndert, came over as cook with Hendrik Hudson. We have an iron spoon of doubtful authenticity, said to have descended from him. Sometimes I have paid the penalty of this ancient and distinguished origin, by receiving stupid compliments on my old Dutch blood, as if that species of blood were better than any other. That sort of nonsense I have always answered by informing the flatterer that the first bearer of my venerable name was a cook; the second, a tanner; the third—well, the least said about the third the better; and the fourth, a barber. My grandfather, a very worthy saddler, in old Queen's street, was the first of the series that was ever able to buy and hold real estate. My father increased upon his purchases, and, when the property came into my possession, I, in turn, added to its extent as fast as I could. In forty years, this property has become valuable; and I now find myself and my lots occupying a large space on the tax rolls.

"It is a curious fact, and illustrates the uncertainty of human events, that my success is the result of accident, and is not in the least due to my judgment or foresight. Every kind of business that I have engaged in—and I have tried several kinds—has failed. Sniggs, Buffet & Co. almost finished me; and, if I had not backed out as I did, the better part of my estate would have been sacrificed. Among those who know me, I pass for a very shrewd business man, who has made a fortune by his numerous failures. This tribute to my abilities is flattering, but I must disclaim it. But I am tiring you with these petty details of my life."

"Not at all, really," said Marcus Wilkeson, who enjoyed the old gentleman's frankness.

Mr. Van Quintem paused, and began to show signs of fatigue. He asked for a cordial which stood on an old sideboard with great lion's feet, near his visitor's chair. Having sipped of its contents, he expressed himself relieved, and resumed his story:

"As I was saying, I found my whole happiness in my wife, and in this house. With the exception of a few friends of my youth—now all dead—she was my only society. Like me, she was fond of retirement and of books. You, sir, can appreciate the quiet, satisfying pleasure which we derived from books, for you, too, are a constant, happy reader; and you have fine books, as I know by the size of them. You see, I have been observing you closely," he added, with a smile. The old gentleman's smile was sweet, but relapsed into a mild expression of sadness.

"Not more closely than I have observed you," said Marcus. "I have often wondered what stout old quartos you were reading. To tell you the truth, I inferred, from the dimensions of the books and your white cravat, that you were a clergyman." Marcus might have added, that the old gentleman's flowing white locks and benevolent features had contributed to the illusion; but he had already discovered that Mr. Van Quintem, like himself, was averse to compliments.

The old gentleman took the remark goodnaturedly. "This is not the first time," said he, "that my old-fashioned fancy for a white cravat has led to that mistake. You will find very little of the body of divinity in that library. When I recover from this illness so as to hobble about, we will look over my little collection together."

Marcus said that nothing could give him greater delight, unless it was to show his friend his own humble library.

"Thank you," returned Mr. Van Quintem; "and I promise to run over and look at it when I am well enough to go out." The haste with which the old gentleman made the last remark, and the fact that he did not invite his visitor to examine the library then and there, led Marcus to think that the old gentleman had some private trouble on his mind, which he wished to diminish by imparting to another. Marcus was right.

The old gentleman heaved a sigh, and resumed:

"For ten years after my retirement, my wife and I lived on in the calm, happy manner that I have described. We had no griefs—not even that one which most commonly afflicts parents, the loss of children. Yet I sometimes think, sir, that it would be far better for some children to die in their youth and innocence, than to grow up and become bad men, and torture and almost kill their parents with ingratitude and unkindness." Marcus guessed what was to come.

"We had but one child—a boy—born long after I had given up all hopes of having an heir. I need not tell you, sir, what a joy he was to us in his infancy; for you, too, I presume, are a husband and a father."

Marcus replied confusedly, and as if it were something to be ashamed of, that he was neither the one nor the other, though he hoped some day (here he was exceedingly awkward) to be both.

The old gentleman was so wrapped up in his own thoughts, that he did not seem to notice the reply. He again braced himself in the chair, as if he would, by that act, gather strength to proceed.

"Of course, I called the child Myndert. He was the seventh of that name; and I used to think, even when he was a toddling little baby, what plans of education would be best suited to develop his talents. I know that a parent's partiality is a magnifying glass of high power; but, to the best of my belief, he was a most precocious child. I think so now, as I look back upon the days of his prattling innocence.

"After a great deal of debating, my wife and I concluded to make a lawyer of him. He was to be the first lawyer in our family annals; and we fondly pictured to ourselves that he would become an eminent judge, or that he would step from the bar into political life, and shed honor upon his country and his family as a statesman. I know how ridiculous these imaginings must seem to you, and I recall them only to show you how deeply our hearts were wrapped up in that boy.

"When our little Myndert was five years old, my wife died." Here the old gentleman clutched the arms of the chair firmly with both hands. "Our son had been very sick for a week before, and my dear Clara had nearly worn herself out watching over and nursing him. A severe cold, which she caught while going to the druggist's in a rain, did the rest. She died with one arm around me and the other around little Myndert; and her last words were a blessing on the boy, and a request that I would always love him for her sake." The old gentleman's eyes glistened with tears, and his lips twitched convulsively. Marcus evinced his sympathy in the fittest way, by keeping silence, and fixing his eyes on the floor.

"Well, sir, not to be tedious, I lavished my whole heart upon that child. His presence seemed to be some consolation for the great loss I had sustained. His features were so like hers, in all except the eyes, that I seemed to see her through him; and thus, in a peculiar sense, I loved him for her sake, indeed. He was petted and caressed from his very cradle. Ah, there was my error; but who can blame a father for over loving his only son, and that one motherless!

"He early showed indications of a fierce temper and a sul len pride, in which respects he resembled not his mother, but her father, who, with the exception of these two faults, was a good and just man. I have heard of cases in which strong mental traits jump over a generation, and appear in the next one. I thought, and still think, that my son's singular peculiarities might be explained in that way. If you will bear with me, sir, I will give you some illustrations of his character.

"When he was nine years of age, a dear friend, now dead, advised me not to injure so precocious an intellect by too much cultivation, but to put the boy on a farm, where he could divide his time between healthful work and youthful sports, and would be kept away from the contaminating influences of the city. I agreed to make the experiment, though reluctantly, for I could not bear the thought of parting with my child. An old family acquaintance who owned a farm in Dutchess County, and had no children, was willing to take my boy.

"Little Myndert liked the idea of going into the country, and for two weeks he behaved very well; and his acting father wrote me, that if I could spare the boy, he would like to adopt him as his own. But the next letter, a week afterward, brought a different story. It was while Myndert was not put to work, that he behaved so well. But when the farmer gave him a little hoe, and asked him to grub up a few weeds in the garden, the lad threw it down, and said to the farmer, 'I hate you.' This was his favorite expression to those who aroused his displeasure when a child. The good man was astonished at this insubordination, and tried to persuade Myndert to do as he was told. But persuasion was useless; and so were the threats with which the farmer tried to frighten him. As for whipping the boy, he was, like me, too soft-hearted to do that.

"So Myndert became the master there, as he had been here. His real nature now came out. From that time until the worthy farmer sent the boy home in despair—ten weeks later—he was the wonder and terror of the neighborhood. Chickens, goslings, and young ducks were killed; boughs of apple trees and other fruit trees were broken down; strawberry beds were entered, and the plants pulled up by the roots; the windows of the village church and schoolhouse were broken with stones; and three fourths of these acts were traced to little Myndert. He always denied the charges, and put on an air of innocence, which deceived many persons.

"The cunning which he exhibited in doing these malicious acts, and trying to divert suspicion from himself, was truly wonderful in a child of his age. One day he was caught by a farmer in the act of killing some young chickens; and the owner was so mad, that he whipped the boy soundly. That very night the farmer's wood shed was set on fire from the outside; but a heavy rain came on, and put out the flames. The traces of the fire were plainly to be seen next morning; and the farmer found proofs enough, I fear, to have convicted my son of a felony.

"My friend informed me of all these facts in a very sorrowful letter, and I hastened to take my son once more under my own roof.

"Here I tried every method that a father's love could devise to reform him. But all was useless. He seemed to have no idea of truth or honor, of affection or duty to me. When, at times, I thought he was showing signs of improvement, I always found, afterward, that he was only concealing his mischievous acts more carefully. I call them mischievous, though the word 'malicious' would perhaps describe them better; for they were all undertaken in a spirit of evil, and not of fun." The old gentleman here rested, and refreshed himself with a sip of the cordial.

"But it would take days to tell you of all my troubles with that boy, and I will briefly refer to the rest of them.

"By the advice of another friend (for I have never taken any step in the treatment of my child without first seeking for friendly advice), I sent him, when twelve years of age, to a celebrated school in Massachusetts, where the discipline is very strict. I had a personal interview with the master, and requested him, as a favor, to chastise Myndert, if all other means failed to subdue him. Though I could not bear to whip him, I was willing that he should suffer a proper punishment, inflicted in the right spirit, from others. At this school he conducted himself properly for about three weeks, and was taking a high rank as a scholar, when his natural tastes asserted themselves, in all sorts of wicked pranks on his fellow pupils, on the teachers, and on people in the village. The master at first expostulated, and then gave Myndert a good thrashing. That night the master narrowly escaped being hit by a large stone thrown through his bedroom window. Next morning my son was missing, and for three weeks no trace of him could be found. I advertised in newspapers, describing him, and offering large rewards for his recovery. I had the same notice printed on bills, and stuck up all through the country. I employed detectives to trace out the runaway. A month passed, and no tidings. I was in despair. Toward the close of the fifth week, one of the detectives struck a trail on Cape Cod, and, after a patient search, found the young rascal living, under the assumed name of Carlo, with a fisherman, in a little seaside hamlet. As the fishing season was a good one, and men were scarce, the fisherman had gladly received my son as an apprentice for his board. The novelty, excitement, and sometimes danger of the pursuit pleased Myndert greatly, and the old fisherman said that he was a good hand for a boy. When the detective found him, however, he was beginning to be tired of his strange occupation (nothing pleases him long), and he consented to come home on condition that I would not scold him, and would give him plenty of pocket money. I had been weak enough to authorize the making of these promises.

"The return of my prodigal son made me happy. As I had promised, I did not reproach him, and gave him all the money that he wished. He was not old enough to know how to spend money viciously. His tastes, though costly, were comparatively innocent. From childhood he had always been very fond of new clothes, and he indulged that passion to the utmost. At twelve years of age, he was called the 'Young Dandy' all through this part of the town; and I sometimes heard of his attracting attention on Broadway.

"He was so well satisfied with my generosity, that he consented to receive two short lessons daily from tutors at the house, and surprised them, as he did everybody, with his wonderful aptitude for learning.

CHAPTER II.

BUYING GOOD BEHAVIOR.

"For three years I bought my son's good behavior with unlimited pocket money, and foolishly thought that his nature had changed. Occasionally he would do malicious acts to his tutors, or to my housekeeper or servants; but these occurred less frequently as time rolled on, and at last ceased. At fifteen years of age, he was sufficiently advanced in learning to pass a college examination, and I determined to send him to college. He was delighted at the proposal, for he had begun now to appreciate the advantages of education. Anticipating that he would have trouble with the Faculty, I selected a college which was distinguished for its means of learning, and was yet very lenient in its discipline. Myndert easily obtained admission, and at once took high rank in his class. Knowledge came so easy to him, that he had plenty of leisure, and I feared that his old vicious habits would break out again. Greatly did I rejoice not to hear a single complaint of him during his first term. But, alas! I found, when he returned home, that he had learned to drink and gamble, and that the large sums of money I had sent him had been squandered in carousals, and over the card table. Still he maintained the first position in his class, and of that I was proud.

"I remonstrated against his vices. He admitted that there was some truth in what I had heard, mixed up with a great deal of exaggeration; and justified his conduct by saying that it was the fashion, and he could not keep out of it if he would. His good health and naturally high spirits did not appear to be in the least affected by dissipation, and I gladly allowed myself to believe that many of the reports about him were false.

"The next term was still more expensive; and I found out that the larger portion of my heavy outlay went for liquor and gambling. Still he kept a high grade in his class—taking the second rank instead of the first; and the Faculty either were ignorant of his misconduct, or did not think it worth punishing. Through his first, second, and third years at college, these were his only vices. His constitution, though strong, was gradually undermined; and, at the end of his junior year, he showed unmistakable signs of bloating, became very irregular in his attendance on recitations, and had sunk to be the fifteenth in his class. I had hopes that he would pass through his fourth year safely, and get a diploma. But, at the very beginning of that year, he kept drunk, and absented himself from recitations for a fortnight, and, when called before the Faculty for a mild reprimand, cursed them with the most horrible oaths, defied them, and left their presence. They had no choice but to expel him from the college; and, a week after, he was brought home to me nearly dead with intoxication.

"A month's illness followed, which brought him almost to the grave. Though, at the time, I prayed with all a father's love for his recovery, I have since thought—oh, how often!—that it would have been far better for him to have died. But he was spared; and, having been thoroughly frightened by his narrow escape from the effects of drunkenness, he vowed, on his recovery, that he would never touch another drop of liquor. This pledge he kept for some months after his health was fully restored.

"Having decided to educate him for the law—the only profession that he did not hold in contempt—I procured a place for him in the office of Mulroy, Biggup & Lartimore, an excellent firm with whom I had had some dealings.

"Myndert entered upon his study of the profession with such ardor, that I was obliged to caution him against ruining his health. But he only laughed, and said he wanted to make up for past follies. I had never before seen him in a penitent mood, and I was delighted. Mr. Mulroy, who has had a hundred pupils in his time, told me that he never had a more promising one than Myndert. He was a regular and constant attendant at the office, and spent all his evenings at home. The natural strength of his constitution came to his aid, as if to encourage him in his efforts to reform; and, notwithstanding his severe studies, he began to look in better health than he had ever been. Thus things went on six whole weeks, and I was happy, and busied myself in framing plans for my son's advancement in life.

"He told me, one day, that he had joined a club of young law students, who met every evening and discussed legal points, held mock courts, and thus sought to familiarize themselves with the duties of their profession; and asked me if I approved of it. He sought my approval so rarely for anything, that I freely gave it, cautioning him again, however, to be careful of his health. He laughed at my apprehensions. But I was pained to see how soon my fears proved true. Within a fortnight, the rosy color of his cheeks had disappeared, and his eyes were palpably sunken, dull, and marked with a sickly blue beneath. He never returned home till midnight, and sometimes was out till three o'clock in the morning. I scolded him for devoting so much time to his law club; but he said that the members were, like himself, enthusiastic students, and that he was always the first to leave their fascinating debates and mimic trials. A week later, I marked the familiar bloat in his cheeks, and suspected the truth.

"Placing a watch upon his movements—no easy matter, for he is very shrewd and cautious—I soon found out that the law club was a myth, and that his nights were passed in the wildest debauchery. He had not only resumed all his old vices, but had acquired new ones.

"When I reproved him, as I did with just indignation, he threw off the mask of concealment, which he said he was tired of wearing, and became the same bold, defiant, reckless boy that he always was; while I continued to be the same weak, foolish, fond parent. I cannot recount the tortures inflicted upon me by my son since that fatal discovery. He has not only abandoned all his law studies (having been expelled from the office of Mulroy, Biggup & Lartimore for grossly insulting a young female client), and utterly ruined his own body and soul, but, by his acts, he has brought shame upon several families.

"When this new series of outrages came to my knowledge, I threatened to disinherit him. He laughed at me. He knew how I loved him for his mother's sake, and, with that hold upon my affections, he defied me.

"To heartless indifference he gradually added insults, and often cursed me, his own father, in this very room, where his mother has rocked his cradle a thousand times while she listened to my reading of an old poem or novel. The last of his crimes of which I have heard, was brought to my knowledge about six weeks ago. It was a piece of treachery the most villanous, and I told my son, in plain words, what I thought of it. I was weak and nervous from an illness which is hereditary in my family, and I reprimanded him with more severity than usual. I told him, that if God, in His infinite mercy, spared him, yet he was not secure from just punishment from the friends of those whom he had wronged, and that the human vengeance, which had been so long postponed, would surely come. He looked at me with malice in his small gray eyes (not his mother's eyes), and, when I ceased speaking, raised both hands to heaven, and, with the most horrible blasphemy, called down its curses upon me; and then he swore, that if I crossed his path, or thwarted his plans, or refused him money, he would kill me.

"Just before he uttered this monstrous threat, I sprang from my chair with horror, and caught him imploringly by both hands. I would have saved him from that dreadful act, but I was too late. I saw him wrench away his right hand, and raise it to strike me back. . . . . . I knew no more, until Mrs. Frump, my niece, who has had charge of my household during the past three years, entered the room, and found me stretched insensible on the floor."

"I saw a part of the sad scene," said Marcus Wilkeson, who had listened with mingled indignation and compassion to this strange tale. "Your son was standing by that window, and you were sitting near him, also within sight of me. I distinctly saw you catch your son's hands with your own; he wrenched the right one away, and raised it; then you fell, but he did not strike you, or attempt to. As you dropped to the floor, he glanced anxiously through the window, saw me watching him, and then pulled down the curtain."

"Then he did not strike me to the floor! I never believed he did, for there was no bruise or other mark upon my head. Thank God, my son was spared the commission of that crime! Bad as he is, he would not strike his own father."

And the poor old gentleman's heart found meagre comfort, for a moment, in that thought.

"A few words more, and I am done. The shock brought my disease to a crisis. For over a month my recovery was doubtful. But my naturally tough constitution, skilful medical attendance, and the unceasing care of Mrs. Frump, brought me safely out of it. The devotion of that good, light-hearted woman was truly affecting. She never left my bedside, night or day, except for a few hours' rest; and even to-day, when, as you see, I am well enough to sit up and talk, and, in fact, am perfectly restored to health, it was only by almost pushing her into the street that I could get her to go out for a day's shopping—a luxury which the good soul had denied to herself during all my illness."

("I must tell Maltboy about this excellent woman," thought Marcus.)

"My son did not come near my sickbed, and I have not seen him since that unhappy day. He has visited the house daily, and shut himself in his room for several hours. How he occupies his time, I cannot imagine, but am sure that it is only in studying or practising evil."

"Possibly I may throw some light on that mystery," said Marcus. "I have seen him, from my convenient window, enter his room, day after day, generally in the afternoon, sit down at his table, and write for over an hour steadily."

"That is strange!" exclaimed the old gentleman. "He has given up the study of law. He has no taste for literary labor. He writes a beautiful hand, and would not waste time in trying to improve his penmanship. It is singular, indeed."

"His work, whatever it is, does not seem to satisfy him; for I have observed that he no sooner fills a page with writing, than he burns it to ashes by the gas jet, which he always keeps faintly lighted above his head."

"Some more villany, I am sure," said the old gentleman, with a deep sigh. "We shall find it out by its terrible consequences, in due time. He has plenty of leisure to cultivate his vices, but not a moment to seek my forgiveness (which, God knows, I would freely grant, if he would only ask it). He cannot even throw away a word upon Mrs. Frump, to find out whether his own father is dead or alive."

The last thought gave acute pain to the wretched parent. Tears again sprang to his eyes, and Marcus feared that he was about to witness that saddest sight in nature—an old man weeping.

But, by an effort, Mr. Van Quintem stifled his emotion, and, turning suddenly upon his visitor, cried, in a voice of despair:

"Tell me, sir, in Heaven's name, what *shall* I do with my son?"

CHAPTER III.

THE YOUNG MONSTER.

FROM boyhood, it had been Marcus Wilkeson's fortune (or the reverse) to attract confidence, and to be sought out for advice. And it had most generally happened that he was requested to bestow the last valuable article in cases where inexperience absolutely disqualified him from giving it.

He had found, however, that, when people ask for advice, they expect to receive it, although they reserve to themselves the right, and, in ninety-nine cases out of a hundred, exercise the privilege, of rejecting it.

But Marcus had gathered, from the old gentleman's story, that the error of his dealings with the rebellious son lay in his constantly seeking advice from everybody, and taking it, too, instead of adopting some firm, consistent, and independent course of his own toward that unfilial monster. Furthermore, Marcus knew that the son was already beyond the reach of reform. For the future peace of his venerable friend, and for the good of society, he could have conscientiously recommended two things:

First, the immediate hanging of Myndert Van Quintem, jr. Second, his imprisonment for life in a penitentiary warranted to be strong enough to hold him.

Neither of these courses being practicable until that young man had entitled himself to the benefit of one or the other of them in the legitimate way, Marcus Wilkeson had nothing to offer, and so he told the old gentleman.

Mr. Van Quintem was disappointed. He looked up wistfully, and said:

"Can't you suggest something?"

Thus appealed to, Marcus angled in the deep waters of his mind, and fished up this inadequate idea:

"Let him travel a couple of years in Europe."

"I have proposed it," returned the old gentleman, "but he won't, unless I give him five thousand dollars, and an unlimited letter of credit. This I refused. Besides, to tell the truth, I do not wish to exile the boy, but to reform him at home."

Marcus was too polite to say bluntly that that was impossible; so he cast in his line again at random, and drew out this worthless suggestion:

"Stop all his pocket money, and tell him plainly that you will disinherit him unless he reforms."

"My dear sir," replied the old gentleman, "that might do with some sons, but not with mine. He would obtain money by theft, or even a worse crime, and bring disgrace upon my gray hairs. He might go even farther—for he has threatened it, as I told you—and murder me in revenge. Besides, he is on short allowance now. I give him only thirty dollars a week—less than a quarter of what he used to receive from me. Much as his conduct deserves punishment, I could not reduce him to beggary, you know."

This useless discussion was cut short by the precipitate entrance of the subject of it. Mr. Van Quintem was greatly surprised at the sudden apparition, and his face exhibited signs first of astonishment, then of indignation, then of pleasure, in quick succession. But before his erring son had advanced halfway toward the father's chair, the father turned his head slightly away, as if not daring to trust himself to an interview.

The son took one sharp survey of Marcus, and then slipped his right hand insinuatingly in that of his father, which hung over an arm of the easy chair. Mr. Van Quintem turned his face farther away, but Marcus observed that his fingers closed upon the hand which lay within them.

"Are you quite well, my dear father?" asked the son, in a low, hollow voice, not meant to be overheard by the visitor.

"I am, thanks to God, and the doctor, and my niece," said the father, stealing a side look at his son.

"And no thanks to me, I know that. I feared, my dear father, after what had occurred, that you could not bear the sight of me. Therefore I kept away from your bedside."

"That is a lame excuse, Myndert," replied the father. He spoke in a voice intended to be audible to Marcus Wilkeson.

A gleam in the son's sunken eyes, and a new pallor on his bloated cheeks, indicated his displeasure at the turn which this conversation was taking. He withdrew his hand, and said, in a deep whisper:

"I did not think you would quarrel with me, when I called to congratulate you on your recovery."

Mr. Van Quintem wavered a moment. Then, looking at the calm face of Marcus Wilkeson, as if to gather strength from it, he replied:

"My son, such language is not respectful to your father. You know, as God knows, that I have been too indulgent with you."

The son coolly twirled the ends of his mustache—which protruded from each side of his mouth like the antennæ of a catfish—and gazed impudently in his father's face. Then he turned about, and bestowed another scornful, analyzing look on the tranquil Marcus.

"That is a friend of mine, Myndert, and I have no secrets from him. Mr. Wilkeson—my son."

Marcus politely rose, and offered his hand to the young man, who accepted it reluctantly.

"I have seen you before, I believe," said he. "Across the way, eh?"

"I dare say," was the reply. "I sometimes sit at the window, reading."

Myndert then abruptly faced his father, and Marcus resumed his chair.

"Since you have no secrets from this gentleman," said the son, "allow me to ask if you could conveniently spare five hundred dollars this morning?"

The old gentleman hesitated; then reassured himself by an observation of Marcus Wilkeson's face, and said:

"No, my son; I can no longer encourage this extravagance. Where is your last monthly allowance?"

"Gone, of course," answered the son, in a loud and insolent tone. "Do you expect to keep me on miserable driblets like that?"

"Thirty dollars a week, and board and lodging, are enough for any reasonable young man, Myndert. I cannot give you more."

The son glared on his father and Marcus Wilkeson (holding the latter chiefly responsible for the refusal) with amazement.

"Since you are obstinate, then, make it three hundred." The son had often been able to obtain half or two thirds of what he originally asked, as a compromise.

Again the old gentleman wavered; and it was not until he had looked Marcus Wilkeson straight in the eye, that he answered, striking the arm of the chair with his thin white hand:

"Not one cent!"

The tumid cheeks assumed a sicklier white, and the small, offensive eyes sparkled with a fiercer fury, as the son replied:

"Very well, sir. Be as stingy as you please. Take the advice of your new friend here, and cut off my beggarly monthly allowance, too. But remember, I must have money, and I will have it!"

Had Marcus Wilkeson not been present, the father might have been brought to terms by this vague but dreadful threat. But now he shook his head, as an intimation that nothing could move him.

"You have taken your own course, sir," continued the son, through his closed teeth. "I shall take mine. Don't forget my last words. As for you, sir," turning to Marcus Wilkeson, "we shall probably meet again."

Marcus urbanely responded that nothing could give him greater pleasure. The son, darting a last malignant look at his father, whose face was happily averted, strode out of the room, slamming the door, and afterward the street door, with increased emphasis.

When he had gone, the father said to his visitor, feebly:

"Have I done right?"

"Precisely. Your conduct was firm, prudent, and will have a good effect."

"I hope so—I hope so. But don't you think, now, I was a little too severe—to begin with, I mean? I fear that my son will be driven to crime; and that would kill me."

"I regard his threats as only empty words," replied Marcus. He has found them useful heretofore, and he tries them now. Having learned that they do not longer frighten you, he will never employ them again. That is one point gained. If he is really bad enough to commit a crime for money, your misjudged kindness will not prevent him, but will rather encourage his evil disposition."

"There is truth in what you say," replied the old gentleman, faintly; "but I—I—fear."

The protracted conversation, and the suppressed agony of the past few minutes, were too much for the old gentleman to bear on his first day of convalescence. He suddenly turned very pale, and his head drooped. Marcus threw open a window, and held the cordial to his lips. As Marcus was applying this restorative, without any perceptible benefit, the door opened, and Mrs. Frump ran in, red in the face, and quite out of breath.

"Excuse me, sir. I am Mrs. Frump, Mr. Van Quintem's niece."

"I am Mr. Wilkeson, a friend of Mr. Van Quintem," said Marcus, hastily introducing himself; "and I am glad you are come."

"Yes, I see. Fainted away. Revive in a moment. Fresh air. Cordial. Quite right. Now a little water on his forehead."

Mrs. Frump made her sentences short, to accommodate her breath.

As she passed a cool sponge across the patient's brow, she said:

"I knew it would be so. He has been here. I saw him round the corner. Looking pale and mad."

"You are right, madam. He *has* been here."

Mrs. Frump's pleasant little eyes shone with unnatural anger, and there was a presage of wrathful words in her quivering lips. Mrs. Frump was desperately trying to keep back certain private opinions that she had long entertained, but proved unequal to the effort. She burst out with:

"He's an undutiful son, sir. A monster, sir. And he's killing his poor father. He's——"

"Ah! what?" said Mr. Van Quintem, opening his eyes, and looking wildly around, like one who wakes from a horrible dream.

"It's I. Your niece—Gusty," replied Mrs. Frump, changing her assumed harsh tones into her natural soft ones "And I think you had better go to bed. Please take hold, Mr. Wilkeson, and assist him to the next room." She added, in a whisper, "Don't talk with him any more to-day."

Mr. Wilkeson nodded, raised his eyebrows to signify that

he appreciated the advice, and proceeded at once to aid Mrs. Frump in her benevolent task. The old gentleman had considerably revived by this time.

"You are right, my dear Gusty," said he, looking fondly at his niece. "You are always right. And you are right, too, sir," he added, turning to Marcus. "Ah, if I had known such a good adviser years ago."

Marcus, remembering Mrs. Frump's injunction, made no answer to this remark.

When the old gentleman had been led tottering into the adjacent parlor, which was fitted up as his bedroom, and placed comfortably on a high prop of pillows, Marcus drew out his watch, made an amiable pretence of very important business down town, and bade his venerable friend "good-by."

"I had hoped you could stay longer; for I feel that you are a true friend, and I can confide my sorrows to you," murmured the old gentleman, taking his guest fondly by the hand.

But Marcus, fortified by another significant look from Mrs. Frump, declared that business was imperative, and he must go. He would call to-morrow, without fail, and hoped to find his friend as cheerful as a cricket. The old gentleman smiled at the absurdity of that hope, and said he should depend on seeing him to-morrow.

So, shaking hands warmly with Mr. Van Quintem, and bowing most respectfully to Mrs. Frump, Marcus took his departure, and meditated, as he walked slowly home, on the strange occurrences of the day.

CHAPTER IV.

WESLEY TIFFLES.

One evening, shortly after the events narrated in the last chapter, the three bachelors, having finished dinner, and escaped from the grim presence of Miss Philomela Wilkeson, took their accustomed seats and pipes in the little back parlor.

The curtains were drawn, the gas was lighted, the fire burning brightly, and, upon these outward tokens of cheer, the three bachelors reflected contentment and happiness from their six eyes. In his own opinion, each of the three had unlimited cause to be happy; and not even that killjoy of the household, Miss Wilkeson, could mar the completeness of their felicity—when she was not present.

Fayette Overtop was blessed with the thought, that in Mrs. Slapman he had found, at last, that rare bird for which he had patiently hunted through the valleys and uplands of society—"a sensible woman." The intellectual sympathy which was enkindled between them on the memorable occasion of their first meeting, had grown warmer at each successive interview—first at a supper party, second at a *conversazione*, and third at a private theatrical and musical entertainment, to all of which Mr. Overtop had been invited, with the particular compliments of the liberal hostess.

During this pleasant acquaintance, Mr. Overtop had made the extraordinary discovery that Mrs. Slapman was married, and that the thin little man whom he saw dodging up the stairs on New Year's day was her husband.

It would be difficult to explain, on behalf of Mr. Overtop, a phenomenon which Mr. Overtop was never able to explain to the satisfaction of the gossip-loving public, or of his best friends. We therefore content ourselves with merely stating the fact, that Mr. Overtop's admiration for Mrs. Slapman was purely intellectual; that he was fascinated by her vivacious intellect, and not by her substantial person; by the charm of her manners, and not of her face. He looked upon Mrs. Slapman as a masculine mind and soul, of uncommon depth, made powerfully magnetic by its enshrinement in a feminine form. Overtop once told Matthew Maltboy, that he knew, in his own experience, the meaning of Platonic love. But Matthew, who was a sad materialist even in his sentimental moods, laughed at him, and winked. Overtop positively felt hurt at this unkind reception of his confidences, and never again alluded to the state of his feelings toward Mrs. Slapman, until subsequent occurrences made it necessary in self-defence.

With Mr. Slapman he was not personally acquainted; but he had ascertained privately, from a musical frequenter of the house, who invariably brought his flute with him, and who was understood to be the oldest friend of the family, that Mr. Slapman owned a large property in wild land in Pennsylvania, not a hundred miles from New York; that he was improving it, and selling it out in building lots, and had already cleared a handsome fortune; that he was a strict business man, and looked after his affairs in person, passing between New York and Slapmansville (the name of the new settlement) twice a week, and spending the larger part of his time at the latter place. Also that, next to avarice, which was his crowning trait, his chief fault was jealousy. It galled him to think that his wife had obtained a settlement in bank from him before marriage, which enabled her to indulge her tastes for society; and it enraged him still more to observe how much she was loved and admired by others, when he had purchased her exclusively for his private love and admiration. He it was who was to be sometimes seen stalking through the parlors with a pale face, or running up and down the front staircase in a state of great nervous agitation. None of Mrs. Slapman's visitors had the pleasure of his personal acquaintance; and it was considered a point of good breeding not to allude to him in her presence.

For this misguided man Fayette Overtop felt a real pity. He yearned to expostulate with him gently, as a friend. Taking Mr. Slapman's hand in his own, he would have said:

"Your wife is a precious gift to the world. Seek not to check the outflow of her ardent nature. Thank Heaven that you are the custodian of such a treasure, not to be selfishly monopolized by yourself, but held in trust for the benefit of society."

Overtop's meditations, on this particular occasion, pertained to the style of the costume which would most become him as the lover of Mrs. Slapman, in an original play to be enacted at her house toward the close of the week. The question was chiefly of knee breeches. Overtop was mentally debating whether he ought not, in justice to his thin legs, to substitute an ampler style of integuments.

Matthew Maltboy had also been invited to this *soirée dramatique* (as Mrs. Slapman's large pasteboards expressed it). A fat man was a necessity of the play. Mrs. Slapman was not cordial to Matthew, regarding him as an excessively commonplace person, and had invited him to her social gatherings out of courtesy to Overtop; but her artist eye saw in him a fitness for the fat man. Matthew was delighted with the implied compliment to those talents for the stage which every man supposes himself to possess in some degree, and cheerfully undertook the part.

The proprieties of costume did not in the least perplex Mr. Maltboy, as he lay on the sofa digesting his dinner, and puffing out smoke rings by the dozen. His thoughts were mildly fixed on that delightful Miss Whedell. Five times he had been graciously permitted to visit the lady at her house, and to discover a score of new charms at each interview. A large experience in love making assured him that the object of his idolatry was not wholly indifferent to him. The paternal Whedell had hobbies. Matthew had studied them, like a skilful strategist, catered to them, and felt quite sure that he had that revered individual on his side. But, in the midst of these pleasant imaginings, there rose the dark and baleful image of Chiffield!

Marcus Wilkeson was also pondering—pleasantly, if one might judge from the contented smile upon his lips. The subject of his thoughts was one which, for reasons that seemed good to him, he still kept secret from his fellow bachelors. He had freely told them of his singular adventure at the house of the old gentleman opposite; but not a word of the inventor and his daughter, and of the private school at Miss Pillbody's. Not even the minute and sometimes tedious accounts which Overtop and Maltboy gave of their private thoughts and experiences, could induce Marcus to reciprocate their confidence. For the first time in his life he wore a mask before his companions, and prevaricated, and became, on a small scale, a humbug.

The sharp ringing of the doorbell broke in upon the quiet reflections of the three bachelors. Mash, the cook, who was at that moment reading the fifteenth chapter of "The Buttery and the Boudoir: A Tale of Real Life," in her favorite weekly, threw down the paper in a passion, bounded up stairs, and admitted John Wesley Tiffles, or Wesley Tiffles, as he always subscribed himself on promissory notes and other worthless paper. Mr. Tiffles chucked Mash familiarly under the chin (resented with a scornful look by Mash, who had learned from "The Buttery and the Boudoir" to set a proper value on herself), and then walked straight to the parlor, like one who knew he was a welcome guest.

And he was right. For when he opened the door, and disclosed to the three bachelors the well-known laughing eyes, hopeful face, and spare figure of Wesley Tiffles, they hailed him with enthusiasm. He was a walking cure for despondency, although he sometimes charged too high, in the shape of borrowed money, for his professional services. But neither of the three bachelors had yet sustained that pecuniary tax which Wesley Tiffles always levied upon his friends, just before leaving them forever. They formed a part of his reserve corps, which had latterly been sadly thinned out in Mr. Tiffles's desperate contest with the world.

Mr. Tiffles shook hands with Marcus Wilkeson, giving him the grip of some unknown Order, slapped Overtop on the back, and playfully pulled the whiskers of Maltboy. Then he filled a pipe, threw himself into a chair, adjusted his legs in the true form of a compass, and opened his coat ostentatiously. All this in about ten seconds, and with a geniality that defied reproof. He was the very embodiment of cheer.

"Prepare to be astonished," said Mr. Tiffles, after his third whiff. "I have a splendid idea." The three bachelors smiled, and nodded an intimation that they were prepared.

"I have had some impracticable notions in my time; but this *is* good, and you'll say so. You know that dog, Mark, two doors below—the large yellow one, with cropped ears, and a tail like the handle of a shaving brush?"

Mr. Wilkeson replied that he had the pleasure of the animal's acquaintance.

"Well, as I was passing the dog's house on my way here, I slipped in the snow. The dog, always on the alert for victims, took a mean advantage of my situation, and jumped after me through the open gate. I scrambled to my feet, but not before he had fastened his teeth in my right leg——"

"Good heavens! was he mad?" cried Overtop, who had a horror of dogs, and made wide circuits about them in the street.

"Can't say as to that," replied Wesley Tiffles, "but advise you to keep shy of him for the future. I was about to say that he bit me through the leg of my trowsers. And on that very instant, as if by inspiration, I caught—not the hydrophobia, but a magnificent idea. Having got on my pins, I kicked the dog into his front yard, and immediately worked the idea into shape. You'll be sure to like it."

Marcus Wilkeson, speaking for self and friends, said he had no doubt of that. Mr. Tiffles's ideas always possessed the merit of novelty.

"That means that they have no other merit!" returned Tiffles, laughing. "Very true of most of them. I confess all my failures. But here is an idea which even you, skeptic as you are, will grant to be not only novel, but great. You have all observed, gentlemen, the immense differences in dogs. There are white, black, brown, gray, yellow (like our suggestive canine friend two doors below), tan-colored, mouse-colored, striped, and spotted dogs. There are round dogs, square dogs, long dogs, short dogs, tall dogs, and low dogs. There are full-grown dogs that weigh less than a pound, and others that kick the beam at a hundred pounds. There are dogs that are pretty much all tail, and there are dogs that have no tail to speak of. Among all the dogs that you meet in the street, do you ever see two exactly alike ? "

Fayette Overtop, who spoke from extensive and minute observation, unhesitatingly said "No."

"True ! Nature never repeats herself in dogs. In so doing, Nature works directly for my benefit, as I will show you. Now, in the second place, as you are probably aware, there is an ordinance forbidding unmuzzled dogs to run in the streets during the hot months——"

"An excellent law," interrupted Overtop.

"If caught at large without muzzles, they are taken to the public pound, and, unless redeemed by the owners within twenty-four hours, are drowned in a tub——"

"Serve 'em right," remarked the hydrophobiac bachelor.

"Now, I am *slightly* acquainted with some members of the Common Council" (he laid emphasis on the word "slightly," to imply that he was on terms of the closest intimacy with them), "and can easily obtain from them the privilege of catching all the stray dogs, and taking them out of the country next summer."

"Which would be very benevolent to the dogs ; and, regarded from their point of view, your idea is a noble one," thoughtfully observed Marcus Wilkeson. "But I don't, at this moment, exactly see how you are benefited by it."

Mr. Tiffles smiled with the consciousness of power, and chidingly said :

"You are dull this morning, Mark—quite dull. Strike, but hear ! In a word, then, I propose to exhibit two or three hundred of these dogs, in some country where there are *no* dogs. I would give them strange names, put them in cages, and call them the 'American Menagerie of Trained Animals.' A person who had never seen dogs, would suppose each one to be a different species from the others—just as the lion, the tiger, and the leopard are different, though all belonging to the one cat family. Now, there is my idea. What do you think of it? Of course, you laugh, at first."

Roars of laughter from the three bachelors had formed the chorus of Wesley Tiffles's closing sentences. Marcus Wilkeson, as became his age, was the first to recover himself.

"The idea is a splendid one. None better. But there is one slight difficulty in the way. Where are you to find your country that has no dogs? If there were such a happy land on the face of this earth, Overtop would have hunted it up long ago, and moved there."

Overtop laughingly replied, "That's so." He then informed Mr. Tiffles, while admitting the theoretical excellence of his idea, that every nation had its dogs as well as its fleas. Those two friends of man were impartially distributed over the terrestrial globe. Overtop referred to the standard Cyclopædias, and several works on Natural History, in proof of his assertion.

"Can't be! can't be!" retorted Wesley Tiffles, who was at first disposed to defend his brilliant idea. But brilliant ideas were a common growth of his fertile mind, and, like all things easily produced, he held them cheaply. The moment that evidence, or the test of practice, showed them to be fallacious, he gave them up, and drew upon his brain for others. So, after a second's reflection, he added:

"Perhaps you are right. Dogs are not exactly in my line, after all. But the idea, *as* an idea, was magnificent."

As Wesley Tiffles spoke, he repeated the act, for the twentieth time, of throwing back his overcoat (a little seedy), and opening his vest, as if to draw attention to his shirt front, whose natural whiteness was toned down by a delicate neutral tint. Immediately afterward, he placed his hand on a small breastpin in the centre of the shirt front, and turned it to the right and left. It sparkled for the first time in the rays of the fire, and revealed to the experienced eyes of the three bachelors simultaneously, that Wesley Tiffles was the wearer of a real diamond.

"Excuse me," said Marcus Wilkeson, who divined that Tiffles wished his diamond to be remarked upon, "but that is pretty!"

"Pretty! What?" said Tiffles, looking about the room.

"That diamond."

"Oh! the diamond. Perhaps you would like to look at it?" (hands it round for inspection). "Cost forty dollars. Rather a hard draw on my exchequer" (that was Mr. Tiffles's word for a friend's pocket); "but I considered it a most judicious investment for a young man just going into business."

The novelty of this idea was not lost on Fayette Overtop. "Pray explain, Tiffles," said he.

"Cheerfully," said Tiffles, replacing the gem in his shirt front, after it had been duly handled and admired. "Nobody will acknowledge that he is taken in by a diamond. He will say, 'Anybody can buy a diamond, by saving up thirty or forty dollars; and why should I believe a man to be rich who wears one?' Yet, in his heart of hearts, he does believe it, unless the possessor of the diamond has the bad taste to dress flashily. Then he passes for an impostor, and people will doubt, even against their own senses, the genuineness of the stone. But let him dress plainly, as I do," continued Mr. Tiffles, stroking down the left leg of his black trowsers, shiny with wear, "and that little diamond shall stand, in the eyes of the whole world, as the representative of a fat bank account, a brown stone house, and a couple of corner lots."

Marcus and Matthew laughed, but Fayette Overtop, who absolutely revelled in paradoxes, said, "True, Tiffles, true!"

"Don't think," pursued Tiffles, "that I expected to impose on you with it. You know that I am a poor devil, living on my wits." (Tiffles was delightfully frank with his intimate acquaintances.) "I hold out this glittering bait, not for my friends, but for my old foe and natural enemy, the world. You must know that I am on the eve of a grand speculation—probably the grandest I have ever undertaken."

"Another plan of advertising with large kites by day, and

pictorial lanterns attached to their tails at night?" asked Marcus Wilkeson.

"Or another Submarine Pneumatic Parcel-Delivering Tube to Brooklyn?" asked Matthew Maltboy.

"Or an Association for the Cultivation of Mushrooms in Dark Cellars?" asked Fayette Overtop.

"Capital hits!" replied Wesley Tiffles, who took an unfeigned delight in a friendly allusion to his failures. "But allow me to inform you definitely, that those unfortunate speculations are not to be revived. Like the lightning, I don't strike twice in the same place. No; the project upon which I am now engaged is one so eminently practical, so free from all that is visionary, that you will wonder how I thought of it. That project is a PANORAMA OF AFRICA!"

CHAPTER V.

THE PANORAMA OF AFRICA.

THE three bachelors concurred in the opinion that the idea was a good one; but Marcus Wilkeson suggested that the field was too large.

"I thought you would like the general proposition," said Tiffles. "But, bless you, Mark! I don't mean to paint the whole continent, from stem to stern, so to speak; only the undiscovered part of Central Africa—say from Cape Guardafui on the east to the Bight of Benin on the west."

"But how the deuce," asked Matthew Maltboy, "are you, or anybody else, going to paint what has not been discovered?"

Tiffles could hardly suppress a smile at the simplicity of the question. "Why," said he, "that's easy enough. Don't all the geographers tell us that the interior of Africa is made up, so far as known, of alternate deserts and jungles, like the patches on a coverlet? Very well. I conform to this general principle of the continent. I put half of the canvas in desert, and the rest in jungle, and I can't be far out of the way. Take the idea ?"

"Perfectly," said Matthew Maltboy; "but if you have nothing but alternate deserts and jungles, it strikes me your panorama will be a little monotonous. Perhaps I am wrong." (Maltboy always offered suggestions timidly.)

"I have thought of that, and guarded against it. I shall fill the jungles with animated life—elephants, lions, tigers, panthers, leopards, rhinoceroses, hippopotamuses, giraffes, zebras, crocodiles, boa constrictors, and other specimens of natural history indigenous to that delightful region."

"Good!" cried Overtop; "and if you will take a hint from me, you will show your elephants in the act of being caught by natives, or engaged in combats with each other; your lions fighting your tigers or your rhinoceroses; your hippopotamuses engaged in death struggles with your crocodiles; and your boa constrictors gobbling down your natives—or, if that is objectionable on the score of humanity, your monkeys."

"Thank you for the hint; but the expense, and the necessity of completing the panorama at an early day, put it out of the question. To paint accurate representations of these animals engaged in their innocent sports, would occupy the time of a first-class artist for months, and cost an enormous sum."

"Ah, I see," interrupted Overtop, who liked to show that he snatched the meaning; "you will put your animals in recumbent attitudes—sleeping, perhaps, in the depth of jungles, shaded from the fierce rays of the equatorial sun."

"You have guessed it," said Tiffles, with a broad smile. "Most of them will be just there—out of sight. The others will be suggested rather than introduced. Elephants will be signified by their trunks appearing above the tops of the dense undergrowth. Lions, tigers, and other quadrupeds, by the tips of their tails. A boa constrictor will be expressed by a head, a coil, and a bit of tail showing at intervals. The one horn of the rhinoceros will always tell where *he* is. I shall have two small lakes (they are scarce in Africa) for my hippopotamuses and crocodiles. If they exhibit only small portions of their heads above the surface, that is not my fault. It is the nature of the beasts, you know."

"Ha! ha! That is what I call Art concealing Art," said Overtop.

"So it is," returned Tiffles; "and it will be appreciated, I doubt not, by those who affect the school of Severe Simplicity in painting."

"One thing more," said Marcus Wilkeson. "Do you intend to take the panorama through the country, and lecture on it?"

"I do. And here let me say, that I read up the law of false pretences long ago. I shall style myself Professor Wesley on the bills. That I have a right to do, as my full name doesn't look well in type. Actors and singers do the same thing every day. I shall call myself a great traveller. This is strictly true. I have been North to Boston, West to Detroit, and South to Baltimore. I shall not say that I have been in Africa, or that the sketches were taken on the spot. If my audience choose to infer *that*, that is their business. If any one doubts the accuracy of my panorama, I can say triumphantly, 'Prove it!'"

"Excellent, but a little risky," said Marcus Wilkeson, who could not help admiring the audacity of the plan. "Your next great difficulty will be to satisfy audiences after you have got them together, as I dare say you will, by some brilliant system of advertising. I have heard—perhaps you have—of audiences breaking furniture, smashing chandeliers, and tarring and feathering people."

"All that has been thought of," was the reply. "Before I leave the city, I shall give a private exhibition of the panorama to a few ministers of various denominations, in the lecture room of some up-town church. Ministers, you know, are debarred by their profession from attending the opera and theatres, and will catch at the chance to see a panorama for nothing. In private life, they are capital people, as a class—I have known several of them—and will willingly certify that the panorama is a highly moral, instructive, and interesting exhibition. I think I can rely on my persuasive powers for that much. These certificates I shall print on my posters and handbills. They will draw moral audiences. Moral audiences do not break furniture, &c., &c. Comprehend my line of argument?"

"Perfectly," said Marcus; "and very ingenious, *as* an argument."

"I thought you would like it. And now, to drop the subject, I want you three fellows to come up to my rooms, No. 121, third floor, Bartholomew Buildings, Broadway—you remember—and see this great work of art, early next week."

"Is it nearly finished?" asked Marcus.

"Yes—in my mind's eye. That is the main thing. The painting has not yet been begun. It will be a very simple matter. The canvas will be about four hundred feet long. One half of it will be a dead level of yellow paint, for desert; and the rest, perpendicular stripes of green paint, for jungle. A good artist, with a whitewash brush and two tubsful of paint, ought to do up the whole panorama in two days. The heads and tails of animated life, the two small lakes, and a few other objects of interest, such as the sun, the moon, birds flying in the air, &c., could be put in afterward by an artist of higher grade. And, by the way, now I think of it, I may as well open with a sunrise off Cape Guardafui, and a distant view of the Straits of Babel Mandel, give a passing glance at the sources of the Nile, which lie in that undiscovered region, a brief glimpse at the Mountains of the Moon, and wind up with a splendid sunset in the Bight of Benin. It——"

Mr. Tiffles's observations were cut short by the sudden entrance of Miss Philomela Wilkeson. She shot rapidly into the room, but, when her eyes rested on Mr. Tiffles, she recoiled with maiden modesty, and stepped back as if to beat a retreat. Then, recovering her self-possession in a small measure, she stepped forward again, and said, in the blandest of tones, with just the least virgin coyness:

"I thought perhaps I had left my scissors here this afternoon."

Messrs. Wilkeson, Overtop, and Maltboy asserted, without rising from their seats, that they had not seen her scissors, and doubted very much whether the scissors were in that room. But Wesley Tiffles, who was the most polite and obliging of mortals when there was a lady in the case, rose respectfully upon her entrance, and insisted upon searching the apartment for the missing tool.

Miss Wilkeson, thus being placed under obligations to Mr. Tiffles, was compelled to take personal cognizance of him, which she did with the nearest approach to a blush that she was ever known to make. "I beg, sir, that you will not trouble yourself. I—I do not think the scissors are here, after all."

"That can be ascertained only by searching, miss," replied Tiffles. Then he glided about the room in his own nimble fashion, looking behind the two vases on the mantelpiece, raking over the littered burden of the table in the corner, and peering and poking into every place where there was the least likelihood of finding a stray pair of scissors; Miss Wilkeson all the while deprecating any further search.

Mr. Tiffles suddenly stopped, like a dragonfly in the midst of his angular dartings, and said: "Since your scissors are not to be found, it is fortunate that I have a pocket pair, which are always at your service." Mr. Tiffles produced the ill-omened article, and handed it to her. This called out a new lot of thanks, regrets for having troubled him, apologies, and a peremptory refusal to take his scissors, immediately followed by their acceptance, and a promise that she would take the best care of them, and return them to the owner on his next visit.

Then was the auspicious moment for Miss Wilkeson to have retired with dignity; but she stood at the door, twirling the fatal scissors in her hand, and waiting either to say something which did not come spontaneously, or to have something said to her.

Marcus Wilkeson saw a subtle motive in this awkward tarrying at the door, and, having no objection to gratifying it, he straightway introduced Mr. Wesley Tiffles to Miss Philomela Wilkeson. Mr. Tiffles put himself into the form of an L, like a professional acrobat; and Miss Wilkeson executed a courtesy in the old, exploded style. Then, as if appalled at what she had done, she backed into the entry as fast as she had come from it.

Mr. Tiffles, upon whom the small events of life made no impression, thought no more of Miss Wilkeson that evening, but smoked three pipes, told two funny stories, sang one comic song, and then went home, having previously exacted from the three bachelors a promise to call at his rooms and see at least one half of the panorama completed, on the following day week.

Since Miss Wilkeson had been an inmate of that house, she had seen Wesley Tiffles perhaps a dozen times, in the entry or on the doorsteps, and had been impressed with his gentlemanlike air, his quick black eyes, and his deferential manner toward her. Everybody is supposed to have a realized ideal somewhere, if he or she could only find it. Such was Wesley Tiffles to Philomela Wilkeson. Let it be confessed at once. The lost scissors were all the time quietly resting at the bottom of Miss Wilkeson's workbag, and she knew it. The prevalent frailty of human nature must be her excuse.

She had obtained not only an introduction to Wesley Tiffles, but a pair of scissors which must be returned to him, and were therefore a bond of friendship. But Miss Wilkeson forgot the fatality which the proverb attaches to gifts or loans of that particular article of cutlery.

BOOK FIFTH.

MANŒUVRES.

CHAPTER I.

STOLEN—MORE THAN A PURSE.

ONE morning, as Marcus Wilkeson was idly turning the pages of a blue-and-gold favorite, the doorbell rang. In accordance with some mysterious law of acoustics, the sound was full three minutes descending the kitchen staircase, entering the keyhole of the kitchen door, and striking on the tympanum of Mash, the cook, who was sitting by the fire, reading the twenty-fifth chapter of "The Buttery and the Boudoir: A Tale of Real Life." When Mash became fully conscious (which was not till the end of the chapter) that the bell had rung, she expelled a sigh from her fat chest, and wiped the tears from her eyes with the end of her clean apron, and then went to the door with a noble resignation to her lot. There she found a stout elderly woman, bearing a note for "Marcus Wilkeson, Esq."

"Lor'! how slow you are!" said the stout woman, handing the letter to her.

Mash, who had read, in the twenty-third chapter, of the overwhelming way in which the heroine cook had answered an insult by dignified silence, said not a word in reply, but took the note, and slammed the door in the stout woman's face.

The exclamation "Bah!" and certain indistinct mutterings which were audible through the panels, convinced Mash that, by her self-denial, she had won a moral victory. It was with a feeling of excusable pride that she walked into the back parlor, and delivered the note to Marcus Wilkeson.

"Thank you, Mash," said he. It was a singular illustration of his excessive politeness, that he was no less grateful for paid services than for free.

Mash retired, thinking to herself that, if Mr. Wilkeson were only a pirate, a smuggler, a guerilla chieftain, or a dashing fellow in some unlawful, dangerous business, a few years younger, he would be a perfect hero.

Marcus did not recognize the handwriting of the address. Tearing open the envelope, he read the following lines, hastily scrawled on a bit of blue paper:

"Wednesday, A. M.

"Marcus Wilkeson, Esq.:

"Sir: Please come over and see me immediately. I have something important to communicate.

"Your obedient servant,

"Eliphalet Minford."

"Something must be wrong," said Marcus; and startling thoughts then occurred to him. "Has her hard studying brought on illness? It can't be. She was well enough last evening. What can be the matter?"

Marcus Wilkeson's temperament was of that unfortunate nervous sort which is thrown off its balance by the slightest shock. His frame trembled as he put on his overcoat and hat; and, when he looked in the mirror, he noticed that his face was paler than usual, and his eyes were glassy. "Pooh! what a sensitive fool I am!" said he.

He walked hurriedly to Mr. Minford's, and mounted the long, creaking staircases, two steps at a time, tormenting himself all the way with vague apprehensions of evil.

When he entered the room, without knocking (as was his

custom of late), he found the inventor standing in front of his machine, with bare arms, hard at work. Marcus nervously said, "Good morning," and stepped forward to shake him by the hand, but stopped when he saw that Mr. Minford averted his face, and did not move.

"I wished to show you a letter which I received a few minutes ago," said the inventor, still not facing Marcus, but busily filing off the rough edge of a brass wheel fresh from the mould. "There it is, on the table."

Marcus caught up the letter, and read the following:

"NEW YORK, Wednesday Forenoon.

"MR. MINFORD:

"RESPECTED SIR: Allow a true friend and well wisher to ask a few questions. Who is this Mr. Marcus Wilkeson that has suddenly taken such an interest in your family affairs? What is his private history? Why is he relieving you from all trouble and expense in the education of your beautiful child? What are the man's *real* motives? Would it not be well to spare your eyes from your invention long enough to look into these matters a little? Pardon the suggestion. The office of a spy, and a secret accuser, is an unpleasant, and, perhaps, a thankless one. I should never have assumed it, but for the fact that your ardent devotion to science may render you the easy dupe—and your daughter the innocent victim—of a designing and heartless man of the world. I do not ask you to believe the writer of an anonymous note, and therefore I make no specific charges against this Wilkeson; but merely ask you to inquire into his private character, and, above all, his MOTIVES, for yourself.

"ONE OF MANY."

Though Marcus Wilkeson was as innocent as a child, in deed and thought, of the baseness hinted at in this letter, he felt that he was looking guilty. Astonishment and indignation kindled in his eyes; but a flush of shame mounted at the same time to his cheeks. Marcus had often said, that if he were tapped on the shoulder in the street, and charged with a petty theft, he would look guilty of grand larceny until he could regain command of his feelings. This diseased sensitiveness, inherited from his mother, was the curse of his physical and mental organization.

His shame was increased by a consciousness that the inventor was stealthily watching him, and studying the enlargement of those horrid red spots on his cheeks.

When Marcus finished the letter, he put on an expression of outraged innocence—which matched poorly with the flaming tokens of guilt—and said:

"These are infernal lies, sir; and, if I knew the coward who wrote them, I would cram them down his throat."

"Of course they are lies," returned Mr. Minford. "Every anonymous letter writer is a liar—until it is proved that he tells the truth. I shall believe none of these low aspersions on your honor, Mr. Wilkeson, without conclusive evidence." As the inventor said this, not emphatically, Marcus saw that he believed all that the letter had insinuated.

By this time, Marcus had got his constitutional devil a little under control. There was something of real boldness and honesty in his eyes, as he answered:

"This is a distressing subject to talk or think of. But now that it has been brought before us, I demand a full investigation. Go, wherever you will, among those who know me, and inquire into my character. Recall everything that has occurred between us since the beginning of our acquaintance. Ask your daughter if I have ever spoken a word to her, or cast a look at her, which could justify these infamous insinuations. Thus much I ask of you, in justice to me."

"And I refuse, sir," said the inventor. "I will not insult you by an unworthy suspicion. The world is full of impertinent people, and we can no more stop their gabble, than that of swallows in the air. This nameless fellow signs himself 'One of Many.' That is probably a lie. But if there were thousands like himself prying into your and my affairs, I should not care. As for motives, none but fools and misanthropes trouble themselves about *them*."

The inventor tossed off the last sentence contemptuously. But Marcus knew that he did attach a great importance to motives; although he could not fairly be ranked either among the misanthropes or the fools. He therefore replied:

"The whole world is welcome to inquire into my motives. As I understand them, they are: First, I take pleasure in your society, sir, because, like myself, you are a quiet, thinking man. Second, you have a hobby—your machine, there—and I admire people with hobbies. Third, I am fond of children, and—and—your daughter is a very pleasant, intelligent child. Fourth, you have insisted on selling me an interest in your invention, in return for a small loan, and that fact would draw me here, if nothing else did. These are motives enough to satisfy the most inquisitive mind, I should think."

Marcus said this with an attempt at a light laugh. But there was one motive not yet confessed—a motive which could hardly be called a motive, for it lay dim and half-formed within his brain. He had never, in his moments of self-inquisition, acknowledged its existence to himself. How could he, then, venture to disclose it to another? It was the suppression of this immature motive, that brought back that look of deceit and guilt to Marcus Wilkeson's ingenuous face.

This unfortunate physiognomical revelation was not lost upon the keen eyes of the inventor. But he said:

"Mr. Wilkeson, let us not say another word on this ridiculous subject. I am ashamed of myself for showing you the letter. I ought to have thrown it into the fire."

"There I differ with you, my dear sir," said Marcus. "You did perfectly right, and I am glad that I have had the opportunity to define my position here clearly, once and for all." Marcus could not avoid saying this much in mere civility to the inventor, but he indulged the private opinion that that gentleman should have burned the anonymous note.

"Who can have written this scoundrelly thing?" continued Marcus, turning over the letter, and then the envelope, for the twentieth time each, and minutely examining them.

The note was written on a half sheet of common letter paper. The manufacturer's stamp in the corner had been cut off, and the size of the half sheet further diminished by paring down one of the sides. The writing was what is known as "backhanded," in strokes which appeared at first sight to be of a uniform lightness. On inspecting it very closely, Marcus discovered a tendency, in this backhanded penmanship, to ascend from the line; and also that, in a few instances, the downward strokes on certain long letters were a trifle thicker than on others. That the writing was a man's, Marcus had no doubt, though he would have been puzzled to give the reasons which led him to that conclusion. The envelope was the ordinary prepaid-stamped one issued by the Government, and therefore could not contribute to the identification of the anonymous writer. The superscription was in the same backhand, and was peculiar in nothing but a small curved flourish, like Hogarth's line of beauty, beneath the words, "New York City."

"The rascal has carefully disguised his hand," said Marcus, "and does not mean to be found out. I can say nothing more positive, than that it is written by somebody who has never corresponded with me. My memory of autographs happens to be pretty tenacious."

"And I am positive that it is written by no acquaintance of mine, or of my daughter's, for we have none—except you. As the case now stands, it is a mystery, not worth the exploring."

"Again I differ with you," said Marcus. "Whoever wrote this false letter, has powerful motives of hostility to me or you, or, perhaps—worse still—to your daughter. I must try to smoke him out of his hiding place. Meanwhile, I trust, sir, you will see the propriety of concealing this unpleasant matter from Miss Minford."

"Certainly, Mr. Wilkeson, certainly. As for myself, it is forever dismissed from my mind; and I cannot blame myself sufficiently for having troubled you with it." Mr. Minford here proffered his hand, which Marcus cordially shook, rejoicing to observe no trace of suspicion in the inventor's clear gray eyes.

"Allow me to retain this letter for the present," asked Marcus. "It may serve as a clue to the detection of the concealed scoundrel. I also beg that you will show me any other anonymous letters of the same character that may reach you."

Mr. Minford laughed. "The stove door is the pigeonhole where all such nonsense ought to be filed away. But just as you please. If any more come to hand, you shall see them. They may amuse you, as they do me. Ha! ha!"

Marcus echoed the laugh, but feebly. Then it occurred to him that Pet would soon be home, and he felt a strange aversion to meeting her, after what had happened. He therefore pleaded a pressing engagement at eleven o'clock (which it then was), and took his departure from the inventor's roof, but not without a warm and seemingly sincere invitation to "call soon."

CHAPTER II.

CONSOLATIONS OF HIGH ART.

MARCUS walked slowly toward Broadway, musing and unhappy. To a man of his delicate and hyper-sensitive nature, an event of this kind was a vast disturbance. He felt that this anonymous letter was but the forerunner of a long series of troubles. That prescience which nervous people have of misfortunes portrayed to him a future black with disappointments and dangers.

"Hallo, Mark! What's the matter? You look as sad as a low comedian by daylight!" Previous to this salutation came a ringing slap on the left shoulder.

Marcus rather liked familiarities; but the slap, coming on him when his nerves were unstrung, startled him. He turned sharply; but the stern and indignant face wreathed into amiable smiles, when he saw that the lively gentleman behind him was only Wesley Tiffles. Everybody liked Wesley Tiffles; even those who bore the burden of his unlucky financial schemes uniting in cheerful testimony to his charming, companionable qualities. His presence was like a ray of sunlight to Marcus Wilkeson's beclouded mind; and when Wesley Tiffles hooked an arm in his (as he did to everybody on the second day of their acquaintance), Marcus felt his perplexities passing away from him, like electricity on a conducting rod.

Wesley Tiffles and his single diamond (the latter from the background of a third day's shirt) shone on him together; and Marcus laughed merrily in reply:

"I don't look sad now," said he. "I'm glad to see you, Tiffles. What are you driving at *now*, eh?"

This question was continually poked at Tiffles. He changed his business so often.

"At the panorama of Africa, to be sure," said Tiffles. "It is a great idea, and I am constant to it, although several capital schemes have occurred to me since I first thought of it. But Africa deserves, and shall have the precedence."

"Oh! yes—I remember. And how far have you got along with this great work?"

"It's almost finished, thank you. Patching is the artist. You know Patching, of course—one of the most promising painters of the modern school. There were several Patchings very much praised by the Sunday papers, at the last National Academy Exhibition, though the hanging committee put them either among the dirt or the cobwebs. This conspiracy against Patching is far-reaching. It would seem as if his rivals of the Academy actually went about town calling upon people, and cautioning them *not* to buy Patchings. Indeed, to such an extent has this outrageous attempt to put down a fellow artist been carried, that I know of but one Patching to be publicly seen in the city. It is an attic interior—a sweet thing, quite equal to Frère, and hangs behind a bar near Spring street. Perhaps you would like to examine it?"

"Hem! Not to-day. Some other time," answered Marcus, who, strangely enough, interpreted the question as an invitation to drink at his (Marcus's) expense.

"I did not mean to-day," said Wesley Tiffles. "Any time will do. Well, I have engaged this brilliant but neglected creature to paint my panorama. At first he refused—as I expected. He said that it would hurt his reputation. I argued to him, that, the larger the picture, the more the reputation; and said that I would put his name on the bills in type second only to my own. But he could not bring himself to see the matter as I did, and consented to paint it only on condition of profound secrecy. Price, one hundred dollars. You will therefore understand (Tiffles lowered his voice) that what I am saying to you is strictly confidential—as, indeed, all is that I say about my panorama. Secrecy alone gives value to these grand, original ideas."

Wesley Tiffles was always unbosoming himself to the world, and informing each individual hearer that his disclosure was strictly confidential.

"I give you my word," said Marcus. He wondered where Tiffles raised the money to pay the artist, but did not like to ask him.

"Now I have caught you, you must come and see how we get along. The work is going on at my room in the Bartholomew Buildings, only a few steps from here." (According to Tiffles, the Bartholomew Buildings were only a few steps from anywhere, when he wanted to take anybody to them.) "Patching will object to bringing in a stranger; but I can pass you off as a capitalist, who thinks of taking an interest in the panorama. Good joke, that!"

Marcus drew back a little at the joke; but Wesley Tiffles had proved so great a relief to his low spirits, that he determined to keep on taking him, and expressed his ardent desire to see the panorama.

The couple, arm in arm, sauntered into Broadway, and down that thoroughfare. Tiffles nodded to a great many acquaintances, and Wilkeson to a very few. People whom Tiffles did not know personally, he had short biographies of, and he entertained Marcus with an incessant string of anecdotes and memoranda of passers by. The walk was leisurely and uninterrupted, with two exceptions, when Wesley Tiffles broke suddenly from his companion, rushed into the entry of a photographic establishment, and examined numerous square feet of show portraits with profound interest. Marcus explained these impulsive movements on the supposition that Tiffles sought to escape from approaching duns. He noticed that that individual, while observing people who streamed by him on either side, kept one eye, as it were, about a block and a half ahead. In some parts of the world, Marcus might have objected to walking publicly with a man of such an eccentric demeanor. But he was well aware that, in New York, a citizen's reputation is not in the least degree affected by the company that he keeps.

They soon arrived at the Bartholomew Buildings—a rickety five-story edifice, which had been altered from a hotel to a nest of private offices. The basement was a restaurant, the first floor a drygoods store, and thence to the roof there was a small Babel of trades and professions known and unknown. No census taker had ever booked all the businesses and all the names under that comprehensive roof.

In the upper story of this building, at the end of a long, hall, the floor of which was hollowed in places by the feet of half a century, was the room, or office, as he called it, of Mr. Wesley Tiffles. There was no number, or sign, on the door, but only a card bearing the inscription, in a bold hand, "Back in five minutes." Mr. Tiffles always put out this standing announcement whenever he had occasion to absent himself from his office for an indefinite period. At the top of the door there was a swinging window. which was ever close fastened, and covered with four thicknesses of newspapers. Though door and window were shut, there came from this room, as if through pores of the wood and the glass, a strong odor of tobacco smoke. A voice within could be heard softly humming an operatic air.

Wesley Tiffles opened the door with a latch key, saying, "All right!" in a loud voice, as he did so. Marcus entered with him into a blue cloud of smoke heated to a sickly degree by a small coal stovê with a prodigious quantity of pipe. Even Marcus's hardened lungs found it difficult to breathe.

The room was about twenty feet square. It had been a part of the laundry when the building was a hotel. The walls, from the floor to the low ceiling, appeared to be hung with a strange, dim tapestry. A second glance convinced Marcus Wilkeson that this seeming tapestry was the panorama, which was fastened on stretchers along three sides of the room, and rolled up in a corner as fast as completed. At the farther end of the room, barely visible through the smoke, was the figure of a man in a torn and dirty dressing gown, and an enormous black felt hat with a huge turn-up brim, of the kind supposed to be worn by the bandits of the Pyrenees. The back of the man was turned to Marcus Wilkeson, and he was making rapid dabs on the canvas with a long brush, frequently dipping into one of a series of pails or pans which stood on the floor by his side. He was smoking and humming the operatic air at the same time; and he pulled his great slouched hat farther over his eyes, as a signal for impertinent curiosity to keep its distance.

Wesley Tiffles whispered something about the eccentricities of genius, and then said:

"Mr. Patching. Allow me. Mr. Wilkeson. A capitalist, who thinks of taking a small interest in the panorama. Confidential, of course."

The artist turned round during these remarks, and presented the original of a portrait which Marcus remembered to have seen—dressing gown, hat, and all—in a small print-shop window in the Sixth Avenue. Touching the face he might have had doubt, but there was no mistaking the pattern of the dressing gown and the amazing hat. He also had a faint recollection of the thin face, the Vandyke beard, and the long, tangled hair at Mrs. Slapman's, on New Year's, but was not positive as to their identity. Mr. Patching's individuality lay chiefly in his hat.

The artist placed a moist hand, with one long finger nail like a claw, at the disposal of Marcus Wilkeson. The latter gentleman shook the member feebly, and distinctly felt the sharp edge of the long finger nail in his palm. It was an unpleasant sensation.

"Happy to meet a *confidential* friend of Tiffles's," said Patching. "Painting panoramas is not exactly what I have been used to. An artist's reputation is his capital in trade, you know." He spoke slowly and languidly, as if hope and happiness were quite dead within him, and he had consented to live on only for the good of high Art.

"I understand," said Marcus. "The secret shall be inviolate."

"Nothing but my old friendship for Tiffles here could possibly have induced me to undertake the job. My enemies—and I have them, ha! ha!" (he said this bitterly)—"would like nothing better to say of Patching, than that he had got down to the panorama line of business. It would be a pretty piece of scandal."

"My lips are sealed, sir. But it strikes me, as a casual observer, that there is nothing to be ashamed of in this beautiful work of art." Marcus Wilkeson had the amiable vice of flattery.

Patching shrugged his shoulders, and made a contemptuous gesture toward the canvas with his outstretched brush. "A mere daub," said he. "One step higher than painting a barn or a board fence—that's all."

"Yet the true artist adorns what he touches," said Marcus.

Patching accepted the homage calmly, as one who knew that he deserved it. "A very just and discriminating remark, sir. I have no doubt that a person thoroughly familiar with my style would say, looking at this panorama, 'It has the severe simplicity of a Patching.' I consented to paint it, as Tiffles well remembers, only on condition that I should not wholly abase myself by abandoning the style upon which I have built up my reputation."

Tiffles, thus appealed to, corroborated the statement with a solemn bow.

The artist continued: "Fortunately, the subject is one peculiarly adapted to my genius. For instance: the desert of Sahara is a dead level of sand. It is a perfect type of severe simplicity in the highest sense. It exhibits no common display of gorgeous colors, such as poor artists and the ignorant crowd rejoice in. As far as the eye can see, there is a serene stretch of yellow sand, without even a blade of grass to break its awful immensity." (The artist, being on his favorite theme, took his pipe out of his mouth for the first time, and spoke with warmth.) "Look at that bit of desert, now. Does it not convey a perfect idea of solitude and desolation?"

Marcus Wilkeson glanced at about ten feet of straight yellow paint (which was all of the desert of Sahara not rolled up in the canvas), and said that it did—which was perfectly true.

"There are one hundred feet more, which you don't see, just like it. Another artist would have put in an oasis, or a stray hyena, or the bleached bones of an unfortunate traveller. *I* did not. Why? Another would have worked up a sunset, or a moonrise, or a thunder storm, to give variety to the sky. *I* did not. Why? The sky over my desert is an uninterrupted blue. There is not even a bird in it. There is nothing, in short, either on the ground or in the air, to take away the mind of the spectator, for one moment, from the sublime idea of a desert—an object which, considered æsthetically, is one of the grandest in the universe. This is severe simplicity. It is the highest school of Art."

"And the cheapest," observed Tiffles; "which is an important consideration when you have an acre or two of canvas to paint. It would cost a deal more to put in the sun and moon, travelling caravans, and other objects of interest, here and there."

"Incidentally it may be the cheapest," said Patching. "But that is a question for capitalists, and not for artists to determine. True Art never thinks of the expense."

"It always seemed to me to be the easiest school of Art," said Marcus Wilkeson. "I suppose, now, that you can dash off twenty or thirty rods of this a day."

Patching smiled with a lofty pity. "So I can. Not because it is the easiest, though—far from it; but because I happen to have a genius for quick and sure touches. You, not being a professional artist, think the execution of that scrap of desert and sky an easy matter. Perhaps you fancy that you could do it." There was the least infusion of satire in the artist's tone.

"Oh, no!" replied Marcus Wilkeson, who ever shrank from wounding the self-love of a fellow creature. "I am not rash enough to suppose that I could do it. I merely observed that it seemed—to my inexperienced eyes—an easy matter. A few strokes of yellow paint here, for sand, and a few strokes of blue paint there, for sky. But I am not even an amateur, and so my opinion goes for nothing."

"I admire your frankness," said Patching. "Now let me convince you practically. Be good enough to stand near this window with me."

Marcus moved to the spot indicated by the artist.

"Here," said Patching, "you are at about the same distance from the desert as the front row of spectators will be. Now look at it critically."

Marcus shaded his eyes with his left hand, cocked his head over his right shoulder, in the true critical style, and gazed on the scene.

"Do you see the harmony—the TONE, I may say—in the desert?" asked Patching, after a short pause.

"I think I do," responded Marcus, willing to oblige the artist.

"And the spiritual, or INNER meaning of the sky?"

"Ye-yes. It is quite perceptible."

"These are the effects of severe simplicity. But you must understand that a single mis-stroke of the brush would have spoiled all the harmony in the desert, or reduced the sky to a mere inexpressive field of blue vapor. Why? Genius alone can achieve such grand results by such apparently simple means. You comprehend?"

"Perfectly," said Marcus Wilkeson.

"Then I shall take a real pleasure in showing you more of the panorama which is already completed and rolled up. With this idea of severe simplicity in your mind, you will be prepared to appreciate the work."

"I believe I have already remarked, that Mr. Wilkeson is a capitalist, and comes here expressly to look at the panorama," said Tiffles, with a wink at the artist.

"With every respect for him as a capitalist," returned Patching, "I see in him only the ingenuous student of Art, whom it is a happiness to teach."

The first instalment was a continuation of the desert with which Marcus had been already regaled. Patching begged him to observe the unfaltering harmony of the sand, and the protracted spirituality of the sky. Then came a jungle.

"You will note the severe simplicity here," observed Patching. "No meretricious effects. Nothing but strokes of green paint, up and down, representing the density of an African jungle. Yet how admirably these seemingly careless strokes, laid on by the hand of genius, convey the idea of DEPTH! You do not fail to notice the DEPTH, I presume?"

"I see it," said Marcus.

"*That* is severe simplicity," replied the artist.

At this point, Marcus noticed a brown something bearing a strong resemblance to the swamp stalk, known among boys as the cattail. "Excuse my ignorance of African plants," said he; "but what is that?"

The artist smiled. "Another happy illustration of my theory," said he. "It is the tail of a lion bounding through his native jungles. Why? The effect of suggesting the lion, so to speak, is much more thrilling than that of painting him at full length. Genius accomplishes by hints what mere talent fails to achieve by the utmost elaboration. You will not deny that that vague revelation of the lion's tail inspires a feeling of mystery and terror, which would not be caused by a full-length portrait of that king of beasts?"

Marcus Wilkeson did not deny it, but said that perhaps everybody could not identify the object as a lion's tail.

"That has all been thought of," said Tiffles. "I shall explain the panorama, you must understand. When I come to the lion's tail, I shall tell the audience what it is, and go on to give a full account of the lion, and his ferocious habits. This will gratify the women and small boys quite as much as seeing the lion *in propria persona*."

"Precisely. Very good," was the laughing acknowledgment. "And what is that thing, twisted like a piece of grapevine above the tall grass at this point?"

"The trunk of an elephant. Look a little farther on, as the canvas unrolls, and you will observe the white tusk of a rhinoceros protruding from the jungle with wonderful effect. Why? The two animals are advancing toward each other for mortal combat."

"I shall describe their terrific struggles," interrupted Tiffles. "Have read up Buffon for it."

"More lions' and elephants' tails, you observe," continued the artist; "also more rhinoceroses' tusks. It is well to have enough of them, to illustrate the teeming life of the African jungle. Also the head of a boa constrictor. Likewise the tail of one. Here we come to a change of scene. Mark how wonderfully a few strokes of dark-green paint, put on by the hand of genius, impart the idea of a pestiferous swamp. That odd-looking object, like a rock, is the head of a hippopotamus. A few feet beyond, you notice two things like the stumps of aquatic weeds. Those are the tails of two hippopotamuses engaged in deadly strife at the bottom of the swamp. The heads of crocodiles are thrust up here and there. Severe simplicity again."

The panorama, from thence nearly to the end of it—or rather the beginning—was a repetition of jungles and deserts, varied by an occasional swamp, all diversified with the heads and tails of indigenous animals. The last hundred feet was the river Gambier, over which Patching had introduced a sunrise of the most gorgeous description, at the earnest request of Wesley Tiffles.

Patching explained: "In my opinion, such effects are tawdry, and detract not only from the severe simplicity, but from the UNITY which should pervade a painting of this description. Of course, I wash my hands of all these innovations upon the province of high Art."

"And I cheerfully shoulder them," said Tiffles. "I know what the public want. They want any quantity of sunsets, crocodiles, lions, and other objects of interest. If we had time and money to spare, and I could overcome Patching's scruples—do you understand?—I would put 'em in twice as thick. Men of genius, like Patching, cannot be expected to be practical."

The artist shrugged his shoulders, and smiled.

Tiffles then repeated his invitation to Marcus to accompany him on his first expedition into the interior of New Jersey; but Marcus positively declined. Tiffles said he would send him a note a day or two before the panorama started, and hoped that Marcus would conclude to go, just for the fun of the thing.

Marcus then shook hands with Patching—who made his long finger nail amicably felt—and with Tiffles, and withdrew to the entry, followed by the latter individual.

Tiffles closed the door. "By the way," said he, as if the thought occurred to him then for the first time, "can you spare thirty-five dollars to-day? Pay you on the—let me see—on the first of next month. By that time the panorama will be fairly under headway, and coining money." (Tiffles always fixed his days of payment with great particularity.)

Marcus, without saying a word, produced his pocket book, and counted out thirty-five dollars. Tiffles had already borrowed from Overtop and Maltboy, but had generously spared the oldest of the three bachelors. Marcus felt that his time had come, and he would not meanly avoid his destiny. He placed the money in Tiffles's hand.

"Give you my note?" asked Tiffles.

"Oh, no!" said Marcus; "make it a matter of honor."

Tiffles pocketed the funds, placed his hand over his heart, and replied that it should be. "But, now I think of it," he suddenly added, "I want exactly sixty-three dollars—do you understand?—to see me through with this panorama. Suppose you make it twenty-eight dollars more."

Marcus smiled, and said that he didn't understand; whereat Tiffles laughed outright, to show that he took no offence at the refusal; and creditor and debtor parted with mutual good wishes.

CHAPTER III.

LOVING AFAR OFF.

The boy Bog had now become, professionally, a creature of the night. He was abroad at the same hours as the burglars and garroters, and other owls and weasels of society. Fink & Co. (Bog was the Co.) had secured the bill posting for three theatres and one negro-minstrel hall. This they called their heavy business. Carrying the huge damp placards, had already given to Bog's shoulders a manifest tendency to roundness, which he was constantly trying to overcome by straightening up. Fink, who was the veteran bill poster of the town, was as round shouldered as a hod carrier. But Bog thought of somebody, and stood as nearly erect as he could.

The firm also obtained rather more than their share of ordinary bill posting, from doctors, drygoods dealers, and other people who find their profit in continually addressing the public from the summit of a dead wall, or the muddy level of the curbstones. This they called their light business. As it required neither strength nor practised dexterity of manipulation, the firm intrusted it to assistants.

There were a dozen of these, all stout, hulking young fellows nearly as old as Bog. They took a fancy to bill posting, and worked industriously and faithfully at it, because it was nocturnal, mysterious, romantic. The half dollar which they each received for a night's labor, enabled them to lounge about the streets all day in glorious indolence. Sometimes there was a prodigious rush of business, and then the firm were obliged to hire an extra force of boys.

Once, when a quack undertook to take the public by storm with his "New and Sure Cure for Dyspepsia," Fink & Co. put a colored poster as large as a dining table on every wall and high fence below Sixty-first street; small oblong bills every ten feet along the curbstones of Broadway, Bowery, Wall street, Fulton street, Cortlandt street, and Third, Fourth, Fifth, Sixth, Eighth, Madison, and Lexington Avenues; besides throwing cheap circulars, folded, into the front yards of about four thousand residences in the fashionable quarters of the town—all in a single night. This immense job took one hundred boys.

Bog had been in this partnership since the first of January. It was now near the close of March. The firm had been very successful. Bog had comfortably supported himself and his aunt (whose rheumatism got worse in steady proportion as his business improved), and had invested more than two hundred and fifty dollars in a Wall-street savings bank.

With this money at his disposal, Bog might have thrown away the greasy cap and old coat and trowsers, spotted with paste, in which he pursued his occupation. But when Bog was at his business, he was not above his business. And he felt none the less attached to his old clothes because they were two inches too short in the legs and arms, and pinched him a little in all directions.

But Bog had a better suit, made of neat gray cloth, which he wore upon occasions. These occasions happened daily between three and four P. M. During that interval, it always fell out that Bog had no work to do which he could not postpone as well as not. And whether it rained or shone, the occasions brought him, like an inexorable fate, through the street where Miss Pillbody's school was situated. He would first stride smartly up the opposite sidewalk, whistling, and cast ardent glances at the lower windows of Miss Pillbody's school, shaded by green curtains with gold borders.

After going two blocks in that direction, he would cross the street, whistling yet, and march boldly up the other sidewalk, past Miss Pillbody's school, as on an enemy. But if there had been anybody to watch him closely—as there was not on that thronged street—that body would have seen that Bog's cheeks began to blush, and his eyes to be cast down, and his whistle to be fainter, as he hurried by the neat three-story brick building with the polished doorplate and handsome curtains.

Then he would loiter for a while in front of McFeeter's grocery, two corners remote, and gaze from that safe distance with intrepidity upon the abode of enchantment; after which he would screw his courage up to the point of marching past the house back and forth again, and would then resume his position at McFeeter's, and wait until four P. M., or about that time, when the envied door of Miss Pillbody's establishment would open, and an angel would dazzle upon his sight, with a music book in her hand instead of a harp, and a jaunty little chip bonnet on her head instead of a golden crown. If the harp and crown had suddenly taken their proper places, and a pair of spangled wings had blossomed right out of her shoulders, and the radiant creature, thus equipped, had spread her pinions and soared up to heaven, the boy Bog would hardly have been surprised. As this angel came down the happy front steps to the blessed pavement (Bog's mind supplying these adjectives), Bog would color up, and sneak off at his best walking pace in the opposite direction. He felt that, if Pet ever saw him, and should ask him what he was doing in that neighborhood, he should melt away in perspiring confusion on the spot.

He called at Mr. Minford's twice a week, to indulge in the hollow form of asking if he could do anything for him. There he confronted Pet, with that trembling figure and those averted eyes which an inexperienced thief may show before the man that he has robbed. But Pet knew not of the adoring spy.

One afternoon, the boy Bog had made his second detour, and was approaching the corner of the favored block, when a novel idea struck him. The very night before, Bog had posted bills of the play, "Faint Heart Ne'er Won Fair Lady." The gigantic lettering arose in his mind's eye, like the cross in Constantine's. He had never seen the drama, and he did not know to what extent Ruy Gomez pushed his audacity, and won the Countess by it. But the name of the drama held the moral of it; and the moral, as applied to Bog's case, was: "Stop at this corner, and take a good view of the house." To do this, in Bog's opinion, was the height of boldness. But he thought of the huge parti-colored lettering, and he did it.

He stopped at the corner, and leaned recklessly against a hydrant. He looked at the house with a deliberation that amazed himself. At the same time, as a matter of instinctive caution, he kept his left leg well out toward the side street, so that he might retreat, should the door suddenly open and disclose the seraphic vision. He consulted his large bull's-eye silver watch (a capital timekeeper), and found that it was half past three o'clock, and he never knew her to be out before four.

This reflection emboldened him. "Faint Heart Ne'er Won Fair Lady," he thought again, and brought back his left leg to an easy position, crossing it with his right one against the hydrant. Then he feasted, with strange composure, upon the house.

Neither Bog nor a much wiser metaphysician could explain it; but the house, and all around it, seemed to be glorified by the loved one within. The newly painted door was bright with love; the polished doorplate and bell handle glistened with love. The name Pillbody looked, somehow, musical and winning, because the owner of that name was the teacher and dear companion of Pet. The carved stone roses over the door seemed to be truly the emblems of love. It was a silly notion; but, in Bog's eyes, love imparted a not unpleasant expression to the grim lions' faces that looked down from the roof. But the green window curtains with gold borders were the most significant symbols of love, in his eyes. Bog felt that curtains of any other color would be wholly out of place in that house. The patch of a garden, scarcely bigger than a bathroom, in front of the house; the single fir tree that grew up in the middle of it; the black iron railing; the door steps, and the pavement—all took their share of beatitude from the joy within. Bog could hear love rustle in the boughs of the young maple, that stood in its long green case like a fancy boot top, at the edge of the sidewalk.

CHAPTER IV.

LEGERDEMAIN.

As Bog was resting against the hydrant, absorbed in this delicious revery, and totally indifferent to the consequences, he was startled by a slight tap on the shoulder. He turned quickly, and saw—the man he hated—the man who pretended (Bog would never admit that it was more than a pretence) to save Pet from the falling boards.

"Well," said Bog, looking on this man as his mortal enemy, "What do you want of me?" He spoke in the gruff, defiant manner peculiar to children of the city.

The man's livid face and lead-colored eyes and white teeth

all combined in a reassuring smile. "Nothing," said he, "my good fellow, but to do an errand."

"I say, now, who'd you take me for, hey?" answered Bog, shaking his head at the man, and feeling a tremendous desire to knock his shining hat off.

The man looked up and down Bog's cheap gray suit, and at his neatly polished shoes and his clean slouching cap, and then said:

"No offence meant, my lad. But I thought you wouldn't object to earning a quarter. You're only to deliver a letter at that house; that's all." He pointed to Miss Pillbody's.

"Hey—what house?" asked Bog, turning pale, with a strange and jarring combination of rage, jealousy, envy, and insulted dignity.

"The one with the bright doorplate, green curtains and gold borders. I thought you were looking at it as I came up."

"N-no, I wasn't. And what if I was, hey?"

"It strikes me you're rather touchy, my young friend," said the man, with his conciliatory smile. "Here's the letter, now, and a quarter. It's only a few steps. No answer required."

As Bog caught sight of the letter, done up in the long, rakish envelope which had just begun to come into fashion, and faintly perfumed, a lucky thought occurred to him.

The man saw that he wavered. "Only a step," said he. "And here is the quarter." He offered it to Bog between a thumb and finger.

"Why don't you deliver the letter yourself?" asked Bog.

"Oh! oh! for family reasons," answered the man, hesitating. "Miss Pillbody there is my aunt, and the lady to whom this letter is addressed is my cousin. The old woman and I have had a sort of falling out about the young one, you see. These little difficulties will occur in the best-regulated families. Come, take the letter. I'm in a hurry."

Bog allowed the letter to be thrust into his hand. He looked at it, and saw, as he expected, that it was addressed to "Miss Minford, Present." The direction was in a beautiful commercial hand, which was at once more hateful in his eyes than the most crabbed of writing.

"All right," said he. "I'll deliver it. Poh! never mind the quarter. I won't take it." Bog moved toward the house as he spoke.

"You're a queer fellow, but a good one. Well, you'll accept my thanks, at any rate."

He waited at the hydrant until Bog had delivered the letter.

Bog walked straight to the house, and up the steps, although his face was pale, and his knees trembled.

He rang the bell with a decisive pull, and, as he did so, glanced at the strange man, who nodded approvingly at him.

He suddenly turned his back on the strange man. With a quick movement of the fingers of his right hand, he thrust the letter up his coat sleeve. The next instant he whipped a handkerchief out of an inside breast pocket, and, with it, a stray copy of a new "Dentifrice" circular, which he had been distributing the night before. This circular was folded to about the size and shape of the letter. With the handkerchief he wiped his face, upon which there were real drops of sweat. The circular he slipped into his right hand, and then turned toward the strange man again, to show that he still held the letter. This bit of legerdemain took about three seconds.

In three seconds more, Bog heard footsteps approaching in the entry. What if his angel should come to the door? The thought sent a horrible, sickly sensation all over him, and the solid rock seemed to tremble beneath his feet.

The door opened, and something quite the opposite of an angel presented itself. It was Bridget; and her red hair was dishevelled, her face flushed to the parboiled tint, and her dress uncommonly damp and frowsy. A mop which she held in her hand explained everything.

"A circular, if you please," said Bog, in a quivering voice, poking the folded paper at her.

"A succular, is it? Miss Peelbody told me not to take

any succulars for her. So 'way wid ye." Bridget put her hand on the door, and was about to swing it to.

"It isn't for Miss Pillbody at all," said Bog, fearful lest the strange man should see it refused, "but for your own pretty self."

Bridget smiled, for she was conscious that the compliment was deserved. She relaxed her hand on the door. "Fut is it?" said she.

"Hush!" said Bog, in a whisper; "a circular about the rights of servants, issued by the 'Servants' Mootual Protecting Society.'" (Bog thought of the name on the spur of the moment.) "Please take it—quick."

Bridget snatched the circular out of his hand, and was about to look at it, bottom side up, for she had not yet attained to the mystery of reading, when the musical voice of Miss Pillbody was heard at the back of the entry. "Bridget—what is wanted, Bridget?"

"Nothin', ma'am, but one of these succular men. Bad luck to him! Here, now, take it."

She made a feint of handing back the circular to Bog, but concealed it, with the other hand, in her capacious bosom.

"Heaven bless ye!" said she, in a low voice, and then slammed the door in his face.

Bog came down the door steps quickly, and saw the strange man make a bow and a gesture of gratitude at him, and then disappear suddenly round the corner. Bog's first impulse was to follow him at a distance; but his curiosity to inspect the slender, perfumed letter, overcame it.

When Bog reached the awning in front of McFeeter's store—a sort of haven or putting-in place for him—he pulled out the letter, and was about to read it. Then it occurred to him that the situation was too much exposed. The strange man might come back, and see him with the open letter in his hand. Bog would have enjoyed a personal collision with him on any pretext; but to be caught in the act of reading the letter, would spoil the strategical advantage that Bog now had over him.

Bog moved on down a side street, and took his stand behind a huge wooden column surmounted by a gilded mortar and pestle. Here he was about to rip open the envelope, but a glance across the street discovered a policeman looking at him. Bog felt guilty and awkward. He coughed, and thrust the letter into his pocket, and moved on again. The exciting events of the morning had made Bog intensely nervous. He did not stop this time until he had gained his home.

His aunt was sitting in the front room, reading a book through a huge pair of silver-rimmed spectacles. There was a thick fold of flannel about her neck, and she smelt strongly of embrocation. As Bog rushed into the room, she groaned audibly, and laid down the book, as if it were a wicked enjoyment.

"I'm so bad to-day, Bog," said she. "Them shootin' pains 'll be the death of me."

Bog responded not a word, but dashed across the apartment, and, entering his little sleeping room, closed the door, and bolted it.

"Unfeelin' creetur!" said his aunt. She stopped groaning, and took up her book and read again.

Bog seated himself on his hair trunk, and drew out the letter. There was a slight discussion within him on the abstract question of his right to open it. After turning it over twice, the question was decided in the affirmative. He slit the envelope with his thumb, and brought to light a billet faultlessly written, as follows:

"Frederick Lynville begs to present his compliments to Miss Minford, and to assure her, from the depths of his heart, that his feelings toward her are only those of the purest admiration for the matchless charms of her mind and person. He takes this method of explaining himself, because he has observed with great sorrow that Miss Minford has shown a desire to avoid him on several recent occasions, when they have accidentally met in the street. It was Mr. Lynville's blessed privilege, under Providence, to save Miss Minford's life; but he would not be selfish and base enough on that account to obtrude himself on Miss Minford's notice. Mr. Lynville would die sooner than be guilty of that discourtesy. He is not presumptuous enough to ask an answer to this letter. His only object in writing it, is to inform Miss Minford that he will not venture again upon the impropriety of speaking to her first when they next meet. Miss Minford will therefore be free to drop his acquaintance, or continue it, as she thinks best. Whatever fate she may decide for him, her happiness will still be his constant prayer."

Bog was ill versed in the art of complimentary letter writing. But the villany here seemed to be clumsily concealed. That the letter was full of danger to the object of his boyish idolatry, he had no doubt.

But why did Pet avoid this Frederick Lynville? Did she really dislike him? Or——. The thought of his own shyness toward the beautiful girl came into his mind like a flash. To avoid might be—to love.

The poor boy dropped the letter, and covered his face with his hands, and wept.

Love is not always selfish; and goodness is sometimes its own reward. In that bitter hour of his first real misery, Bog did not regret his kindness to the Minfords, or take credit to himself for having nobly concealed from their knowledge those little weekly gifts of money which he sent to them through the mail, when they were in poorer circumstances. He was not for a moment base enough to think that Pet would look with kinder eyes on him, if she but knew of his secret benefactions—which, up to this time, neither she nor her father had suspected, and which they would never learn from his lips.

BOOK SIXTH.

MYSTERIES OF THE NIGHT.

CHAPTER I.

THE UNKNOWN HAND.

MARCUS WILKESON made no effort to discover the writer of the anonymous letter, because he knew that such an effort would be in vain. He called on Mr. Minford once in two or three days now. The inventor always took occasion to refer to the letter, and assured Marcus that it was not worth remembering, or talking about. "Why, then, did he talk about it?" Marcus asked himself. His eyes were not blind to watchful and suspicious glances which the old man directed to him, at times, under cover of those shaggy, overhanging eyebrows. Nor could he help noticing a strange reserve in the bearing of Pet toward him. It was not mere modesty, or timid gratitude, but DOUBT, as he read the signs. Marcus was convinced that the father had put his child on guard against something, though he might not have mentioned the existence of the anonymous letter. This thought distressed him acutely.

But his troubles, as well as his joys, he kept to himself. The miser puts his broken bank notes and his good gold under the same lock and key.

One evening, early in April, Overtop and Maltboy observed a peculiar expression of sadness on the face of their friend.

He had eaten nothing at dinner, but had drunk more than his usual allowance of sherry. He had kept his eyes fixed on the table as in a revery, and had scarcely spoken a word. Miss Wilkeson, in her solemn state opposite the boiled chickens, was hardly less social.

After dinner, Marcus took to his pipe with a strange sullenness, and smoked furiously. His two friends, closely regarding him, saw that he was unhappy, but wisely forbore to make him more unhappy still by obtruding their condolence on him. The day had been rainy and cold. They knew that Marcus's spirits were barometrically sensitive to the weather, like those of most persons who look at it through a window.

They had noticed, as they came home, that he was reading that sweetest of elegies, the "In Memoriam" of Tennyson. And the two friends thought that the melancholy weather and the melancholy poem together fully accounted for the gloom on his brow.

Marcus sat for some minutes meditating. Then he heaved a sigh, which was distinctly audible to his two friends. Then he left the room without saying a word, and went up stairs.

Presently he was heard to come down; but, instead of returning to the little parlor, he went into the street, and closed the door with a sharp slam. At the same moment, the cold rain of the April night beat noisily against the window.

"Sly old fellow!" said Maltboy.

"Up to something, depend on it," said Overtop.

Marcus walked rapidly toward the inventor's house. "My fate is decided to-night," he muttered.

His long strides soon brought him to the house. The old building wore a gloomy look. He did not speculate on the reason of this. It was probably because there was no light visible in any of the front windows, and very little light in the street lamps. The gas burned low and blue, and flickered in the wind.

Ringing the bell, Marcus was admitted by one of the numerous children belonging to somebody in the house (Marcus could never determine to whom), and walked up to the inventor's room. His heart beat with strange emotion as he rapped at the door. For a moment he was sorry that he had come.

"Come in," said the inventor, in a voice more sepulchral than usual.

Marcus entered the apartment. The inventor received him with a feeble shake of the hand, bearing no resemblance to the hearty one which he used to bestow in the early days of their acquaintance. Marcus noticed that Mr. Minford's hand was hot. He also observed that his eyes were preternaturally lustrous, and that the circles under them were deep and dark. His cheeks were deathly pale, saving a little red spot in the centres. He looked like a man in a state of fearful mental exaltation and nervous excitement.

Marcus was not in the habit of worrying people upon the subject of their ill health; but the inventor looked so palpably bad, that Marcus could not forbear to say, in a tone of anxiety, "You are unwell, sir."

"Oh, no! Quite well, I assure you," said the inventor, with a weary smile. "Though I should be sick, perhaps, but for the glorious hope that bears me up. I have not eaten, or slept, for forty-eight hours."

"But, my dear sir, this is trifling with your health."

"I acknowledge it. But we must make sacrifices, if we would master the UNKNOWN. Newton lived on bread and water when he wrote his immortal Principia. He condemned himself to the coarse fare of a prison, in order that his intellect might soar untrammelled to the stars. I have improved on Newton—I eat nothing. As for sleep, I grudge a single hour of it which comes between me and the completion of my great work."

"But how long can you stand this dreadful strain upon your powers?"

"Till daylight to-morrow, with safety. By that time I shall have overcome the last obstacle. Of this I am confident.

Then, ho! for unbounded wealth and undying fame. The toil has been severe, but the reward will be glorious."

"I congratulate you," said Marcus, "on the near approach of your final triumph. And, in order that I may not delay you a single moment, I will bid you 'good-night.'" Marcus rose, but he hoped that the inventor would ask him to stay.

The inventor did so. "Pray don't hurry, Mr. Wilkeson; I would like to have a brief conversation with you. A few minutes only." He drew a chair to the side of Marcus, and seated himself.

"Mr. Wilkeson," he said, in a deliberate voice, as if he were repeating carefully-considered words, "it is unnecessary for me to say that I have the highest opinion of you. Providence seems to have sent you to me at a time when I was in the greatest need. You saved me from starving. The world will be as much indebted to you for my grand invention, as it was to the generous patronage of Queen Isabella for the discovery of America."

"Pooh!" interrupted Marcus, blushing.

"The praise is none too high," continued the inventor. "It is true, I have repaid your advances of money tenfold, by giving you an interest in my future but certain fortune. But that does not diminish my gratitude."

Marcus knew that this flattering exordium meant something serious. It was a favorite theory of his, that danger, or any kind of anticipated disagreeable thing, was best met half-way. So he said, with a feeble attempt at a smile:

"I infer from this ominous opening that you have received another lying anonymous letter about me. If I am right, Mr. Minford, be good enough to let me see it at once, according to your promise."

"You have guessed correctly, Mr. Wilkeson. I have received a second anonymous letter, which I intended showing to you after a further brief explanation. But I can readily appreciate your anxiety to read it without delay. Here it is." He drew forth a letter, and handed it to Marcus.

Marcus immediately recognized the envelope and the address as similar to those of the first letter, which he still had in his possession.

He pulled the letter nervously from its yellow sheath, and read as follows:

"MR. MINFORD:

DEAR SIR,—Pardon me for intruding on you a second time. But, as a friend of virtue, I must warn you of continued danger to your daughter from the acquaintance of Mr. Wilkeson, your pretended benefactor. If you are any longer in doubt as to the vile intentions of this man, conceal yourself from observation within sight of Miss Pillbody's school, any fair afternoon, about half past two o'clock, and watch his actions. If his suspicious conduct, at that time and place, does not give a sufficient significance to my warnings, then take the trouble to go to ———, Westchester Co., where he was born, and search into his infamous history. Take heed—I warn you again—lest, in your devotion to science, you forget that you are a father.

"ONE WHO WOULD SHIELD THE INNOCENT."

While reading this letter, Marcus was conscious that the eyes of the inventor were fixed piercingly upon him. That consciousness caused his head to bow, and his cheeks to crimson with shame. It is the curse of this morbid sensibility, that righteous indignation at a foul slander upon one's good name springs up only after the victim has shown all the accepted evidences of guilt.

There was one reason why a man much less sensitive than Marcus should have been thrown off his balance by this letter. It was a fact that every afternoon, at half past two o'clock, rain or shine, with bachelor-like punctuality, he passed up and down in front of Miss Pillbody's school, and looked sentimentally at the closed blinds, thinking unutterable things. He was also addicted to standing at the hydrant on the corner, and gazing hard at the house, wishing that he could see through its brick walls. Then he would cross the street, and pace up and down on that side, taking views of the house at every variety of angle. This was precisely what the boy Bog did daily about an hour and a half later. Now, although Marcus felt, in his heart, that these pedestrian exercises—absurd to everybody but a lover—were perfectly harmless in their purpose and effect, he was aware that, to a man like Mr. Minford, looking at them suspiciously, they would appear to be connected with some stealthy and base design.

As to the imputations upon his former history, Marcus could freely challenge the closest scrutiny; which is more than most men can do into that long record of juvenile frailties and escapades which ushers in the sober book of manhood. But here again the devil of sensitiveness asserted his supremacy. Marcus had had a twin brother (who died years before), a duplicate of himself in all respects but two. Marcus was quiet, studious, honest, and frank; while Aurelius was quiet, studious, less honest, and infinitely crafty. Marcus had, on several occasions in his boyhood, been accused of petty offences which Aurelius had committed, but which that cunning youth had unblushingly denied. These, so far as Marcus supposed, were nothing more serious than robbing orchards or melon patches. Still it was possible that some graver wrong—more worthy of the title "infamous"—committed by his wild, shrewd brother, might be brought to light by some deep explorer among the traditions of his native village, and charged upon himself. This possibility, and the difficulty of refuting a serious accusation under such circumstances, brought a second flush of guilt to the face of Marcus Wilkeson as he read the letter.

These harassing thoughts, which fill so much space, written out, are but a small part of those which were suggested with electric suddenness.

Marcus's first impulse was to say: "I love your daughter, Mr. Minford, with my whole heart and soul. It is my first

9

and my only love, singular though this confession may sound from the lips of a man of thirty-six years. The proudest and happiest day of my life would be that on which I could marry her, with her dear love and your fatherly consent. This love, which is as pure as the angelic creature upon whom it is lavished, fully explains my visits here, and whatever else is mysterious in my conduct. But, before declaring myself to your daughter, or asking her hand of you, I have desired to see whether it were possible to inspire her with love for a man so much older than herself. For, much as I love her, I would not seek to marry her without a return of love—not mere respect, esteem, or gratitude. That is the problem I have been waiting to solve."

A confession to this effect was on the tip of his tongue. To have made it, would have been like tearing open his breast and showing his heart. But he would have made it, whatever the pain, if, on looking nervously up from the letter, which he had now finished, he had not met the cold, searching eyes of the inventor. He instantly shut his lips upon the outcoming confession, and said, with as much indifference as he could awkwardly assume:

"I hope, sir, you have taken the trouble to investigate these ridiculous charges." But Marcus inwardly hoped he had not.

"I have sir," responded the inventor, gravely. "Had the accusations been vague, like those in the first letter from this unknown person, I should have dismissed them from my mind with a laugh. But they were so specific, and the truth or falsity of them was so easily ascertained, that I thought it my duty, in justice to my daughter, yourself, and to me, to look into them. It was a painful task, but I have done it."

"And what have you learned?" asked Marcus, making a transparent feint to look at ease.

"I will tell you frankly; though I wish to say, in advance, that my discoveries, though they might justify some suspicion, do not prejudice me in the least against you. I have no doubt that you will be able to explain everything." But so spoke not the eyes of the inventor.

"Well, then, to make a short story of this unpleasant affair, I have watched your promenades in front of Miss Pillbody's school three afternoons in succession. I will spare you the details, though, so clearly are your movements back and forth imprinted on my memory, that I could recount them all to you, if necessary. It is sufficient to say, that I am forced to believe that my daughter is the magnet which draws you to that neighborhood, and keeps your eyes riveted on that house. This is all I have to say on the first point in the letter."

CHAPTER II.

IN VAIN—IN VAIN.

THIS was Marcus Wilkeson's golden opportunity, and he manfully determined to seize it. But, as he was on the point of blurting out the stifled secret, that cold, pale face—which resembled marble in all but the drops of sweat upon the brow—chilled him again. At the same moment, the hopeless absurdity of love and marriage between a girl of seventeen and a man of thirty-six, occurred to him in all its force. Stupidly sensitive being that he was, he thought that this icy, intellectual Mr. Minford would laugh at him.

"I confess, sir, that these wanderings seem 'singular,' as you term them. But all the habits of old bachelors are regarded as singular, I believe. Now, it has been my daily habit, since I retired from business, to lay down my book at two o'clock, and take a little out-door exercise. Miss Pillbody's school is not far from my house; the street is pretty clean for New York, and the sidewalks are tolerably dry. Therefore I select that neighborhood for my daily walk—my—my 'constitutional,' as they call it. If, in so doing, I should occasionally cast my eyes—in fits of absent-mindedness, I may say—on Miss Pillbody's school, that is not strange, considering—considering the interest that I take in your daughter's education. It strikes me, my dear sir, that this seeming suspicion is easily cleared up." Marcus smiled to think how adroitly he had extricated himself.

But there was no smile on the shroud-colored face of the inventor.

"The explanation is *plausible*" (Mr. Minford emphasized the word), "and I will not attempt to set it aside. God alone knows all the motives of human action. Now, to the second, and more serious implication of the letter. I have visited your native village, and inquired into your early history. Though you moved to the city over fifteen years ago, and have returned to your birthplace but once since, so far as I could ascertain——"

"Allow me," said Marcus. "My absence from my old home may seem strange, but it is occasioned by no shame or disgrace. My father, mother, and twin brother died and were buried there. By my father's failure, shortly before his death, the old family mansion passed out of his hands, and was afterward torn down to make room for a railway depot. This extinction of my family—for I am now left without a relation in the world, excepting a half-sister—and this destruction of our old home, have made my native village horrible to me. When I visited the scene of desolation, ten years ago, the village seemed to me like a huge graveyard, in every part of which some happiness of my boyhood was entombed; and I vowed that I would never go near it again. In the matter of family recollections, I am exquisitely sensitive."

"I respect your feelings, sir," said the inventor, "and regret that I should be the means of reviving these painful recollections. But I have a duty to perform."

"And I will no longer delay you in its performance. Now be kind enough to let me know the worst at once. I can stand it." Marcus unconsciously sat up more erect, as if to brace himself against a shock.

"On my arrival in the village, my first act was to seek out some of the oldest inhabitants. I found that most of them distinctly remembered you, and your brother—Aurelius, I think, was his name. You will pardon me for telling you the exact result of my inquiries, but I found that these old inhabitants, without a single exception, gave you a very bad name, and your brother a very good one."

Marcus was about to explain, that his brother and himself were images of each other; that the former was crafty, and full of mischief, and that he (Marcus) had been made, on fifty occasions, the innocent scapegoat of his brother's little offences. But he forbore. He had cheerfully received reprimands, and even chastisements, for his brother while living; and he would not blacken his memory when dead. He merely smiled a sad smile, and said, "Ah?"

"Many of the offences charged against you by these old gossips, were petty and excusable. But there were others, committed by you when you were at or near manhood, exhibiting, if true—understand, I say, *if* true—a moral depravity for which no extenuation can be found. Some of the charges were not sustained by adequate proofs, and those I set down as idle rumors. But there was one of which the proof was abundant and most positive. No less than five persons gave me circumstantial accounts—all agreeing with each other—of your betrayal and ruin of Lucy Anserhoff."

"Lucy Anserhoff!" echoed Marcus, in real amazement. "I have a faint remembrance of an old lady by that name, and a pretty girl who was her daughter. But as God is my judge, I never wronged her." Still there was that expression of guilt, which did not escape the scrutinizing glance of the inventor.

Marcus could have hunted up evidence to transfer the burden of the imputed wrong to the memory of the dead Aurelius. But should he commit this profanation of the grave—as he regarded it? The voice of brotherly love—for he had tenderly loved his erring brother—said, "No." Would any amount of proof satisfy the nervous, doubting man before him? He feared not. Therefore Marcus Wilkeson did an act of awful solemnity, to prove his innocence. And, because the doing of it thrilled his sensitive soul, as if he had thrust himself into the terrible presence of the Infinite, he weakly supposed that the most suspicious of men would unhesitatingly believe him.

He stood up, turned his eyes to the ceiling, raised both hands, and said, in a deep, trembling voice:

"May God strike me dead, if I am guilty of this offence, or any like it, or of any thought of wrong toward your daughter."

Marcus sat down, pale, and caught his breath quickly. He was awe-stricken by his own act.

"That is a solemn adjuration," said the inventor, after a short pause, "and should not be lightly taken."

Marcus looked well at Mr. Minford. Unbelief was written in every hard line and wrinkle of that white, deathlike face. "Do you doubt me now?" he asked, sharply. His sensitiveness on the subject of personal honor and veracity was painfully acute. He had never told a lie in his life.

"Oh! no," replied Mr. Minford; "I do not say that I doubt you" (in a tone expressive of the greatest doubt). "I shall be truly glad to receive counter proofs from you."

"You have heard my solemn appeal to God, sir. Between gentlemen of honor that should be sufficient."

The inventor's thin lips (from which the last drops of blood had disappeared within the last half hour) curved in a satirical smile. Marcus interpreted it as a reiterated doubt and a sneer upon his honor. For the moment he lost control of his temper, and was about to make a remark that he would have regretted immediately after, when the door yielded to a gentle pressure, and Pet entered the room.

Her face was pale. Her eyes were dull, and the lids hung droopingly, weighed down by twenty-four hours of wakefulness by the bedside of her sick teacher. The faint blue crescents beneath—those strange shadows of the grave, which sometimes seem the deepest when the eyes above are giving the brightest light — imparted a frail, delicate beauty to her countenance. They were the last master-touches of Nature in working out that portraiture of wearied and sleepy loveliness.

As she put her foot in the room, Mr. Minford and his guest telegraphed a truce with their eyes, and assumed a cheerful look.

Little Pet timidly ran to her father, and kissed him, and then shook hands with Marcus. He observed a shrinking in her touch. She averted her eyes.

"Your clothes are damp, and your feet wet, my darling," said the father.

"Are they?" answered Pet, looking down at her saturated garments and glistening shoes. "I had not noticed them. Oh! I am so happy that she is well now. The doctor called at the house just before I left, and said she was out of all danger. He ordered me home."

"Very sensible of the doctor. Another hour of this watching might have killed my poor child."

"So I took a last look at my dear teacher—who was asleep—and kissed her, and came right away through the rain."

"It was foolish to do that without an umbrella and overshoes, my child. But, as you were always forgetful of yourself, your father will not be forgetful of you, at any rate." The inventor glanced significantly at Marcus. That glance, so full of distrust, entered his soul. He longed to say something —if only a word of common civility—to the young girl; but he felt that there was now an impassable barrier between them.

"But what is the matter, Pet?" exclaimed the father. She had dropped into a chair, and her head fell on one side. He sprang to catch her. So did Marcus. But the inventor reached her first, and seized her in his arms, directing another of his speaking looks at Marcus.

Pet roused herself at the touch of her father's hands, sat erect, and opened her large blue eyes. "I am so sleepy," she said.

"Of course you are, my blessed; and to bed you must go at once. That is my prescription. But, first—always first—a cup of tea."

The inventor darted to the stove, snatched up the teapot, poured out a cup of the universal restorer, scalding his forefinger in the hurry, milked and sugared it just right, and bore it to his daughter, who was nodding again. She drank it dutifully, like medicine.

Children do not comprehend tea. We have to grow up to it. It is the appointed balm of fatigued and sorrowing middle age.

In its function of medicine, the strong draught revived her, giving a twist to her pretty features, and sending a lively shudder through her slender frame. Pet rose from her seat quite briskly.

"Now to bed. To bed at once. No delay. And mind you put on all the blankets, and your heavy shawl a-top of them."

"Yes, father."

Marcus blushed, twirled his hat, and made a motion toward the door.

"You need not go, Mr. Wilkeson," said the inventor. "I beg that you will not. I wish to settle up that little unfinished business with you to-night."

Marcus saw that the inventor was in earnest. He coughed, and hesitated what to say.

But, before he could say anything, Pet had kissed her father, and said "Good-night," in a faint voice, to the guest, and already had her hand on the knob of the door which led to her little sleeping room.

"Remember, darling—all the blankets, and your shawl. To-morrow morning you will wake up bright and happy, and ready to enjoy a little surprise that I shall have for you." He jerked his thumb toward the machine.

Pet understood him, and smiled sadly. "You need bed more than I, father," said she.

"Nonsense, child!" replied the old man, with a hollow laugh. "It is not for the patient to prescribe to the physician There, good-night, now."

He kissed her again with more tenderness. "Remember," said he, "there is a little surprise in store for you to-morrow."

Pet said, "Heaven bless you, father," murmured another "Good-night," and disappeared within her sanctuary, closing the door after her.

"Now, Mr. Wilkeson," said the inventor, "we can finish our conversation."

His voice sounded like a voice from the tomb.

CHAPTER III.

THE CLASHING ORBS.

THE rain had ceased, and the moon was out. The dark, massy clouds that floated between her and the earth were doing their ghostly, phantasmagoric work. At one moment, clear, white light, like a shroud; at another moment, darkness, like a pall. An owl, lighting on the spire of Grace Church in his flight over the city, might have seen the white edge of the shroud, or the black edge of the pall, advancing in well-defined lines over the housetops, and the parks, and the two rivers, swiftly succeeding each other.

It was as if the mighty invisible demons of the night were capriciously trying the effects of cerements on the sleeping city. It was as if they were perplexed between the soft beauty of the shroud and the sombre majesty of the pall. A woman could not have tried on two shawls more often and more indecisively, before making up her mind to buy.

Little Pet's sleeping room, like every room that faced the south, that night, was full of strange, spectral effects. The scrolls and the roses on the cheap yellow curtains that hung in the windows, were changed to hideous faces of variable size and ugliness. Their grotesque shadows on the floor mingled with other faces—horrible as antique masks—wrought by the magic of the moon from the gigantic flowers that adorned the narrow strip of carpet by the bedside. Her dresses, suspended from a row of hooks in the corner—and showing, in gentle swells and curves, the lithe, graceful form of the little wearer, like moulds,—would have looked to any open eye, that dreadful night, like women hanging against the wall. This startling idea would have been helped along by two or three shadowy bonnets depending from pegs above them. The white somethings carelessly tossed over a chair near the head of the bed, were no longer the garments of youth, beauty, and innocence, but graveclothes, cold, shining, shuddering, in that deathly light. The touch of the moon, like the presence of a sexton, suggested mortality.

The narrow, single bed, with its four black posts, looked like the fatal trestle, or bier. The slender body which lay upon it was still as death. The head nestled motionless in a deep indentation of the pillow. A slanting ray of the moon, coming between one of the window curtains and the window, fell upon the face, and showed it white and waxen; the lips, still red, parted to the gleaming teeth; and the eyes not quite covered by the lids. One beautiful round arm curved above her head, and some of her soft brown hair rested in the little open palm. The other stretched down toward the centre of the bed, as if fearlessly to invite the touch of those weird things with which imagination peoples the solemn night—which the wakeful eye, in the still, small hours, sees moving in the darker corners, or passing swiftly by the bedside, or hovering in the air, wearing the semblance of one's dead friends, or filling large portions of the room with some formless presence of unutterable malignity and woe.

It was only sleep to which the moon thus gave the pale polish of death. The gentle murmur of a childish breath broke the silence. The heavy bedclothes slowly rose and fell with the mysterious pulsations of warm life beneath. At intervals, a shudder shook the little figure of the sleeper, her breath came louder and quicker, and her arms moved with sudden starts. Pet was dreaming, under the joint influences of an excess of blankets and a cup of strong tea.

She was alone in infinite space. Above, below, on all sides, was a leaden atmosphere. Neither sun, nor moon, nor stars illumined it, but only some dull, phosphorescent light, which seemed to be born of the murky, stagnant air. It was such a strange, sickly, wavering gleam as she had seen above decaying wood, fish, and other substances. All around was absolute stillness. Not a swallow waved his wing nor an insect hummed in that barren immensity. Nature was hushed by some deadly spell.

Yet the dread silence portended the near approach of HORRORS. She knew what they were, for she had been in this frightful region often before, and was familiar with its dread phenomena. They came. They were only two little black specks—like motes in the sunbeams—scarcely visible to her strained vision at first. She gazed upon them with the fascination of a charmed bird on the two small jet eyes of a serpent; but with this difference, that she knew the terrible peril that they brought. The moment that these two motes became visible to her in that dimly lighted mist, they commenced revolving around each other.

They revolved slowly, and increased in size as they rolled on. The slowness of the motion and the swelling of the motes were elements of horror. But she could not take her eyes from those two black objects revolving like binary stars, until her breath should cease to come and go, and her heart to beat. As the motes enlarged, their orbits widened. And they grew and grew, performing greater and more awful circuits—still slowly, still noiselessly. The eternal, unbroken silence was another element of horror. The doomed spectatress of this solemn, maddening whirl would fain have shrieked, or even whispered, to break the silence, but she could not. Either her powers of articulation had disappeared in that region of universal dumbness, or the dead atmosphere was waveless, and could vibrate to no sound. She knew, by harrowing experience, the scene that was to come, and she prayed inwardly to God to strengthen her for it.

The two black objects swelled and swelled in even proportions, until they became as large as a full moon just seen above the horizon; then to the size of two full moons, and a dozen, and a hundred, and a thousand. Still black, still noiseless, still revolving slowly, like a tardy but certain doom. Then a quarter of the leaden space was filled with their gigantic bodies, and the lurid air was darker. Then a half of the heavens was blotted out. She grew faint and sick, as she moved her head to the right and left, and up and down, and watched the dizzy revolutions of those vast orbs, between which she knew that she was to be crushed at last, as by the nether and upper millstones. Her inarticulate cries to God were unheard. It seemed as if there were no God for that accursed part of the universe.

Majestically, slowly, silently ever, the orbs increased. Two strips of the sky could be seen constantly changing positions, but always opposite to each other. These were the gaps, fast narrowing, which were to be filled up by the swelling worlds before her destruction was accomplished. Her long familiarity with the movements of this stupendous enginery of death enabled her to calculate to a nicety when the crash would come. She lay like the bound victim under the guillotine, watching fer the axe to descend.

The blackness of darkness above and beneath and around her . . . . . a suffocating compression of the stagnant air . . . . . a thrilling consciousness of the close approach of the two cruel orbs . . . . . a superlative stillness . . . . . and then a mighty attrition, in which the mortal part of the poor girl was about to be ground to atoms, when she . . . . . awoke.

She threw back the heavy blankets that oppressed her

chest, as if *they* were the crushing danger. She looked overhead, expecting to see a whirling globe within a foot of her face. But she saw only the ceiling, made visible by the pallid light of the room. Then she knew that she was in her own little room, and that this frightful adventure was only the old, old dream, that came to her two or three times a year, as far back as she could remember—the same always, without addition or curtailment.

CHAPTER IV.

A VISION OF HORRORS.

LITTLE Pet was not the least superstitious; because her father had taught her from infancy to pay no heed to dreams or signs; and because he had allowed no housemaid or fussy old woman to inoculate his young daughter with her own senseless and cowardly fears. Pet smiled at the momentary terror which the strange old dream had caused, closed her eyes, and addressed herself again to sleep. But, first, she drew up the weighty blankets over her little frame, as her father had told her to do. She had already found out by experience, that a hot application of blankets was the best remedy for a young cold.

A low murmur, as of conversation, came from the adjoining room. Then she remembered that Mr. Wilkeson was there when she had come to bed. She said to herself: "It cannot be late; for he never stops after ten o'clock." Then she began to think of some matters which had recently perplexed and distressed her greatly. But she was so sleepy, that the thoughts came into her little head confusedly, and, several times, merged into dreams, and then came out again. The low murmur of the talk outside, like the distant hum of a waterfall or a mill, was sedative. The act of listening to it—as she did for a few moments with natural curiosity—was provocative of sleep.

* * * * The conversation suddenly grew louder. The hollow voice of the inventor, and the deep bass of Marcus Wilkeson, could be heard alternating quickly. These words reached little Pet:

THE INVENTOR. "We have had a long conversation, Mr. Wilkeson, and I will end it by saying that it is best for us to separate, now and forever."

MARCUS (*bitterly*). "As you please, sir; but it is hard that a man's reputation should be at the mercy of any scoundrel who knows how to write a libel, and has not courage enough to acknowledge it."

THE INVENTOR (*pettishly*). "I have told you a dozen times, that I despise anonymous letter writers. They are ever liars and cowards."

MARCUS. "But you respected this one enough to adopt his suggestions."

THE INVENTOR. "So the magistrate uses hints that may be furnished him by professional thieves, for the detection of crime. But he, none the less, loathes those who would inform upon their comrades."

MARCUS. "You believe, therefore, only what you have seen or heard for yourself."

THE INVENTOR. "Nothing further, I assure you. In all matters of proof, it is my nature to be suspicious."

MARCUS. "But none of these accusations against me have been proved."

THE INVENTOR. "Why protract this painful conversation? It is sufficient for me to say that we must part.—(*Excitedly.*) Good heavens, sir! am I not the guardian of my daughter, and warranted in accepting or rejecting acquaintances for her? Must I make long explanations to everybody that I don't see fit to admit into my house and my daughter's society? Is not this a free country, sir?"

MARCUS (*with deep despair in his voice*). "Perfectly free, sir. I admit your rights. And I hereby pledge myself not to intrude upon you or her—at least, until you are convinced of the great injustice of your conduct toward me, and invite me again to your house. But there is one thing more!"

THE INVENTOR (*impatiently*). "One thing more! will this dialogue never end? Well, sir. What the devil is it?" Then he added, as if aware of the coarseness and gross impropriety of that expression. "Excuse me, sir, but it is late, and my machine is waiting."

MARCUS (*slowly and firmly*). "One moment, sir. I have sworn my innocence before God, with the most solemn oath known to man. I may have misconstrued your remarks, but I thought you still doubted me. It is my misfortune to be extremely sensitive upon the point of honor. Having relinquished your acquaintance and that of—of—your daughter, it is now my duty to ask whether you presume to question my oath?"

THE INVENTOR (*with increased impatience*). "Why should I be bored with this cross-examination? I have never said I doubted your oath."

MARCUS (*quickly*). "That is not an answer. Do you believe me, or disbelieve me? Am I a liar and perjurer, or not? In one word; yes, or no!"

THE INVENTOR (*laughing nervously*). "Will you bully me in my own house, sir? There is the door. Out of it!"

There was a noise like the opening of a door.

MARCUS (*between his teeth*). "Never, sir. Never, until you retract your imputation upon my honor."

THE INVENTOR (*losing all control of himself*). "Curse your honor. If you had been more careful of it in your native village—where you are best known—it would not trouble you now. Come, there are the stairs."

MARCUS. "Once more. Do you believe my oath, or not?"

THE INVENTOR (*shouting*). "No! no! a million times, no! since you drive me to it. I believe you to be a crafty scoundrel, who has been trying to ruin my daughter. Out, sir, now—out!"

Then was a sound of two men clenching, and struggling

toward the door. A noise followed like that caused by the sharp closing of the door; but the two men were still in the room, for their scuffling and their short, quick grunts of exertion could be heard with increased distinctness. The noise indicated that one was pushing the other toward the centre of the room. Then followed the dull, nauseating sound of blows, apparently struck with fists upon heads and chests, mingled with noisier but still partly suppressed groans, and defiances.

The conversation which preceded this struggle, had come to Pet's ears with such distinctness, and made such a terrifying impression upon her mind, that it seemed as if she could see the combatants.

At the time when the clenching commenced, the vision was faint, as if she were looking into a dark room. But, as the struggle proceeded, the room seemed to be gradually lighted up for her; and every grapple, every blow, every facial contortion of this horrible contest, were plainly visible. And yet she was not in the room, but lying in her little bed, bound as in the awful dream of the clashing orbs. She knew she was there, and yet she felt that her eyes, all her faculties of observation, had been somehow transferred to her father's room, and that she was actually seeing and hearing the commission of a murder there.

She tried to cry aloud, but her jaws were closed. She would have risen, entered the room, and thrown herself between the frenzied men, but neither hand nor foot could she move. Her body was fastened to the bed as if with adamantine chains, while her mind and soul were the voiceless spectators of a tragedy of which she knew that she was the cause. She could not even open her eyes. If she could have loosed but a muscle from the rigidity of the trance, she knew that her whole frame would be relaxed in an instant. Then she would have bounded—oh! with what speed—into the other room, where her immortal part was helplessly watching the conflict, and interceded at the risk of her life. Alas! Prometheus was tied to the rock not more firmly than she to that bed of anguish!

The struggle went on. The inventor, though past the prime of life, and worn down by excessive thought, had some strength left. Its duration was brief; but it was not to be despised while it lasted. He grasped the tall figure of Marcus Wilkeson by the neck with one arm, and with the other struck dozens of blows upon his face and chest. The comparative youth and freshness of Marcus were unable to free him from the strong hold of this vigorous old man. Pangs of terror shot through the heart of the poor girl as she saw that her father was about to become a murderer. Then the tide of fortune changed. Marcus, bruised and black in the face, and panting with exertion, released himself from the inventor's clutch, and, in turn, caught him by the throat. With his long arm he held the furious old man at a safe distance. The unhappy girl was now agonized with fears for her father's life.

"This is madness. Let us stop it." Thus Pet heard Marcus Wilkeson say, in panting accents.

What demoniac spell was it that prevented her from shrieking—"Stop it. In God's name, father, stop?"

"Never!" said the undaunted old man. "Never, till I have thrown you headlong down stairs! Liar! Villain!"

With that, Pet saw her father hurl himself, with the ferocity of a tiger, on Marcus Wilkeson. Such was the suddenness and impetuosity of the movement, that Marcus was pushed back several feet toward the door, from the centre of the room, where the most obstinate part of the struggle had taken place.

But the old man's supremacy was short lived. The younger and stronger man suddenly stooped, caught the inventor with both hands under the arms, and thrust him toward the corner occupied by the mysterious machine. The inventor would have fallen on it, and perhaps have been instantly killed by contact with some portion of the brass or iron work, but for the interposition of the screen. This broke his fall. He scrambled to his feet, full of rage, and foaming at the mouth.

Marcus stepped back, and said, "Now let it cease."

Pet saw her father snatch something that looked like a club, from some part of the machine.

"This is my answer," he said, and precipitated himself with fresh fury upon Marcus.

The younger man had expected the attack, and braced himself for it. He caught the inventor by the arm that held the club, or other weapon. They wrestled for its possession—the inventor with frenzy in every feature, Marcus with fixed determination, and silently.

The weapon was now aloft—now below—now shifted in the twinkling of an eye to the right, and now to the left. At one time the inventor seemed to be on the point of securing it; at another, Marcus. Suddenly Pet saw it whirl like a shillelah above her father's head, with a strange noise like the quick winding of a clock. Then she heard a dull sound, as of striking a board with a brick, and—she saw her father fall to the floor. At the same moment, the light in the room went out, and all was darkness.

The pent-up agony at last found utterance. She shrieked, and, instantly, her eyes were open, and her limbs free. She jumped out of bed, and was about to rush into the chamber of horrors, when she saw the bright light of the gas yet shining through the crack beneath her door. She listened. The house was still as the grave. Not a sound from all the world outside, except the striking of a fire alarm for the seventh district. The deep notes vibrated upon her quickened hearing like a knell.

Then she remembered that, in the vision, the light had disappeared. Here it was gleaming under her door as brightly as ever. "Pshaw! what a silly girl I am!" said she. "It was a nightmare. That's all." She raised her hands to her face. It was hot and dripping.

"Father prescribed too large a dose of blankets. No wonder I had this horrid dream."

But, notwithstanding the presence of the light, and the absence of all noise, such as would be caused by the murderer in leaving the room and going down stairs, the impression of this tragic vision upon her mind was not to be dismissed with a "Pshaw!"

Pet would have derived much relief from opening the door and looking in, and seeing, with her own waking eyes, that her father was alive, at his usual seat in the corner. She placed her hand upon the latch.

But then she remembered how her father had laughed at her, two or three times before, when she was a younger girl, and not so wise as now, and had rushed into his room screaming with fright from a nightmare. She prided herself on having outgrown childish fears.

She also remembered that her father had told her, two days before, that he was engaged in the most difficult mathematical calculations, day and night, and, kissing her, had playfully said that she must not disturb him.

"He is thinking over his problems now," thought little Pet. "Dear father! I *do* wish he would give up that hateful machine. It will be the death of him. But he said I must not disturb him, and I will not. Mr. Wilkeson must have gone home a long time ago; and dear father is thinking, as he calls it, with his hand on his forehead, in the old corner. Let me take one little peep through the keyhole, and go to bed again."

Pet stooped, and looked through the keyhole. Within her range were the chair where Marcus Wilkeson had sat that evening, and the nail where—with bachelor-like precision—he always hung his hat. Neither Marcus Wilkeson nor his hat were in their accustomed places. "What silly things these dreams are!" thought little Pet. The keyhole did not command the corner of the room where the machine stood, and where the inventor pondered and toiled; but Pet felt as certain that he was there, coaxing thoughts out of his pale brow with that habitual caress of the hand, as if she had seen him.

"Good night, dear father," she whispered, softly. "May Heaven watch over your labors, and keep you from all harm."

With this pious prayer, she slid into her warm nest. But,

before adjusting her limbs for sleep, she threw off a portion of the heavy blankets which had weighed upon her, and was soon sound asleep, and dreaming of a garden in which all the roses were beautiful new bonnets.

Still the moon played her ghastly metamorphoses in the little chamber. And the figures on the carpet and the figures on the curtain writhed in horrible contortions of glee, as if they rejoiced over a calamity which had befallen that house.

CHAPTER V.

WHAT THE MORNING BROUGHT.

THE child woke about seven o'clock. She knew the time by the sun's rays upon the window curtains. In that strong, cheerful light, the phantom faces had shrunk back to great red bunches of flowers again. She thought of the absurd dream, or vision, as of something that had happened ages ago, and wondered that she had been foolish enough to be frightened by it.

There was no noise in her father's room. But that was not strange, for he rarely retired to bed before three o'clock in the morning (even when he did not sit up all night), and slept till eight. His sleep, though short, was sound; and it was Pet's custom to prepare breakfast in her father's room without waking him.

She washed her face, which looked rosy and bewitching in the little cracked mirror, and dressed her hair in two simple bands down the cheeks, and put on a white calico dress with small red spots, and a white apron bound with blue. This was the dress that her father loved the best. She looked in the glass, and examined her damaged reflection with a charming coquetry, and said, "Pet, child, you are looking well to-day. Now for breakfast."

Pet walked to the door, humming her last music lesson in a low voice.

She placed her hand upon the latch, and opened the door softly. As it swung on its hinges, and she began to obtain a glimpse of the room, she noticed the gas still burning, though the daylight filled the apartment. This was strange. A shud der passed through her frame, and her cheeks began to pale.

"Pooh! what nonsense!" she said. She pushed the door wide open.

Was it another mocking, maddening vision that she saw? She rubbed her eyes in wild affright, and then raised her hands aloft with a piercing shriek.

There, before her, lay the dead body of her father. In the centre of his ghastly forehead was a small wound, from which the blood had trickled over the temples, bedabbling his thin gray hairs, and forming a small red pool by his side. Near him, on the floor, was a club with an iron tip, which had done the dreadful deed. She recognized it at once as a part of the machine.

The monstrous vision of the night was true! Her father was dead! Mr. Wilkeson was his murderer! She was an orphan!

These agonizing thoughts flashed through her brain in the single instant. She felt her head turning, and her limbs failing under her. She had only strength to shriek, "Murder! murder! Help! help!" and then she fell headlong and senseless upon her father's dead body.

BOOK SEVENTH.

JOURNEYINGS AGAINST FATE.

CHAPTER I.

PEA-SHOOTING AS A SCIENCE.

Be it said to the credit of Wesley Tiffles, that he always paid bills promptly when he could borrow money to do it. The funds that he had raised from Marcus Wilkeson, and others, for the panorama, had been faithfully applied to that great object. If he could have borrowed money from other people to repay those loans, that act of financial justice would also have been done; and so on without end, like a round robin.

When Tiffles bestowed the last instalment of compensation upon Patching, that individual shrugged his shoulders, and smiled. "The paltry price of artistic degradation," said he. "Remember, I would have done this job only for a friend. The world must not know it is a Patching—though I fear that even on this hasty daub I have left marks of my style which will betray me."

"You are safe, my dear fellow," said Tiffles. "I have already ordered the posters and bills; and the name of Andrea Ceccarini will appear thereon as the artist. Ceccarini has an Italian look, which is an advantage; and, you will pardon me for saying, is rather more imposing than Patching."

The artist was sensitive touching his name. It had been punned upon in some of the comic papers. He could not take offence at the innocent remark of a friend, but he felt hurt, and vindictively rammed the large roll of one-dollar bills into his vest pocket without counting them. (Whenever it was practicable, Tiffles paid his debts in bills of that denomination. He had a theory that the amount looked larger, and was more satisfactory to the receiver.)

As Tiffles saw how lightly the artist regarded the money, not even counting it, he felt a momentary pang at the thought that he had paid him.

The panorama of Africa had not only been finished and paid for, but it had been exhibited to a large number of clergymen of all denominations, at the lecture room of an up-town church. The clergymen, being debarred from attending secular amusements, as a class, had gladly accepted the invitation of "Professor Wesley" (Tiffles's panoramic name), and brought with them their wives and a number of children apiece.

The panorama was rigged up at the end of the lecture room, in front of the desk, under the personal supervision of a former assistant of Banvard's, and worked beautifully, saving an occasional squeak in the rollers.

Tiffles, in his character of Professor Wesley, told his story glibly and with perfect coolness, interspersing the heavier details with amusing anecdotes, which made the ministers smile, and brought out a loud titter of laughter from the ministers' wives, and tremendous applause, inclusive of stamping and the banging of hymn books, from the ministers' children.

One of the children, with the love of mischief peculiar to that division of the human family, had provided himself with peas, and, taking advantage of the partial darkness in which the panorama was exhibited, shot those missiles with practised aim at Professor Wesley, and now and then hit him in the face. The lecturer kept in good humor; and when, after a smart volley of peas, Rev. Dr. A—— arose, and suggested that these disturbances were disgraceful, and, although he did not wish to meddle with the household government of his brethren, he thought that the children who were guilty of such outrages ought to be taken home, soundly whipped, and put to bed—when Rev. Dr. A——, moved by just indignation, did this, the lecturer smiled, and blandly said: Oh, no; he wasn't annoyed in the least (at the same time receiving a pea on his left cheek). He would trust to the generosity of his young friends not to fire their peas too hard; and he hoped that the reverend gentleman would withdraw his suggestion.

Cries of "All right, brother!" "We'll keep the boys quiet!" "Go on! go on!" went up from all parts of the room. Rev. Dr. A——, yielding to the pressure, sat down, and received, at that moment, one pea on the right eye of his gold spectacles, and another square on the end of his nose. The two peas were fired by his second son John, who had been delivering this invisible artillery all the evening from the other end of the identical pew in which the Rev. Dr. was seated. He groaned in the spirit, and muttered something to Mrs. Rev. Dr. A—— about the degeneracy of other people's children, which made that lady chuckle low, under cover of the night; for she knew that her second son John was the pea-shooter, and had made vain efforts to stop him, by pinching his leg, though the good matron could not help laughing at every fine shot achieved by her promising boy.

Professor Wesley "went on," as requested, and so did the pea-shooting, until John's stock of ammunition gave out.

The lecturer had ransacked the Society, Astor, and Mercantile libraries, and stuffed himself with facts touching the interior of Africa, so far as that mystery had been explored. Fortified with these facts, and a lively imagination, he found no difficulty in satisfying the curiosity of his auditors on every point; and answered questions of all sorts, which were fired at him even thicker than the peas, without the least hesitation.

When the exhibition was over, every clergyman present

signed a certificate declaring that they had been highly entertained and instructed by the Panorama of Africa, and Mr. Wesley's able lecture; that they considered the painting a masterpiece of moral Art, and cordially recommended it to the patronage of an enlightened public.

CHAPTER II.

BY STEAM.

TIFFLES had selected, as his first field of active operations, the State of New Jersey. His large number of relatives (the Tiffleses were prolific on the female side) and friends, and occasional creditors, scattered through New England and New York, effectually barred him from all that territory. New Jersey, then Pennsylvania, then the West—those were the great topographical features of his campaign.

For his initiatory performance, he had chosen a quiet little town less than thirty miles from the city, on a line of railway. If his panorama was to be a hopeless failure at the very outset, Tiffles wanted to be within striking distance of New York. He was sanguine of success; but, like a prudent general, he looked after his lines of retreat.

To this small town in New Jersey, with which the fate of the great enterprise was to be indissolubly linked, Tiffles had sent a large stock of posters and handbills. He had previously corresponded (free of expense both ways) with that universal business man of every American village, the postmaster, and, through him, had engaged Washington Hall—the largest hall in the place, capable of holding six hundred people—at five dollars for one night, with the refusal of two nights more.

The name of the hall and the night of exhibition were written in blank spaces on the posters and handbills with red chalk, in a fine commercial hand, by Tiffles himself; and, for a small consideration, the postmaster had agreed to stick up the posters on every corner; also on the post office and the three town pumps; and to distribute the handbills in every house. These labors the P. M. did not undertake to perform personally—though he had plenty of leisure for them, as well as for the local defence of the National Administration, which was his peculiar and official function—but he turned them over to a semi-idiot, who occasionally did jobs of that kind, and who was willing to trust for his pay to the coming of Professor Wesley.

The last letter from the postmaster ran thus:

"Yure's of the 6th resevéd, and contense, including $3 for my pussenel expenses, dooly noted, Washinton Hall has been moped out for you and is clene as a pin, six new tin cannel sticks have been put up in the antyrum by the propryetor, this is lyberul, all the hanbils has been distributid, and the posters stuck up, sum of em wrong side down, owin to the bilposter bein a little week-minded, which will be a kind of curosity, and an advantije to you I think. I have sent tickets to the village pastures and their famylis, as yu requested and they red the notises last Sunday and advised everybuddy to go. I have gut public opinion all rite for yu here, now cum on with yer panyrammer of Afriky.

"Yure's trooly,

"B. PERSIMMON, p. m."

This was cheering; and Tiffles only hoped that he would be able to secure so faithful an ally in every postmaster, for he had decided to do this preliminary work through that variety of public functionary, until the success of the panorama would justify hiring a special courier to go in advance and smooth the way for him.

All these preparations having been satisfactorily made; and the panorama, with the curtains, the lighting apparatus, and the other properties, having been forwarded in three enormous boxes to the scene of the impending conflict with public opinion, Tiffles made ready to follow. And, on the eventful morning of the —— of April, 185–, he might have been seen at the Cortlandt-street ferry, accompanied by Patching, who had graciously consented to see how the "thing worked" on its first public trial.

Patching pulled his enormous hat still farther over his eyes, so that he might not be recognized. This gave him an extremely questionable aspect; and the ticket taker at the ferry peered under the huge brim suspiciously as Patching came in. He also attracted the attention of a detective in citizen's clothes, and was a general object of interest to all the people congregated in the ferry house and waiting for the boat.

"This is fame," muttered Patching, glancing at his scrutinizers from the shadow of the far-reaching hat. "This is what people starve and die for. It is a bore." He struck an attitude, as if unconsciously, folding his arms, and appearing to be in a profound revery. Then, after another cautious glance about, he turned to Tiffles, by his side, and said:

"It is useless. I am recognized. But remember your solemn promise. I had no hand in the painting of it."

"Not a little finger, my dear fellow," cheerfully replied Tiffles, who had given the artist similar assurances of secrecy five times that morning.

At that moment a hand touched Tiffles familiarly on the shoulder. He turned suddenly, for he was always expecting rear attacks from creditors. He saw Marcus Wilkeson.

"Best of friends," said Tiffles, with unfeigned joy, "I am glad to see you. Of course you are going with us, though I hardly dared hope as much when I sent you the invitation."

"To tell the truth, Tiffles, I had no intention of going, till this morning, when it suddenly occurred to me that a little trip in the country, and the fun of seeing your panorama and hearing you lecture, would drive away the blues. I had a bad fit of them last night."

Here Patching turned, and looked Marcus in the face, without seeming to recognize him. It was his habit (not a singular one among the human species) to pretend not to remember people, and to wait for the first word. Marcus indulged in the same habit to some extent, and, when he saw Patching looking at him without a nod or a word, he also was blank and speechless.

"Don't you remember each other?" said Tiffles. "Mr. Patching. Mr. Marcus Wilkeson."

The gentlemen shook hands, and said:

"Oh, yes! How do you do? It is a fine morning. Very."

"So much paler than when I last saw you, that I didn't know you, positively. Little ill, sir?" asked Patching. The artist was sure to observe and speak of any signs of illness on the faces of his friends and acquaintances. Some people called him malevolent for it.

To be told that one looks pale, always makes one turn paler. Marcus, extra sensitive on the point of looks, became quite pallid, and said, with confusion:

"I have not been well for several days, and my rest was badly broken last night."

Tiffles had also remarked the unusual deadly whiteness of his friend's complexion, and the air of lassitude and unhappiness which pervaded his face, but he would not have alluded to them for the world. He never made impertinent observations of that sort.

"Unwell?" said Tiffles. "I had not noticed it. In the morning, all New York looks as if it had just come out of a debauch. Wilkeson will pass, I guess." This calumny upon the city was Tiffles's favorite bit of satire, and it had cheered up many a poor fellow who thought himself looking uncommonly haggard.

Marcus smiled languidly, and turned away his head with a sigh. As his eyes swept about, they encountered the gaze of the man in citizen's clothes, previously noticed. At first, Marcus thought he had seen this man somewhere before; and then he thought he was mistaken. The man evinced no recognition of Marcus, and, an instant after, his sharp glance wandered to some other person in the large group waiting for the boat.

Here the boat came into the slip, and, after bumping in an uncertain way against the piles on either side, neared almost within leaping distance of the wharf. A solid crowd of passengers stood at the edge of the boat, with their eyes fixed on the landing place, as if it were the soil of a new world upon which they were to leap for the first time, like a party of Columbuses When the distance had been diminished to about four feet, the front row of passengers jumped ashore, and rushed wildly up the street, as if impelled by a rocket-like power from behind. These people could not have been more eager to get ashore, if they had come from the other side of the globe on business involving a million apiece, to be transacted on that day only.

In fact, they were only lawyers, tradesmen, mechanics, and clerks, living in Jersey City, and going over to New York on their daily, humdrum business. It was not the business that attracted them, but the demon of American restlessness that pushed them on. They went back at night in just the same hurry, and made equally hazardous jumps on the Jersey side. They were mere shuttlecocks between the battledoors of Jersey City and New York.

Tiffles and Patching lifted up the thin carpet bags which reposed at their feet, and which contained an exceedingly small amount of personal linen and other attire, and went on board the boat, followed by Marcus, who was unencumbered with baggage. They entered the ladies' cabin. The thick crowd of people pressed into the cabin in their front and rear, and all about them, and scrambled for seats. There was a general preference for the part forward of the wheelhouse, because it was a few feet nearer New Jersey than the aft part. The rush to obtain these preferred places was like that of the opera-going world for the front row of boxes at a *matinée*. Ladies who obtained eligible seats, settled themselves in them, spread out their dresses, put their gloved hands in position, and smiled with a sweet satisfaction at ladies who had got no seats. Those ladies, in turn, looked reproachfully at the gentlemen who were comfortably seated. And those gentlemen, with the exception of a few who rose and gracefully offered their seats to the youngest and prettiest of the ladies, in turn looked out of the windows, or at the floor, or at a paper, intently.

A stranger to the ferry boats and customs of the country would have supposed that the passengers were bound for Europe instead of the opposite shore of North River.

Marcus Wilkeson, Tiffles, and Patching did not participate in this contest for seats, but walked through the fetid and stifling cabins to the forward deck, where fresh, bracing air, glorious sunlight, and a cheery view of the river were to be had. But these charms of nature were apparently thrown away on the trio. They all leaned over the railing, and looked steadily into the water. Tiffles was thinking up his lecture, and other matters of the panorama. Patching was misanthropically reviewing his career, and exulting in future triumphs over his professional enemies. Marcus was engrossed with some sad theme which, once or twice, brought tears into his eyes. A burst of noble music, a fine sentiment in a poem, a poor woman crying, keen personal disappointment, or any acute mental trouble, had this strange effect on the optics of Marcus Wilkeson.

The bell rang; voices shouted, "All aboard!" the gang-plank was drawn in; several belated people jumped on, at the risk of their lives, after the boat had left the wharf, one man vaulting over ten feet; and the voyage for Jersey was commenced.

Three minutes later, the inmates of the cabins began to go forward and pick favorable positions for jumping off on the other side. The scramble to evacuate the seats then was as sharp as the scramble to possess them, three minutes before. A few more rounds of the wheels, and the boat thumped in the usual way against one row of piles at the entrance of the Jersey slip, and then caromed like a billiard ball on the other, each time nearly knocking the passengers off their feet, and shaking a small chorus of screams out of the ladies.

When the boat was within a yard of the wharf, the jumping commenced; and all the able-bodied men, most of the boys, and some of the ladies, were off before the boat butted with tremendous force against the wharf, shaking both wharf and boat to their foundations, and giving to the people on both a parting jar, which they carried in their bones for the rest of the day.

Once safely on the wharf, the scramble was continued in various directions and for various objects. Marcus, Tiffles, and Patching indulged in the eccentricity of not scrambling; and, when they reached the Erie Railroad cars, they found every seat taken, some by two persons, but many by one lady and a bandbox or carpet bag, which was intended to signify to the inquiring eye that the lawful human occupant of that half of the seat was absent, but might be expected to come in and claim it at any moment.

The three companions understood this conventional imposture, and politely claimed the spare half seats from the nearest ladies. The fair occupants looked forbidding, and slowly removed their bandboxes, baskets, and other parcels, to the floor beneath, or the rack overhead; and the disturbers of their peace and comfort ruthlessly took the vacated seats, with a bow, signifying "Thank you."

The seats thus procured were some distance apart; and so the three companions were precluded from conversing with each other. This suited the taciturn mood of each that morning. As for the ladies who filled the other half of the three seats, they might as well have been lay figures from a Broadway drygoods store; conversation with them being prohibited by the etiquette of railway travelling. A man may journey two hundred and fifty miles in a car, with his elbow unavoidably jogging a lady's all the way, and still be as far from her acquaintance (unless she is graciously inclined to say something first) as if the pair were leagues apart. This is proper, but peculiar.

The strange sadness that possessed Marcus that morning was intensified as the cars rolled on. There is something in the monotonous vibration of the train, and the recurring click of the wheels against the end of the rails, that provokes melancholy. Marcus looked out of the window at the flying landscape, and the distant patches of wood which seemed to be slowly revolving about each other, and was profoundly wretched. He was totally unconscious of the sharp, pale, nervous face by his side.

The owner of the face was about thirty-five years old, though the lines on her brow and cheeks added an apparent five years to her age. If she had been put upon her trial for murder, the police reporters would have discovered traces of great beauty in her countenance. An ordinary spectator, having no occasion to spice a paragraph, would have made the equivocal remark that she had once been handsomer.

This lady was dressed plainly, comfortably, and in good taste. Her hands, ungloved, were shapely, but red and hard with manual labor. On the second finger of the left hand was a little gold ring, much thinned by wearing. The eyes of this lady were regarding the unconscious Marcus obliquely, with a singular expression of mingled recollection and doubt. Sometimes her glance would drop to the ring, as if that were a link in the chain of her perplexed reflections. A sudden jolt of the car, as the train ran over a pole which had fallen on the track, roused Marcus to the existence of this face and those eyes.

As he saw the eyes sternly bent on him, he thought that his staring out of the window, past the lady's profile, might have offended her. So, with a cough which was meant to serve as an apology for the unintentional rudeness, he turned his face away, and continued his gloomy revery among the odd patterns of the oilcloth on the floor of the aisle.

Still the thin, nervous lady watched him obliquely.

A ride of three quarters of an hour brought them to their destination, as they learned from a preliminary howl of the conductor through the rear door of the car. The engine bell rang, the whistle screamed, the clack of the wheels gradually became slower.

"Only one minute. Hurry!" howled the conductor again.

Marcus, Tiffles, and Patching were out of their seats and at the door with American despatch. Before the car had quite stopped, they had jumped off. Marcus did not notice that, behind him, was a woman struggling between the two rows of seats with a bandbox, a workbasket, an umbrella, and her hoops, all of which caught in turn on one side or the other. Nor did the conductor observe that this burdened and distressed lady was trying to make her way out; for, after looking from the rear of the train, and seeing that three persons had landed, and that there was nobody to get on, he concluded that it would be a waste of time to stop a minute, and so rang the bell to go ahead. The engine driver, equally impatient, jerked the starting lever, and the engine bounded forward like a horse, giving a shock to the train, and nearly upsetting the woman, who was still wrestling with her personal effects between the rows of seats. With a sudden effort, she freed herself, opened the door, and stood upon the platform.

The engine had wheezed three times, and she hesitated to jump. She screamed shrilly. The sound entered the ears of Marcus Wilkeson, who was whisking dust and ashes off his clothes with a handkerchief. He ran forward, and saw the predicament of his pale and nervous fellow traveller. She screamed again, as the engine wheezed for the eighth time.

Marcus extended his hand. "Jump!" said he; "I'll catch you."

She did jump, much to the surprise of Marcus and the two lookers on—thereby indicating decision of character.

Marcus caught her in his arms—bandbox, basket, and all—and the train hurried on.

"Thank you, sir," said the lady, with some confusion. Then she walked rapidly down the road toward the village, like one who lived there.

"A customer for the panorama, perhaps," said Tiffles. "I'm glad you landed her safely." Tiffles had got through his thinking, and was exhilarant again. He laughed so pleasantly, that even Marcus relaxed his grim visage, and smiled.

"Not a bad ankle, that," observed Patching, looking at the rapidly retreating form of the rescued woman. Patching, artist-like, was always discovering beauties where nobody else looked for them.

Marcus had no eye for the charms of nature that morning, and he responded not to the remark which the artist had addressed to him. Whereupon Patching determined not to speak to Marcus again that day.

They followed the mysterious female down the road which led to the village. On the fences, every few rods, were plastered posters announcing the "Panorama of Africa" for that evening, at "Washington Hall"—"Tickets, twenty-five cents"—"Children under twelve years of age, half price," &c., &c. As B. Persimmon, P. M., had said, in one of his letters, some of the posters were stuck upside down. This circumstance did not seem to prevent the population from reading them; for the party observed at least two boys (half prices) in the act of spelling them out between their legs.

Tiffles was so absorbed in the contemplation of the posters, Patching in a critical survey of the scenery on both sides of the road, and Marcus Wilkeson in an introspection of his troubled heart, that none of them observed how often the thin, nervous female, walking rapidly ahead, looked over her shoulder at one of their number.

CHAPTER III.

PIGWORTH, J. P.

The village was composed of the usual ingredients, in the usual proportions. Law, drygoods, liquor, blacksmithing, carpentry, education, painting and glazing, medicine, dentistry, tinware, and other comforts of civilization, were all to be had on reasonable terms. There were four churches with rival steeples, and two taverns with rival signs. The village contained everything that any reasonable man could ask for, except a barber's shop. It takes a good-sized town to support a barber's shop.

As they marched into the village, they were conscious of attracting general attention. Men looked out of the doors, women out of the windows, and boys had begun to fall in procession behind.

"Them are the performers," said one boy to another "Wonder what that feller with the big hat does?" observed a second. "Turns the crank, guess," was the response.

Patching pulled his hat farther over his eyes, and smiled gloomily at Tiffles. "They little think who I am," he murmured.

"What a solemncholy mug that tall chap's got," said another youthful citizen. This made Marcus try to laugh genially at the boys. But in vain.

"Say, Bill, isn't that little feller's shirt out o' jail?"

Tiffles made a personal application of this remark. It was his constant misfortune to suffer rents in portions of his garments where their existence was least likely to be discovered by himself. As he could not publicly verify the suggestion of the impertinent small boy, he buttoned his coat tightly about him.

How their identity with the panorama of Africa had been established, was a mystery. Small boys divine secrets by instinct, as birds find food and water.

The two taverns were the National House and the United States Hotel. Although the signs were large and clean, the taverns were small and dirty. There was no choice between them, except in the fact that the United States Hotel was directly opposite Washington Hall. Therefore the adherents of the panorama cast their fortunes with that place of entertainment for man and beast—particularly beast.

Mr. Thomas Pigworth, the landlord, was seated on the stoop of his hostelry, discoursing of national politics to a small group of his fellow citizens, who were performing acrobatic feats with chairs in a circle about him. Pigworth was a justice of the peace, and was always dressed in his best clothes, so as to perform his judicial functions at a moment's notice, with dignity and ease. He was tall, thin, baldheaded. T. J. Childon, landlord of the "National," said hard things, as in duty bound, of his rival. Among others, that he had kept himself lean by running so hard for office for the last ten years. To which slander Pigworth retorted, that Childon was fat (which was true—a fine, plump figure was Childon's) only because he ate everything in his house, and left nothing for his customers.

The three newcomers mounted the rotten wooden steps to the stoop. Mr. Pigworth left his group of auditors, came forward, and received them with the affability of a retired statesman.

"The landlord?" asked Tiffles.

"I keep the hotel," said Pigworth, with a smile which intimated that he kept it for amusement rather than profit.

"Room and board for three of us?" asked Tiffles.

"Certainly," said Pigworth, with the air of a man who was doing them a favor. "Ef you want only one apartment, I can give you the one occupied last week by the Hon. Mr. Podhammer. You have heard of him?"

"Of course," responded Tiffles, to cut short the conversation.

"He spoke in Washington Hall, there, on the Cons'tution. He is smart on some things, but THE CONS'TUTION he doesn't understand—not a word of it. I told him so."

Tiffles was about to ask why, if the Hon. Mr. Podhammer didn't understand a word of the Constitution, he had the audacity to lecture on it; when he remembered that it was no uncommon thing for lecturers to talk of what they don't understand—himself of Africa, for instance.

"Be good enough to show us the room," said he.

"I say, Judge" (Pigworth, being a justice of the peace, was universally styled thus), cried a voice from the group, "do you, or do you not, indorse my sentiments?"

Pigworth turned majestically, and spoke like an oracle:

"I do not indorse your sentiments. I wish it distinctly understood, that I do not indorse them. I indorse nothing but the Cons'tution. That instrument I indorse to any extent. Are you satisfied now?"

This speech was hailed by cries of "Good! good!" "That's so!" "Sound doctrine, that!" "The Judge knows what's what!" Only one person, the questioner, a young man with a preternatural head, was unappeased.

"A single word more," said this young man. "Do you, or do you not, subscribe to my views on the Homestead Law?"

Pigworth looked at the three comers as if to say, "Mark how I crush him now." Then, pointing his long right arm at the rash youth, he replied, slowly, but with fearful distinctness: "I do not subscribe to your views. Sooner would I lose this right arm than subscribe to them. There is only one view that I subscribe to. That view to which I subscribe (the Judge spoke with increased dignity here, and rose on his toes)—that view is found in the Cons'tution. You would do well to study the Cons'tution, my young friend."

This withering rebuke was greeted with shouts and clapping of hands from all but the young man, who muttered something about humbug, and looked glum.

The landlord had another excoriating remark, which he might have flung at the young man and finished him up, but he magnanimously forbore.

"Now, my friends," said the landlord, patronizingly. He ushered them into a dirty entry, and piloted the way up stairs.

"From New York, I suppose?" said the landlord. "Any political news?"

"Really, sir, we don't meddle with politics," replied Tiffles, sharply.

The landlord looked at him with an expression of pity "Oh! to be sure not. You belong to the pannyrama. I recolleck that the last circus folks that come here never talked about politics. Are you Professor Wesley?"

"I am," said Tiffles.

"I merely wanted to say," continued the landlord, "that six of my lodgers are goin' to the pannyrama on my recommendation. I have a wife, sister-in-law, and five children."

Tiffles took the hint. "I will hand you a complimentary ticket for yourself and family," said he.

"Oh, no! by no means!" replied the landlord. "I wouldn't think of taking it."

Mr. Pigworth then ushered his guests into the large, uncomfortable apartment known as the "best room" in all country hotels. The ceiling was low; there were three windows with small panes, the sashes of which rattled in the wind; a rag carpet covered the floor; an old bureau, topped off with a dirty white cloth, a rickety table similarly draped, four cane-bottomed chairs, and a huge wooden spitbox filled with sawdust, stood at intervals around. Two single beds occupied opposite corners.

With reference to the beds, Mr. Pigworth remarked:

"Podhammer and Gineral Chetley slept in that air one. Colonel Hockensacker and Judge Waterfield in t'other. There was four other mattresses put down here that night, each of 'em with two of our most distinguished citizens on it. That convention was worth to me a good hundred dollars."

With every respect for the precedent established by Podhammer and associates, Marcus Wilkeson preferred to sleep alone, as he had done for twenty years. He privately expressed to the landlord a desire for one of the mattresses which had done duty during the convention.

The landlord smiled, evidently regarding the request as eccentric and unreasonable, but nodded "All right." As for Tiffles and Patching, having shared the same couch several nights during the incubation of the panorama, the problem of how to distribute three men among two beds gave them no concern. Pigworth then retired.

Marcus Wilkeson's first act was to open the windows, and mix some fresh air with the damp and mouldy atmosphere of the apartment. Patching's first act was to light his pipe, and throw himself on the nearest bed for a smoke. Tiffles's first act was to inspect the rent which the impertinent small boy had discovered, and make temporary repairs with a pin. Having done these things, and arranged their toilets hastily in a mirror with a crack running through it like a streak of lightning, the three adventurers sallied forth, and crossed the street to Washington Hall.

CHAPTER IV.

STOOP.

WASHINGTON HALL was the only place of public congregation, excepting the churches, in the village. It was used on Sunday by a small but clamorous religious sect; on Monday by a lodge of Free Masons; on Tuesday by a lodge of Odd Fellows; on Wednesday by the Sons of Temperance; and for the balance of the week was open to any description of exhibition that came along. It was originally built for a loft, and its reconstruction into a public hall was an afterthought. It was situated over a drug store, and was owned by the druggist, Mr. Boolpin, who was universally regarded as the meanest man in the village.

As the three drew near the door, Mr. Boolpin, strongly smelling of aloes, and carrying a pestle in his hand, came out to greet them. He, in common with all the inhabitants, knew that the "pannyrarmer folks" were in town. The small boys had borne the glad intelligence all abroad. A number of citizens, who had been lying in wait, issued forth with Mr. Boolpin, and looked hard at the three.

"The proprietor of the hall," said Mr. Boolpin, intro ducing himself.

"My name is Wesley," responded Tiffles. He then introduced Patching as Signor Ceccarini, and Wilkeson as Mr. Wilkes. Patching chuckled inwardly at the thought of the incognito, and imagined the sensation that would be produced by the accidental revelation of his real name. Marcus felt a momentary humiliation at having consented to this innocent imposture.

Mr. Boolpin, having shaken hands solemnly with the three, asked them to walk up stairs and look at the hall. They accordingly followed him up a series of creaking steps.

"Everything in apple-pie order," said Mr. Boolpin. "The three boxes containing the panorama right side up with care, you see. I had them carted from the depot. Cost me a dollar. People thought they were coffins. Ha! ha! Six new tin candlesticks, you observe; also the ceiling whitewashed; also ten extra seats introduced, making the entire capacity of the hall three hundred and fifty—giving twelve inches of sitting room to each person. No extra charge for these fixings, though I made them expressly on your account. There are some things about this hall to which I would call your attention. Boo! Boo! Hallo! Hallo! No echo, you perceive. Likewise notice the fine view from the window." Mr. Boolpin pointed to a swamp which could be distinctly seen over a housetop toward the east. "The ventilation is a great feature, too." Mr. Boolpin directed his pestle toward a trap door in a corner of the ceiling, through which a quantity of rain had come a night or two previous, leaving a large wet patch on the floor. "It's almost too cheap for fifteen dollars a night."

"For what?" asked Tiffles.

"For fifteen dollars," replied Mr. Boolpin, twirling his pestle playfully. "Of course, not reckoning in the one dollar that you owe me for cartage. It's too cheap. I ought to have made it twenty dollars."

"Why, Mr. Persimmon, the postmaster here, engaged the

hall for five dollars. Here is his letter mentioning the price." Tiffles produced the letter, and pointed out the numeral in question.

"It's a 5, without any doubt," rejoined Mr. Boolpin; "but Persimmon had no authority to name that price. I distinctly told him fifteen dollars. But here he is. Perhaps he can explain it."

The three turned on their heels, and beheld, standing at the door, a short, dirty man in a faded suit of black, and a cold-shining satin vest. He wore an old hat set well back on a bald head, and his cravat was tied on one side in hangman's fashion. One leg of his trowsers was tucked into the top of his boot; the other hung down in its proper position. The man's face and hands wanted washing. This was Mr. Persimmon, postmaster. The secrets of his popularity were: First, his addiction to dirt; second, his eccentricities of dress, heretofore enumerated; third, a reputation for political craft and long-headedness, not wholly unfounded, as his ingenuity in procuring the passage of resolutions supporting the policy of the Administration, in all the conventions of his party since he became postmaster, fully proved. This political sage walked about town with Post-Office documents and confidential communications from Washington sticking out of all his pockets, and under the edge of his hat. He had a slight stoop in the shoulders, which the local wits said had increased since he undertook to carry the Administration.

"Professor Wesley?" remarked Persimmon, extending a grimy hand. "Happy to see you."

"Your most obedient," said Tiffles, a little stiffly, for the fifteen dollars annoyed him. It was a small sum to borrow, but a large one to pay.

"Have you such a thing as a morning newspaper about you?" asked the postmaster. "Our bundle missed the train. As you may naturally imagine, sir, I am anxious to see how the grand mass meeting went off last night in your city. Perhaps you wos there?"

Tiffles had never attended such a thing in his life; although he was aware that two or three grand mass meetings were held every week about all the year round, and a dozen nightly in times of political excitement. "No," said he; "but will you be good enough to tell me how much you hired this room for?"

Persimmon thought how culpably ignorant some people were of the great political movements of the day, but did not say so. Descending from politics to the subject in hand, he replied:

"Oh! fifteen dollars, of course. You will find it stated in my last letter to you." At this moment (no one of the three observing the act), the long-headed postmaster tipped a slight wink to Mr. Boolpin, who returned that signal of mutual understanding.

Tiffles handed the letter to the postmaster, pointing out the figure 5.

"Can I believe my eyes?" said the postmaster. "True enough, it is a 5. Confound my absent-mindedness in not puttin' down a 1." It may here be said, that similar instances of mental aberration were discovered in Mr. Persimmon's accounts toward the close of his official term.

Tiffles was staggered, as he reflected that it would take sixty full tickets to pay the single item of rent. He had less than half a dollar in his own pocket. Patching was, as usual, reduced to his last five-dollar bill. Marcus had incidentally observed, a few minutes before, that he had left his wallet at home, and had only a handful of small silver about him. Suppose the panorama should fail on the first night, and be detained for debt! Tiffles had not thought of that.

Tiffles remonstrated, entreated, suggested compromises, but all to no purpose. Boolpin was iron. The best arrangement that Tiffles could make, was to postpone the final settlement of the terms until after the performance. To that, Boolpin had not the least objection.

"One thing more," said Boolpin. "If there is a row, and

any seats or windows are broken, you are to pay the damages."

Tiffles laughed faintly. "Oh! of course," said he. "But you never have rows here, do you?" He put the question with disguised interest.

"Sometimes," carelessly replied Mr. Boolpin. "There was a legerdemain man got his machinery knocked to pieces, and his head broken. The mob was quite reasonable about the furniture, and smashed only ten seats and sixteen panes of glass. I charged the Professor twenty dollars for damages, but took off two dollars on account of his illness. Poor fellow! he was laid up more than a month. Then there was a band of nigger minstrels, called the 'Metropoliganians.' They were regular humbugs; and so the mob took them, and tarred and feathered them in the back lot. Damage to furniture on that occasion was only sixteen dollars; and I got every cent of it, by holding on to their trunks. There have been a good many such little affairs in this village. I mention these two cases only as examples."

"And yet no people in the world is more peaceable, nor more easily satisfied, than the people of this town," said the postmaster. "They only axes not to be imposed on. That's all."

"A kinder-hearted people don't live on the face of this earth," added Boolpin, stating the case in another way; "but you mustn't give them less than twenty-five cents' worth for a quarter."

Tiffles replied to the effect that he would give them a dollar's worth apiece; but, in his heart, he foresaw, with that remarkable prescience which is occasionally vouchsafed to mortals, that the panorama of Africa was doomed to be a bad failure; and he bitterly regretted that he had not tried some one of a dozen other immense speculations which he had thought of. But he determined to give one night's exhibition, whatever might be the consequences. "I may as well die for an old sheep as a lamb," thought Tiffles.

During this conversation, Patching was secretly studying the effect of the swamp, visible from the eastern windows; and Marcus was looking at the cracked wall in a fit of abstraction.

Tiffles had observed several times, that morning, a youth, or man, of singular aspect, following him. Occasionally, on turning around suddenly, he would see this person at his elbow. Looking behind, at the close of the colloquy with the landlord, he again saw the strange youth, or man. The being was nearly six feet high, and powerfully built, like a strong man of twenty-five. His face was childish even to the degree of silliness. The mouth opened like a flytrap; the eyes were small and intensely guileless. Only a few wrinkles, and a few hairs, which grew wide apart on his cheeks and chin, indicated his manhood. But the oddest feature was the falling away of his forehead, at an angle which a dirty greased cap, pulled over his brow, could not conceal.

"Well, sir, what do you want?" said Tiffles.

"If you please, sir," said the singular being, in a cracked voice, "yure the pannyrarmer, a'n't ye?"

"Not exactly, my lad, but I own it. And who are you?"

"My name's Stoop, if you please, sir."

Mr. Boolpin broke out with a laugh, which made the building reverberate. "It's the village idiot," said he. "He goes by the name of Stoop, which is short for Stupid. Ha! ha! Come, now, clear out, Stupid, and don't be bothering the gentleman."

The boy-man began to whimper, when Tiffles, recollecting an allusion to a semi-idiot in one of the postmaster's letters, said:

"Stay, my lad; I believe I owe you something."

"For pastin' up two hundred posters, fifty cents; and distributin' five hundred bills, twenty-five cents. Totale, seventy-five cents." The idiot did not hold out his hand for the pay, and Tiffles conceived an instant esteem for him. An idea came to Tiffles. This idiot, as he was called, had shown intelligence in reckoning. He might have a deal of good sense under that dull exterior. Tiffles had observed, in his travels, that *the* idiot which Providence assigns to every town and village, is not always the biggest fool in it. This idiot might have sufficient intellect to turn the crank of the panorama, and render muscular aid in other respects. At any rate, he was able-bodied enough.

"My lad," said Tiffles.

"Stoop, if you please, sir."

"Very good. Stoop, I think I can find some work for you behind the scenes to-night. Can you turn a crank?"

"I've done it to grindstones, sir."

"It's the same principle," said Tiffles, laughing. "I'll engage you."

The idiot took off his greasy cap, and swung it in the air with joy. A smile irradiated his great, coarse face, and his small eyes twinkled. "Gosh golly!" he cried; "I'm goin' to be one of the performers. I'm so glad!"

He said this, in a spirit of juvenile exultation, to the dozen boys who stood gaping in at the doorway. This innocent bit of boasting provoked their derisive laughter, and a quantity of playful epithets and nicknames, which the idiot endured with marvellous patience, until one dirty little boy put the thumb of his left hand to his nose, twirled the fingers, and said, "Boo! boo! boo!" This act had the same effect on poor Stoop as the shaking of a red handkerchief at a bull. It enraged him. He sprang at the youth, and, but for the sudden closing of the door by the offender, who had judiciously kept a hand on the knob, would have chastised him on the spot.

The door not only arrested his progress, but suddenly checked his wrath. "I'm very sorry, indeed, Professor," said he; "but Gorrifus! it makes me so mad!"

Messrs. Boolpin and Persimmon laughed heartily. "He's a perfect idiot, you see," remarked the former. "Coming the nose system at him always makes him mad."

Tiffles did not understand how that was any proof of idiocy; but, to prevent the recurrence of any difficulty between his new assistant and the populace of small boys, he thought it best to take possession of the hall, and lock the door. He therefore signified to Mr. Boolpin that they would at once proceed to put up the panorama. Tiffles threw off his coat, thereby intimating that he would go to work at once.

Messrs. Boolpin and Persimmon inquired, as a matter of form, whether their further assistance was needed, and were answered in the negative. Whereupon they retired—Mr. Boolpin uttering a farewell caution against driving more nails in the wall than were necessary, and not to cut the floor under any circumstances—and the panorama and its adherents were left alone.

Mr. Boolpin had driven the uproarious boys before him with his pestle, administering smart taps to the reluctant ones. Tiffles suffered no further annoyance from them that day, save an occasional "Boo! boo!" shouted through the keyhole, and followed by an immediate scampering of the perpetrators down stairs. This well-known sound always roused the idiot to fury; and the peaceable persuasions, and even the gentle violence of Tiffles, were needed to keep him from relinquishing his work and springing to the door.

He was a most intelligent and useful idiot. He could measure distances more accurately than either of the three, and could ply the saw, hammer, plane, or hatchet (Tiffles brought all these tools with him) like a carpenter. His strength and skill were so great, that Tiffles found himself gratefully relieved from the necessity of lifting, or directing. Marcus Wilkeson, who had also thrown off his coat with a manful determination to do a hard day's work, in the hope of tiring out and driving away the sadness that possessed him, put on the garment again, and sat on a front bench, vacantly staring like an idiot at the idiot, and all the while thinking, gloomily, of New York. Patching stalked about the hall, and criticized the work as it progressed, from numerous angles of observation; but even he confessed that he could make no improvement on Stoop's highly artistic disposition of things.

The idiot worked on steadily and swiftly, and only two things interrupted him. The first was the "Boo!" yelled through the keyhole, as heretofore described. The second was the unrolling of portions of the panorama as they were taken out of the boxes, fastened together, and attached to the rollers.

As the canvas was unwound, Stoop would drop his saw, or hammer, or other tool, and gaze, with his large mouth and small eyes wide open, at the pictorial marvels successively disclosed. "Blame it!" said he; "a'n't that splendid?" or, "By jingo! look at that!" or, "Thunder! don't that beat all?" The tigers' tails and the elephants' trunks, the alligators' snouts and the boa constrictor's convolutions, he recognized at once. He had "read all about 'em in Olney's Jogriffy."

"He is an idiot of taste," thought Patching. "I wonder what they call him an idiot for?" thought Tiffles. "It's a pity all the people aren't idiots," said Marcus Wilkeson to Tiffles. "Your panorama would be patronized and appreciated then." It was Marcus's first approach to a joke that day.

By four o'clock in the afternoon the Panorama of Africa was all up, the rollers and the curtain in good working order, and everything ready for the eventful night. Stoop had taken a lesson at the wheel, and turned it beautifully. Tiffles had arranged a system of signals with him. One cough was "Stop;" two coughs were "Go on;" one stamp was "Slower;" two stamps were "Faster." Tiffles and Stoop rehearsed the system several times, the one being before the curtain, in the position of the lecturer, and the other behind it, at the crank. Nothing could be more satisfactory.

"Only one thing puzzles me," said Tiffles to his friends. "Why do they call this smart fellow an idiot?"

CHAPTER V.

AN AUDIENCE ANALYZED.

THE eventful night came on. Tiffles and friends fortified themselves with a poor supper, including numerous cups of weak black tea, at the hotel, and repaired, full of anxiety and misgivings, to the hall. The idiotic but intelligent Stoop had remained in charge of the panorama, and feasted himself, intellectually, upon the splendors of that work of Art, as disclosed by a single candle in front.

All the candles in the hall and the entry were then lighted up, and produced quite a gorgeous illumination of the four windows fronting on the main street. This having been done, Marcus (who, having a more extensive acquaintance with the faces of bank bills than either of his friends, had kindly consented to act as money taker and cashier) took his seat in a little box with a pigeon hole in it, and his entire stock of loose change, amounting to seventy-five cents in silver, spread before him. Tiffles stood within the door of the hall, to see that nobody came in (especially small boys) who had not paid. Stoop remained behind the scenes, and was positively instructed to stay there. Patching wandered up and down the hall, as if he were an early comer, and had paid his quarter, and had no personal knowledge of or interest in the panorama.

Performance was to commence at 8 o'clock. Doors were open at 6½. Some time previous to that hour, the stairs leading from the street door to the hall were lined with the lads of the village, who amused themselves with making jocular remarks about "the man in the cage there" (meaning Marcus), and "t'other man at the door, whose shirt was out of jail" (meaning Tiffles). Marcus smiled grimly at his assailants through the small pigeon hole; and Tiffles, who felt reckless in the sure view of a failure, laughed heartily at them, returned jokes as bad as they sent, but, in the height of his humor, begged them distinctly to understand that they could not get in without paying. At which the juvenile chorus sarcastically replied, "P'r'aps not;" "Mebbe you're right;" "You'll have to stop up the keyhole, Mister;" "Mind I don't get down the chimbley," &c., &c.

At precisely forty-seven minutes past six, the first man made his appearance. He was a thick-set, pompous individual, with a gold-headed cane and gold spectacles, and climbed up the stairs with dignity and difficulty. He was followed by a pale little woman, four small children, and a stout, red-haired nurse, bearing in her arms a baby, which was laboring under an attack of the intermittent squalls. Marcus reconnoitred the party through his pigeon hole, and nervously jingled the seventy-five cents in his hand. Tiffles stepped forward to the head of the stairs, in order that he might not be wanting in personal respect to his first patron.

As this thick-set man ascended the stairs, the boys hushed their voices; but Tiffles distinctly heard several of them say, "It's the Square." Though apparently awestruck in his presence, the boys did not forget to play a few practical jokes on "the Square's" children, such as slapping them, and pinching their legs as they clambered wearily up. A peal of cries from his tortured offspring, particularly the baby, who received a pin in a sensitive part of its little person, so enraged "the Square," that he would have beaten all the boys with his gold-headed cane, had they not jumped away, laughing, and got safely out of the building, only to be back again the next minute.

"You should not allow these boys to hang around the stairs, sir," said the pompous man, planting his foot on the topmost step, and bringing down his cane on the floor with the ring of a watchman's club. "It's trouble enough to come to your panorama, without being annoyed by all the young vagabonds in the village."

"I'm sorry, sir," replied Tiffles, inwardly laughing, "but it would take six strong men to regulate the little rascals."

"Then you ought to employ six strong men, sir. It's your business to see that your patrons are not insulted."

Tiffles could only smile deprecatingly.

"Every exhibition in this hall, for a year past," continued the man, "has been a humbug—an outrage on the common sense of mankind. Perhaps yours is an exception, though, to be candid, I have my doubts of it. Do I understand, sir, that you have travelled in Africa?"

Tiffles indulged in the unjustifiable deception of nodding his head.

"And you mean to say that the sketches for this panorama were taken on the spot?"

"Yes, sir; on the spot—in a horn."

"In a horn! What's that?"

"A technical phrase, sir, which it is hardly worth while to explain at length. Briefly, however, I may say, that no more ingenious or satisfactory mode of taking sketches has been invented."

"Oh! never mind the details. I hate the jargon of Art. I only wished to assure myself that I am not to be imposed on. Well, I think I will risk it, and go in. You can put us on a front seat, I suppose?"

"First come, first served," said Tiffles, amiably, for he had reckoned up, and found that this party brought him a dollar and a quarter, counting the children as half prices, and the baby free.

"Under these circumstances we will go in, though I must confess I expect to be disappointed. You will excuse my plain speaking." The thick-set gentleman thereupon thrust a hand into a pocket, and produced—not a huge roll of bank bills, or a half pint of silver, as Marcus, who eyed him sharply through the pigeon hole, had expected, but—a card, which he poked at Tiffles.

Tiffles recognized it at the first glance. It was one of thirty complimentary tickets that he had caused to be distributed among the leading men of the village that morning, by advice of the landlord; and it bore the name of "C. Skimmerhorn, Esq."

"Welcome, sir, welcome!" said Tiffles, as he observed the dollar and a quarter disappear from his mental horizon, and felt that, but for his indomitable good nature, he would like to kick C. Skimmerhorn, Esq., down stairs. And Tiffles, nobly concealing his disappointment, showed C. Skimmerhorn, Esq., and his domestic caravan to the best front seat. As he turned back to the door, he heard that gentleman say to his spouse, "That fellow looks like a humbug."

A stream of people on the stairs gladdened his eyes. In one sweeping survey, he figured up three dollars. But they proved to be three clergymen, with faded wives, large families, and female relatives stopping with them. Each of the clergymen graciously informed Tiffles, on delivering up his family ticket, that a panorama was one of the few secular entertainments that he could consent to patronize. They doubted very much whether they could have been persuaded to come, but for the recommendation of their evangelical brethren in the city.

Tiffles bowed acknowledgment of the empty honor, and ushered the three clergymen and families to the front row of seats, of which C. Skimmerhorn, Esq., and his train, occupied as much as they could cover by spreading out. Mr. Skimmerhorn recognized, in one of the clergymen, his beloved pastor, and proceeded, in a pleasant, off-hand manner, and a loud voice, to give a few of the reasons which inclined him to pronounce the panorama a humbug.

"Being deadheads," sarcastically observed Tiffles to Marcus Wilkeson, "of course they come early, and take the best seats."

The next customer was a poor but jovial mechanic, having a red-faced little wife slung on his arm. This humble individual paid down fifty cents in bright new silver to the grim treasurer, entered the hall, and took seats about halfway up. "It's a splendid affair, Sally, this 'ere pannyrammer, I'll bet anything." "Sha'n't we enjoy it, John!" returned that healthy young woman.

More work for the amiable Tiffles, but none for the melancholy Wilkeson. Two more clergymen with families, the County Judge, the local railroad agent, all the members of the Board of Freeholders, and several other people, who, according to the landlord of the United States Hotel, were highly influential in moulding public opinion, and were in the habit of receiving free tickets.

"Very good for a school of comparative anatomy," said Tiffles to Marcus (in facetious allusion to the deadheads), "but decidedly bad for my panorama."

Marcus responded with a dreary smile through the pigeon hole.

Then there came a few more mechanics and other plain people, and then a streak of fortune—an entire young ladies' seminary, headed by the preceptress, and divided into squads, each commanded by an assistant teacher acting as drill sergeant. They were admitted at half price (as per advertisement), and brought five dollars and sixty-two cents into the treasury. Tiffles rubbed his eyes at the sight of such a troop of blooming faces, and his hands at the thought of the grand accession to his cash box. The female seminary was accommodated with the two front rows of the best seats left.

Following the seminary, in an unprecedented sequence of luck, was a boys' school, that came whooping up the stairway like a tribe of young Indians, in charge of a venerable sachem in spectacles. In the rush and excitement of the moment, several of them ran toll—a circumstance of which the old gentleman did not take cognizance when he settled with Marcus Wilkeson for their admission at twelve and a half cents *per capita*. Marcus had not noticed it, and Tiffles was far too generous to make a fuss about a few shillings.

Then a party of six flashily dressed young men, who threw away their cigars as they came up stairs, and thrust their quarters through the pigeon hole at Marcus Wilkeson, as if they were good for nothing—which proved to be true of two of them. Being informed of the fact by Marcus, the owners of the counterfeits winked at each other, and whispered, "No go," and then offered a broken bill on a Connecticut bank. This also proved "no go," whereat the sharp practitioners winked again and laughed, and this time paid out good current coin. These were some of the fast men of the village. They took seats behind the female seminary.

Luck changed again, and brought in the landlord, Mr. Persimmon, P. M., Mr. Boolpin, and three more free tickets, with their wives and families. Mr. Boolpin whispered in Tiffles's ear, that he hoped there wouldn't be a row; but it was a hard-looking crowd that had just gone in ahead of him. And there were plenty more of them coming.

The latter observation proved true. The next minute, the stairs swarmed with a jovial party, under the leadership of a gorgeous person, who wore in the middle of his snowy shirt front a cluster diamond pin larger than a ten-cent piece. This was one of the gentlemanly conductors on the railroad; and the mixed company which he had the honor to command, was composed of ticket sellers, freight masters, brakemen, civil engineers, and clerks of liberal dispositions and small salaries in various walks of life. The party was slightly drunk, but not offensive. The gentlemanly conductor paid for himself and associates out of a huge side pocket full of loose silver. They rolled up the hall, and took the nearest spare seats to the female seminary.

Seven and three quarters P. M. arrived. The people in the hall began to stamp with a noise like thunder. Tiffles had marked the heavy boots of the conductor, and could recognize them in the din. Several deep hisses varied the monotony of the performance. There were no persons coming up stairs. The small boys, Tiffles observed with astonishment, had vacated the building some time before, and could now be heard whispering quietly around the door below.

CHAPTER VI.

HUMORS OF THE MANY-HEADED.

Tiffles knew that his time had come, and he accepted the crisis.

Requesting Marcus to pocket the funds, shut up the shop, and leave the door to take care of itself, Tiffles marched boldly to his doom. Previous to extinguishing the candles in the exhibition hall, he went behind the curtain, and there found the idiot sitting patiently at the crank, and rehearsing, in a low tone, the code of signals which had been adopted. Patching was also there. He shrugged his shoulders in the French style as Tiffles came in, but said not a word. Tiffles proceeded straight to a bottle which stood on a window sill, and took a long drink from it, and then passed it to Patching, who mutely did the same, and, in turn, handed it to the idiot, who pulled at it with great gusto, in the manner of a rational person.

Feeling that it would be superfluous to repeat his instructions to so sagacious an idiot, Tiffles immediately presented himself before the audience again, with a long stick, or wand, for pointing out the beauties of the panorama.

"Ladies and gentlemen, I am about to exhibit to you the Panorama of Africa. You have all heard of Africa."

Voice. "Consider'ble."

"True, my friend; therefore you will be well prepared to enjoy the pictorial attractions which I am about to unfold."

Voice. "H'ist the rag."

"My friend—who has no doubt paid his quarter—I respect your request. The rag *is* about to be h'isted. But, before that ceremony is proceeded with, I would ask the gentlemen sitting nearest the candles to be good enough to blow them out."

Never was request more cheerfully complied with. There was a scramble of six or seven tall young men to each candle; and, at several of the candles, a brisk but friendly struggle took place between rival aspirants for the privilege. The room was then in total darkness, save a small gleam which came through the partly opened door from a solitary tallow in the entry, and the dull reflection of the panorama lights through the curtain.

Some of the effects of this sudden extinguishment were extraordinary. The female seminary all screamed slightly. The boys' school all laughed, and several were heard to say, "Prime fun, a'n't it?" The railroad conductor and his friends coughed fictitiously, and said, "Oh! oh!" "A'n't you ashamed!" "Look out for pockets!" "Thief in the house!" and other playful things, which put the entire audience in good humor. But the strangest and most unexpected occurrence, was a grand rush, as of a herd of wild bulls, on the stairs, accompanied by the dousing of the one remaining light in the entry. Another moment, and over a hundred of the choicest juvenile spirits tore into the hall, and knocked over each other and everybody else in a frantic contest for free seats. The young ladies' seminary screamed in concert, and all the elderly ladies cried, "Oh my!" "Good gracious!" "What's that?"

"Only the boys," said Tiffles, with unruffled composure. "Let them come. It is a moral entertainment, and will do them good."

After a pause of about three minutes, giving the boys time to seat themselves, and the screams, mutterings, and laughter of the rest of the audience to die away, Tiffles said:

"Now, ladies and gentlemen, I will introduce you to sunrise in the Bight of Benin."

This was the preconcerted signal for the raising of the curtain, which office was performed by Patching, without a hitch. The gorgeous proem, or introduction to the panorama, was then for the first time disclosed to the public. Patching blushed as he thought of the vile pandering to popular taste of which he had been guilty.

There was a dead calm for a minute. Tiffles was silent, in order that he might not interrupt the quiet admiration of the spectators. The spectators were silent, because they could not exactly understand the scene, and did not know whether to laugh, hiss, or applaud. The silence was broken by a boy in the back part of the hall:

"I say, Mister, is that a cartwheel on top of a stone wall?"

"No, sonny, not exactly," said Tiffles. "What your uneducated eyes mistake for a cartwheel, is the rising sun. The objects that your immature judgment confounds with spokes, are rays. Your stone wall, it is hardly necessary to inform riper intellects, is a distant range of mountains. It is one of Ceccarini's happiest efforts."

"Hurrah for Checkerberry!" cried another lad, mistaking the name of the high (imaginary) Italian artist.

"Are we to understand, sir, that this is a rolling prairie in the foreground?" asked a deep voice, which Tiffles at once recognized as emanating from C. Skimmerhorn, Esq.

"Oh! no, sir; it is the Bight of Benin; and I must say, though, perhaps, I am too partial, that Ceccarini never did a better thing."

"The *what* of Benin?" asked the voice.

"The Bight—or, in other words, as you may not be familiar with geography, the Bay of Benin."

"Then why not say Bay, sir?" replied C. Skimmerhorn, Esq., stung with the allusion to his want of geographical knowledge. "Why this mystery about terms!"

There were cries of "Go it, Square." "Dry up, old boy!" "Propel with the show!" &c., &c. Tiffles adopted the latter suggestion, and without answering the lawyer's insinuation, proceeded to point out the natural appearance of the waves, the truthfulness of the distant mountains, the absolute fidelity of the sunrise. "And here let me answer an objection in advance. It may be said that this sunrise does not look like a sunrise in Jersey. Admit it. Neither do the snakes (*sensation*)—neither do the snakes which I am about to exhibit (*increased sensation*, and Oh! me's! from the Young

Ladies' Seminary) resemble the familiar green or striped serpent of your own peaceful fields. Neither do the tigers, which I shall presently have the honor of showing to you (*renewed sensation*), bear any marked affinity to the serene woodchuck that burrows in your happy hills. The sunrises and sunsets, the boa constrictors, the tigers, and the other phenomena of Africa, are all immense, gorgeous, and peculiar. They must be judged by themselves, and not by comparison. My hearers will be kind enough to bear this in mind, as we go on."

He then went on to repeat a great many statistics concerning the population and resources of Africa. He had read up for these facts and figures, under the impression that they would interest the solid portion of his audience. But he soon found out that he interested nobody (perhaps because the solid portion of audiences is a myth), and finally yielded to general requests of "Push ahead!" "Fire away!" "Start your train!" (the latter from the gentlemanly conductor and friends.)

Tiffles therefore whistled once, and the panorama commenced moving slowly and steadily. The idiot, the rollers, and the lights, all worked well.

From the Bight of Benin, the voyaging spectators took an excursion up the river.

The uninterrupted stretch of deep blue for water, and light blue for sky, and green for the farther bank, with occasional palm trees looking like long-handled pickaxes, seemed to satisfy them. At any rate they looked on, and found no fault in words; which both Tiffles and Patching took for an auspicious sign. Tiffles kept step with his explanations.

His method was this. When the palm tree came in sight, he would give a minute account of that noble tropical growth, and the many uses to which it and its products could be put. When a flock of wild ducks appeared sailing majestically on the river, he would entertain his auditors with a circumstantial description of how the natives caught wild ducks. A boat or hollow log, with a human figure, suggested a reference to the progress which the African had made in marine architecture and the science of navigation. In this way, Tiffles thought he was beguiling his customers. Some low sounds, like suppressed hisses, soon convinced him of his error.

"I beg your pardon, Professor," said a thick-set voice, which he always recognized as coming from C. Skimmerhorn, Esq.; "but it seems to me that this portion of your panorama is a little monotonous. I presume that in this suggestion, I express the sentiments of my fellow citizens here assembled." Cries of "Go on, Square!" "That's so!" mingled with a vigorous stamping of feet and catcalls from the boys in the background, proved, alas! the truth of the conjecture.

Tiffles coughed twice for the idiot to stop, and was sagaciously obeyed. "In behalf of Africa," he remarked, "representing her, as I may say, on this occasion, I would beg leave to apologize to the learned gentleman for the poverty of her scenery, at this stage of the panorama. If Africa had been aware of the learned gentleman's preferences, she would, doubtless, have got up some stunning effects for him in places where now you see only a river, a sky, and a strip of green bank, all unadorned, precisely as they are."

The exquisite irony of this retort pleased the audience, and elicited general though faint applause, and several cries of "Shut up, Skim!" "Got your match, old boy!" "Oh! let the man go on!" The last remark issued from the gentlemanly conductor, and fell with peculiar pleasure on Tiffles's ears.

"One word more, and I am done," resumed the lawyer, who was professionally calm amid scenes of disturbance. "I only wish to elicit the truth. Have you, and your artist (Mr. Chicory, I think you call him), or either of you, actually gone over the scenery here represented. We wish to understand that point!"

"We have, both of us, gone over this scenery repeatedly." This was true, as both Tiffles and Patching, anticipating some such question, had stepped over the canvas back and forth, in rolling and unrolling it, several times. "Is the eminent counsellor satisfied?"

"Oh! yes," said C. Skimmerhorn, Esq., in a voice which signified that he knew the panorama was a humbug, but, unfortunately, couldn't prove it.

One cough, and the panorama started again—but a little too fast. Tiffles stamped once, and the idiot reduced the speed, until it was too slow. Two stamps brought it right. The river soon disappeared in a swamp, where the alligators' heads protruding above the water gave Tiffles an opportunity to describe several terrific combats which he had enjoyed with those pugnacious creatures. This entertained the audience for several minutes.

"Have you no full views of alligators, sir?" asked a voice which Tiffles presumed, from its solemn inflection, to come from a clergyman.

"None at all, sir. The African alligator persists in keeping out of sight. You never see anything but his head—except his tail, as represented here." Tiffles pointed with his wand to something that looked like the end of a fence rail sticking out of the water. "True Art, sir, sacrifices effect for Truth."

"Certainly, sir. Truth is what we are all after," replied the clergyman. But there was an indefinable something in his voice that indicated a wish for more alligator—much more.

The swamp ended in a dry jungle, interspersed with palm trees, elephants, lions, tigers, and serpents. Tiffles counted upon interesting his audience here. Snakes were first on the list. Two heads, with expanded jaws and forked tongues, were looking at each other above the jungle, and two tails were interlocked, also above the jungle, a few feet off. This conveyed the idea of two boa constrictors fighting. Other heads and other tails—there was always a tail for every head—stuck up at regular intervals about. He stopped the panorama with a cough, and said:

"The entire population of this particular jungle are—boa constrictors of unprecedented size and ferocity."

Tiffles heard a rustle of fans and dresses not far off. It

was the whole female seminary shuddering. There was also a general movement throughout the audience as of people adjusting themselves to obtain a good sight.

"These boa constrictors, so admirably delineated here,"—commenced Tiffles.

"Where?" said the voice of a country gentleman. "I don't see any bore constructors."

"Nor I." "Nor I." "Trot 'em out!" "Show 'em up!" "Produce your snakes!" Such were the remarks that resounded through the hall.

"Oh, no!" "Don't!" "Please don't!" emanated from several girlish voices.

"My fair auditors have no cause for alarm. I have no living snakes to show. I might have captured several hundred, and brought them to this country and exhibited them, but, in deference to the well-known aversion cherished toward snakes by cultivated communities, I forbore to do so. The only boa constrictors that I have, are now before you. These are their heads. These their tails" (indicating the termini of the snakes).

Now, the spectators—or a large number of them—had suffered fearful expectations of seeing real snakes. When, therefore, it was announced that these harmless daubs, resembling, at a distance, some variety of tropical vegetation, were the only snakes they were to see, there was a feeling, first, of relief, and then of disappointment.

The disappointment manifested itself in low hisses, and exclamations, such as "Humbug!" "Gammon!" "Swindle!" Tiffles made several beginnings of excellent snake stories, of which he was the hero, but was checked by the tumult. Finding the snakes were not popular, he determined to try the tigers, lions, and other beasts of prey farther on. He coughed once emphatically, and the canvas moved like clock-work.

Before it had journeyed five feet, somebody on the front row of seats coughed twice in precisely the same manner as

Tiffles. The idiot, supposing the signal came from his employer, stopped. Tiffles, perceiving the mistake, coughed again, and the motion was resumed; when a double cough resounded from the front seat, and the motion ceased.

Then Tiffles realized that his system of signals was understood by somebody. What should he do? He could not stop the free, universal right to cough. Therefore he stepped to the corner of the curtain, raised it, and said, in a voice loud enough to be heard by the audience, "Stoop, whenever I want you to 'stop,' or 'go on,' or 'faster,' or 'slower,' I will say so. You understand?"

"Puffickly," replied the gifted idiot.

"I say, boys, Stoop's in there," shouted the somebody that had coughed.

"Stoop!" "Stoop!" "Bully for Stoop!" "Come out o' that, Stoop!" was shouted all over the house; but Stoop remained faithful to his post, and calmly ground away at the crank.

Suddenly it occurred to some boy to yell, "Boo! boo!" whereat the other boys laughed, and took up the chorus, "Boo! boo!"

The canvas moved less steadily, slackening for a moment, and then shooting ahead, as if the propelling power were the subject of strange perturbation. The roguish boys, and the men too, and, chief of them, that practical humorist of a conductor, observing this, screamed, "Boo! boo! boo! boo!" all the louder. Tiffles knew that the critical time had come, and philosophically laughed at the ruin of his last grand project, as he had laughed at the ruin of forty other grand projects in their day.

The panorama stopped without a signal this time. A hoarse voice screamed, "Gorryfus! Gosh thunder! By jimminy!" The curtain was jerked aside, and Stoop rushed into the hall like a fury. Coming out of a place partly lighted into one totally dark, his first move was to run blindly into Tiffles, nearly knocking that gentleman off his legs.

"Hold on, Stoop! Hold on!" shouted Tiffles, with what was left of his breath. But the idiot only screamed, "Gosh thunder! Gorryfus!" and darted for the main aisle, intending to run a muck among his persecutors. There was a general scrambling of the boys to avoid this incarnated wrath. The whole female seminary, and all the ladies present, screamed together.

CHAPTER VII.

SCENES NOT IN THE BILLS.

The enraged idiot struck out right and left, without hurting anybody—the objects of his vengeance contriving to elude him in the dark. Most of the sturdy blows which he dealt, using his arms like flails, fell upon the railings of the seats, and only bruised his hands. Just as he had caught a boy by the collar, and was about to take a twist in his hair, the door opened, and a light appeared. It came from three candles borne by three men.

This apparition caused the furious idiot to suspend hostilities on the instant.

All eyes were turned toward the three men. All voices were hushed. There was a whisper in the air that something strange was about to happen.

The man who entered first was a stranger, who moved and looked about in the quick, nervous way born of city life. The other two men were well-known residents of the village. Some of the audience had had unpleasant cause to know them.

Having locked the door, and stationed his associates in a position to command the windows, the stranger walked quickly up the aisle, bearing his lighted candle, and said, in a loud voice, which fell strangely on the hushed assemblage:

"Marcus Wilkeson will be kind enough to give himself up. Upon my honor, he cannot escape." This was said with a charming politeness.

A tall figure arose at the wall end of one of the back seats.

"I am Marcus Wilkeson. What do you want with me, sir?" His voice trembled, and his face was livid.

"To go with me to New York, Mr. Wilkeson," said the tall stranger, quickly. "Thank you for your promptness in answering. The only clue that I had, was the hasty measure I took of you this morning, when I was watching for an escaped convict at Cortlandt-street ferry. Perhaps you remember seeing me there, sir?"

Marcus, though the sudden shock had almost stunned him, at once recalled the man who had eyed him narrowly at the ferry that morning.

The two other candle bearers had stepped forward as Marcus declared himself, and were about to lay hold of him, when the first man smilingly pushed them back, and said:

"Don't touch him. It's all right. Mr. Wilkeson is a gentleman, and will go quietly."

To Marcus he said, apologetically:

"Two Jersey constables I got to assist me. They don't do things exactly in the style of Detective Leffingwell."

Marcus recognized the name; and so terrified was he at the thoughts which it conjured up, that his tongue clove to the roof of his mouth. The scene was like a horrid dream.

"Everything is regular, sir," continued the detective. "We have a requisition for you from the Governor of this State. It was obtained by telegraph from Trenton. You will excuse my dropping on you in this way; but I wanted to take you to New York to-night, as the inquest meets again at ten o'clock to-morrow morning."

"The inquest!—what inquest? Tell me, in God's name!" said Marcus, finding his voice at last.

"Inquest! There must have been a murder committed.' "What is it?" "Tell us, Mr. Policeman." The question was asked on all sides.

"Now I *didn't* want a scene," said Detective Leffingwell, politely, "and I won't have one. Mr. Wilkeson and I understand each other. The word 'inquest' dropped out of my mouth before I thought."

"As heaven is above us, we do not understand each other!" said Marcus. "Tell me, pray tell me at once, or I shall go mad."

"Anything to please you," replied the officer; "but I can't bear these explanations in public. It isn't my way of doing business." He then leaned forward, and whispered in the ear of Marcus.

"Great God!" was all that Marcus could say. Then he sank to the seat, and bowed his head in agony.

Tiffles, who had forced his way to his friend's side during the excitement, threw his arms about him, and said:

"Never mind appearances, Marcus. I'll stake my life you are innocent of the charge, whatever it is."

"Oh! you're a humbug," remarked C. Skimmerhorn, Esq.

"Call me and my panorama a humbug, if you please; but Mr. Wilkeson is a gentleman and a man of honor." Tiffles's face beamed with a strange kindness. He looked up, and saw the idiot standing near him. His small eyes filled with tears as he gazed with an expression of intelligent pity at the crushed man. Tiffles could have hugged the idiot, not only as the most sensible man, but the best-hearted one he had seen in the village.

C. Skimmerhorn, Esq., would have retorted severely, but his attention, and that of all the crowd, was drawn, at that moment, to a citizen who came forward, and, in a state of breathless excitement, said he guessed he knew what it all meant. He was in New York that afternoon, and read, in one of the evening papers, an account of a dreadful murder committed on an old man named Minford. The supposed murderer, the paper said, was a Mr. Wilkes or Wilkson.

"Now I hope you are satisfied," said Detective Leffingwell, looking around with contempt at his hearers.

A slight scream was heard from the corner of a seat near by. From the beginning of this unpleasant affair, it was observed that a plainly dressed woman—a seamstress accom panying the family of a Mr. Graft—had become very pale and nervous, and had been seen to move uneasily in her seat. This woman had fainted away. She it was who had stared sc strangely at Marcus in the car that morning.

Mrs. Graft and her two daughters promptly removed the fainting woman to the entry, where the fresh air soon restored her, and she was sent home.

"No wonder the women faint away, when you crowd round here so stupidly," said the officer, momentarily losing his temper. "Please step back, now, and let Mr. Wilkeson and me get out. We must leave for New York by the next train —and that starts in fifteen minutes." The detective referred to his watch. "Are you ready, sir?" tapping Marcus gently on the shoulder.

Marcus rose, and displayed a face haggard with grief.

They all whispered, or thought, "He is guilty."

"I am ready," said he; "but I call heaven to witness that I know nothing of this crime."

The detective bowed courteously, and then said:

"I also have summons for Mr. Tiffles and Mr. Patching, gentlemen connected with this panorama, as witnesses. They will please step forward."

"I am Mr. Tiffles," said that person. "Wesley is my panoramic name."

This disclosure caused a small sensation. "I knew the man was a humbug from the start," whispered C. Skimmerhorn, Esq., to a friend at his elbow. "I'd like to prosecute him for swindling."

"And I am Mr. Patching," exclaimed the artist, presenting himself.

It should be here stated, that, when the disturbances of the evening first set in, Patching, in pure disgust at the bad taste of the audience, had quietly dropped himself out of the second story window at the rear of the stage, and had been skulking in the back lot ever since. Having heard, outside, of the arrest of Marcus Wilkeson, on an unknown charge, he had plucked up courage and friendship enough to reënter the hall, and tender his aid and consolation to that unhappy man. He came in just in time to hear his name called.

"So that's the chap they called Chicory, or Checkerberry," whispered C. Skimmerhorn, Esq. "Anybody can see he is a swindler by his slouched hat, and beard. *Shouldn't* I enjoy having a good case against him!"

Pigworth, J. P., landlord of the United States Hotel, and Mr. Boolpin, proprietor, came forward with their little bills, and demanded immediate payment. This financial difficulty was arranged in one minute by the genius of Wesley Tiffles. After paying Stoop one dollar and a half (that excellent idiot crying, and vowing that he didn't want it), the rest of the proceeds, deducting enough for fares to New York, were divided equally between the two other creditors; and the panorama and all the appurtenances were left as a joint security for remaining obligations. The panorama was worth twice the debts, to be cut into window shades. After some grumbling, Messrs. Pigworth and Boolpin accepted the terms.

Five minutes later, the polite detective and his party started for New York. There was a great number of people at the station to see them off, but only one to say "good-by." That one was the man-boy Stoop, who cried as if his great, simple heart would break.

BOOK EIGHTH.

A DRAMATIC INTERLUDE.

CHAPTER I.

THE OVERTURE.

It was the last of a delightful series of dramatic nights at Mrs. Slapman's; and her house was quite filled with embodied Poetry, Travels, Dramatic Literature, Music, Art, and the Sciences.

The dramatic arrangements of Mrs. Slapman's house were simple, but effective. A curtain, with rings, hung across the north end of the parlor, established the confines of the stage, which was on a level with the floor, and covered with green baize to represent rural scenes, or a three-ply carpet to indicate refined interiors. Against the wall were rollers, from which scenes could be dropped, affording perspectives of country, or streets, or gilded saloons, as the necessities of the drama required. There were six of these scenes, all painted by Patching (to oblige Mrs. Slapman) in his leisure moments, which were numerous; and they all exhibited evidences of his style. Six sets of flies, or side scenes, matching with the rear views, had been executed by a scene-painter's assistant, whom Mrs. Slapman had taken under her patronage, and were thought, by some persons, superior to Patching's efforts. Such was the belittling criticism to which that great artist was constantly subjected. There was a space of about four feet between the top of the curtain and the high ceiling. The light from the parlor chandelier directly in front, aided by six gas jets behind the scenes, made the whole performance and performers as clear as noonday.

This miniature theatre was constructed of portable frames, which could be put up or taken down in half an hour, and was the ingenious invention of the scene-painter's assistant. When it was removed, the only traces of its former presence were two brass-headed spikes in the walls, from which the side curtains depended.

These spikes imparted anguish to the mind of Mr. Slapman whenever he gazed upon them. Mrs. S. had heard him say, that "some people would look well hanging up there." By "some people," he was supposed to mean the gentlemen who participated in her dramatic entertainments. Mrs. S. bore the cruel remark meekly, merely replying that perhaps he had better try the strength of the spikes first, by suspending himself from one of them.

The audience, usually numbering about fifty, were seated in chairs, which filled the parlor, with the exception of a space of ten feet in front of the stage. A fair view of the entire proceedings could be had from all but the two back rows of chairs, the occupants of which were compelled to imagine the attachment of feet and ankles to the several characters of the drama.

From the left wing of the stage a door opened into the hall, affording communication by the staircase to the ladies' and gentlemen's dressing rooms on the floor above. On the third floor (it was known to some of the guests) was the private apartment of Mr. Slapman. A strong smell of cigar smoke, as of one fumigating sullenly and furiously, was the unvarying proof of his presence in the house. On this eventful night, he had been seen, at an early hour, pacing up and down the hall of his third floor, belching forth clouds of smoke, like Vesuvius just before a fiery eruption.

People who were in the sad secret of Mrs. Slapman's household sorrows, looked at each other and smiled, but said nothing; for it was a point of good breeding not to allude to him in conversation. The newer guests, unaware of the melancholy facts in the case, supposed that the restless gentleman on the third floor was some one of Mrs. Slapman's eccentric friends, working out an idea. Mrs. Slapman paid no attention to her jealous spouse, imagining that he would smoke away his wrath quietly, as usual, and not interfere with the evening's amusement. Hitherto, on occasions, he had done nothing more disagreeable than to open the parlor door furtively, cast one wild look inside, and then suddenly withdraw his head, gently slamming the door after him.

The play of the evening was written "expressly for the occasion" by a gentleman who had produced one melodrama at a Bowery theatre, and failed to produce a large number of melodramas at all the theatres in Broadway. Mrs. Slapman, a true patroness of genius, kindly permitted this gentleman to prepare all her charades, and gratified him, on several occasions by bringing out some of the minor plays from his stuffed portfolio.

By eight o'clock all the chairs were filled, and the actors and actresses were still lingering over their toilet. After waiting ten minutes longer, and crossing and uncrossing their legs repeatedly, the audience stamped and whistled very much in the manner of an impatient crowd at a real theatre. Mrs. Slapman relished these little ebullitions of natural feeling, because it made the illusion of her "Thespian parlor" (as she called it) more complete.

At eight and a quarter o'clock, the orchestra, consisting of two flutes and a violin, issued from behind the curtain, and seated itself before some music stands ranged against the wall. The performers were amateurs (two bookkeepers, and a cashier in private life), and could not have been hired to play for any amount of money, though they were always willing to favor a few friends. Mrs. Slapman humored them in this whim, and they played regularly at her private theatricals.

After a few nods and facetious remarks to their friends in the audience (familiarities from which a paid orchestra would have been totally cut off), the musicians dashed into a new overture, composed by Signor Mancussi, also "expressly for the occasion."

This musical composition had been rehearsed the week previous in the presence of a select party of amateurs and critics, and had been pronounced, by the sub-editor of a weekly paper, "remarkable for its breadth and color." Under these circumstances, the overture was listened to with much interest at first, which abated as the music progressed. Touching the merits of "color" and "breadth" there might be some grounds of doubt, but none whatever concerning its "length."

It lasted until twenty minutes of nine; and, toward the close, faint scrapings of dissatisfaction were heard, which would have been more audible had Signor Mancussi not been present. As the last twang of the fiddle died on the air, M. Bartin was heard by several persons to say, "Bah! a bad hash from Rossini and Auber." The remark was reported to Signor Mancussi, and did not tend to enhance his friendly regards for the other gentleman.

CHAPTER II.

CURTAIN UP.

At eight and three quarters P. M. the curtain was rung up, and discovered a rustic scene, in the midst of which Mrs. Slapman (Fidelia) was seated. She was dressed in a white frock with low neck, and a flat hat, and was trimmed out with red ribbons in all directions. She looked young and pretty. Only an anxious knitting of her eyebrows revealed the cares and troubles of intellect. Mrs. Slapman was applauded by a unanimous clapping of hands. She was seated in a red-velvet rocking chair, at a small but costly table, on which stood an expensive vase filled with flowers. These properties, though few, were intended to signify boundless affluence and luxury. Fidelia languidly waved a jewelled fan, and sighed. "Will he never come?" said she.

She had hardly made this remark, when, by a singular coincidence, Alberto (Overtop) entered from the left wing, and threw himself, with as much grace as his tights would permit, at her feet. She emitted a small shriek, and gave him her hand to kiss, which he did with ecstasy. Alberto was habited like an Italian gentleman in good circumstances; and no one would have suspected his poverty, if he had not commenced the dialogue by an affecting allusion to his last *scudi*, which brought tears to the eyes of the fair Fidelia.

Such trifling questions as lovers alone can ask and answer then passed between them; and at last came the solemn interrogatory from the kneeling Alberto: "And will you always love me, dearest?"

Fidelia turned her meek orbs toward the ceiling, raised her hand, said "*Forever!*" and was about to add, "I swear," when Bidette (Miss Wick) rushed upon the scene with the intelligence, "He comes."

"Who?" asked Alberto.

"My father!" shrieked Fidelia. "Go—that way." She pointed with her small alabaster hand to the left wing.

Alberto vanished as per request, while Fidelia, with well-affected calmness, commenced humming an opera air, and fanning herself. Bidette, the favorite maid, pretended to readjust a flower in her mistress's hair. These feminine artifices were to throw the coming father off his scent.

But the father (Mr. Johnsone, the junior of a small book-publishing house) was sharp eyed, though he lacked spectacles. As he emerged from the right wing, he caught a distinct view of a pair of soles disappearing in the distance, and benignantly asked: "Who is that, my child?"

The child answered: "Only the postman, pa."

"Where is the letter?" he asked.

"Please, sir," interrupted Bidette, observing her mistress's confusion, "there wasn't no letter. He mistook the house for another, sir."

The father nodded his head to express his complete satisfaction with this explanation, and then told Bidette to leave the spot, as he had something of the utmost importance to tell his daughter. Bidette pouted, and withdrew, giving a bewitching shake of her striped calico dress, to signify her hatred of brutal fathers. This touch of nature drew plaudits from those among the audience who were but slightly acquainted with Miss Wick. The others looked on with critical indifference.

The father took a chair, thrust out his legs like a reigning prince, and proceeded, in a story of unnecessary length, to tell his daughter that he owed one hundred and seventy thousand florins to Signor Rodicaso, and would be a ruined man in forty-eight hours if that sum were not paid. Life, in that event, would be simply insupportable. He had procured a pistol to blow out his brains, but had subsequently concluded to make one more effort to save himself. He would, therefore, appeal to his daughter, *as* a father, and ask her to marry Signor Rodicaso, and so liquidate the debt, to-morrow. He did not wish to influence her choice—far from it—but, if she did not consent, he should feel under the painful necessity of shooting himself on the spot.

The father produced a pistol, and held it to his left ear.

Fidelia, looking like a marble statue of grief, said, in a low but perfectly audible voice: "Stay! I will wed him." This was enunciated with the calmness of despair. Not a gesture, nor a twinge of the features, nor an accent to indicate emotion of any kind. It was in quiet efforts like these that Mrs. Slapman excelled.

When the applause elicited by this stroke of genius had ceased, Mr. Chickson (Signor Rodicaso) came rather awkwardly upon the stage. His eyes (and, it might be added, his legs) rolled absently about, as if he were endeavoring to recall his part, or were in the inward act of composing a poem.

"Your future husband, Fidelia," said the father.

Fidelia rose from her seat—still imperturbable.

Chickson advanced with a sliding motion, and then paused, as if he had forgotten what to do. Mrs. Slapman was heard to whisper something (probably the cue), but he only rolled his eyes heavily in response. A look of displeasure marred her serene features, and, instead of fainting away in Signor Rodicaso's arms, as she should have done, she dropped into the embrace of her father, taking that personage quite unexpectedly, and nearly knocking him off his chair.

Chickson projected himself forward at the same time to catch her, and, in so doing, lost his balance, and just escaped, by an effort, from sprawling on the floor.

Then he looked helplessly at the audience; and there was no longer any doubt entertained that Chickson was slightly intoxicated. Getting drunk, now and then, was an infirmity of Chickson's genius.

The stage manager had the good sense to ring down the curtain on this painful scene, and, the next moment, there was a dull sound, as of somebody falling on the floor behind the green baize.

After an interval of fifteen minutes—protracted by the "unexpected indisposition" of the poet, and the consequent necessity of intrusting Signor Rodicaso to other hands—the curtain rises again, and discloses Alberto in a humble cot, surrounded by three-legged stools, and other evidences of extreme poverty. He is seated on a rickety table (in preference to the greater uncertainty of the stools), his arms are folded, and his head droops upon his breast.

In this attitude, he begins to soliloquize, and informs the audience (what they did not know before) that, from a clump of shrubbery, he had seen fully as much as they of the preceding scene. He does not blame Fidelia. Oh! no. In her cruel dilemma, she could do no less. But he curses—and curses again—and continues to curse for some time—that Fate which deprives him of the "paltry means" (one hundred and seventy thousand florins) to buy off the "heartless monster" (Rodicaso). Having wreaked himself upon Destiny to his own satisfaction, he suddenly remembers that he has not eaten anything for thirty-six hours. He feels in all his pockets successively, but finds nothing. He then draws from his bosom a portrait of his father, set with antique gems. He gazes upon it reverently, kisses it, and says: "Shall I part with this sacred memento for vulgar bread? Never! Let me die!" He restores the portrait to his bosom, folds his arms again, inclines his head, and shuts his eyes, as if preparing to expire comfortably.

All this time, a fat red face, belonging to a corpulent body, has been watching the depressed lover from the right wing. As Alberto utters the last sad ejaculation, a thick hand attached to a short arm raises a kerchief to a pair of small eyes in this fat red face, and wipes them. Then the stout gentleman reflects a moment, nods his head approvingly, draws forth a wallet, opens it slowly, takes out some paper that rustles like bank notes, produces a memorandum book, writes a few lines on one of the leaves hastily with a pencil, tears out the leaf, encloses the leaf and the bank notes in an envelope, emerges with his entire figure into the full light of the stage, walks stealthily toward Alberto with a pair of creaking shoes that would have waked the soundest sleeper, places the note on the table by his side, raises his hands to heaven, murmuring, "God bless the boy!" and retires in the same feline but tumultuous manner.

This mysterious visitor was Bignolio (Matthew Maltboy), a rich money lender, uncle of Alberto, and commonly reported to be the "tightest old skinflint in Venice."

After a pause, scarcely long enough to allow his uncle's heavy footsteps to die away in the distance, Alberto came out of his revery. His first act was to look at the ceiling, then at the floor, then all about him—everywhere but at the note on the table. At last, when nothing else remained to be scrutinized, his eyes naturally fell upon this valuable communication.

"What is this?" he asked. Then he answered his own question by opening the letter, and reading it, as follows:

"VENICE, Oct. 16, ——.

"DEAR NEPHEW:

"I have watched you, and know all. You are indeed the son of your father, and, I am proud to add, the nephew of your uncle. Enclosed are sixty thousand florins. Go to Jinkerini Bros., on the Rialto, and buy up judgments that they hold against Rodicaso for three times that amount, and offset them against old Corpetto's debts. Rodicaso conceals his property so well, that none has ever been found to satisfy these judgments. Drive a sharp bargain, and show yourself a chip of the old block. Keep the balance for your wedding gift.

"Farewell—till we meet again.

"BIGNOLIO."

"Dear, dear uncle!" exclaimed Alberto, carefully buttoning up his pocket over the funds, and kissing the letter in transports of joy. "And only yesterday he would not lend me a *scudi* to get my dinner. Generous man! how have I wronged him! Now, Fate, I will floor thee and Rodicaso together."

[Exit Alberto, rapidly, by shortest land route to the Rialto.]

Overtop's acting, throughout this difficult scene, was of a superior order. Nothing could be more natural, for instance, than the buttoning up of his pocket over his uncle's gift. But neither that, nor the other strong point, where he exulted in the finest tragedy tones over the anticipated downfall of Fate and Rodicaso, produced the slightest sensation among his hearers. Matthew Maltboy paid the penalty of his intimate relations with Overtop, by an equal unpopularity. His fine rendition of the character of Bignolio might as well have been played to a select company of gravestones.

There was a necessary interval of twenty minutes for the fitting out of the stage—during which time the amateur orchestra performed selections from "Semiramide," but, happily, not loud enough to interfere with the easy flow of conversation all over the room. The second flutist, while looking over his shoulder angrily at the garrulous audience, executed a false note, which almost threw the first (and only) violinist into fits. In turning round to rebuke the errant performer, the violinist struck his elbow against a similar projection of the other flutist, and knocked a false note out of that gentleman too, besides momentarily ruffling his temper. This little episode diffused unhappiness over the entire music.

CHAPTER III.

ACT SECOND.

THE spectators had been told that there were imposing stage effects in the second and last act; and they were not disappointed. The entire front was filled with furniture, real mahogany and brocade, leaving barely room for human beings to walk about. The background was a perspective of pillars, conveying the idea of unlimited saloons, all opening into each other. Three Bohemian vases, filled with natural flowers, were placed on pedestals in places where they would be least in the way, if it were possible to make such a discrimination. But the great feature of the scene was a magnificent paper chandelier of nine candles, which hung from the centre of the framework, and made every spectator, while he admired, tremble with fear that it would set the house on fire.

At a small table in front, covered by a rich cloth, sat the heroine, dressed in a gorgeousness of apparel that mocked her misery. Beneath the gems that studded her bosom, there was supposed to be unappeasable wretchedness; and the white brow, covered with a spangled wreath, was presumed to ache with mental agony. She was pale and beautiful. Murmurs of applause ran round the apartment.

By her side was the faithful Bidette, armed with a bottle

of salts. She bent affectionately over her mistress, and asked if she wanted anything.

"Nothing, my child—but death," was the thrilling reply.

Bidette was taken somewhat aback. She made a respectful pause. Then she said:

"But, my dear mistress, though you do not love Signor Rodicaso——"

"In Heaven's name, stop, child! You are piercing my heart with a hot iron. Name not love to me. Henceforth I erase it from the tablets of my brain. Now go on" (with tranquil despair).

"I was about to say, dear mistress, please, that Signor Rodicaso has a splendid town house, and a beautiful country seat (they say), and thousands of acres of land, which will all be yours——"

The eloquent grief of her mistress's face checked the maid.

"Bidette," she said, "I shall want but a small portion of all his lands."

"What do you mean, dear mistress?" asked the frightened maid.

"Only enough for—a grave," was the harrowing reply.

This dreary dialogue was here interrupted by the appearance of the father in tights, knee buckles, velvet coat, ruffles, a powdered wig, and a general air of having been got up for a great occasion. He carefully picked his way through the furniture to his daughter, and kissed her on the forehead.

"Are you happy, my dear daughter?" he asked.

"Happy? Oh! yes, father, I am *so* happy! See how I smile." So saying, she made a feeble attempt to smile, which was a most artistic failure, and brought out another tribute of applause.

The father, not detecting the sad irony of the smile, replied:

"It is indeed fortunate that you are enabled not only to achieve your own happiness by this marriage, but also to redeem what is dearer to me than all else in this world—my mercantile credit. But here they come."

"Here they come," was the cue which was to bring in Signor Rodicaso and party; but the Signor was momentarily delayed by the giving way of two buttons in his doublet. When he had repaired damages with pins as well as he could, he emerged into view, accompanied by a notary and a pair of friendly witnesses. The Signor, this time, proved to be the author of the play, who had kindly consented, at five minutes' notice, to take the part in which the hapless Chickson had broken down. Stealing behind, in the shadow of the others, was distinctly seen (by all except the people on the stage) the burly form of Uncle Bignolio.

To satisfy the conventional idea of dramatic concealment, his left leg was plunged in obscurity behind the scenes, while the rest of his figure stood out in bold relief. He was observed, by those who watched him narrowly, to send a pleasant wink and nod to Bidette, who responded with a scarcely perceptible pout.

On the entrance of Signor Rodicaso and friends, Fidelia rose, turned toward them, and made a profound courtesy, as if to signify her abject submission. Signor Rodicaso bowed with equal profundity, and straightway proceeded to make a speech to the lady, in which he spoke of the wild idolatry that he had long felt for her, and alluded most disparagingly to his own merits. If the Signor's statements could be relied on, he was totally unworthy of an alliance with the beautiful Fidelia; in fact, was a "dog who would be proud only but to bask in the sunshine of her smile."

This singular address, extending over "one length," or forty-five lines, excited little less astonishment on the stage than in the audience. For it was not set down in the acting copy, but had been improvised by the author, to better the part of the Signor, which, as originally written, was destitute of long and effective orations.

Fidelia smiled, and could only reply to this unpremeditated

effusion by several modest inclinations of the head. The other actors and actress turned aside to conceal their grins. Uncle Bignolio alone fulfilled the requirements of his part, by casting Mephistophelean leers at the Signor, and now and then stealthily shaking his fists at him.

The father, not being apt at off-hand oratory, did not attempt any response to this speech, but merely bowed, to express his perfect agreement in everything that had been said, and waved his hand toward a table in the rear of the stage, as if to say, "Let us proceed to business."

The notary, taking the hint, seated himself at the table, opened his black bag, drew forth a document from it, and spread it out. Then he dipped a pen into an inkstand, and said:

"We now await the signing of the contract of marriage between Signor Alessandro Arturo Rodicaso, gentleman, and Signorina Giulia Innocenza Fidelia Corpetto, only daughter of Signor Francesco Corpetto, merchant."

In the absence of any definite information on the Venetian formula adopted in such cases, the author had selected this style of announcement as being sufficiently stiff and imposing.

Signor Rodicaso sprang forward with joyful alacrity to sign the contract, dashing off his name in two strokes, as is the invariable custom on the stage.

The climax of the drama had now arrived, and everybody stood aside for the wretched Fidelia. Mrs. Slapman proved equal to the great occasion. Directing one look to heaven, as if for strength, and pressing a hand over the jewelled bodice which covered her bursting heart, she walked with firm steps toward the fatal table. Never in her life had she been more grandly simple. It was sublime!

As Fidelia came up to the little table, she faltered, and leaned upon it to support herself; then, with a nervous motion, grasped the pen. Several times she dipped the pen in the empty inkstand, and each time her face assumed a look of more settled anguish. Then, bracing all her nerves for the decisive act of woman's life, she put down the pen boldly on the paper, and made one up stroke. Before she could make the other down stroke which was necessary to complete her signature, a wild figure, with hair dishevelled, and other evidences of hasty purpose, burst upon the stage.

Fidelia paused; all stood back; and gentlemen who had swords laid hands on them.

"Who is this?" asked the father, with mercantile calmness.

"Who dares thus break in upon my happiness?" inquired Signor Rodicaso.

"Know you not, young man, that you are committing a breach of the peace?" remarked the notary, regarding the intrusion with the eye of a lawyer.

The wild figure answered them all at once: "I am Alberto, and I come to rend this impious contract—thus—thus—thus!" (snatching the parchment from the table, tearing it to pieces, and trampling on it).

Fidelia, astonished at the turn events were taking, leaned back in her chair, and looked on silently. Her time for fainting had not yet come.

"Draw and defend yourself, caitiff!" exclaimed Signor Rodicaso, brandishing his sword.

"Anywhere but in the presence of a lady," was the sarcastic reply. "Besides, I have claims on you, which, perhaps, may teach you to respect me."

"Claims! Thou liest! What claims?"

"These! Hast seen them before? Ha! ha!" shouted Alberto, shaking a bundle of papers in the face of his rival.

"Allow me to examine them, if you please?" asked Signor Rodicaso, with forced calmness.

"No, you don't," was the response. "But I'll tell you what they are. They are judgments to the extent of one hundred and seventy thousand florins—dost hear? one hundred and seventy thousand florins—against you, which I have bought for less than quarter price from Jinkerini Bros., No.

124 Rialto. With them I offset the sum which this unhappy but excellent merchant" (pointing to the father) "owes you. Here, sir; now you are released from yon monster's clutches." (Hands package of judgments to the father, who, overpowered by the scene, takes and holds them in dumb amazement.)

An expression of silent joy begins to steal over the face of Fidelia. But her time for fainting had not yet come!

"Boy!" said Signor Rodicaso, with a composure that was perfectly wonderful, "there is another hand than thine in al' this work. Thou art but the poor tool and I despise thee!'

"Here is the hand!" exclaimed the uncle Bignolio, draw ing out his leg from its seclusion, and bringing his whole bodj into full view. "Dost know it?" He held up his right hand, to carry out the idea of the author.

"It is the hand of Bignolio the usurer," said Signor Rodicaso, despondingly, seeing now that the game was clearly against him.

"Bignolio the usurer!" exclaimed the father, still wrapped in amazement.

"Bignolio the usurer!" murmured Fidelia, whose woman's wit divined the mystery of his appearance. But her time to faint had not *yet* come.

"Bignolio the usurer!" cried the notary, witnesses, and Bidette in chorus.

"Yes," returned that gentleman; "Bignolio the *usurer*, who now is proud to claim the dearer title of 'own uncle' to his nephew Alberto. That nephew he this day receives into his partnership, and proclaims his only heir. Come to my arms, adopted son!"

Alberto flew to his uncle, and was silently embraced. Even at this moment, sacred to the interchange of the noblest affections, several persons in the audience distinctly saw the uncle's left eye wink over Alberto's shoulder to Bidette, who responded to the unwelcome familiarity, this time, with an indignant frown.

12*

The nephew gently uncoiled his uncle, and addressed himself to the father:

"Respected sir, I have long loved your daughter, and am not totally unprepared to believe that she may, in some slight measure, reciprocate my affections. I humbly solicit her hand in marriage."

The father, with the characteristic decision of an old man of business, had already made up his mind. Alberto, the young partner and heir of the rich usurer of Venice, would be a more manageable son-in-law than the middle-aged though wealthy Rodicaso. The father said words to this effect in an "aside," and then replied aloud:

"Her hand is yours; and may your union be crowned with felicity. Come, children, and receive a parent's blessing."

"My bitter curse be on you all! Boy, we shall meet again!" shouted Rodicaso, striding off the stage, and followed by the notary for his pay, and by the laughter and scorn of the rest of the company.

Fidelia's little cup of earthly happiness was now full. Her time for fainting had arrived at last. Everybody moved to clear a space for her. She rose, and walked with an unfaltering step toward Alberto. There was no overdone rapture in her gait; no exaggerated ecstasy in her face. As a practised critic remarked, "her calmness was the truest expression of her agony of joy."

Alberto advanced halfway with a lover's ardor, and extended his arms. Then was her time to faint; and she fainted with a slight scream, sinking gently upon a faithful breast.

The father raised his hands above the couple, and blessed them in the correct way, never seen off the stage. Uncle Bignolio wiped his eyes, and murmured, "Dear boy! How much he looks like his father now!"—a remark somewhat out of place, considering that Alberto's back was turned to the uncle. Bidette hovered near the happy group, and danced for joy.

It was a touching tableau, and the spectators applauded it

in a way that tickled the heart of the author, who was watch ing the effect through an eyehole of the left wing.

CHAPTER IV.

HOW THE PLAY ENDED.

JUST as the curtain was to be rung down on the end of the play, a mad clatter of boots was heard behind the scenes. Then a man, dressed in complete black, and excessively pale, jumped upon the stage. His black hair was tossed all over his head, and his black eyes were rolling wildly. Thus much all the spectators saw at a glance.

The strange man's first intention appeared to be to dash at the happy couple; but, if so, he checked himself, and, standing at a distance of four feet from them, uttered these words: "Scoundrel! what are you doing with my wife there?" The man's whole figure could be seen to tremble.

Many of the spectators, supposing this was a part of the play—though they did not see its precise connection with the plot—applauded what was apparently a fine piece of acting.

"Good!" "Capital!" "Bravo!" were heard from all parts of the room, mingled with stamping and clapping.

The man darted looks of concentrated hate at the audience.

"Who is he?" "How well he does it!" "What splendid tragedy powers!" were some of the audible remarks that this called forth.

It was also observed that a wonderfully natural style of acting was instantly developed among the other *dramatis personæ*. Fidelia sprang from the arms of Alberto, and put on a lifelike expression of insulted dignity, mingled with astonishment. Alberto took a step away from the ghastly intruder, and was evidently at a loss what to do. His face was eloquent with bewilderment and mortification. The father looked confused and sheepish, and put his hands into his pockets. Bidette screamed a little, and fled to the opposite scenes. Uncle Big nolio whistled and smiled, and was evidently amused at the occurrence.

All this, done in five seconds, so delighted the spectators, that they cheered, and cheered again. "As good as a theatre!" ejaculated a new friend of Mrs. Slapman's, on the front row.

The strange, disorderly man plunged forward with one leg toward Alberto, and then drew himself back suddenly, as if in a state of harassing indecision. (Applause.) Then he cast a diabolical look (worthy of the elder Booth in Richard III) at the young lover, and shrieked, "Wretch! villain! I will—I will——" He hesitated to add what he would do, but shook his fists in a highly natural manner at the object of his hate. (Great applause.)

"Sir!" said Fidelia, stretching her proud young form erect, like a tragedy queen, "How dare you, sir!" (Boisterous applause, and this remark from an elderly gentleman: "The picture of Mrs. Siddons!")

The singular individual in black was seen to tremble with increased violence. His eyes rolled more wildly, while his face took on a chalkier hue. He stepped back, as if to insure his retreat. Then, mustering all his resolution, he said:

"M-Mrs. M-Mrs. Slapman, you—you ought to be a-ashamed of yourself!"

The real character of the strange actor was now made evident, and the whole house was hushed in awe and expectation. There was not a man or woman present but knew too well the folly of mingling in a family quarrel. So they held their tongues, and enjoyed the scene.

Mrs. Slapman turned to the audience. She was pale, but perfectly composed. She said:

"Ladies and gentlemen, this is my husband, a very quiet and well-behaved man, whose only fault is excessive nervousness. This fault, I am sorry to say, he encourages, by constantly smoking cigars and drinking strong black tea. He has been indulging in both of these stimulants to-night, till he is quite beside himself. I trust you will excuse and pity him. He has no other vices that I know of."

Then, turning to her husband, whose hands had now dropped listlessly by his side, she added:

"My dear, bathe your head, and go to bed immediately."

He struggled to say something in the presence of this calm embodiment of satire, but could not. Hanging down his head, and looking very silly, he slinked off the stage.

"Now, ladies and gentlemen," said Mrs. Slapman, "after an interval of fifteen minutes, we will proceed with the comedietta of 'A Morning Call,' as if nothing had happened."

When she had said this, Mrs. Slapman fainted—this time in earnest. She was caught in the arms of Fayette Overtop, who immediately, and with the utmost delicacy, resigned her to the arms of Miss Wick (Bidette), and of several other ladies, who came upon the stage and proffered salts, cologne, and other restoratives.

The gentlemen present, actors and audience, unanimously decided that the best thing for them to do, under all the circumstances, was to leave the premises.

This they did as soon as they could, reserving all discussion of the painful event of the evening for the free air of the street.

As Overtop, very serious, and Maltboy, very jovial, were about to descend the steps to the sidewalk, they were met by a messenger, who desired them to go with him immediately to the station house to see some friends (names forgotten) who had been arrested, and had sent for them.

Thither they went, and experienced the greatest surprise of the evening.

BOOK NINTH.

THE INQUEST.

CHAPTER I.

CORONER AND JURY.

The post-mortem examination had been held; and three doctors had sworn that deceased came to his death from a great variety of Greek and Latin troubles, all caused by a learned something which signified, in plain English, a blow on the head. Coroner Bullfast was so struck with the clear and explicit nature of the medical evidence, that he had it reduced to writing for his private regalement.

The post-mortem examination, and the testimony of the three doctors, and of all the people in the house (except Patty Minford, daughter of the deceased)—whose joint knowledge upon the subject amounted to nothing more than hearing somebody with heavy boots come down stairs about midnight—occupied the whole of the first day. Patty, or Pet, was so thoroughly unnerved by the events of that horrible night, that the coroner found it impossible to take her evidence on that day. She had fainted twice before she could make Coroner Bullfast clearly understand that Marcus Wilkeson, her benefactor, and her father's best friend, was THE MURDERER. Having learned thus much, the coroner had put the police on the track of Marcus Wilkeson, and had postponed the further examination of the chief witness.

Mrs. Crull, on learning of the tragic affair, had gone in person to the house of death, and taken Patty to her own home.

The remains of the unfortunate inventor had been removed to the nearest undertaker's for interment, at the expense of Mrs. Crull. The apartments had been diligently searched, and the personal effects of the deceased examined, under the direction of the coroner. A number of documents had been discovered, which, in the coroner's opinion, threw a flood of light on the motives that led to the crime. A few dollars and a bull's-eye silver watch, found on the dead body, precluded the idea that the murder was done for plunder. With that quickness of perception for which Coroner Bullfast, like most of his official kind, was celebrated, he had formed his theory of the murder, and tremendously strong must be the future testimony that could shake it.

On the morning of the second day, Coroner Bullfast and the jury reassembled, about ten o'clock, in the room where the murder was committed.

The coroner was a jovial man, with a bulging forehead, a ruddy nose, a large diamond breastpin (a real diamond, of that superlative style only seen in its perfection on the shirt fronts of aldermen, contractors, and Washington Market butchers), and the native New York manner of speaking, which is sharp and mandatory. The coroner began life as a stone mason, gained early distinction as a fireman, controlled several hundred votes in his ward, became a member of a political committee, and got a coronership as his share of the spoils. He had aspired to be a police justice, or city inspector, or commissioner of the Croton Board. To either of these positions, or, for that matter, to any position indefinitely higher, he felt himself perfectly equal. But other members of the committee (which was a kind of joint-stock company for the distribution of offices) had prior and stronger claims than Harry Bullfast, and so he was put off with a coronership. He felt the slight acutely, but, like a prudent man, determined to so keep himself before the public in his performance of the office, as to make it a stepping stone to something much higher—the city comptrollership, or a seat in the State Senate, or in Congress, or (who could tell?) the governorship of the commonwealth—that grand possibility which every ward politician carries in his hat.

The coroner was seated in the inventor's private armchair, with one leg thrown over the side of it, and the other stretched on the floor. He was chewing tobacco with manly vigor, and cracking jokes with a facetious juryman, who was assistant foreman of the Bully Boy Hose, of which the coroner was an exempt and honorary member.

The jury was composed of six men whom the coroner had picked from the large number of idle spectators found by him at the scene of the murder when he was first summoned. Two of them chanced to be acquaintances of his. As to the rest, the coroner had not the remotest idea. They might have been beggars or pickpockets, for aught that he cared. They looked stupid, and he liked stupid jurors.

"Them sharp fellers that thinks they knows more'n the cor'ner, is a cussed nuisance," he often had occasion to remark.

The jury sat near one of the windows, in a semicircle of chairs which had been borrowed from the first and second floors. Pending the resumption of their melancholy work, such of them as could read were reading newspapers containing reports of the first day's proceedings, from two to ten columns long, wherein the scene of the "Mysterious Midnight Tragedy," as one paper called it, was represented in the most ingenious manner by printers' rules cut to show the dimensions of the rooms on the third floor, the position of the fireplace, bed, washstand, chest of drawers, unknown machine in the corner, and other things which had no bearing whatever on the affair. The other jurors, who could not read at all, or had an insuperable aversion to that laborious occupation, were rolling their quids in silence, and looking wise.

At a long table in the centre of the room were seated several young gentlemen, dressed with singular independence of style. From one point of view they looked like actors, bearing about them signs of fatigue, as if from heavy night work. Observed again, they resembled young lawyers of indolent habits and scanty practice, who had just dropped in to watch the case.

From their conversation, no clue to their professional identity could be gathered. They were cracking jokes, propounding conundrums, and telling stories humorously broad to each other. Everything was to them a legitimate amusement. The proceedings of the day before were peculiarly rich in funny reminiscences; and one tall, bright, curly-haired fellow was evoking roars of suppressed laughter by his capital mimicry of two of the dullest witnesses. Another was drawing comic profiles of a sleepy juryman on a scrap of paper. He had previously dashed off a very happy sketch of the coroner, and shown it to that functionary, who had "haw-hawed," and pronounced it "devilish good," and, in turn, presented the young artist with a fine Havana cigar, which he playfully put in his mouth and chewed the end of. Yet there were, about these young gentlemen, signs of business, which an intelligent observer might have easily interpreted. From the outside breast pockets of each of them protruded a number of pencils; and, from their lower side pockets, thick memorandum books with gray covers, or stiffly folded quires of foolscap.

They were the reporters of the press—the gamins and good fellows of literature;—fellows of inexhaustible resources, who carry their wits literally at their fingers' ends;—who can do more than extract sunbeams from cucumbers; for they can make up thrilling facts out of nothing;—who can thread their way through a crowd where a tapeworm would be squeezed to death;—whose writing desk is usually another man's back; and who sketch out a much better speech between an orator's shoulder blades than he is making in front;—whose written language is a perplexity compared with which Greek is a relax ation and Sanscrit a positive amusement;—who deal in adjectives, and know their precise value, and how to administer them, as an apothecary knows the drugs that are boxed and bottled on his shelves;—who are less men than parts of an enormous mill grinding out grist to be branned and bolted in the editorial rooms, made into food in the printing office and press vault, and served up hot for the public's breakfast next morning.

Clever, witty, insatiable fellows they, for whom a planet ought to be set apart, where all the murders are wrapped in impenetrable mystery, and the smallest railroad accidents are frightful catastrophes.

The east side of the room, where the dead body had been found, was preserved inviolate from the broom, mop, and other touch, until the inquest was over. The strange machine stood in its accustomed place, flanked by the screen. It had been extensively handled and looked at, and passed for a new kind of clock. Two large weights (which had fallen to the floor) and the interplaying cogwheels gave force to that conjecture.

A large purple spot on the floor showed where the old man's life had ebbed away. Close by this spot, precisely where it had been picked up, lay the long oaken club with the iron tip, which, it was supposed, had done the dreadful deed. There were small splashes and spots on it too.

The fun of the reporters, the chat of the coroner and his friends, the readings and airy meditations of the jurors, were all suddenly checked by the appearance of Marcus Wilkeson, escorted by two police officers, and Messrs. Overtop and Maltboy, Patching and Tiffles. All five had passed the night in the station house—Messrs. Patching and Tiffles from compulsion, as witnesses, and possible accomplices, and Overtop and Maltboy as guides, philosophers, and friends. All looked seedy and criminal, as if there were something in the atmosphere of station houses to give a man the semblance of a vagabond and an outcast. Marcus Wilkeson was very pale, and, when he looked across the room, as he did upon his entrance, by a singular impulse, and saw the great blood mark and the club on the floor, he trembled with emotion.

The keen eyes of the coroner caught these signs, and he immediately brought in a mental verdict of "guilty." Some of the jury observed the same signs, and thought them suspicious. The reporters looked upon Marcus Wilkeson without emotion or prejudgment. They were so accustomed to seeing murderers, that they regarded them simply as a part of the business community—a little vicious, perhaps, but not so much worse than other people, after all. One reporter, attached to an illustrated paper, dashed off the profile of Marcus Wilkeson, under the cover of his hat, and caught the dejected expression of his face to a nicety.

CHAPTER II.

STATEMENT OF THE PRISONER.

THE coroner received Marcus with that air of consideration which magistrates instinctively bestow upon persons charged with great crimes, and informed him, with some respect, that he was brought there to make any explanation that he saw fit, touching his connection with "this 'ere murder."

The party were then accommodated with seats near the jury, and facing the reporters. As Marcus looked up, and saw those practised scribes sharpening their pencils, his heart sank deeper within him. The vision which had troubled him all night, of a broadside notoriety in all the city papers, rose before his mind, clothed with fresh horror. The dull sound of sharpening those pencils was like the whetting of the executioner's knife.

The proper course was to have accepted an unsworn statement from the prisoner; but the coroner always administered oaths when prisoners were willing to take them. The repetition of that jargon with a profane conclusion (for so it seemed, in the slipshod way that it was said), which the coroner called an oath, was a positive pleasure to that official. As Marcus desired to take the oath, the coroner rattled off the unintelligible something, and handed him a Bible, which the prisoner pressed reverentially to his lips. Marcus, being now supposed to be sworn, proceeded, with what firmness he could muster, to answer the numerous interrogatories of the coroner. That official chewed hard, and, as it were, spit out his questions.

His testimony, in substance, was this:

That he was a friend of the deceased, and had loaned him one thousand dollars to complete a machine upon which he was engaged—pointing to the unfinished pile in the corner. That his relations with the deceased and his family (Marcus did not like to mention Pet's name) were entirely agreeable, until an anonymous letter, charging him with improper motives in visiting the house, had poisoned the mind of the deceased against him. [The giving up of this letter to the coroner, who read it to the jury, and then tossed it over to the reporters for copying, was a hard trial, but Marcus had resolved upon meeting all the troubles of the case halfway.]

The coroner here produced the second anonymous letter, which had been found on the person of the deceased, showed it to Marcus for identification, and then threw it to the reporters, as one would throw a choice bone to a cage full of hungry animals.

Marcus explained that he had made every effort to discover the authorship of the letters, without success; whereupon the coroner shut his eyes knowingly, rolled his quid from right to left, and said that he was "investigatin' 'em" himself.

QUESTION BY A JUROR. "Wos the letters postpaid?"

ANSWER. "They were."

The juror took the reply into his profoundest consideration.

Marcus, resuming, stated that, on his last visit—the night of the supposed murder—he had found Mr. Minford very much disturbed in mind by the unjust suspicions aroused by these letters. He had accused witness of the vile intentions referred to in them. Witness had denied the imputations with emphasis. The discussion was becoming quite warm, when the daughter of the deceased entered the room, and, being worn out with watching by the side of a sick friend, retired to bed in the adjoining chamber. The conversation, broken off by her entrance, was then continued, much in the same vein. Mr. Minford was in a distressing state of nervous excitement that evening, and talked loud and wild. Witness made an effort to keep his temper, and did so, though the peculiar injustice of the accusations were enough to arouse any man's anger. He reserved his show of wrath for the author of the anonymous letters, if he could ever catch him. He would not say that he had not replied to the deceased with some warmth of manner. But as to threatening him, or hurting one hair of his head, witness had not done it—so help him God!

QUESTION BY A JUROR. "Was the key of the door in the keyhole that night?"

ANSWER. "I don't know."

COMMENT BY FACETIOUS JUROR. "Be me sowl, I thinks that whishkay had more to do with it than the doorkay. Don't you, Harry?"

CORONER. "Bully for you!"

Clothing himself again with dignity, the coroner asked:

"Der yer mean to say, Mr. Wilkingson, that yer didn't kill this man? Remember, now, yer on yer oath!"

The horrible bluntness of the question nearly felled Marcus to the floor. He placed his hand on his brow, now pale with the acutest anguish. Then he rose, and, looking upward said:

"As God is my judge, and as I hope for heaven, I am innocent of this murder, or of any part in it."

"If you please, Mr. Coroner, this gentleman and myself are counsel for the accused," said Overtop.

"Oh! you're his counsel. Then the other two are the chaps arrested as 'complices?"

Patching writhed at this. Nor were his feelings relieved by observing, with an oblique glance, that the artist of the illustrated paper was in the act of taking him.

"I protest," said Wesley Tiffles, rising to his full height, and throwing out both arms for a comprehensive gesture, "I protest against this arrest and detention as illegal. If the coroner will give me but a short hour of his valuable time, I can——"

CORONER (*puffing up*). "The gentleman will be good enough to shut up for the present. When we are ready, we will hear what he has to say."

TIFFLES. "I protest, sir. I wish the gentlemanly and intelligent reporters to note that I protest——"

CORONER. "Are you, or me, boss here, hey?"

TIFFLES. "Oh! you, of course, sir." The protestant then sank into his seat, not wholly disappointed, for he had gained his object of making a little newspaper capital by tickling the reporters. He had also remarked, with pleasure, that, while he stood erect, with both arms outstretched, the artist had secured his full length. Tiffles was fond of notoriety, however achieved; and he saw a good opening for it in this case.

Overtop here suggested that it would be easy to prove their client's innocence. He would respectfully request his Honor to procure the testimony of Miss Patty Minford, if she could be found. As she went to bed in the adjoining room early that evening, she must have heard some noise in connection with the murder—if, indeed, a murder had been committed. Overtop's legal education taught him to doubt everything.

Coroner Bullfast was touched with the title of Honor, so skilfully applied by Overtop; and he answered, with uncommon sweetness:

"I am expecting Miss Minford every minute, sir. She will speak for herself. For the present, sir, I am sorry to say that it was on her testimony alone that Mr. Wilkingson was 'rested."

A look of new surprise and horror passed over the pale

face of Marcus, and Overtop and Maltboy exchanged glances of astonishment.

"Now, Mr. Wilkingson," continued the coroner, taking a fresh chew, "please drive ahead with yer statement—if yer choose to. Yer not bound to say anythink, yer know."

An intelligent Juror. "Will Mr. Wilkeson tell us about what time he left this house that night, and where he went?"

Marcus raised his sunken head, and shook it, as if to dispel a stupefaction. Then, in a faint and trembling voice, he replied that he looked at his watch just before bidding Mr. Minford "good-night," and observed that it was fifteen minutes past eleven o'clock.

Question by a Juror. "What kind o' watch do you carry?"

Answer (*exhibiting the watch*). "An English hunter—lever escapement—full jewelled."

At any other time, Marcus would have smiled at the impertinence of the question, but he answered it gravely.

He then went on to say, that Mr. Minford had not replied to his "good-night." That he repeated the salutation, and extended his hand as a token of unbroken friendship. That Mr. Minford refused to take it, and said that he had one last favor to ask of him (Marcus), and that was, never to cross his threshold again. That he (Marcus) responded, "I forgive you, sir. When, on reflection, you think that you have done me injustice—as you will, at last—send for me, and I will still be your friend." That he received no answer to this, save a shake of the head, and immediately went down stairs into the street. He was feverish, and his brain was in a whirl. Hardly knowing what he did, he walked the streets hither and thither. He could not tell what streets he traversed, but he kept up the exercise till he was tired. Then he became calmer, returned home, entered the house with a latch key, and went to bed without waking any of the inmates. On going to bed, he observed that his watch marked one o'clock.

An intelligent Juror. "You must have passed a large number of people in the streets between eleven and one o'clock. Did you see no one whom you knew?"

"No one; but at a corner some distance from here,—I could not say what corner,—I noticed a policeman sitting on a barrel in front of a grocery, smoking. He was a short, fat man, and his legs hardly reached to the pavement. I remember him the more particularly, because I stopped and lighted a cigar at his pipe. Just at that moment, the City Hall bell commenced striking a fire alarm."

"What was the district?" asked the juror who was assistant foreman of the Bully Boy Hose.

"The Seventh. I counted the strokes. I walked on rapidly, and soon came up with another policeman, who was leaning against a grocery store. I said to him, 'A cold night, Mr. Policeman,' and I think he would remember that circumstance, if he could be found. Just after I had passed him, the alarm bells struck the last round. Three or four rounds had been struck."

The assistant foreman of the Bully Boy Hose, having referred to a memorandum book which he drew from a breast pocket, here exclaimed:

"The alarm was at twenty-five minutes of twelve. Nothing but a chimney in Whitehall street. We run into Twenty's fellers, comin' back, and had a nice little row. Ever belong to the department, sir?"

Marcus answered "No;" and the pyrophilist looked compassionately upon him, as upon one who had never known true happiness.

"If you never run with the mersheen," observed the coroner, "you do' 'no' wot life is. As for me, sir, it's my boast and pride that I have been a member of the New York Fire Department for more'n twenty years. It wos the backin' of the boys that made me a coroner; and, thank God! I'm never ashamed to tell 'em so."

The coroner spoke truly. So far from being ashamed to

"tell 'em so," he was always "telling 'em so," never missing an opportunity, at political meetings, to inform the firemen that he was "one of 'em," and that no mark of honor, even from the President of the United States, was equal to his fireman's badge. The continual "telling of 'em so" had aided in procuring for him his present official distinction, and was destined to earn higher honors for him at a future day.

The coroner tore off a fresh chew from a half hand of Cavendish which had been well gnawed at all the edges, and told Marcus that he might "fire away" again.

Marcus then proceeded to state that, on the morning after the eventful night, he woke up early. His dreams had been horrible, and his waking reflections were no less distressing. The thought that Mr. Minford should have suspected him, thus unjustly, of the basest of crimes, and that they, who had been such good friends, should have parted in a way that effectually cut off reconciliation; and the other thought, that this mischief had been wrought by some unscrupulous enemy, when he had always fondly believed that he never could have a foe in the world—these thoughts, occurring with great force to a nervous and sensitive man, nearly maddened him. He felt that if he remained in the house that day, as usual, and brooded over his troubles, he would grow crazy. While he was pondering what to do, his eyes chanced to fall on an invitation which he had received from Mr. Wesley Tiffles, to meet him at the Cortlandt-street ferry at seven and a quarter o'clock that morning, and accompany him and his panorama of Africa to New Jersey. The day before, when this invitation came to hand, he had determined not to accept it; but it now seemed to offer him a capital chance to see some excitement and fun. As these remedies were precisely what his mental malady required, he jumped to dress himself, and hurried out of the house, seeing nobody as he made his exit, and leaving no word of explanation. He took no luggage, except a clean collar, as he intended to return the following day. He was even so careless and forgetful as to leave his purse behind him, and found, on reaching the ferry, that he had barely two dollars in his pocket.

Question by a Juror. "Wos they bank bills; and, if so, what bank wos they on?"

Marcus answered the question to the best of his knowledge, and the juror sagely nodded, and took the reply under treatment.

"I say, Tubbs," cried the coroner, "wot's the use of askin' them kind o' questions?"

Tubbs looked up from his ruminations, somewhat confused. The politic Overtop—that model of a rising lawyer—here put in a word for Tubbs, and said that the question, in his opinion, was a very pertinent one, for it went to test the memory of his client. If Mr. Wilkeson had just committed murder, he would hardly be in that calm frame of mind which is necessary to the recollection of small facts. He hoped that the ingenious gentleman would ask many more such questions. By these judicious remarks, Overtop gained one fast friend for his client on the jury.

CHAPTER III.

JUSTICE GOES TO DINNER.

Wesley Tiffles was then examined. He commenced with an eloquent dissertation on the rights of man, and his own rights in particular, but stopped when he saw that the reporters tucked their pencils behind their ears, and waited for facts. The moment he began to talk facts—which are to reporters what corn is to crows—down came the pencils from their perches again, and went tripping over the paper.

Mr. Tiffles's testimony would have consumed two hours, or two days, perhaps, if he had been allowed to go on unchecked. But the coroner had been invited to dine at a Broadway restaurant, with a few political friends, at three P. M. So he concluded, after Tiffles had talked five minutes, that he knew nothing about the murder, and could throw no light on it, and told Tiffles that he was not wanted further.

"And you mean to tell me, sir, that I am not to be locked up in the station house to-night," said Tiffles.

"No, unless yer want ter be."

"Of course not—of course not." But the interior Tiffles was disappointed at this sudden and unromantic termination of his case. A few more nights in the station house, or in the Tombs, would have given him capital material for a book, of which he had already projected the first chapter. He sat down, and execrated his ill luck.

Patching, the artist, was then interrogated, to the extent of two minutes, and corroborated Tiffles's testimony as to the sad and strange appearance of Mr. Wilkeson on the day after the supposed murder. Patching was then informed by the coroner that his further attendance at the inquest would not be required.

Patching, on rising, had assumed the attitude of Paul before Felix, as set forth in some ancient cartoon; and in that position of mingled innocence, dignity, and defiance, the artist of the illustrated paper got a spirited sketch of him. Had Patching dreamed how capitally his long hair, peaked beard, thin nose, and bony forehead would be taken off, in a rough but faithful character portrait, he would have sunk in confusion. Happily, the newspaper artist was sitting almost behind his more pretentious brother of the canvas, and the latter knew not what had been done, until, the following week, he saw a striking intensification of himself staring into the street from numerous bulletin boards and shop windows.

Before sitting down, Mr. Patching begged to explain to the jury, and to the public through the reporters (who did not take down a word of the explanation), that he had painted the panorama of Africa to oblige his friend, Wesley Tiffles. It was hardly necessary for him to say, in this community, that he was more at home among higher walks of Art.

"Are you a sign painter, Mr. Patching?" asked the coroner.

"No, sir; I am not," said Patching, with dignified contempt.

"Perhaps you're a carriage painter, then? Them's the fellers for picturin'. The woman and flowers on the Bully Boys' hose carriage wos well done. Hey, Jack?"

"That it wos, Harry," returned the assistant foreman of the Bully Boys. "If Patching can do that sort o' thing, he'll pass."

Patching fixed looks of professional indignation on the coroner and the assistant foreman, and sat down gloomily, amid the suppressed laughter of the irreverent reporters.

The coroner then looked at his watch, and, finding that the time was within half an hour of dinner, said that the inquest would be adjourned till the following morning, at ten o'clock.

"But, your Honor," said Overtop, "—that is, if you will allow me to make the suggestion—couldn't you give us an hour longer? Nothing has yet been heard from Miss Minford, who, you said, was expected to be in attendance to-day. Will you be good enough to send to Mrs. Crull's house for her?"

"Really, I can't wait," replied the coroner. "The young lady must be sick, or she would have been here before now."

"But—pardon me, your Honor—we are anxious to have Miss Minford brought on the stand this afternoon, believing that her testimony alone will acquit our client."

"You believe so, because you do' 'no' what it is. But, as I said before, it wos on Miss Minford's statement that Mr. Wilkingson there was 'rested. And the best advice I can give him is to take a good night's rest, and get his nerves ready for the young woman's testimony to-morrow, for it'll be a staggerer." The coroner consulted his watch again, with evident impatience, and rose from his seat.

Overtop essayed to speak again; but the coroner interrupted him with, "The inquest is 'journed till to-morrer, at ten o'clock. Mr. Policeman, you will take the prisoner back to the station house."

This speech was torture to Overtop and Maltboy, who, believing firmly in their friend's innocence, were convinced that a full investigation of the case that day would procure his acquittal. They turned eyes of exhaustless friendship and sympathy toward him.

Marcus was in that half-comatose state which is the stupid reaction from an intense and painful excitation of the nerves. He was morbidly calm. The opinion of the coroner, that Miss Minford's testimony would be a "staggerer," had no more effect on him than it would have had on the most phlegmatic reader of the case in next morning's paper.

"Then, your Honor, we must ask you to take bail," said Overtop.

"Can't take bail! Can't take anything but my dinner, to-day! For the third time, I say, the inquest is adjourned." The coroner hastily put on his spring overcoat.

Overtop was tempted to make a fierce reply; but the legal discretion in which he was educated restrained him.

The word had gone forth. The jurors rose, yawned, and grasped their hats. The reporters jammed their notes into their pockets, and precipitately fled from the room. The policeman escorted Marcus Wilkeson and his counsel, and Tiffles and Patching, to the carriage which brought them, and which still stood in front of the house, an object of tragic interest to a large crowd of men, women, and children, who had remained about the doorway during the inquest, and could not be dispersed by the policemen.

"Which is he?" "Who's the murderer?" whispered twenty voices, as the party emerged from the stairs upon the sidewalk.

"That's him! That chap with the big hat and long hair. You could pick him out of a million," said a shrewd observer.

"What ugly eyes he's got! They're sharp enough to stab ye," added a shop girl.

"I seen some pirates hung, when I was a little gal," remarked an old woman, "and they were pooty compared to him."

The object of these and other remarks was the unhappy Patching, who had not yet got over his wrath at the coroner, and was scowling and compressing his lips very like a murderer.

The policeman and his companions, all but the spell-bound Marcus, could not help laughing at these ridiculous mistakes. But Patching turned upon the crowd, and delivered among them one withering look of scorn, which fully confirmed them in the belief that he was a murderer of the deepest dye. And when the carriage rolled away, it was followed by a volley of groans, mixed with a few pebbles, handfuls of mud, and other missiles which happened to be lying around loose.

"Here, boys, don't act that way," said the coroner, who had just made his appearance on the sidewalk. "Let the poor devil go. It's a case of murder, clear enough; and he won't slip through my hands easy, I can tell ye, if he *is* rich." The coroner spoke good-naturedly, for he saw several of his political adherents among the throng.

"That's the talk!" "Good boy!" "You're the feller for us!" were some of the warm responses.

The coroner smiled, as he stopped to light a cigar from the pipe of a dirty admirer, and then, bowing obsequiously to the group, he stalked off in a rowdy way in the direction of his expected dinner.

CHAPTER IV.

LIGHT IN THE PRISON.

On the return of the prisoner and friends to the station house, Marcus was gratified to find a number of old business acquaintances waiting for him in the ante-room. They were men whom he had known in his Wall-street epoch, and had always set down as good-enough friends in prosperity, but cold-shouldered creatures in an hour of trial. He was mistaken, as many men are mistaken, in judging the hearts of business men from their white and careworn faces. They came with warm hands, sympathetic words, and offers of bail money and other aid, if wanted. There were short notes from two or three other old fellows whom he had not seen for years, telling him that they were at his command.

These expressions of good will touched Marcus to the heart. He learned that, in the self-conceit of his retired and studious life, he had done injustice to these citizens of the whirling world. With a thousand thanks for the kindness of his callers, he told them that their friendly services were not needed; that his innocence would surely be made to appear; and that, to the day of his death, he should never forget them. Upon this assurance, repeated two or three times, his business friends withdrew with characteristic business impetuosity, wishing him a speedy release from his disagreeable position—which is the roundabout phrase for prison.

A policeman, who had charge of the station house during the absence of his superior officer, here informed Marcus that an old lady and a young one, an old gen'leman and a lad, had called. The old gen'leman and the lad would drop round again during the evening. The old lady and the young one were waiting for him in the captain's room.

He entered the captain's room—his companions staying outside—and saw, as he expected, his half-sister Philomela, and a young woman dressed in the height of cheap fashion, who was no other than Mash, the cook.

His sister rose, and extended her hand to him severely, and said, with a solemn voice:

"Brother Marcus, I am sorry to see you here. I hope you are not guilty of this crime?"

"Hope?" said Marcus, stung to the quick. "Why not say at once that I am guilty? It is strange that the only relative I have on earth should be the first to doubt my innocence."

"Oh, no, Marcus! You do me injustice there. I do not for a moment doubt your innocence. But you know I always advised you to give up your moping habits at home, and go into active business, like other men of your age. If you had been in business now, you wouldn't have had time to get mixed up in the affairs of this old man Minford and his daughter, and would have escaped this disgrace. I trust, Marcus," she added, emphatically, "I trust this will be a lesson to you."

Poor Mash, the cook, had been playing with her bonnet strings, and trying to check her tears. But the unnatural effort was too much for her, and she burst out crying.

"Oh, Mr. Wilkeson!" she said, between her sobs, "I—I'm so sorry to see you here; b-but I—I know yer innocent. Boo-boo-hoo!"

"Thank you, Mash," replied Marcus, quite affected at this sudden outbreak of sympathy. "*You* speak like a true woman. But don't cry any more, my good girl. I shall be released to-morrow." Marcus said this confidently—though he had not the least idea how his acquittal was to be obtained.

"Oh! I hope so—I—hope so, Mr. Wilkeson. Boo-boo-hoo-I—I wish I could g-go to prison in your place. Boo-boo-hoo!"

Mash had derived this preposterous idea of vicarious imprisonment from the story of "The Buttery and the Boudoir," which was now drawing near its conclusion, and gradually killing, or marrying off, its heroes and heroines.

Marcus could not help smiling at the romantic notion. Miss Philomela laughed sarcastically, and exclaimed:

"You must take pattern from me, girl, and control your feelings. My brother doesn't want crying women about him at this time."

"Don't be too sure of that, sister. Tears come naturally from a woman. They are her best evidence of sympathy, and therefore precious to one who needs it."

Mash, the cook, gave vent to a fresh shower of tears at this encouraging remark, and made Miss Philomela shrug her shoulders in disgust.

"Oh! *don't* be silly, Mash!" said Miss Philomela, losing all patience with the cook.

"I—I—boo-boo-hoo!—can't help it, marm."

"Nonsense!" said the superior female. "As for you, Marcus, you should not encourage such folly, when you have troubles that demand our sober and earnest attention. With reference to the past, I might say a great many things, but I forbear. To be serious, now—for once in your life—what can I do for you?"

"Will you do what I ask, faithfully?" asked Marcus.

"Yes, faithfully. I promise."

"Then, my sister, be so good as to go home immediately, and send me a spare shirt and a change of clothes. Mash can bring them. And, lest another interview should prove too severe a trial for your female sensibility, I beg that you will not come here again. If I want you very much, I can send for you."

"You are very unkind—very unkind. But I will not make any remarks. You know that nothing would give me greater pleasure than to serve my brother. For, though you have faults—I suppose you will not deny that you have some little faults—you are still my brother."

Marcus smiled, and thought how foolish it was to quarrel with the whimsical but not bad-hearted woman. "Well, sister Philomela, you can see for yourself that I am not ill used here. Comfortable bed, rousing fire, and warm meals from the restaurant round the corner! The lieutenant* who is in command of this station house turns out to be an old friend of my boyhood, and treats me more like a guest than a prisoner. And I must say, that, but for the idea of a prison, I could live as pleasantly here as at home. Even you can do nothing to lighten my captivity. But I promise, that *if* I am held by this coroner's jury—which, of course, I shall not be—and am sent to the Tombs, then I will tax your sisterly affection to the utmost."

At the mention of that dreadful place, the "Tombs," Mash

* Called sergeant of police under the recent Metropolitan Act.

broke into sobs again. The touching experiences of Gerald Florville in that house of despair—as set forth in "The Buttery and the Boudoir"—were poignantly brought to her mind.

Miss Philomela looked serious as the Tombs loomed up in her mind, and she would have said something condoling, but for the irritating conduct of the cook, who annoyed her so much that she decided to leave. She abruptly shook hands with her half-brother. "It is very easy," said she, "to point out how certain mistakes might have been avoided. But let the past go. If you are not acquitted to-morrow, I shall call here again, notwithstanding you don't seem very desirous to see me. Now, good-by. Come, hurry up, Mash!"

Marcus shook hands with his half-sister, and also with Mash, who wept afresh.

In the ante-room, Miss Philomela saw Overtop and Maltboy, upon whom she bestowed a half smile, and Tiffles, whom she treated to a cordial grimace, not unmingled with a blush. Tiffles, on his part, was profoundly polite, and inquired if she were going home. Learning that she was, he remarked that he had occasion to walk in the same direction, and accompanied her as she left the station house. Mash followed at a short distance behind, not because she did not think herself fully as good as Miss Philomela, but because she wished to indulge unchecked in the mild luxury of tears.

A new visitor was now announced. He was a curly-headed, neatly dressed boy of nineteen years. His face was one that is handsomer in promise than in fact. Marcus recognized him as the boy Bog, whom he had not seen for several weeks. The boy had developed a remarkable talent for making money honestly. For two months he had attended a night school, and was fast correcting his awkward English, and attaining to other knowledge. Prosperity and schooling together had given him quite a polish. The rough boy was coming to be a presentable youth.

He advanced timidly toward Marcus, who shook hands with him. He sat down before the fire, and commenced fumbling his cap in the old way. With the exception of that trick, and his shyness, there was little of the original boy Bog about him.

"Mr. Wilkeson," said he, giving his cap a twirl, "I am very sorry to see you here; because, I may say, I *know* you are innocent."

The positive manner in which the boy asserted this, charmed Marcus. "I thank you, my dear Bog," said he; "but how do you know it? For, though I am innocent, I may have some trouble in proving it."

The boy drew a small folded note from his pocket. "I'll explain, sir," said he.

Marcus here called in his counsel, Messrs. Overtop and Maltboy, and his good friend the lieutenant of police, who had just arrived in the outer room, in order that they might hear the explanation.

The boy was embarrassed by his audience; but the anxious look of Marcus, and a few kind words from the lieutenant of police, reassured him. Bog then proceeded to tell what he knew of the strange young man's acquaintance with Miss Patty Minford—which was very easily told, since it did not amount to much—and concluded by opening the letter given to him by the young man for delivery to Miss Minford, and handed it to Marcus.

Marcus glanced at the writing, expecting that it would resemble tnat of the first anonymous letter addressed to Mr. Minford, which he drew from his pocket for comparison. But the writing was totally different in inclination, thickness of the downward stroke, and all other respects. He read it aloud, his counsel and the lieutenant of police listening attentively.

"I don't know much about the case yet," said the lieutenant, "but, jumping at a conclusion, I should say that this sneaking chap was jealous of your intimacy with the Minford family; that he wrote the anonymous letters to the old man, in a different hand, and that he either committed the murder, or knows something about it. His motive for annoying Miss

Minford I can understand—for this city is full of just such well-dressed scoundrels; but the motive of the murder I can't comprehend. But mark me—this fellow has some knowledge of it; and we must hunt him up. And, first, let us compare the letters."

Marcus handed the two letters to the lieutenant, who, with Overtop and Maltboy, gave them a close examination. One was written on faint blue paper in a buff envelope; the other on white paper in a white envelope. Every curve, cross, and dot was minutely compared; but not the faintest resemblance between the two letters could be discovered. "No more like than chalk and cheese," said the lieutenant. "My theory is knocked on the head."

"Let me examine the envelopes again," said Overtop. They had inspected them less carefully than the contents.

As soon as Overtop had placed the two envelopes side by side, his eyes lighted up with the pleasure of a great discovery. "What fools we are!" he exclaimed. "There it is! Don't you see? Don't you see? A regular Hogarthian line of beauty under the name on each."

All stared at the envelopes, and at once recognized the similarity between the graceful curved lines. They looked somewhat like the letter S laid on its side; and more like the arm of a rocking chair.

Marcus had a sudden inward vision of the writer. One of those convictions which defy all logical analysis flashed upon his mind.

"Do you know where this strange young man lives, Bog?" asked Marcus.

"No, sir. I follered—I should say followed—him two or three times, because I thought he wasn't acting just right toward Miss Minford (here Bog blushed). He always went into drinking houses and billiard saloons, and once into a place where they say the worst kind o' gambling is allers—I mean always—going on. But he knew me by sight, and I was afraid he would ask me about that letter which I didn't deliver for him. So I had to follow him a good piece behind; and sometimes I lost track of him. Then, again, he would keep a tramping round from one drinking place to another—but never getting drunk that I could see—till twelve or one o'clock at night. By that time I felt I ought to go home, and so I never tracked him to his lodgings, if he has any. But it's my belief he travels in the night, and sleeps in the daytime, like the cats."

"Good, so far," said Marcus. "You have already given us a general description of this fellow's dress and appearance. Now, tell me whether his face is pale, his mustache small and curved up in points, his eyes light gray, and never looking straight at you; his nose small, thin, and sharp; and, now I think of it, has he not got a small scar on one of his cheeks?"

"Why, Mr. Wilkeson," exclaimed the boy Bog, "that's the very chap!"

"Who is he?" asked the lieutenant of police, "that I may have him arrested at once."

"He is the son——"

CHAPTER V.

THE SORROW OF WHITE HAIRS.

At that moment the door opened, and the venerable form of Myndert Van Quintem appeared before them. Marcus cast a hasty glance, importing silence, at his companions, and rose to receive his old friend.

Mr. Van Quintem's face expressed the tenderest compassion. He clasped Marcus's hand, and said:

"My young friend, it deeply grieves me to see you here; for I feel—I may say I know morally—that you are innocent of any part in this murder."

"Thank you for your confidence," said Marcus. "I hope, when Miss Minford and certain other witnesses are examined to-morrow, to prove my innocence conclusively."

"So you will, I am sure. When I say that I know you are innocent, I found my belief on my short but pleasant acquaintance with you. But I cannot guess, from the evidence at the inquest yesterday and that of to-day—just published in the afternoon papers,—who committed the murder, or what was the motive of it. Have you any clue to the mystery?"

"Yes—yes," replied Marcus. "We think we have a clue; but so slight, that it is hardly worth mentioning. My friends here are going to follow it up."

"And in order that we may do so without any delay," said the lieutenant, "please give us the name of that sneaking letter writer."

Marcus coughed, looked at the lieutenant knowingly, and said, "Oh, *that's* no consequence. It's a false scent. Depend on it."

The old gentleman, as he entered the room, had caught Marcus Wilkeson's words. "He is the son—" and had observed the slight confusion with which Marcus had stopped saying something. He now noticed the glance enjoining silence, which Marcus had directed at the lieutenant of police.

Mr. Van Quintem turned pale, as a harrowing suspicion came into his mind. "Mr. Wilkeson," he said, in a trembling voice, "will you answer me one question truly?"

"I—I will," replied Marcus.

"Then tell me, in Heaven's name, do you know of anything that connects my son with this monstrous crime? I have had a dreadful presentiment, all along, that he had something to do with it. The end of his wrong career will be the gallows. I have dreamt of it for years. O God! that I should have begotten such a profligate and miscreant into the world!"

The old man made another pause, and then said, with a calmness that surprised his hearers. "Now I am ready to hear all."

"And you shall," said Marcus, "though it pains me, my dear friend, to tell you what we know of your son. I will say, however, that there is no proof directly connecting him with the murder."

"He is cunning and covers his tracks," said the wretched parent. "I know him well."

Marcus then exhibited the letters. Mr. Van Quintem compared them carefully, but could not detect the least trace of resemblance. But, on examining the envelopes, at the suggestion of Fayette Overtop, he at once recognized the Hogarthian curve as a mark which he had always observed on his son's letters.

"I could almost swear to this mark; and yet it is possible that he did not write the letters. Bad as he is, I will wait for further proofs. Please tell me all else that you know, Mr. Wilkeson."

"With regard to the letter written to Miss Minford," said Marcus, "there is, unhappily, but little doubt; as this lad, who was well acquainted with the Minford family, can inform you."

The boy Bog, very reluctantly, and with many awkward breaks, and swingings of his cap, repeated the history of the first letter, and described the young man's person most minutely, and told how he had followed him in his wild rambles about the town.

The old man listened sadly and quietly; only now and then interrupting the boy's narrative with questions that were seemingly as calm as a judge's interrogatories.

"He is a murderer. Something in the air tells me that he is," murmured the old man. "And he is my son."

The inexpressible heart-broken sadness, with which he uttered these words, brought tears to the eyes of his hearers.

"It may be, my dear Mr. Van Quintem, that your son did not write the anonymous letters to Mr. Minford, notwithstanding the point of resemblance which we think we have detected. While sitting at my window, I have often noticed him in his room scribbling at a desk, as if he were practising penmanship. Perhaps, if you examine the contents of the desk, you may get some further light on the subject. It is wonderful—most peo ple would say impossible—that a man should write two letters so entirely dissimilar as these."

"My son always excelled in writing. It was one of the branches that he took prizes in at school. I will examine the desk; but I fear I shall only confirm my strong suspicions that he is a murderer. O God! O God! Why did he not die with his sainted mother! Far better would that have been. It is a hard thing, gentlemen—it is a very hard thing; but if this boy of mine does not surrender himself to the hands of justice to-morrow, I shall—I shall—myself denounce him to the——"

The afflicted man, overcome with the terrible conflict between a sense of public duty, and a lingering, inextinguishable parental affection, fainted and fell into the arms of Marcus, who sprang to catch him.

While he was still insensible, the lieutenant of police, and the boy Bog, slipped out of the room, and started off on a search for Myndert Van Quintem, jr.

CHAPTER VI.

WHAT PAPER, TYPES, AND INK CAN DO.

When Marcus and his counsel, accompanied by the faithful lieutenant of police, arrived in a close carriage at the scene of the inquest, at the hour of adjournment next morning, they saw a convincing illustration of the power of paper, types, and ink.

The morning journals, with whole leaded pages of evidence, and new diagrams of the house and fatal room; and the enterprising illustrated weekly, with portraits of the deceased, the prisoner, his counsel, Tiffles, Patching (great hat and all), Patty Minford, the coroner, the foreman of the jury, a full-page design of the murder, as it was supposed to have taken place, representing the infuriate Wilkeson, club in hand, standing over the prostrate body of the inventor, from whose forehead the gore was pouring in torrents—all these delightful provocatives of sensation had done their full and perfect work.

At that moment, Marcus Wilkeson was known to the world of readers in New York, and the whole country round about, as the murderer of Eliphalet Minford.

On the second morning of the inquest an immense crowd of people were assembled in front of the house. They had been collecting since five A. M., when a party of six Jerseymen, having sold off their stock of nocturnal cabbages at Washington Market, had taken position of vantage before the house, from which they and their wagons were afterward dislodged with great effort by a squad of police. Some butcher boys, also returning from their night's work at market, were next on the ground, and selected adjacent awning posts and trees, as good points of observation. Mechanics and shop girls, going to their labor, recklessly postponed the duties of the day, and stopped to stare, awestricken, at the house.

A knot of people in a street, is like a drift of wood in a river. It chokes up the stream, and catches all the other wood that is floating down.

The police had in vain tried to clear out this human throng. They had waged the following contests with their fellow citizens, since six o'clock A. M. :—first, they had driven the Jersey market wagons to the street corner below; second, they had tumbled the butcher boys out of the trees, where they hung like a strange species of fruit; third, they had cleared a space of ten feet square in front of the house. Having done thus much, the police paused from exhaustion, and endured the jokes of the populace with philosophic disdain.

Three policemen guarded the door, within which no one was admitted but the coroner, the jury, witnesses, a few political friends of the coroner, who exhibited passes from him, and about twenty-five reporters, fifteen of whom really belonged to newspapers, and the remainder had a general connection with the press, which could never be clearly defined and established. To the magic word "reporter," accompanied by the flourish of a pencil and a roll of paper, the three policemen smiled obsequiously, and unbarred the way. Seeing how well this plan worked, two gentlemen of inelegant leisure, and at least one pickpocket, provided themselves with rolls of paper and pencils, and, giving the password, were admitted.

As the carriage rolled round the corner of the street, bringing Marcus in full view of these acres of men, women, and children—all waiting for him—the little courage which he had plucked up failed him, as plucked-up courage generally does. The sound of mingled laughter, jokes, oaths, and exclamations of impatience reached his ears.

"Great heavens!" he cried; "and I am to face all these people!" If his features could have been seen, at that instant, by some person who thought himself skilled in physiognomy, he would have been unhesitatingly pronounced guilty of several murders. Marcus sat in the rear part of the coach, and he leaned back to avoid observation.

As the carriage entered the outskirts of the throng, they became aware that it contained the man of their desires. Five small boys, who had run all the way from the station house, had brought the exciting intelligence. The vehicle was at once surrounded by clamorous people.

"Say, Mister, wich is the murderer, hey?" asked a red-shirted fellow of Matthew Maltboy, whose corpulent figure squeezed the thin form of Fayette Overtop into a corner of the front seat.

Maltboy was not quick at thinking; but, on this occasion, a brave thought came into his head before he could turn to the speaker. "I am the prisoner," said he.

"I knowed you wos," was the red-shirted reply, "by your —— ugly face."

"Thank you," said Matthew, meekly.

"That's the chap that killed the old man—him with the big chops," said the red-shirted individual to his numerous red and other shirted friends about.

"What! that fat cuss with the pig eyes?"

"Zackly!"

"He's the puffick image of his portrait in the ——— Weekly, isn't he?"

"Like as two peas."

There was truth in this; for the artist who sketched the portraits, had inadvertently placed Marcus's name under Matthew's portrait, and *vice versa.*

"Well," said another man, an expert in human nature, "I'd convict that fellow of murder any time, on the strength of his looks. Never were the worst passions of our nature more prominently shown than in that bad face." Having said which, the speaker looked about for somebody to contradict him, and was disappointed in finding no one.

Marcus Wilkeson said: "Here, Matt, none of that generous nonsense, if you please. I am the prisoner, my good people." As Marcus spoke, he stretched forward, and exhibited his face to the gaze of the red-shirted querist and his companions.

"No, you don't!" said that fiery leader. "This blubbery chap is the one. We knows him by his picter."

"No use disputing them, Mark," said Maltboy, with his indomitable smile.

The friendly struggle was soon terminated by their arrival at the house. Here the human jam was tremendous; but the police, under the direction of the lieutenant, succeeded in getting their convoy safe within the entry. The door was then closed, and five sturdy policemen stood outside to guard it.

On entering the room, everybody and everything were found just as they had been the day before—a day that seemed to Marcus a month ago. The jury were idling over the newspapers, or lazily turning their quids. The coroner, who looked a little the worse for his dinner of the day before, was bandying jokes with the facetious reporters. The other reporters were sharpening their pencils and laying out their note books. Some—the younger ones—were listening with a species of reverence, which they would soon outgrow, to the official jesting of the coroner. Others were squabbling over the right and title to certain chairs which possessed the extraordinary advantage of being a foot or two nearer the coroner than the other chairs. This is a grave cause of dispute among the reporters, and has been known to give rise to a great many hard words, and threats of subsequent chastisements, which are always indefinitely postponed.

The coroner nodded, and said "good morning" to the comers, and assumed a temporary official dignity, by taking down his right leg from the arm of the chair over which it gracefully depended. He also fortified himself, by thrusting a sizable chew into a corner of his mouth, as if he were carefully loading a pistol.

But neither the coroner, nor the jury, nor the reporters, nor the few private citizens who had obtained entrance by special dispensation, and sat gaping about the room, attracted the attention of the prisoner. Before him was one in whose presence all other persons faded into nothingness—the fair disturber of his peaceful life—the arbitress of his fate—Patty Minford.

CHAPTER VII.

PET AS A WITNESS.

LITTLE PET sat on the low stool which she had always occupied, and which Marcus, in his strange sentimentality, had always considered sacred to her. She was veiled; but, through the thick gauze, he could see that her beautiful face was deathly pale. Her slender frame shook with little convulsions, that made the chair rattle.

"Be calm, my dear child," said a stout, self-possessed woman who sat by her side, and held a bottle of salts conspicuously in her hand. "Remember, you have only to tell the trewth, and let the consekences fall where they may. Tell the trewth, as the old sayin' is, and shame the de—you know who."

Mrs. Crull—for she it was—checked herself with a neat cough. Her three months' private education seemed to have been lost upon her. She could never speak correctly out of Miss Pillbody's sight. Fortunately, her heart needed no education. She had taken the poor orphan girl to her home, and been a mother to her. In that phrase there is an horizonless world of love.

The deep, manly voice of Mrs. Crull carried assurance to the sinking heart of Patty. She took the extended hand, and pressed it, deriving strength from the contact of that strong, positive nature.

"If you please, Mr. Cronner," said Mrs. Crull, "I think you'd better go ahead with her examination at once. Quickest said, soonest mended, you know."

The prisoner and his counsel having taken their seats, the coroner having involuntarily thrown his right leg into the old, easy position, the jury having pricked up their ears, the reporters having cleared spaces for their elbows, the young girl proceeded to give her testimony. She was too nervous to make a clear, connected statement. Sometimes terror, sometimes tears, would choke her voice; but the cheering words and the smelling bottle of Mrs. Crull invariably "brought her round in nc time," in the words of that estimable lady.

Pet told the story of her return home on the fatal night; of her finding Mr. Wilkeson and her father in angry conversation; of her retiring to bed very much fatigued; of more conversation, growing angrier and angrier, which she overheard; of her marvellous vision in the night; of her waking next morning to find her vision true, and her father dead on the floor. All these facts, with which the reader is already familiar, the poor child made known to the jury in a fragmentary, roundabout way, as they were elicited by questions from the coroner, the jury, and occasionally the prisoner's counsel. The narrative of the vivid dream, or vision, produced a startling effect on the coroner, who was a firm believer in every species of supernaturalism which is most at variance with human experience and reason.

In his interrogatories to the witness, the coroner took the truth of the vision for granted. When she testified to the blows which (in her dream) she saw her father and the prisoner exchange, and the battered appearance of Mr. Wilkeson's face, the coroner looked at the prisoner, and was evidently disappointed to observe no traces of a bruise upon his pale brow or cheeks, nor the lightest discoloration about his eyes. But the absence of this corroboration did not, in the coroner's opinion, throw the least discredit on the dream.

But the foreman of the jury, who had been listening with an affrighted look to the marvellous story, and believing it, had his faith sadly shaken by this discrepancy. Having been fireman ten years, and foreman of a hose company six years, he knew by large experience how long it took to tone down a black eye or reduce a puffed cheek. The foreman looked at the smooth, clear face of the prisoner, smiled incredulously, and shook his head at his associates.

Fayette Overtop here acted his part with a skill worthy of a veteran. Instead of making a great ado over this weak point of the dream, he shrugged his shoulders, and smiled faintly at the jury. The jurors, who had been inclined, up to this time, to accept the dream as evidence, without question, now decided that it was nonsense.

Marcus Wilkeson sat and listened, as if the scene and all the actors in it, himself included, were only a dream too. The young girl's evidence, of which he had not an inkling before, would have astounded him, if anything could. But he had reached that point of reaction in the emotions, where a stolid and complete apathy happily takes the place of high nervous excitement. He somehow felt certain of his acouittal, but was strangely benumbed to his fate.

He looked at the witness—the holy idol of all his romantic and tender thoughts in days gone by—with unruffled composure. The marked stoicism of his demeanor was not lost on the reporters, and they noticed it in paragraphs to the effect that the prisoner exhibited a hardened indifference during the most thrilling portion of the evidence.

QUESTION BY THE CORONER (*after thinking it over a bit*). "Who do you say struck the fust blow, miss? Remember, now, you're on oath."

ANSWER. "My father, sir—or rather, I dreamed so."

The coroner was disappointed again, for he hoped that the witness would, on second thought, fix the commencement of the actual assault on the prisoner. "Your father, being old and kind o' feeble, struck a light blow, I s'pose."

WITNESS. "No, sir—a heavy one, I should judge; for it appeared to cut open Mr. Wilkeson's lip, and bruise his cheek. The blood seemed to run down his face in a stream." Here little Pet exhibited signs of faintness, which good Mrs. Crull stopped by an instant application of the smelling bottle.

CORONER. "Mr. Wilkeson struck back a terrible blow in return, I s'pose."

WITNESS. "Yes, sir. He hit my father right in the eye, raising a black and blue spot as large as a hen's egg." The painful recollection of this part of the dream so overpowered the witness, that she burst into tears, but was soon quieted by the motherly attentions of Mrs. Crull.

FOREMAN OF THE JURY. "I don't want to hurt the young lady's feelin's, but this 'ere dream is all nonsense; and it strikes me we're a lot o' fools to be listenin' to it. Why, Harry, you know, as well as I do, that there wasn't no bruise on the old man's face, exceptin' the big one on his forehead. No more is there a sign of a scratch on the prisoner's mug there. It's all gammon."

Three others of the jury nodded in approval of this sentiment. The remaining two shared somewhat in the coroner's reverence for dreams, and awaited further developments.

The coroner turned his quid uneasily. "You can think as you please, Jack," said he: "but we'll see—we'll see." The coroner, like many other men of greater claims to wisdom, used this enigmatical expression when he could not see anything.

A lawyer less crafty than Fayette Overtop would have protested against the reception of this singular testimony at the outset, and at intervals of a minute during its delivery. But he foresaw that, being a dream, it must be full of absurdities, which would surely betray themselves, and help his client. Besides, he was curious to hear all of the evidence, however ridiculous and worthless, against the prisoner.

The witness then proceeded to the close of her testimony, amid the silence of all hearers. The narrative of the dreadful grapple, the struggle for the club, and the death blow given by Mr. Wilkeson to her prostrate father—all delivered with an intense earnestness, broken only by occasional sobs and pauses of anguish—produced a powerful impression. As she finished, and fell, half fainting, into the arms of Mrs. Crull, the coroner nodded his head slowly, and said:

"What do you think of dreams now, Jack? Something in 'em, eh?"

The foreman shared in the general feeling of awe; but he nad given his opinion that the dream was nonsense, and stood oy it. "It's strange," said he. "It's what the newspapers call a ''strordinary quincidence,' that the young lady should 'a' dreamed out this murder so plain. I do' 'no' much about the science o' dreams, but I think this one might be explained somethin' in this way: The young lady heerd the old man and Mr. Wilkeson here talkin' strong, when she come home that night. She went to sleep with their conversation ringin' in her ears. Part on it she heerd in her dreams, and the rest she 'magined. She says she was afraid there would be trouble between 'em when she went to bed. The fight, and the murder, and all that, which she says she saw in a dream, or vision like, might have grown out o' that naterally enough. That's my notion of it, off hand. I've often gone to bed, myself, thinkin' of somethin' horrible that was goin' to happen, and dreamt that it did happen."

THE INQUEST. MARCUS SPRINGS TO HIS FEET.

This was precisely the theory upon which Fayette Overtop intended to explain the dream to the jury when the proper time arrived. He was glad that the foreman had done it instead; for he knew the tenacity with which a man, having given an opinion, defends it. To have so potent an advocate of his client's innocence on the jury, was a strong point.

"Very good, old boy," said the coroner; "but, if the prisoner didn't commit the murder, who did?"

This question, so manifestly unjust, and betraying the coroner's intention to sacrifice Marcus to a theory, roused that unfortunate man to consciousness, and he sprang to his feet. But the wiser Overtop placed his hands upon his friend's shoulder, whispered in his ear, and forced him reluctantly into his seat. Overtop knew that the argumentative foreman could best dispose of the coroner.

The foreman replied to the coroner's question:

"As to who did the murder, that's what we're here to find out. But, for one, I sha'n't bring in no man guilty till it's proved onto him."

The foreman's face was a dull one, but it became suddenly luminous with an idea:

"You say, miss, that you was waked by a noise as of somethin' heavy fallin' on the floor?"

"Yes, sir."

"You s'pose—as we all s'pose—that it was your father's body that fell, when he received his death blow?"

"Yes, sir."

"You say you heerd no one a-goin' out o' the room?"

"No, sir."

"That's not strange; for the murd'rer could 'a' slipped off his boots or shoes, and walked out pufficklу quiet. I noticed, this mornin', and the other members of the jury can see for themselves, that the boards of the floor don't creak when you walk on 'em, nor the entry door neither when you open it. Didn't you never observe that succumstance?"

"Yes, sir; but it did not occur to me when I woke up. I

thought, if the dream had been true, that I should have heard Mr. Wilkeson moving around in the room, or going out of the door. I listened for a long time, as I have already said, and, hearing nobody, I thought the dream was nothing but a nightmare, as father used to call it."

"One more question, miss, which may or may not be of some consekence. Haven't you no idee about what time it was when you was waked up by this noise of somethin' fallin'?"

"No, sir; not the least. It might have been about midnight, I should guess."

"Think a minute, miss, if you didn't hear any sound outside that could give you some idee of the time." The foreman fixed his eyes piercingly on the witness.

She reflected a moment. "Yes—yes; I do remember, that when I jumped out of bed—which I did the very second that I woke up—and listened at the door, I heard the fire bells striking. Now, if anybody could tell what time that happened."

"At precisely twenty-five minutes of twelve," said the foreman, in a solemn voice. "It was for the seventh district—the only 'larm that night. It was a false 'larm, and only three or four rounds was sounded. Did you hear the bell many times?"

"Only two or three, and then it stopped. The sound was very plain, sir, because the bell tower is only a short distance from here, you know."

"Exactly," said the foreman. "You woke up just as Uncle Ith was givin' off the last round."

There was a deep, awestruck silence in the room; for all understood the object of these inquiries.

"Now, gentlemen," continued the foreman, in a trembling voice, "let the prisoner only prove that he was a half, or a quarter, or an eighth of a mile from here when that 'larm was sounded, and I rather think he will clear himself. Where are the policemen that the prisoner saw that night?"

A noise, as of heavy official boots, was heard on the stairs, sending a strange thrill through the hearts of all present.

"God be praised," said Fayette Overtop, "if the lieutenant has found them." It was the first time that the model young lawyer had shown any signs of emotion.

CHAPTER VIII.

THE BENEFICENCE OF FIRE BELLS.

The door opened, and the tall form of the police lieutenant appeared, attended by two patrolmen. The patrolmen, on entering, looked directly at the prisoner, and seemed to recognize him. The police lieutenant appeared to be pleased with his success in finding the witnesses, after a hunt through several station houses; but he was not aware what importance the testimony which they could give had suddenly acquired. The witnesses had been searched for at the suggestion of Fayette Overtop, with the vague hope of making them useful in some way.

The coroner scowled at the witnesses, for he feared that they would prove the man innocent, who, in his opinion, was the murderer. Having adopted this theory at the outset, and staked the whole issue upon it, he felt a natural reluctance to give it up.

The lieutenant explained to the coroner that the two officers could probably throw some light on the prisoner's movements, the night of the murder.

The coroner administered the oath to both of them, as follows:

"Holeup your ri't'an'. You swear to tell truth, th'ole truth, nothin' but truth, s'elpyeGod. Kiss the book."

The men complied with these impressive formalities, and the coroner then proceeded to interrogate one of them—a strapping fellow with an intensely Irish face.

"Name?" said the coroner.

"Patrick O'Dougherty, yer Honor."

The phrase "Yer Honor" produced 'ts customary gracious effect.

"Do you spell O'Dougherty with a 'k'?" asked the coroner.

"Hang me if I knows!" said the O'Dougherty. "I niver spilt it. Spill it to suit yezself, yer Honor."

"Spell it in the usual way, with a 'k,'" said the coroner, turning to the reporters.

"Your residence, Mr. O'Dougherty?"

"Me what?"

"Your residence. Where do you live?"

"Oh! it's fare I live yer want to know. In Mulberry street, near Baxter."

"You belong to the perlice, I believe?" asked the coroner.

"It's quare ye should ax me that!" replied the O'Dougherty, with an enormous smile.

"Because you have the perliceman's hat, club, and badge? You forget," said the coroner, patronizingly, "that courts of justice doesn't know nothin' until it's proved to them. As a coroner, I shouldn't know my own grandmother, until she swore to herself."

"'Tisn't that, yer Honor; but becos yer got me onto the perlice yerself. Don't yer 'member, on 'lection day, I smashed two ticket booths of t'other can'date, in the Sixth Ward, lickt as much as a dozen men who was workin' agen ye, an' din was put into the Tumes over night—bad luck to the Tumes, I say! Well, yer Honor, ye was 'lected coroner by a small vote; an', in turn for me services, ye got me 'p'inted——"

"Ah! oh! I remember, now," said the coroner, somewhat confused. "I did not know you in the perliceman's dress. Well, Mr. O'Dougherty, did you see the prisoner on the night of the murder?"

"I did, yer Honor. It was about twelve o'clock. I was sittin' on a bar'l in front of Pat McKibbin's store, corner of

Washin'ton and ——— streets. I was watchin' the bar'l, yer Honor, becos Pat McKibbin had some of 'em stole lately, ye see."

"Could yer swear to him, Mr. O'Dougherty?"

"Could I shwear to me own mother?—Hivin rest her sowl! Bedad, I shud know him a thousan' years from now. Didn't he shtop and light his siggar at me poipe? And didn't his nose touch me own?"

"Did he look pale and excited?" asked the coroner.

"No, yer Honor; his face was red as a brick, an', though it was a cowld night, he looked to be warm wid fasht walkin'."

"Did he say anythin'?"

"No; he only axed for a light."

"Was his 'pearance 'spicious?"

"No, yer Honor, more'n yer own. No offince to yez."

"That'll do, Mr. O'Dougherty. Next witness."

"If you please, your Honor," said the smooth Overtop, rising, "you have accidentally omitted to ask one very important question. The prisoner stated, on his preliminary examination, you remember, that, when he stopped to light a cigar from the pipe of a policeman, he heard the sound of a fire bell commencing to strike. Miss Minford testifies, that when she was roused from sleep by the noise of her father falling to the floor, she heard the alarm for the Seventh District. McKibbin's store, at the corner of Washington and ——— streets, is more than half a mile from here. In view of these facts, I will, with your Honor's permission, ask Mr. O'Dougherty if he heard the fire alarm that night; and, if so, whether the prisoner was in sight at the time?"

"Shure, an' I heerd it," answered the O'Dougherty. "It was fur the Seventh District. An' wasn't this gin'leman here at the ind o' me poipe, jist when it begun to bang away?"

Overtop cast one triumphant glance at the jury, which was fully reciprocated by the foreman and four others.

"I have no more questions to ask, your Honor," said Overtop.

"Nor I," said the coroner, "as the witness's testimony has no great bearin' on the case, that I can see. What is your name, Mister—er——"

"Thomas Jelliman," responded the second policeman, a stout, bluff, honest-looking fellow. He did not say "Your Honor," and thereby offended the coroner.

"Well, what's yer bizness, anyhow?" asked the coroner, curtly.

"I should think you would remember that I was a policeman," said the witness, looking the coroner straight in the eye.

The coroner, taking a second observation of the witness, recalled him as the identical officer who had arrested him, one Christmas night, for drunkenness, and locked him up in the station house. This little occurrence was before his election to the dignified and responsible office of County Coroner.

"If you don't remember me," said the witness, "I think I could bring myself to your mind easy. On a certain Christmas night, not many years ago——"

"Never mind the particulars, Mr. Jelliman," observed the coroner. "Come to look at yer, I recolleck yer very well. Ahem! What do you know about this 'ere case, Mr. Jelliman?"

"Nothing, sir, except that I can swear to having seen the prisoner, on the night of the murder, at the corner of West and ——— streets. He was smoking a cigar, and walking fast. As he passed me, he said, 'A cold night, Mr. Policeman.' This made me notice him particularly, because it isn't very often that people throw away civilities on us. Just as he turned the corner below me, the alarm bells struck the last round for the Seventh District. They had struck three or four rounds. That is all I know about the affair."

"I have no other questions to ask, Mr. Jelliman," said the coroner, with great politeness.

The coroner was baffled. He had staked the whole case upon the theory of Marcus Wilkeson's guilt, and had made no attempt to procure other testimony than what would prove that supposition. He scratched his head and rolled his quid in a perfect quandary.

Another noise was heard on the stairs, as of several persons hurriedly ascending.

Then the door opened, and an excited group made its appearance. In advance was a slender young man, whose face was pale with debauchery. His clothes were rich, and had an unpleasantly new look. As he stepped over the threshold, he glanced coolly about the room, and, his eyes resting on the coroner, smiled.

"Ah, Myndert, my boy," said the coroner, "what are you here for?"

CHAPTER IX.

AN OLD MAN'S OFFERING.

"HANG me if I know, Harry! It's the old man's work. He'll explain it to you."

Behind this easy young man came a strong policeman, who, immediately upon his entrance, received a nod of approbation from the lieutenant. Behind the policeman walked, with bended white head and tottering limbs, the venerable Mr. Van Quintem. The old gentleman was partly supported, in his infirmity, by the boy Bog. It was a touching sight to see the confiding trust with which the weakness of sixty-eight clung to the strong arm of nineteen. Bog hung down his head modestly, and blushed. He was not seen even to look at the little veiled figure which sat in the middle of the room. But young Myndert Van Quintem looked at it, and bowed with the deepest respect. The bow was answered by a faint nod and a delicate blush. Mrs. Crull observed the interchange of recognitions, and frowned to herself.

"Mr. Coroner," said the old gentleman, straightening himself, and coming forward with a quick step, as one who was about to perform an unpleasant task, and would hurry through it, "this young man is my son. God knows what love I have lavished upon him from the day that he was born, and with what ingratitude he has repaid me. But—but that is neither here nor there. I have come here to deliver him up to you as a prisoner——"

"As a prisoner!" echoed the coroner; and he and all looked amazed at this strange announcement.

"Why should it surprise you? It is a simple act of justice. I have reason to think that my son knows something about this murder" (here the old gentleman's voice faltered); "and my duty, as a good citizen and an honest man, requires me to surrender him. There are other affairs of a private nature between myself and my son—he knows to what I refer—which I am not prepared to make public at the present time." The old gentleman looked significantly at his son, who smiled calmly at him in return.

A chair was brought for Mr. Van Quintem, sen., and he sank into it. The young man seated himself in another chair which was handed to him by the attentive coroner himself.

"Now, Myndert, my good fellow," said the coroner, "if yer knows anything about this affair, fire away."

"Will the coroner be good enough to swear the witness?" asked Fayette Overtop.

"Oh! I'd quite forgot it." And the coroner mumbled his irreverent jargon.

"Two minutes are enough to tell you all I know, Harry," said the young man, in a sweet, effeminate voice. "I happened to save Miss Minford's life, a few months ago—she will give you the particulars, no doubt, if you desire them—and that is the way I made her acquaintance." (Here another respectful bow to the young lady.) "Since then, I have met her, quite accidentally, a few times, and—I do not pretend to conceal it—have gradually come to feel an interest—a brotherly interest, I may call it—in her." (The coroner smiled.) "Having learned from her that she was receiving her education at the expense of Mr. Wilkeson, and that that gentleman was a constant visitor at her father's house, I thought it proper, as a sincere and disinterested friend of the young lady, to make some inquiries into his character. Judging, from the result of these inquiries, that his designs were not honorable toward Miss Minford—Mr. Wilkeson will pardon the expression, but I am under oath, and must tell the truth as to my motives—I took the liberty of writing a note to Mr. Minford, merely cautioning him against Mr. Wilkeson. I did not sign my name to the note, because I was not personally acquainted with Mr. Minford—in fact, never saw him in my life—and did not wish to assume the responsibility, disagreeable to every sensitive person, of interfering in another man's family affairs. The object of the note was to make Mr. Minford cautious. I presume no one will undertake to say that a father can be too cautious concerning the honor of a young and lovely daughter." (Another respectful glance at Miss Minford.) "I am aware anonymous letters are a little irregular, in the opinions of most people. But, when sent with a good motive, I really don't see the harm in them."

"Nor I neither," said the coroner. "It strikes me they're correct enough when the motive's a good 'un."

"But, your Honor, when an anonymous letter is full of lies and slanders, I respectfully submit that it is a piece of cowardly malice, which the law ought to punish with the utmost severity." Fayette Overtop spoke with tranquillity and firmness, looking young Van Quintem directly in the eye, and making him quail.

The judicious phrase, "Your Honor," alone saved Overtop from an explosion of official wrath. "The Court can't allow these interruptions, Mr. Overtop," said the coroner. "Her dignity must be maintained. As for 'nonymous letters, whether it's right or wrong to send them, people will differ. The coroner and the jury is competent to judge for themselves. Go ahead, Myndert."

"As the first letter seemed to have no effect, I sent another, suggesting that Mr. Minford should inquire into Mr. Wilkeson's history in the little village of ———, Westchester

County, where he was born, and lived many years. I learned from Miss Minford that her father visited Westchester County one day, and presume that he made some important discoveries there; for Miss Minford told me, that, on his return, he had forbidden Mr. Wilkeson to come to the house. If there was any harm in putting Mr. Minford on the track to find out the real truth about the man who was a constant attendant at his fireside, I do not see it."

"Nor I neither," said the coroner. "The end, as the sayin' is, justifies the means."

"If your Honor pleases," said the facile Overtop, "we could easily prove that all the reports which Mr. Minford gathered in Westchester County, prejudicial to my client, arose from a confounding of another person with him. But, as this explanation would involve the disclosure of private family affairs, and also the reflection of disgrace on the memory of the dead, my client prohibits me from saying more on the subject. But all this, as none knows better than your Honor, has nothing to do with the case. We ask that my client shall either be proved guilty of the murder, or of some knowledge of it, or released."

Fayette Overtop here looked volumes of confidence at the jury; and five of the jury looked back volumes of agreement with him.

"Nobody can be in a bigger hurry than me, Mr. Overtop," said the coroner, with tolerable good nature. "These 'ere inquests, commencin' in the mornin' and holdin' on a good part of the day, are rather hard on a chap 'customed to his 'leven-o'clock drink. I have to make up for the loss by adjournin' early in the arternoon. Ha! ha! Now, Myndert, my boy, rush her through. You don't know anythin' about the murder, I s'pose. You were somewhere else on the fatal night, of course—and I can guess where. At Brown's, eh?"

Brown's was a notorious gambling house on Broadway.

"Exactly, Harry. I was at Brown's from nine P. M. to four o'clock the following morning. And, if I mistake not, there is a gentleman in this room who can swear to having seen me there, say from ten to eleven." Saying this, young Van Quintem winked hard at the coroner.

"You needn't mince matters," said the coroner. "I was at Brown's that night, and between the hours you name. Being a public officer, I sometimes look into Brown's, and a good many other places, too, to see that nothin' a'n't a-goin' on wrong. Ha! I partickly 'member it, because I accidentally lost about fifty dollars there that night. Ha! ha!"

"I think I recollect the little circumstance," said the witness, with a smile.

"Very likely. Ha! Now, Myndert, of course we all understand that you are innocent; but, to satisfy the public, I guess I'd better summon a few witnesses from Brown's, to prove you were there all night."

"I thought of that, Harry, and requested a number of my friends at Brown's to drop around here, and prove an *alibi* for me. They were very much engaged at the time, or they would have come with me."

"They were playing faro," said the old gentleman, "and my son was gambling with them. Wretched young man, how often have I cautioned you against that vice!"

"The cautioning I don't object to," said the son; "but I consider it unfair to drag a fellow away from a streak of good luck. I was raking in the piles just as you and the policeman, and that mop-headed youth behind you" (he alluded to the boy Bog) "came down on me. Ah! I see the game is finished, and here they are."

Four men, of a highly correct appearance, dressed in quiet good taste, who would have passed in the Broadway muster for merchants of the severest practical variety, entered the room.

They nodded in the most gentlemanly manner to the coroner, and gave a friendly recognition to young Myndert.

"You may be willing to believe these polished scoundrels

under oath; but hang me if I would!" said the old gentleman, with emphasis.

The four gamblers showed their even rows of white teeth pleasantly, and one of them replied:

"You are an elderly gentleman, Mr. Van Quintem, and the father of our young friend; and, of course, you are permitted to abuse us as much as you like."

"It seems to me, Mr. Van Quintem," said the coroner, "that you are rather hard on these gen'lemen, who, so fur as I know 'em, is of the highest respectability. Don't yer want to have yer son prove an *alibi?*"

"I want to have him prove the truth, and that's all. And for that reason I wouldn't credit such evidence as these men will give."

"You would like to have me hanged, my dear father," said the son, mildly; "but I don't think you will be gratified in that amiable little desire. Eh, Harry?"

The coroner grinned, shifted his quid, put on his most serious official look, and said:

"No more of this 'ere jokin', if you please, gen'lemen. A inquest isn't zactly the place for fun."

He then proceeded to swear and interrogate the four new witnesses. They took the oath decorously, kissing the book in the politest, most gentlemanly manner. Their testimony was to the effect that young Van Quintem passed the night of the murder, from ten P. M. till four A. M., at Brown's, and was not absent one minute. They were able to corroborate the fact, by a reference to pocket memorandum books, in which entries such as "Van Q., debit $50," or "Van Q., credit $100," appeared at intervals. As to the general character of the house, upon which several members of the jury asked questions, they testified that it was a species of club house, where a few gentlemen of excellent reputation occasionally met for the purposes of innocent social intercourse. Games of chance were sometimes played at Brown's, to while away an hour; and betting was now and then done, in a strictly honorable and legitimate way. Several of the jurymen would have improved the occasion, to learn all about the internal management of Brown's; but the coroner decided that such questions were entirely "relevant" (meaning irrelevant), and suggested that, as there were no more witnesses, the case might as well go to the jury. The coroner had just consulted his watch, and found that it was four o'clock. He was aware, from the turn things had taken, that he had lost the verdict which he hoped to obtain; but that was no reason why he should lose his dinner. The coroner was not a man of energy; and, being foiled in his efforts to convict Marcus Wilkeson, he had no disposition to pursue the matter further. Besides, he had already achieved a large measure of profitable notoriety from the case; for he had been ridiculed and abused in most of the city papers; and *that* insured him, beyond all doubt, the nomination for and election to the State Senate, for which he was an aspirant at the next fall campaign. Under all these circumstances, the coroner was satisfied.

The jurors, receiving but a shilling a day, and being hungry and tired, were quite willing to wind up the case. After putting their heads together, whispering and nodding about five minutes, the foreman declared the following as their verdict:

"That the deceased, Eliphalet Minford, came to his death, on the night of the ——— day of April, 185–, from a wound inflicted on the head by a club in the hands of some person unknown to the jurors."

Overtop and Maltboy took the verdict as a matter of course, having anticipated it for some time. Marcus Wilkeson, who had been in a gloomy stupor for the past hour, and had expected the worst, looked up in surprise at this lucky dispensation of Fate. Tears sprang to his eyes, and he extended a hand to each of his faithful friends, by whom he was warmly congratulated on the happy issue of the affair. The jurors also came forward with their congratulations. Even the coroner said, "Well, Mr. Wilkeson, I did my pootiest to hold you, because I thought you was the murderer; but the jury doesn't indorse my 'pinion, and I gives in." Mrs. Crull, who had been watching Marcus narrowly, and was firmly impressed with the conviction of his innocence, came forward with a warm hand, and tried to think of a proverb suitable to the occasion, but could not. Patty Minford removed the veil from her face, and looked at her benefactor. She made a motion as if to rise and go toward him. Then an expression of doubt stole over her features; and Marcus, who observed her at that moment, knew that the vision of the night was still before her, and that she could not hold him guiltless though a dozen juries had released him. This thought touched Marcus with sadness, which all the congratulations of his friends could not disperse.

A faint cry was heard. Old Mr. Van Quintem had fallen from his chair, and would have dropped upon the floor, but for the strong arm of the boy Bog. He was in the act of rising from his seat for the purpose of offering his hand to Marcus, when the vertigo, from which he was an occasional sufferer, seized him.

"Poor old gentleman!" said Marcus, forgetful of all else, and rushing to the side of his venerable friend. Directing that the windows be opened, Marcus, aided by the boy Bog, bore the senseless form to the fresh, cool air. The grateful breeze, and a cup of cold water applied to his brow, soon restored the wretched father to a beginning of consciousness.

As he lay there, more dead than alive, in the arms of his two friends, the ingrate son, having lighted a cigar, looked coldly over the shoulders of the bystanders at the senseless figure of his father, and said, in the sweetest voice:

"Poor old fellow! He has only himself to blame for kicking up all this row. I told him it would be too much for his nerves; but he would insist on dragging me up here. I forgive him from the bottom of my heart."

The bystanders looked on in amazement at this speech.

The son continued: "I'm glad to see that he is in good

hands. Upon my word, nothing would give me greater pleasure than to help a little; but I fear that, when the old man came out of it, and saw me over him, he would go off again. So I guess I had better leave."

And young Van Quintem sauntered cheerfully out of the room, in company with his four friends from Brown's. The coroner had been waiting at the foot of the stairs for them; and the party adjourned to the nearest drinking saloon, when the coroner, overjoyed at having got rid of a tedious and embarrassing case, stood treat for one round.

But who killed the inventor?

The papers and the police, after groping for weeks in search of the answer, turned it over to the solution of Time, with the comforting assurance that MURDER WILL OUT.

BOOK TENTH.

DONE ON BOTH SIDES.

CHAPTER I.

A FISHER OF MEN.

Mr. Augustus Whedell was a gentleman who had been living handsomely for three years on his wits.

There was nothing remarkable in Mr. Whedell's personal appearance, with the exception of his wig. It was his fond belief that this wig looked like natural hair; but everybody knew it was a wig across the street. He also wore a gold double eyeglass, which he handled as effectively as a senorita her fan. Most of his loans, credits, and extensions, had been obtained by the dexterous manipulation of that eyeglass.

Mr. Whedell twirled the dangerous instrument, and opened and shut it with more than his usual grace, one evening toward the middle of April. He was about to broach a disagreeable subject to his daughter, who, blooming, and exquisitely dressed, sat by the fire and yawned.

"My dear Clementina, you are now twenty years old, and ought to be married. Delays are dangerous. What do you think of Chiffield?"

Mr. Whedell spoke bluntly, and to the point, because he

was addressing his own daughter, and also because short speeches suited his natural languor.

"He's a horrid dancer!" said that young lady.

"Granted. But when he does dance, he jingles money in his pocket."

"He's a perfect fright, pa. You won't deny that?"

"I won't deny that he is a plain, substantial gentleman. He has immense feet, and he is a little bald. What of that?"

"Oh! nothing," replied Clementina, in a tone that signified "Everything."

Her father caught the irony of the remark, and said:

"My dear child, I know the natural leaning of your sex to handsome men. You are like your mother there. But remember, they never have any money—as a general rule. I won't undertake to explain the curious fact. But fact it is, you will admit that."

"Very likely. But I hate this old Chiffield."

Mr. Whedell smiled, twirled his double eyeglass a few dozen times round his forefinger, and said:

"My darling daughter, listen, and you will appreciate the advantages of this match."

Clementina frowned, and bit her finger nails.

"My child," continued the fond parent, "I have always concealed my troubles from you. They can no longer be kept a secret. This house is not mine. Most of this furniture is unpaid for. The last month's bills at the butcher's, baker's, and grocer's are still due. I have exhausted my credit, and don't know where to raise a dollar. That is my 'situation,' as the newspapers say."

Clementina turned pale with amazement, and could not say a word.

"You are willing to hear me? I will explain further. Three years ago, my old friend Mr. Abernuckle failed. He owned this house, and, wishing to save it from his creditors, he had previously made a sham sale of it to me. I have occupied it free of rent. On the strength of this house, I got credit for furniture, for clothes, for our bread and meat. On the strength of this house, I have borrowed money enough to keep my principal creditors at bay. On the strength of this house, we occupy to-day a very fair position in society. On the strength of this house, I propose to marry you."

His daughter still looked on with open mouth, like one stupefied.

"But, to do this, no time must be lost. My friend Abernuckle has at last settled with his creditors at fifteen per cent., and wants possession of the house on the 1st of May. On that day this will be our home no longer."

There was a fearless pull at the door bell. "It is a creditor," said Mr. Whedell. "I will face him."

Mr. Whedell went to the door, and returned in a few moments. "It was the butcher," said he. "He had called twice to-day, and, not finding me in, takes this unusual hour to ask for a settlement. The old excuses would not do. What do you suppose I told him this time?"

"I can't imagine. Something dreadful, I suppose," was the shuddering reply.

"The man had to be got rid of. We must have meat. I was at my wits' end. So I took the liberty of telling him, confidentially, that my daughter would marry a wealthy merchant in a few days, and asked him, as a favor, to let the bill run on to the 1st of May. On that day he should positively be paid. The man grumbled at first, but finally said he would give me one more trial, and then went away. Neatly arranged, wasn't it, my dear?"

Mr. Whedell would have been delighted with one word of approval (even a qualified one) from his daughter, but she would not, or could not speak it.

"You listen attentively, my darling. I am glad to see it. This plan worked so well with the butcher, that I shall try it on with the upholsterer, the baker, the grocer, the tailor, and the rest of my long list of creditors. I shall stake all on the 1st of May. To save us from a grand explosion, and to obtain a roof for your head and mine on the 1st of May, you must marry immediately."

Miss Clementina Whedell, like many other people, had an unsuspected strength of character which only a great occasion could call out. "It is perfectly atrocious," said she, at length, "and I am making a grave sacrifice of my happiness; but I suppose I must do it. Are you sure this Chiffield is rich?"

"Now, you are my own dear daughter!" said Mr. Whedell, tossing his double eyeglass up and catching it, as was his custom when exulting. "Your question is a prudent one, and worthy of you. I am happy to inform you that Chiffield is worth one hundred and fifty thousand dollars."

Clementina smiled faintly, though she tried to look like a martyr.

"I learn this from the tax rolls. When Chiffield first began to call here, and showed a profound interest in my conversation, I knew that he was after you, and I thought it best to look into his resources. The tax rolls, which are the best possible evidence, show that he has ten lots in Harlem, with a cottage tenement on each of them, and several acres now rented to German gardeners in the Twelfth Ward. These are rated in a lump at seventy-five thousand dollars, which is a low estimate. So much for the real estate. Now the personal property of Upjack, Chiffield & Co. is valued on the same tax rolls (which always understate it) at three hundred thousand dollars. Suppose Chiffield to own a one-fourth interest only, and there you have the item of seventy-five thousand dollars more. Grand total, one hundred and fifty thousand dollars. A nearer figure would probably be two hundred thousand dollars; but I will not build castles in the air for you. Chiffield is only forty—which is, in fact, young. He is healthy and energetic. The firm are making money. He will yet be a millionnaire. Confess, now, that I have chosen wisely for you."

Here another decisive pull at the door bell. Mr. Whedell answered it in person. Returning, he merely said, giving his double eyeglass a fillip, "The furniture man. Have fixed him for the 1st of May. So far, the plan works well."

"But are you sure, pa," asked the discreet Clementina, "that Mr. Chiffield will offer himself?"

"Positive; because he has always been so very attentive to me. When men flatter, and study the hobbies of the father, they are after the daughter in earnest. Mr. Chiffield's very figure—the cut of his jib, so to speak—is that of a marrying man. Only you must give him some little encouragement. Not keep him at a distance, as you have hitherto done."

"But he may not be anxious to marry before the 1st of May. Then what?"

"Poor thing! how little you understand mankind! He will marry you at twenty-four hours' notice, if you will let him. All men are alike impatient and unreasonable in such matters. It is the women who hold back—after they are safely engaged."

"La, pa! how knowingly you talk!"

"I flatter myself I know something of the human species," returned Mr. Whedell. "Ah! another ring. Too faint for a creditor. Mr. Chiffield, perhaps."

CHAPTER II.

PLAYING WITH THE LINE.

THE conjecture was correct. But with Mr. Chiffield came Matthew Maltboy. They had arrived on the door steps at the same moment, coming from different directions.

Mr. Whedell received Chiffield with his heartiest grip, and inflicted only a mild squeeze on the hand of Maltboy, whose appearance at that time he considered decidedly unfortunate. The father thought he had observed in Clementina signs of preference for that corpulent young lawyer. He was pained to see that Clementina barely extended the tips of her fingers to Chiffield, while to Maltboy she gave her whole palm with great cordiality. Not only this, but she encouraged Maltboy to take a seat by her, and commenced talking with him of the opera, of balls, of new music, of fashions, of the last novel, rattling away on these subjects as if her whole soul were wrapped up in the discussion. It was almost a monologue. Maltboy's part consisted of "Yes;" "I think so too;" "We agree perfectly," and adjectives of admiration occasionally thrown in. That musical voice! He could have listened with rapture to its recital of the multiplication table.

Mr. Chiffield and Mr. Whedell had settled themselves on a *tête-à-tête*, and, after some cursory observations on the weather, commenced talking of finance—a theme of which neither of those gentlemen ever tired.

"So money is getting tighter?" said Mr. Whedell, after a pause to digest the awful truth which Mr. Chiffield had imparted to him. "Now I shouldn't be surprised, sir, to hear of failures before long, and in quarters where the public least expect them."

If Mr. Whedell's double eyeglass had been astride his nose instead of swinging in his fingers, he might have noticed a faint paleness blending with the deep yellow of Mr. Chiffield's complexion. That gentleman replied, a little more quickly than was his wont:

"A few small, weak houses may go down, perhaps, but the strong ones will weather the storm easy enough. If our establishment could live through 1847, it is in no danger now."

"And such was the good fortune of Upjack, Chiffield & Co., I well remember," said Mr. Whedell.

Mr. Chiffield bowed his gracious acknowledgment of the handsome historical allusion.

"How is Erie, Mr. Chiffield?"

"Looking up."

"Sure of it?"

"A leading Wall-street man told me, this afternoon, it

would advance three per cent. this week. I have a slight interest in watching it," said Mr. Chiffield, smiling.

"So have I," said Mr. Whedell, smiling also.

During their conversation, and the remainder of their financial dialogue, Mr. Whedell kept one ear, and occasionally one eye, inclined toward his daughter and the favored Maltboy. If there was a hint conveyed in those side glances at his daughter, she either did not notice it, or did not choose to take it. Sometimes Mr. Chiffield looked in the same direction, but casually, as it were, and without one sign of impatience visible in the depths of his calm brown eyes. Mr. Chiffield was not a nervous man.

Matthew Maltboy was so perfectly free from selfishness at this moment, that he would cheerfully have spared a few words from Miss Whedell's delightful monologue for the gratification of his late rival ("late" was now decidedly the word, in Maltboy's opinion) over the way. In the exercise of his large charity and compassion, he pitied that unfortunate, sadly disappointed dealer in dry goods.

This pity, as Matthew used to say in after days, was thrown away. At the end of a brilliant description of a new set of quadrilles which Miss Whedell had danced at a sociable the night before, that young lady said, "Excuse me," and crossed the room to a what-not in the corner, and searched for something among a pile of magazines and pictures. The thought that she was making efforts to please him, tickled Matthew's vanity. While she was overhauling the pile, Mr. Whedell left his seat by Chiffield, and took the one just vacated by his daughter. Matthew received him with the diplomatic courtesy due to the parent of one's enchantress, and made a well-meant if not novel remark on the state of the weather. Mr. Whedell mildly disputed his proposition (whatever it was)—for Mr. W. was always disputatious on that subject—and then passed to the consideration of national politics. "The one topic natually suggests the other," said Mr. Whedell, "for they are equally variable." This was one of the father's few standard jokes; and Maltboy always laughed at it with the heartiness of a future son-in-law. They then grappled with the great theme in earnest.

CHAPTER III.

PULLING IN.

Clementina, having found what she sought, glided to the chair which her father had relinquished, and said, coquettishly, "Now I have come to entertain *you*, Mr. Chiffield. You were speaking of Niagara Falls, the other day. Here are some photographs of them, taken for me on the spot." She handed the pictures to Mr. Chiffield. That gentleman took them with a profound bow, glanced over them, and said, "How elegant!" "What rich scenery!" "How tasty they are got up, a'n't they?" "This is the showiest picture;" "Here's a neat one," &c., &c., &c. Mr. Chiffield had contracted the use of a certain class of highly descriptive adjectives in selling dry goods. Clementina watched him narrowly, and thought how nicely she could manage this heavy fellow.

"How many times have you been to the Falls?" she asked, when Chiffield had shuffled through the photographs twice.

"Three times," said Chiffield, telling a white lie; for he had seen them at morning, noon, and evening on the same day. "And how often have you visited them, Miss Whedell?"

"Oh! so often I can't remember. My last visit was early last autumn. Oh! pa, did we go to Niagara Falls before or after our trip to the White Mountains?"

"After it, my child," replied the father, who maintained a cocked ear toward his child. "Don't you recollect we went from the Falls to Lake George, and stayed there till the first week in November? That was the year we omitted Newport and Saratoga, for a wonder," he added, conveying the idea, in a look to Mr. Chiffield, that such an omission was a marvel in their annual experiences.

"You love the Falls, I suppose?" said Mr. Chiffield.

"Oh! not much. I think they're dreadfully overrated." Clementina was determined not to be won too cheaply.

"So I think," said Chiffield, delighted to speak his real sentiments this time; "though everybody is obliged to praise 'em, because that's the fashion."

"But, though the Falls a'n't much, I must say the balls and hops are delightful. The fresh air there seems to give one strength to dance all night without a bit of fatigue. I bought these pictures because they show the hotels and other places where I have had such delicious dances."

Chiffield execrated dancing, because he had large feet, and egs slightly bowed. He moved in the cotillon or waltz with a certain elephantine ponderousness and sagacity. Therefore she tantalized him with these reminiscences.

"You see the Clifton House, there, on the Canada side? One night I danced eight waltzes, six polkas, four quadrilles, three fancy dances, and wound up, at five o'clock, with the German."

"Wonderful!" observed Chiffield, not knowing what else to say.

"Perhaps you think I was tired? Oh! not a particle. Next night we had a little hop on Table Rock. It was got up on short notice, but perfectly charming, I assure you. There were only two fiddles, and sometimes the noise of the Falls would almost drown the music. The fiddlers had to scrape so hard, that they gave out about three o'clock, and we had to give up the dancing, and go home, very much disappointed."

"Unlucky, indeed!" interjected Chiffield.

"But the next night we had two extra fiddlers. They relieved the other two at midnight, and then we danced till daybreak. Oh! such a glorious time. Next year, when I heard that a part of Table Rock had tumbled into the horrid river, I could have cried."

"It was a great shame, indeed!" said Chiffield.

"Isn't this view of Suspension Bridge natural?" she asked.

"Amazing!" said Chiffield; and he ventured to add that he considered that bridge to be a great triumph of human genius.

"I dare say it is. But I didn't think of that. I was only going to tell you how the gentlemen of our Table Rock party tried to hire the use of the bridge one night to dance on. The owners wouldn't let it. Mean, weren't they?"

"Contemptible!" replied Chiffield.

"We should have had it nicely swept and lighted. The breeze coming down the river would have been beautiful, and the awful noise of the Falls wouldn't have been too loud for the music. But we almost made up for our disappointment. Next night, the gentlemen hired the 'Maid of the Mist'—the little steamboat, you know, that you see in this picture—and we sailed round and round below the Falls all night, dancing all the time. We went so near the Falls twice, that I got quite wet with the nasty spray, and caught cold; but that didn't prevent me from dancing all the next night, at the International. You have a good view of the house in this picture."

"Tasty," said Chiffield.

Mr. Whedell and Maltboy had not lost a word of this conversation, though they had been mutually boring each other with complex sentences about national politics. Happily, the discussion required no mental effort, and left them both free to hear and make mental comments on the dialogue that buzzed across the way.

Mr. Whedell regretted that his daughter should expatiate with such vivacity upon a subject that must be extremely disagreeable to a gentleman of Mr. Chiffield's large figure and steady habits. To the cultivated judgment of Maltboy, it was evident that the young lady was trying to amuse Chiffield merely for the purpose of annoying him (Maltboy). Experience had taught Matthew the best kind of cure for this species of female perversity. He determined to leave the house, and thereby show that he was not to be trifled with.

Availing himself of a pause in the dissertations on national politics, Maltboy pulled out his watch and consulted it. "Why!" said he; "nine o'clock! And I was to be in Fourteenth street by half past eight. Only intended to drop in just to see how you were. You really must excuse me, Mr. Whedell." Matthew rose as he spoke, to show that his mind was made up, and remonstrances would be useless.

"Don't go. Put off your other call," ejaculated Mr. Whedell, at the same time rising, and thereby indicating a perfect acquiescence in the departure of his guest.

"You are in a hurry," said Miss Whedell, calmly, but without objection in voice or eye.

Mr. Chiffield looked calmly at his rival; and none but a skilled student of physiognomy could have discovered a gleam of triumph in his dull, yellow face.

Maltboy was disappointed in the calm demeanor of Miss Whedell; but, strong in his purpose, he walked toward the door, followed by the father. As he passed into the entry, he bowed coldly to the lady of his heart, and drew from her a scarcely perceptible nod.

At this moment, a valuable thought occurred to the paternal Whedell.

"My dear Maltboy," said he, closing the parlor door, "excuse the abruptness of the question; but could you lend me a couple of hundred?"

The question was indeed abrupt, but not altogether unexpected. Mr. Quigg had apprised Maltboy of Mr. Whedell's financial weakness; but the infatuation of the ardent young bachelor had led him to disregard that warning. He was fully prepared to say, "Yes, with pleasure," and he did say so.

"Thank you," said the gratified parent. "Only want it a few days." Mr. Whedell was too great an adept in the art of borrowing, to waste words of tedious explanation and gratitude, which only produce an impression that the borrower does not mean to pay. He accepted Maltboy's reply as a matter of course.

"If not too much trouble, could you give me a check to-night?" asked Mr. Whedell. "Have a payment to make before bank hours to-morrow."

"Most readily, my dear sir," replied the amiable Matthew. "Have you pen and paper convenient?"

"In this room, Mr. Maltboy," said his host, ushering him into a little apartment at the end of the entry, which contained a few books, and was passed off upon a credulous world as Mr. Whedell's library. The gas was lighted, writing materials were produced, and, in less than three minutes, Matthew Maltboy had put his name at the bottom of a check on the ——— Bank, for two hundred dollars. He did so smiling, and with a full consciousness that he had sustained a dead loss to that extent. But he was always too good-natured to deny a friend; and, in this particular case, he felt that he was buying a perpetual free admission to the house, and a usufructuary interest in the fascinations of Clementina. The idea of marriage with that young lady had never occurred to him. He never troubled himself with problems of the future.

"All right," said Mr. Whedell, folding up the check carelessly, and putting it in his pocket. "Shall I give you my note?"

"Oh, no!" said the willing victim, blandly. "Hand it me any time, at your convenience."

"Can return it within a week," responded Mr. Whedell; "but, on some accounts, the 1st of May will suit me best, if perfectly agreeable to you."

"As you please."

"We will call it the 1st of May, then. I regret you are in a hurry, sir. But remember, we are always happy to see you here."

With this pleasant remark ringing in his ears, and fully compensating him for the loss of his two hundred dollars, Maltboy hastened home, but did not tell his friends of his adventure; but he smoked and mused over it agreeably, and was totally unmindful of the truth announced by Mr. Quigg on New Year's day, when speaking of this same Whedell, that "somehow debtors always give the cold shoulder to creditors, as if the creditors owed the money."

Mr. Whedell, left to his own society, flattered himself that he had turned a rejected lover to a good account, and entered his library and sat down in the cold, that he might not, by his presence, mar the harmonious progress of the courtship upon which so much depended, in the parlor.

CHAPTER IV.

THE FIRST OF MAY.

Mr. Chiffield proposed, was accepted, and was married in a Broadway church about the middle of April. The affair was simplicity itself—bridesmaids, groomsmen, costly wedding costume, and the subsequent conventional reception at the bride's residence being dispensed with. The ceremony was witnessed only by the officiating minister, the sexton, the happy father, and about two hundred of the floating population of Broadway, including a number of pickpockets, one of whom sounded the recesses of the coat tails appertaining unto Mr. Whedell and his son-in-law, as they were coming out of church, and found nothing in them.

The Siamese twins of the soul passed from the church amid the sneers, criticisms, and suppressed laughter of the spectators —who united in pronouncing the ceremony a shabby affair, not worth looking at—and, entering a carriage with Mr. Whedell, were driven to the New Jersey Railroad Depot furiously, as if they had been guilty of some crime against society. At the depot, Mr. Whedell kissed his daughter in public, and not without a touch of the melodrama, for which he had cherished a fondness in his earlier days, and wrung the hand of his son-in-law. The train bore the couple away toward the city of Washington, where a portion of that indefinite season known as the honeymoon was to be passed, amid every discomfort that money could purchase. Why they should have gone to Washington in pursuit of bad hotels, and other miseries, when they could have procured them in so many other parts of the country for a quarter of the money, was something which Mr. Chiffield was never able to explain to his own satisfaction.

He afterward bitterly regretted that he had not made the nuptial trip to Newburg, or some place near the city, where the expenses would have been more moderate. But we anticipate.

Mr. and Mrs. Chiffield had been absent ten days. They were expected home on the 28th day of April; but a letter from Clementina informed her father that she had taken a bad cold, was confined to her room, and could not return before the 1st of May. The brief note was written in a crabbed hand, and exhibited spots, which, if not lemon juice, were tears. She made no allusion to her husband, but wound up by saying, "Oh, pa! I am an unhappy girl!"

This intelligence was a thorn in the bed of Mr. Whedell's comfort. Had he not arranged to settle with his creditors on the 1st of May? Was not the owner of the house occupied and used by him to resume possession on that eventful day? And was not everything—even his daily food—dependent on the return of his children, as he fondly called them, with their pockets full of money? What if this infernal cold should keep them in Washington until after the 1st of May? As Mr. Whedell thought of himself, turned adrift, and a wanderer, he invariably tore out a few of the gray hairs which could be poorly spared from his venerable skull.

Mr. Whedell had a deep and unchanging faith in his ill luck; but, this time, he was pleasantly disappointed. The morning train on the 1st of May brought back his children to him. They arrived just as those Bedouins of civilization—the New Yorkers—were beginning to indulge their nomadic propensities. The streets were full of wagons and drays laden with jingling stoves, rickety bedsteads, conspicuous crockery, and other damaged Penates, on the way to new domiciles. Fortunately, the owner of Mr. Whedell's residence had not yet come to claim possession. Creditors are early birds; but the hour—six and a half A. M.—was even too early for them; and only one—Mr. Rickarts, the shoemaker—had called. He had been disposed of in the library, by the servant, under the pretence that Mr. Whedell was not yet up. But Mr. Whedell was up and dressed before six o'clock, and was watching for the expected carriage, through the window blinds of his apartment. He ran down to the door with juvenile briskness to receive the returning ones.

Mrs. Chiffield looked pale and jaded. Her hair was carelessly arranged, and her bonnet awry—unerring indications of fathomless female misery. To the anxious inquiry by her parent after her health, she only replied, "Horrid!" Mr. Chiffield wore the aspect of a man who is disappointed in his just expectations. He gave a hearty grip to the proffered hand of his father-in-law, but he quarrelled with the driver over the fare, and abused him in an under tone, by way of relieving himself.

"And how did you like Washington, my child?" said the fond father, in his tenderest voice.

"I hate it!" said Mrs. Chiffield, hurrying into the house, as if she were running away from her husband.

"Hum. Well, I'm not surprised that she dislikes the capital. I believe most visitors do. Clemmy seems to be a little nervous from travelling, eh?" Mr. Whedell addressed these remarks to his son-in-law.

"Nervous? Perhaps she is just a trifle nervous, sir. All women are."

"True—true! One of the peculiarities of the sex. Well, you have had a pleasant time, I trust?"

"Pleasant time? Oh! yes—delightful! Your daughter is a charming girl, sir, and will make a most excellent wife." Mr. Chiffield spoke as if he were very much in earnest, but the expression of his face was not of rapture.

"She is a treasure, sir—a perfect treasure!" replied the doting parent. "It cost me many pangs to part with her. I trust that we shall not be separated now. Why should we be? There are but three of us—just enough for a happy family." Mr. Whedell was hinting at a home under the future roof of his son-in-law.

"I agree with you perfectly," said Mr. Chiffield, with unaffected eagerness. "Let us live together always. It will suit me exactly." He was thinking of free board and lodging at the house of his father-in-law.

The couple shook hands, mutually pleased at the prospect, and beamed on each other.

A part of this conversation took place in the hall, into which the hackman had borne the travellers' luggage. A pull was heard at the door bell—a loud, confident pull—which Mr. Whedell knew could be inflicted only by a creditor. It would not do to admit his son-in-law into his budget of family secrets just yet. So he said:

"Now, Chiffield, you must need some rest. Let me not detain you, my dear fellow. Your room is on the first floor. I'll show it to you."

Mr. Whedell snatched a carpet bag out of the hand of his son-in-law, and hurried up stairs with him. Having turned that gentleman into the apartment reserved for him, and shut the door, Mr. Whedell paused at the head of the stairs, and listened for the developments below. The servant, after waiting for two or three more jerks at the bell, so as to be quite sure that it was the bell, went to the door, and there found Mr. Numble, the butcher, who supplied the Whedells with meat on the strength of the brownstone front.

Pursuant to instructions, the servant explained that Mr. Whedell was not up, and asked him to walk into the library and wait a few minutes. Mr. Numble growled—as if he scented deception not far off—but allowed himself to be conducted into the library. There he discovered Mr. Rickarts, the shoemaker, taking down the few books which graced the shelves of the library, and evidently pricing them with an unpractised eye. The two gentlemen knew each other, and straightway engaged in a brisk dialogue about the weather.

CHAPTER V.

DEMOLITION OF CERTAIN AIR CASTLES.

The coast being clear, Mr. Whedell hastened down stairs to the front parlor, where his daughter had secluded herself immediately after her entrance into the house. She was lying back on the sofa, with her bonnet on, biting the ends of her gloves, and staring into space. She did not appear to observe her father.

Mr. Whedell seated himself on the other end of the sofa, and reached out his hand, as if he would have taken his daughter's caressingly within it. If that was his intention, it was frustrated by her drawing the hand away. Then the father heaved a sigh, and said:

"Ah, my child, I am so thankful that you have returned to-day. You will save us from ruin."

"*I* save you from ruin!" said Mrs. Chiffield, in a hollow voice. "That's a good joke!"

Mr. Whedell grinned a ghastly smile, as if he did not precisely see the point of the jest. "Joke or no joke," said he, "I must look to you for some money to put off the infernal creditors, who have begun to flock into the house. There's the bell. Hang me, if it isn't another one! To come to the point, then, I wish you would loan me, say two hundred dollars. It is a small amount, but will stave them off a week or two."

"Two hundred dollars!" Mrs. Chiffield opened her fine eyes in amazement.

"That's all. Perhaps you have saved up the amount from your pin money? Or, if you have been a little extravagant, and spent it all, why, then, perhaps you can get it from Mr. Chiffield this morning?"

The daughter laughed bitterly again. "I tell you, father," said she, "that this man is the meanest creature that walks on two legs. He has not spent fifty dollars on both of us, during our absence. As for me, I have never got a cent from him, though I have dropped a thousand hints about new bonnets, dresses, and jewelry."

"Gracious heavens!" cried Mr. Whedell, turning pale "But then," he added, with an effort to laugh, "Mr. Chiffield is a business man, and was an old bachelor. He knows nothing of women's wants. It must be your mission to teach him what they are."

"Pooh!" said the daughter; "I don't believe he has got any money."

"Don't talk so, my child. You put me in a cold sweat."

"Anyhow, I examined his pocket, last night, when he was asleep in the cars, and found only five dollars there."

Mr. Whedell's jaw dropped. "Oh, no! it can't be," said he, at length. "Mr. Chiffield must be a rich man. You remember his fine horses at Saratoga and Newport. You remember how much his society was courted by mammas with disposable daughters. They never patronize poor young men. Their instinct in finding out rich ones is unerring. And furthermore, Mr. Chiffield is a member of a firm twenty years old, who are marked 'A No. 1' on the books of a mercantile agency, that makes it a business to pry into other people's affairs. I paid ten dollars for the information, only a month ago. He must be rich! He must be rich!" Mr. Whedell repeated it twice, as if the repetition put the question of Chiffield's opulence beyond a doubt. "Ha! there goes that dreadful bell again!"

"What you say may be true, but I don't believe a word of it, till I have the proofs," replied the daughter, who seemed to delight in taking a gloomy view of her case. "Why—will you believe it?—I can't get him even to talk about engaging a house in New York. He always dodges the subject, somehow. Upon my word, I think he expects to quarter on you for the balance of his life. That would be rich!"

Mr. Whedell raised his eyebrows, and emitted a doleful whistle. Reflecting, he said:

"You may misjudge him. Perhaps he doesn't like to disturb Love's young dream, by looking into the future. That's all—I'm sure of it."

"Humbug!" ejaculated Mrs. Chiffield.

"Poor thing!" said her father, tenderly. "There—cheer up. Depend upon it, that you have got a rich husband, who will take all our troubles off our shoulders. Stay here, and I will go up stairs and sound him."

Mr. Whedell proceeded to the apartment where his son-in-law was shut up, and found that individual in a deep fit of meditation.

"Thinking—and so soon after marriage?" said Mr. Whedell, with a charming smile.

"Oh, yes; and I was thinking how much happier is a married man than a bachelor."

"You will always think so, I am sure, with my dear Clemmy as your wife. My dear Clemmy! How naturally that phrase comes to my lips. And you are about to take her away. It's a foolish thought, but I hardly know how I shall live without her." Mr. Whedell paused, for effect, and contemplated the vermicular work in the carpet.

"A happy thought strikes me," said Chiffield. "You have a house here, already furnished. Let us occupy it free of rent, and I will pay the housekeeping bills of the establishment. That will be mutually advantageous, and will especially suit your daughter, who, of course, has a child's attachment for home. What do you say to the proposition, respected father-in-law?"

Mr. Whedell did not catch at it with the alacrity that was expected of him. "A capital plan," said he, at length; "but, unfortunately, the house is not mine. I only lease it."

Chiffield's lips puckered up. "That's curious," thought he. "The old fellow must have put his money into bonds and stocks. Well, they are the best-paying investments."

Mr. Whedell proceeded to break the news of his penniless condition to his son-in-law, gently. "Mr. Chiffield," said he, "as a wholesale dealer in dry goods, you must have observed, perhaps at times experienced, the fickleness of fortune."

"Can he suspect?" thought Chiffield. "And what if he does? The truth cannot be concealed much longer. But I will pump him a little further before disclosing all."

"Yes," said he; "our firm, like others, has had its ups and downs; but then, business would not be interesting without some little risks, you know."

The easy manner of his son-in-law convinced Mr. Whedell that no "little risks" had shaken the firm of Upjack, Chiffield & Co. "Ah, yes," said he. "Rich to-day, poor to-morrow—the history of the world. As every person may learn this by his own sad experience, some time or other, he ought to be lenient in judging of those who have become reduced from wealth to poverty."

"Can he mean me?" thought the son-in-law. "Faith! it sounds very much like it. If so, his manner of broaching the subject is truly generous and delicate."

"I agree with you," said he, aloud. "Money does not make the man." It is a safe adage, and Chiffield quoted it intrepidly.

"True—true!" replied Mr. Whedell. "Money is but a small item in the sum of earthly happiness. Take the institution of marriage, for example. What gives to that institution its blessedness—love, or money?"

"Love," responded the unhesitating Chiffield.

"The promptness of that reply shows that he does not expect a fortune with Clemmy," thought Mr. Whedell.

"He must suspect—perhaps already knows—the truth," thought Chiffield. "How kind in him to spare me the least humiliation!"

"That person is truly rich," continued Mr. Whedell, "rich beyond expression, who brings pure love and exalted virtues into the married state."

"Generous father-in-law!" thought Chiffield. "He knows that I am ruined. Yet how nobly he treats me! I may cast away all reserve now."

"It would be an affectation, sir," said Chiffield, aloud, "tc pretend that I do not understand to whom you refer, my dear father-in-law."

"The glorious fellow!" thought Mr. Whedell. "He guesses what I am about to disclose, and yet calls me a dear father-in-law."

Chiffield continued: "Tc save any further circumlocution, sir, and in order that we may fully understand each other, I will say at once, that we are completely—ruined!"

"Ha! What! Who ruined?"

"The house of Upjack, Chiffield & Co. I—I thought you knew it."

"Ruined, sir!" cried Mr. Whedell, livid with horror. He choked for further utterance.

"Yes, sir," said Chiffield, who, being a fat man, was happily calm; "totally ruined."

"You impudent scoundrel! out of this house!" shrieked Mr. Whedell, rising from his chair, and glaring like a wildcat at his son-in-law.

"Be calm," said that phlegmatic individual. "I respect your age."

"Curse your impudence! what do you mean by my age?" (approaching Chiffield in a threatening manner). "I'll let you know, sir, that I am young enough to kick a swindler like you into the street."

"Pray compose yourself, sir," returned the bland Chiffield. "Your surprise and excitement are natural, and therefore pardonable. But my affairs are, after all, not quite as bad as they might be. I have a sure prospective fortune, if not a present one."

"What do you mean, sir?" asked Mr. Whedell, not quite so savage as before.

"That I have talents, energy, a large business acquaintance," said the cheerful Chiffield.

"Humbug!" roared Mr. Whedell. "What is all that stuff good for, without money?"

"Not much, I admit," was the conciliatory reply. "There fore, sir, to come to the point at once, advance me ten thou sand dollars to start in business again, and I will make a fortune in three years. It was the outside speculations of my partners that ruined me. Perhaps you don't know that dry goods are going up, sir? Now's the time to buy."

"This man will drive me mad!" shrieked Mr. Whedell, combing his hair wildly with his hands.

"Regard it in the light of a family investment," suggested the soothing Chiffield.

"You diabolical scoundrel!" yelled Mr. Whedell, in a partial asphyxia of rage; "if I had a million dollars to-day, I wouldn't give you a cent. You should starve first. But I want to tell you—and hang me if it isn't a pleasure, too—that I am a beggar, sir—a beggar, sir—a beggar, sir! By noon to-day I shall be turned out of this house. And, by Jove! I'm glad of it, for then I shall get rid of you." During this *adagio* passage, the speaker shook his fist within a few inches of Chiffield's nose.

The summery Chiffield answered, with a hearty laugh: "I see," said he; "it's a regular sell on both sides. However, neither of us is worse off than he was, since neither of us had anything. As for me, I have gained one point, for I have a tolerably good-looking wife."

Mr. Whedell was about to retort in a vein of unmitigated ferocity, when Mrs. Chiffield, who had been listening in the entry, and could contain herself no longer, rushed into the room, and, brandishing a small clenched hand in the face of her laughing spouse, forcibly observed:

"You sneaking, swindling, cheating, lying, black-hearted, ill-looking pauper, scoundrel, and vagabond!"

"Very prettily said," remarked the imperturbable Chiffield.

"You miserable thief!" continued his matrimonial partner, aiming a blow at him, which he playfully parried; "why didn't you tell me you were a beggar?"

"Why? Because you didn't ask me. For that matter,

why didn't you or your father tell me that *you* were beggars?"

"I sha'n't answer your insulting questions, you mean, deceiving, ugly, ungentlemanly——" (no other epithet suggesting itself.) At this crisis, the infuriated wife burst into tears, and wished several times that she was dead.

"Poor, dear wifey!" said the emollient Chiffield.

"None of your 'poor dears' to my daughter, you jail-bird!" screamed Mr. Whedell.

"Now, don't get excited, father-in-law."

"How dare you call me father-in-law, sir!"

"Perhaps you prefer the more endearing epithet of 'poppy,' sir?"

"Monster! will you leave my house?"

"Have you any good old brandy on hand?" asked Chiffield.

"Brandy! No. If you want brandy, sir, go to the d—l for it."

"Not quite so far, thank you," retorted Chiffield the genial; "but I don't mind walking to the next corner for a smash."

Chiffield rose, put on his hat, and stepped toward the door.

"Good-by, wifey. I sha'n't be gone long."

A growl, bisected by a sob, was the only reply.

"By-by, poppy," said Chiffield, with a flippant wave of the hand.

Mr. Whedell cast at him a look of scorn, to which justice could be done in no known language; and Chiffield, with a bow of exceeding grace, left father and child to their reflections.

CHAPTER VI.

MR. WHEDELL'S CREDITORS IN CONVENTION ASSEMBLED.

THESE reflections, which were neither profitable nor interesting to the parties immediately concerned, were interrupted by a peculiarly vigorous pull at the door bell. Pulls of a startling description had come so often, the previous ten minutes, that Mr. Whedell had quite ceased to notice them. But this long and strong pull caused him to start, and remark, "It must be Quigg."

It was Quigg, who had come to make his last appeal. He was by far the heaviest creditor. The unfortunate servant girl, acting under her general instructions, would fain have shown him into the parlor, where his fellow sufferers, having overrun the library and dining room, were already in strong force; but Quigg, having immense interests at stake, would stand no such nonsense.

"Where is Whedell?" said he. "I can't dance attendance on him all day."

It was always remarked that Quigg put off his slow and stately method of speech, when dealing with obstinate debtors.

The terrified Mary lost her presence of mind, and replied; "In the first floor, front." Quigg mounted the stairs with surprising agility, and gave a hard rap at the door of the first floor front.

Mr. Whedell said, in a voice calm with despair, "Come in." In the few minutes that had elapsed since the retirement of Chiffield, Mr. Whedell had privately determined to give up everything to his creditors, leaving them to divide the spoils among themselves, and then to go out, expend his last quarter on a dose of poison, and end his existence. This resolution, suddenly taken, imparted preternatural composure both to his mind and his face. He could now see his way out of all difficulties—or out of the world, which is the same thing. Clementina, who had not yet risen to that height of philosophy, buried her face in her hands, and sobbed with fresh violence.

Quigg entered, and at a glance saw that he had lost. He stopped short in the bow that he was intending to make.

"Well, Whedell," said he, roughly, "how are things today?" By "things," he always meant money.

"Not a penny," said Mr. Whedell. "I've done my best to pay you, and failed."

"Just as I expected. Serves me right. I never was forbearing with a debtor, that I didn't get chiselled this way. Strike me if I ever make the mistake again. This marriage of your daughter's, which was going to set you up in funds, has proved a fizzle, eh? Instead of taking somebody in, you have been taken in yourself."

Quigg laughed; and then remembering that a delinquent debtor was before him, assumed his wonted serious aspect.

At this allusion, poor Mrs. Chiffield burst into tears again. Mr. Whedell adroitly turned the circumstance to advantage. He pointed to her, and said, "There is my reply."

Quigg felt that he was losing ground on these side issues. "Well, Whedell, we must have a settlement to day. You owe me one hundred and fifty dollars. Turn over all your furniture to me, and we'll call it square."

Mrs. Chiffield doubled her sobs anew. But Mr. Whedell said, "Very good. Take everything, I shall want nothing where I am going."

Quigg had been accustomed to these dark hints from contumacious debtors, and was not to be frightened. "I accept your offer," said he, "and will take everything."

At this moment, a rush, as of many feet, was heard upon the stairs. The owners of the feet appeared to be literally tumbling up in their anxiety to get up. By the time Quigg could open the door, a half dozen flushed persons were ready to step in, and did so, brushing him aside. More than a score of others followed, and all plunged pell mell into the presence of Mr. Whedell and daughter.

"Here we are, Mr. Whedell, by appintment," said the spokesman of the party, Rickarts, the shoemaker.

"I see you are," responded the placid Whedell. "Take seats, if you can find them, gentlemen." This with a real smile, for he thought of the arsenic, and the immeasurable relief that it would afford him.

"We don't want seats, Mr. Whedell; and, if we did, there isn't enough for all of us. We want our pay, and have got tired of waitin' down stairs for it. You put us all off to the 1st of May, you know, expectin', you said, to raise money enough by the marriage of your daughter (excuse the remark, marm, but business is business) to pay off all of us. We found, on comparin' notes down stairs, this mornin', that you had told the same story to everybody. Now, sir, as your daughter is married, accordin' to the papers, and the 1st of May has arriv', will you be good enough to square up?"

Mr. Whedell smiled touchingly. "My good and patient friends," said he, "nothing would give me greater pleasure—I might say, without exaggeration, rapture—than to pay all that I owe, with compound interest thrown in. But, unfortunately for my excellent intentions, I have no money."

"Blast me if that isn't just what we expected! I told 'em, down stairs, that I'd bet ten to one you couldn't or wouldn't raise anythink out of your son-in-law."

"Your name is Rickarts, I believe?" asked Mr. Whedell.

"Yes, Rickarts!" growled the owner of the appellation, "You ought to know it by this time; for I've dunned you often enough."

"True, Mr. Rickarts, but then I have so many creditors, you see, that I cannot be expected to know them all. I merely wanted to observe, Mr. Rickarts, that, at least, *you* have not been disappointed in your expectations. Furthermore, that if you had made a bet of ten to one, it wouldn't have been a bad speculation for you."

Cries of "Pshaw!" "Humbug!" "Swindled!" "Done for!" and kindred expressions, arose from all sides. The spokesman said: "We ha'n't got no time to joke, Mr. Whedell. We have only to remark, now, that the best thing for you to do is to give up your furniture, without the trouble and expense of a lot of lawsuits."

"You are perfectly welcome to the whole of it, my good friends," said Mr. Whedell.

"The deuce they are!" cried Quigg. "Why, you have just turned it over to me!"

"I give it to all of you, singly and collectively, severally and jointly," responded the happy, melancholy man. "Divide it among yourselves, and leave me."

The small creditors, under twenty dollars, took a favorable view of the proposition. One of them immediately jumped on a bureau having a marble top and elaborately carved legs, and expressed his willingness to take that for his pay. Another laid violent hands on the heavy yellow window curtains, and declared himself satisfied. A third commenced ripping up a corner of the carpet, and notified all persons that he claimed *that*. The original owner of the bureau, curtains, and carpet, who had furnished the house, and held an exalted rank among the principal creditors, objected to this summary disposition of the property. Quigg, in very emphatic but improper English, insisted that he had the largest and first claim, and warned everybody on their peril not to remove a thing from the house.

Mr. Whedell reclined in his chair, positively enjoying the spectacle, which was all the more entertaining because the common wrath was now diverted from him. Mrs. Chiffield wept behind her handkerchief. Her bonnet was knocked on one side, and the flowers were seriously disarranged, indicating a real case of distress.

Sauve qui peut was now the motto among all the small creditors. Notwithstanding the energetic objections of Quigg and others, they rushed down stairs into the parlors, where the best furniture was kept, and commenced taking possession. Rickarts, the shoemaker, seated himself on the top of the piano, and said he considered that his'n. But a second after, a man milliner, who had furnished two new bonnets to Miss Clementina on the strength of the brownstone front, took his seat on the other end of the piano, and gave Mr. Rickarts distinctly to understand that he was glued to it. The man milliner was a powerful fellow, and looked as if his proper vocation were hammering stone or rolling iron, instead of handling flowers and feathers. Rickarts murmured something inaudibly, at first but, on taking a second survey of his neighbor, concluded that he would be more desirable as an ally than as an enemy.

"All right," said he; "s'pose we go snacks on this?"

"Agreed," said the man milliner.

Other of the minor creditors, not caring to quarrel for a third or fourth interest in the piano, attached themselves to movable pieces of furniture, such as ottomans, whatnots, etageres, and chairs. One succeeded in unscrewing a large chandelier which hung from the centre of the front parlor, and the gas came pouring through the opening in odorous volumes, while the spoliator waddled off to the door with his prize. Others rummaged the small stock of showy books which consituted the library, and were surprised to find that the most imposing volumes were bound in wood, with gilt backs, and contained nothing but air, which a funny creditor characterized as very light reading matter.

In about five minutes, a considerable amount of portable property would have gone out of the house, but for Quigg's presence of mind. Seeing that decisive action was required, he slipped out of the front door, locked it, and returned in a moment with a couple of policemen, who chanced to be strolling through the street at that hour.

On the way to the house, Mr. Quigg succeeded in persuading the policemen that it was necessary for the peace of society that they should turn all the other creditors out of the house, and leave Mr. Whedell's effects to be divided among them according to the regular legal process. As the officers marched up the steps of the house, it fell out that Matthew Maltboy came sauntering by. Observing the two officers, headed by an excited individual, going into Mr. Whedell's house, it occurred to his benevolent heart that that gentleman must be in trouble. He also felt moved by a desire to hear of his old flame—for such she now seemed at the remote distance of six weeks,—of whose marriage with Mr. Chiffield he had read in the papers with the utmost complacency. Therefore, Maltboy stepped up behind the officers, and was about to follow them into the house. The officers would have kept him back; but Quigg recognized his friend of New Year's day, and asked him in, hoping to get legal advice for nothing.

"An old friend of mine, and of Mr. Whedell's," said Quigg. "Admit him, officers. Perhaps, sir" (Quigg had forgotten his name), "you know something about Whedell's affairs, and, as a lawyer" (with a wink), "can tell me where he has some property snugly stowed away, that I can pounce on. If so, I would cheerfully let the smaller creditors divide the furniture among themselves. Any information—ahem!—will be confidential, you know."

"I am not a shyster!" said the indignant Matthew, alluding, by that term, to the outlaws of his profession.

Quigg was evidently surprised at this unfriendly repulse. "I only made the suggestion for you to think on. No offence meant. Please walk in, sir."

The door being opened, several of the small creditors were discovered, grouped together, with property in their hands. They had made several ineffectual attempts to break the lock, or pry back the bolt. The larger creditors were forcibly remonstrating against this disposition of Mr. Whedell's effects; and a serious row would probably have ensued, but for the timely arrival of the police.

CHAPTER VII.

DEUS EX MACHINA.

One of the officers planted himself against the front door, and gave general notice that no one would be allowed to remove any of the furniture. The other officer stationed himself at the back door, to carry out a similar policy at that point.

These manœuvres caused consternation among the small creditors, and a vivid feeling of approval among the larger ones.

"I am happy to announce," said Quigg, "that the counsel of Mr. Whedell—one of the most distinguished ornaments of the bar—has now arrived, and will take charge of his client's affairs. To those who know the name of——" (Aside) "By the way, your name escapes me at this moment."

"Maltboy," said Matthew, a little flattered with this compliment.

"I repeat, that, to those who know the name of Maltboy, no assurance need be given that Mr. Whedell's affairs will be honorably adjusted." Quigg again winked at the young lawyer.

Matthew, having recovered from the flutter into which he was thrown, was about to disclaim the office thus thrust upon him, when the voice of Mr. Whedell was heard from the first landing. He had come to listen to the disturbance, and smile at it.

"It is my dear Maltboy!" he exclaimed, catching at the straw of a hope. "Thank Heaven! he is here. Yes, gentlemen, he is my lawyer, and I refer you to him for the adjustment of all your claims. Come up, my dear Maltboy."

"Oh! it is dear—good—Mr. Maltboy!" added a voice, qualified by sobs. "How kind of him—to—to come here at this time! Oh—ho!"

Maltboy never could resist Beauty in any condition; and, for Beauty in tears, he would cheerfully lay down his life. He did not deny that he was the counsel and confidential adviser of Mr. Whedell, but rushed up stairs, just in time to receive the falling form of Mrs. Chiffield in his arms.

Matthew felt that he had no moral right to clasp that burden of loveliness; but he took it tenderly in his arms, and followed Mr. Whedell into the room which father and daughter had just left. There he deposited it, with the gentleness of a professional nurse, on the sofa, when it opened its eyes, and faintly said, "Heaven bless you, our benefactor!"

The creditors were pouring into the apartment. "In the name of humanity," said Mr. Whedell, "leave us for a few moments. I appeal to you as gentlemen and Christians."

The appeal produced no effect; those to whom it was made conceiving, perhaps, that it did not apply to them. Maltboy added the remark: "'If you will withdraw at once, I promise you that in fifteen minutes we will proceed to business."

"That's all right," said Quigg, winking again at Matthew. "Let us go, friends."

The proposition was accepted, as the best thing that could be done under the circumstances, and all the creditors retired.

Mr. Whedell then locked the door, and proceeded to inform Mr. Maltboy of the black-hearted treachery of which he and his daughter had been the victims, in the Chiffield alliance. Clementina corroborated the paternal statement with numerous particulars, delivered in a heart-broken voice, showing what an abandoned wretch her husband was. Matthew listened, nodded his head, and said, "The brute!" and the "The monster!" at intervals, looking the while into the deep blue eyes of Mrs. Chiffield, which sparkled with tears. "If he had but been the lucky man!" he thought. But it suddenly occurred to Matthew that these thoughts were a little irregular; and, besides, he had a fresh recollection of the troubles from which Fayette Overtop had not yet emerged. He therefore pulled out his watch, and informed Mr. Whedell that thirteen of the fifteen minutes were consumed. The creditors were beginning to pace heavily in the entry.

Mr. Whedell, taking the hint, came down to business. His affairs were of a kind that were easily settled. He owned nothing except his personal clothing, and a few small articles of furniture. Everything else had been obtained on credit, and either not paid for, or only partly paid for. This statement of affairs occupied one minute.

A minute remained, which Mr. Whedell put to good use. He looked appealingly at Maltboy. So did Mrs. Chiffield.

"My dear friend," said Mr. Whedell, "I find myself, at an advanced period of life, in this cold world, deserted, penniless. You are the only person living that I can call by the sacred name of friend. I have already experienced your noble bounty in a loan of two hundred dollars." (Tramps of creditors becoming louder outside.) "In a word, sir, can you lend me one hundred dollars more? It will at least save me from the self-destruction which I had contemplated."

At the word "self-destruction," Mrs. Chiffield cried aloud, and threw herself on her parent's breast, with a fresh flood of tears.

These tears swept away the last trace of Matthew's prudence. He whipped out his pocket book, and delivered over five twenty-dollar gold pieces to Mr. Whedell. The sight of those beautiful coins seemed to reconcile the wretched man to life.

Mr. Whedell was about to thank his preserver most profusely, and Mrs. Chiffield to burst into a new torrent, when Matthew, to avoid these demonstrations, rose, opened the door, and let in the pack of hungry creditors.

Now Matthew had, in these fleeting fifteen minutes, thought up no plan of settlement. Being taken aback by the sudden reappearance of the creditors, he did not know what to propose.

"Everything fixed, I s'pose?" said Rickarts, the shoemaker.

When Matthew was in strong doubt what to do in any case, it was his invariable custom to postpone. "I think," he feebly suggested, "that we had better postpone final action, say till three P. M. It would give us time——"

"Can't come it!" "No go!" "Now, or never!" were some of the exclamations which went up from the excited crowd.

Matthew was too good natured to quarrel with these insin uations. "My friends," said he, "as you appear to have unlimited confidence in each other, suppose you appoint a committee to dispose of this property, which my client generously" (cries of "Oh! oh!") "turns over to you, and divide the proceeds among yourselves *pro rata*."

The creditors looked at each other suspiciously. A want

of that childlike trust which, in a perfect state of society, should exist between man and man, was unhappily too apparent.

Just then, when Matthew was at his wits' end, the policeman who guarded the front door entered the room, and delivered a note to Mr. Whedell. That gentleman perused it languidly, and passed it to Matthew.

"Good news," said he. "Mr. Abernuckle, the owner of these premises, who was intending to move in to-day, writes that he will not be able to take possession until noon to-morrow. Therefore, I say, let the creditors employ an auctioneer, hang out the red flag, sell, and divide, before that period arrives."

The large creditors were silent—Quigg veiling his dissatisfaction under a look of complete misanthropy—but the small ones, headed by Rickarts, the shoemaker, highly commended it.

"Besides," added a butter man, who had originally been in the mock-auction line, "don't ye see, we can all stay at the auction, and kind o' bid on the things. Hey?" The butter man nodded at the lesser creditors.

The idea took; only a few of the larger creditors holding out against it.

"My friends," again observed Matthew, drawing on his stores of legal knowledge, "you seem to forget that, if my client chose to resist your claims, he could retain a large amount of furniture as household articles under the law, which exempts certain necessary things. But, with rare magnanimity, he gives up all."

The allusion to magnanimity produced some derisive laughs, which slightly nettled Matthew.

"Auction it off," said he, "or we throw ourselves back on our reserved rights."

At this hint, everybody gave in; and a committee, consisting of Quigg, Rickarts, and the butter man, was appointed to make all the arrangements for an immediate sale.

It is not pleasant to pursue this painful theme—the decline

and fall of the Whedell household—farther. Let the historian barely record, that the sale attracted a large crowd, and that by the ingenious side bids of the creditors, the furniture was run up to twice its original value (no uncommon thing at auctions); that the creditors, large and small, were well satisfied with the results; that Mr. Whedell and daughter moved to Boston, and became stipendiaries upon a younger brother, who had made a fortune in the upholstery business, and whom Mr. Whedell had always despised; that Mr. Chiffield took to drink tenaciously in consequence of his misfortunes, and never saw or sought after his wife from the day when he discovered that she was dowerless; that Mrs. Chiffield obtained a divorce from the bonds of matrimony, but had not married again at last accounts; and that Matthew Maltboy, Esq., on looking over the whole episode of his acquaintance with the Whedells, thanked his stars that he had got out of their entanglements on the reasonable terms of three hundred dollars.

BOOK ELEVENTH.

DISCOVERIES.

CHAPTER I.

THE OLD HOUSE REVISITED.

IN the month that followed the acquittal of Marcus Wilkeson, three real murders, a railway collision killing thirty persons, and a steamboat explosion almost as tragical in its results, occurred. The Minford affair was already getting old. Public curiosity, except in the immediate neighborhood of the house, no longer exercised itself upon the problem which all of Coroner Bullfast's powers of analysis had failed to solve.

Marcus Wilkeson might have derived a selfish consolation from the fact that other mysteries and calamities were causing his name, which last month was on the tongue of the whole town, to be forgotten. But he had a nobler and truer source of consolation in his dear books. In the presence of the philosophers, and sages, and historians, and novelists, and poets, and wits, the men of genius of the past, chroniclers of the loss of empires, grave men who taught the vanity of life, and funny men who taught the same lesson in a different way, Marcus felt his pack of sorrows considerably lightening. His first, last, only disappointment in love had subsided into a gentle and not disagreeable melancholy. His trial, and the dreadful notoriety which his name had acquired, had imparted to his mild nature a gentle tinge of cynicism, which improved him.

Marcus was sitting, one morning, in the little back parlor, idly turning over the leaves of an old folio, and looking with a half eye through the closed window at the houses opposite, and thinking what a deal of trouble it was possible to extract from a single block of buildings, when a slight rap was heard at the door. Simultaneously, the door was pushed open, and Wesley Tiffles shot in.

He had brought all his tonical properties with him. Good nature and cheerfulness effervesced from his face. Through the trial, and since the acquittal, Wesley Tiffles had stuck to Marcus. Twice, often three times a day, he called, and was always welcomed by Marcus, and not inhospitably received by Miss Philomela Wilkeson. The interviews between that lady and the romantic speculator usually took place, quite by accident, in the entry, on the arrival or the departure of Mr. Tiffles; but, as it happened, not with the cognizance of Marcus.

On one occasion—at the edge of evening—Marcus went into the entry a few minutes after Tiffles had left the room, and saw that gentleman and Philomela standing in the doorway. Tiffles appeared to be in the act of raising the lady's hand to kiss it; but, if that were his intention, he abandoned it on seeing Marcus, and shook the attenuated fingers instead. Then he coughed, and, saying "Good-night," went down the steps, as if he had not seen Marcus in the gloom. Miss Wilkeson coughed also (why do people always cough?), and, turning to her approaching brother, said it was a cool night, which was not true, as the night was agreeably warm. Marcus had never afterward seen them together, and had forgotten this slightly mysterious circumstance. Wesley Tiffles had, as usual, something enlivening to tell.

"Got the funniest piece of news for you, my dear fellow!" said he.

"Anything funny is always welcome, Tiffles," said he, closing his folio, that he might not appear to obstruct his friend's jocosity.

"I've heard from that infernal old panorama—when I say

infernal, of course I don't mean to imply that it wasn't a splendid idea, if I had had capital enough to see it through—and what do you s'pose the landlord and the other creditor have done with it? You couldn't guess in a month."

"Well, what?" asked Marcus Wilkeson, laughing in anticipation.

"Ha! ha! cut it up, and sold it for window curtains. A friend of mine, who passed through there the other day, says there's a picture of a lion, or a palm tree, or a slice of a desert—principally desert—hung up in every other window. And the best of it is, that they made a good thing of it. The curtains brought at least twice what I owed them. Great heavens! why didn't I think of it myself?"

"Of what?"

"Why, to cut up the panorama into window curtains, when Patching had finished it, and—ha! ha!—peddle them through the country. By Jupiter! that speculation may be worth trying yet. But at present I have my new patent process for——"

Marcus coughed, and opened the book. Tiffles accepted the delicate hint in a spirit of true friendship, and let his new patent process drop.

"Marcus," said he, "I don't wish to revive an unpleasant subject; but have you no idea what the late Mr. Minford was trying to invent?"

"Not the least. I never trouble myself about inventions, as you wel. know, who are full of them. Besides, poor Mr. Minford was not communicative on that subject. He kept the secret even from his daughter."

"You have a claim on the apparatus, whatever it is."

"Yes. Mr. Minford insisted on giving me a paper to that effect, as security for two loans of five hundred dollars each. I took it to please the old gentleman." Marcus felt like groaning, as he thought of the sorrows that he had derived from his connection with the Minford family; but he had just been reading of the consolations of philosophy, and he stifled the rising weakness.

"I have thought, Marcus, that there might be something about that unfinished machine that could be patented for the benefit of Miss Minford. You know I am a good judge of patentable things."

"What do you propose, then?" asked Marcus, concealing, with an effort, the emotions which the mention of Miss Minford always caused."

"That we go to the house together. The legal claim which you hold upon the machine entitles you to see it, if only to ascertain that it has not been stolen."

"The visit you propose is a disagreeable one; but if you think there is a possibility of benefiting Miss Minford, I will go. Not that she is likely to be in want, however, at present, for I understand that a wealthy lady, Mrs. Crull, who befriended her at the inquest, you remember, has taken her to her own house."

Without further words—for Marcus retained his old business habit of forming his conclusions suddenly, and adhering to them — the friends proceeded to the late residence of Mr. Minford.

Marcus had not yet philosophically conquered his dread of recognition in the street as the man who had been suspected of a murder. He buttoned his overcoat up to his chin, pulled his hat over his brow, and walked fast. As he had purposely altered his style of dress since the inquest, he was not readily identified. But he was sympathetically conscious that several persons whom he passed, and who glanced at him, knew him, and that he was pointed out to others when his back was turned.

Reaching the house, they hurried up stairs, hoping to run the gauntlet of the three floors in safety. Luckily, there had been a general move from the premises—the lodgings being less desirable since the supposed murder. The faces which thrust themselves out of the doorways as the two visitors passed, were strange ones.

Marcus felt his heart palpitating, and his face growing pale, as they ascended the last flight of stairs, at the head of which were the room and the mystery. The lodgings had not been taken. The rent had been paid by Mr. Minford up to the 1st of May; and no person had been sufficiently charmed with the apartments to hire them since that date.

Upon the door was a placard, announcing that the key could be obtained by application to the floor below. Tiffles went for it, and returned accompanied by an old woman, who looked as if she knew a great deal which she did not care to tell. She had been requested by the landlord to show the apartments to applicants, but not to whisper a word about the murder; and she was almost bursting with her great secret. While the old woman was wondering how much longer she would be able to hold in, Marcus and Tiffles entered the front room, and quietly closed the door in her face. The old woman grumbled at this discourtesy, but, as she had a superstitious objection to putting her foot in a room where a murder had been committed, she leaned against the banisters of the stairs, and waited for the visitors' reappearance.

The room looked just as it did on the day of the inquest. The faded and worn furniture was all there; the yellow curtains still covered the windows; the clock still hung against the wall, tickless. Marcus's eyes glanced restlessly about the room for a moment, not daring to look at the spot where the old man had received his death blow. But an inevitable magnetism soon brought his eyes to it, and his heart was lightened as he saw that the blood stains had been carefully wiped out.

The door of the adjoining room—the maiden's bedchamber—was ajar. Marcus pushed it open with that slow motion which is a token of delicacy and respect. The general appearance of the room was unchanged, as well as Marcus could recollect from the occasional glimpses of it which he had formerly stolen. The little row of dresses which hung on pegs in a corner, and a few simple ornaments, might have been removed, but nothing more. Marcus felt that he was intruding here, and he closed the door.

In the mean time, Wesley Tiffles had been examining the mysterious machine, which stood undisturbed in its corner, with the protecting screen still standing before it. Tiffles had first wiped off the dust, and then looked into it, and through it, and over it, and under it, with an eye that was predetermined to pry out a secret. Then he felt of every wheel, lever, cam, ratchet, drum, and other portion within reach of his fingers. Everything was immovable. Then he stood aloof from the machine, folded his arms, pursed up his lips, and cocked an eye at it, as if, by the mere force of intellect, he would compel the dumb thing to give up its mystery.

As Tiffles was applying this species of exorcism in vain, Marcus came to his assistance.

"What on earth can it be?" exclaimed Tiffles. "Not a new kind of steam engine; or an electrical apparatus; or a clock; or a sewing machine; or anything for spinning, carding, or weaving—nothing that is adapted to any useful labor. These heavy weights, that have fallen on the floor, would give the works a kind of jerky motion for a few seconds, while the weights were descending. Nothing more. But the ultimate purpose of the machine is a puzzler."

"Mr. Minford always said that it was something that would revolutionize the world of industry—that it was a new mechanical principle of universal application."

Tiffles laughed a little. "Excuse my levity," said he, "but inventors—and I am one of them, you know—always claim that they are about to revolutionize the world of industry. I never knew one of them to claim less than that for a patent flytrap or an improved sausage stuffer. Mr. Minford was a man of genius, I dare say, but he probably overestimated the importance of his invention. Have you any objection to my prying the thing apart at this opening? I want to inspect some of the works that are partly concealed. I pledge myself to put it together again as good as new."

CHAPTER II.

A POSTHUMOUS SECRET.

"Go ahead," said Marcus; and Tiffles, inserting his walking stick in a wide gap between two cog wheels, forced the strange machine apart. A large brass drum upon which a small chain was loosely coiled, fell to the floor. The other portions were not disturbed. Marcus picked up the drum; and Tiffles cast his unerring eye in among the new jumble of wheels and connecting levers that was brought to view.

"Can't make head or tail of it," said he, at length. "Let me see that drum."

Marcus handed it to him. Tiffles took it, like an expert, between a thumb and finger, and tapped it with his stick. It answered back with a muffled clink.

"It is hollow, and contains some soft non-metallic substance. Ah! here we have it." And Tiffles, unscrewing a nicely fitting cap from the drum, drew out a close roll of paper. He unfolded it with trembling fingers.

The upper portion of the paper was covered with neatly drawn diagrams, which bore some semblance to the machine. Beneath, in the fine copperplate hand of the inventor, were these memorable words:

"*Eliphalet Minford's original plan of* PERPETUAL MOTION, *to which he has devoted his fortune, and twenty years of labor. Perseverantia vincit omnia.*"

"*Christmas Day*, 185–."

Then followed a careful technical description of the plan, and a mention of the fact that on two occasions the machine had moved. One occasion was the night of April 10, 184–, when the mass of wheels started with a sudden click, but stopped in three seconds by the clock. The other occasion was daybreak, December 30, 185–, when the works began to move of their own accord, and did not stop for six seconds. This record had evidently been made by the inventor for his private reference, and concealed in the brass drum for safe keeping.

Tiffles read with bated breath; and Marcus listened in astonishment.

"What do you think of it?" asked Marcus.

"I think," replied Tiffles, "with every respect for the memory of the inventor, that he was insane. Perpetual motion, without an exhaustive power—or, in other words, the eternal motion of a thing by its own inherent properties—is a simple impossibility. To cite familiar illustrations of its absurdity, you might as well try to lift yourself by the straps of your boots, or pour a quart into a pint pot. I wasted six months on perpetual motion when I was a boy, and gave it up. Every inventive genius bothers his head with this nonsensical problem, till he learns that he is a fool. Of course, I say this with every possible regard for your deceased friend. He was insane on this point—*quoad hoc*, as the lawyers have it—without question, or he would not have thrown away twenty years on it;—or twenty-three years, I should say, since the paper is dated, you observe, three years ago."

"But Mr. Minford says, in that document, that the machine moved twice. He could have no object in deceiving himself."

"You are wrong there, my friend. Inventors are continually deceiving themselves. Their judgment, their very eyesight becomes worthless in respect to subjects upon which they have labored long and hoped ardently. This machine has evidently been greatly altered from the original plan in the progress of its construction. You observe that these weights do not appear on the diagrams. They were an afterthought—recently put on, I should judge, from the appearance of the cords which hold them. Anybody can see, as I said before, that the weights would move the works spasmodically, so to speak. But this motion cannot be what he alludes to as having taken place on two occasions. Of course, I can't explain what caused the motion on those occasions—if it were a real motion, and not a fantasy of the inventor's brain—but I'll bet my life that any intelligent mechanic could have fully explained it to Mr. Minford at the time. But, mark you, Mr. Minford would never have accepted the explanation. Inventors never take advice."

"So then you are satisfied that this machine is of no value—to Miss Minford—except for old brass?"

"Oh! I don't say that. Mr. Minford, aside from this absurd crotchet, may have possessed real mechanical genius. Let me see if some part of it may not be good for something besides perpetual motion."

Wesley Tiffles peered down among the brazen and steel complexities again. "Sure enough, here it is," said he; "a splendid window fastener."

"I don't see any window fastener," exclaimed Marcus, looking in the direction of his friend's forefinger.

"There—that cam with a small spring and lever attached. Strength and simplicity combined. I have studied the subject of window fasteners—in fact, have invented three or four, which possessed the extraordinary property of never letting the window up or down when you wanted to move it. I recognize, in this window fastener, my ideal. Marcus, you must patent it for Miss Minford. It will be a sure fortune to her. I'll make the drawings and specifications."

Marcus, sadly happy in the thought of rendering any service to that young lady, readily chimed in with Tiffles's views, and said that the patent should be obtained as soon as might be.

It was then agreed that Tiffles should call on Mrs. Crull, on the following day, and inform Miss Minford of the important discoveries which had been made by him—not mentioning the name of Marcus Wilkeson—and should also offer to remove and dispose of the neglected furniture, as the young lady might think best.

As this conclusion was arrived at, the door opened suddenly. The old lady, being apprehensive, from the long stay of the two visitors, that they were ransacking the rooms and hiding portable articles about their persons, had overcome her superstitious antipathy, and opened the door quickly, so that she might catch them in the act. But they were only standing in the middle of the room, earnestly talking to each other.

The old lady muttered an inaudible apology; and the two friends hastened to take their departure.

CHAPTER III.

OVERTOP FINDS A SENSIBLE WOMAN.

Next morning, Mr. Wesley Tiffles, after an inexpensive breakfast at a cheap restaurant in Chatham street, set out on his mission of goodness. He was reduced to his last dollar, but felt opulent in the possession of his diamond breastpin—that tower of moral strength to the borrower. He whistled as he walked, and thought what would be the best name for the new patent window fastener of the future. "Union," "American," "Columbian," "Peoples'," "Washington," "Ne Plus Ultra," and a score more, were turned over and rejected. Finally he settled upon the "Cosmopolitan Window Fastener," meaning that its destined field of usefulness was the whole civilized globe. Patents for it could be and should be obtained in England, France, Germany, Russia, and Spain.

While Wesley Tiffles was taking this rosy view of the "Cosmopolitan Window Fastener," he stumbled upon Fayette Overtop, Esq., who was walking briskly toward his office, and thinking over a hard case in which his services had been secured the day before.

The firm of Overtop & Maltboy had recently come into a small but paying business, in this way: The release of Marcus Wilkeson was generally supposed to have been effected, not by his innocence, but by the skilful and professional, but unprincipled efforts of his legal advisers. Their name was not unfavorably known among the thieves and murderers of the city; and several individuals belonging to those classes of society resolved to employ them when they got into their next little difficulty. And, since the inquest, another thing had greatly contributed to the prosperity of the firm. We allude to the case of Slapman *vs.* Slapman.

This was an action for divorce, with alimony, brought by Mrs. Grazella Jigbee Slapman against her husband, Ferdinand P. Slapman. The ground upon which the separation was sought, was the continual brutality of Mr. Slapman toward his wife.

It was the law and the custom, in cases where both parties to the action were agreed to that arrangement, to turn over this species of litigation to a referee, who took the testimony in private, heard arguments of counsel, and rendered a decision subject to the confirmation of the Supreme Court. The Court had issued a standing order prohibiting all persons from publishing (except with the consent of the parties to the action) any further reports of the cases than a simple announcement of the decree, as confirmed by the Court, for or against a divorce. This order was put forth to protect the public from the contaminating example of matrimonial infelicities; though we are not aware that the number of divorce cases has materially decreased, or the standard of public morality been greatly elevated in consequence thereof.

The case of Slapman *vs.* Slapman was on trial before a referee, by mutual agreement of the parties. The newspapers did not report it; but some of them kept hinting at it in an appetizing way. The gentleman whose "gallantry, &c.," was the "remote cause of the action," was described as "a rising young lawyer, who distinguished himself in a recent inquest before Coroner ———, the thrilling particulars of which are still fresh in the minds of our readers;" or as a "young ornament of the legal profession, whose office was not a hundred miles from the corner of Broadway and ——— street" (the precise location of his office). One paper went so far as to say, that the "triumph which this disciple of Coke had achieved in the late *cause celebre*, was only to be equalled by his invariable success in affairs of the heart, &c., &c."

All this caused Fayette Overtop's name to be known by thousands of people. Persons who were seeking divorces, reasoned, strangely enough, that a man whose "gallantry, &c.," was the cause of a divorce, could materially assist them in severing the matrimonial bonds. Therefore they began to flock to him. He already had five female and two male clients of this description.

When Tiffles stumbled against Fayette Overtop, he at once invited his friend to go with him to Mrs. Crull's. His legal knowledge (of which Tiffles, in common with the public, was beginning to have a high opinion) might be of some service. Overtop had been told by Marcus Wilkeson of the previous day's transactions, and of Wesley Tiffles's intended visit to Miss Minford; and he at once consented to accompany him.

On their way to Mrs. Crull's—whose residence had been ascertained from the Directory—they passed Miss Pillbody's select school. Tiffles suggested that it would be well to call on that young lady, and pick up some intelligence of Miss Minford. She might still be receiving lessons from Miss Pillbody; and might, possibly, be in the house at that moment. Overtop also thought it would not be a bad idea to call there. He had heard much from Marcus Wilkeson in praise of Miss Pillbody, especially of her sensible qualities. Being still in the active pursuit of a sensible woman, he was moved with a real curiosity to see her.

The servant showed the two callers to the speckless little front parlor; and, a minute afterward, Miss Pillbody, looking fresh and neat, her narrow collar white and smooth, and every hair of her heavy brown tresses in its place, made her appearance.

Miss Pillbody entered the room in that noiseless, sliding way, which indicates a constitutional diffidence. Her eyelids involuntarily contracted, so that she might see her callers on a near approach to them. Fayette Overtop, marking her modest demeanor and her short-sightedness, immediately announced his name and that of his companion, and the object of their visit.

At the mention of his name, Miss Pillbody started. She had heard of Fayette Overtop, Esq., through the newspapers, as counsel for Marcus Wilkeson; but not as the philosophic friend of Mrs. Slapman. In reply to questions about Miss Minford, she stated that that interesting young pupil had not taken lessons from her since the death of her father.

Miss Pillbody here indulged in a little artifice. She produced a memorandum book, to see when Miss Minford took her last lesson; and, in order that she might read distinctly, drew out her eyeglasses, and adjusted them with a graceful movement of the arm and hand. Overtop thought that she handled the eyeglasses in a most ladylike manner; and that, when they were astride of her shapely nose, they became her face wonderfully.

When Miss Pillbody had referred to the little memorandum book, she gave one short look at Fayette Overtop. That gentleman, conscious that his face was scrutinized, looked at the wall. Miss Pillbody stole but one glance, and then shut the eyeglasses prettily, and stuck them into an invisible pocket of her waist. She had come to the conclusion that Mr. Overtop was a person of dignified and intelligent appearance. And Mr. Overtop had settled into the opinion that Miss Pillbody was a near approach to that imagined paragon—a sensible woman.

Mr. Overtop was about to make a shrewd remark upon the great superiority of private select schools over all public institutions for the education of young ladies, when Miss Pillbody rose.

"Do you desire any other information, gentlemen?" said she.

"No, I thank you, Miss Pillbody," returned Overtop, who interpreted her question to mean that a pupil was waiting for her somewhere—which was true; for Mrs. Gipscon, a fat lady of forty-eight, was taking her second grammar lesson in the back parlor.

The two callers seized their hats.

"Could I intrust you with a message for Miss Minford, Mr. Overtop?"

"With a thousand," said that gallant man.

"Please, then, give my love to her, and ask her to come round and see me."

Mr. Overtop would have said that he always found it difficult to carry a lady's love to another without keeping some himself; but then he thought that this might be a little bold for a stray caller. So he answered, "With pleasure."

The two visitors bowed, and Miss Pillbody bent her head gracefully toward Mr. Overtop.

"What do you think of the schoolmarm?" asked Tiffles, when they had got into the street.

Overtop did not like the phrase "schoolmarm." "I think Miss Pillbody," said he, "is—a sensible woman."

CHAPTER IV.

INNOCENCE ON A SLIPPERY ROAD.

WALKING with the nervous and unreasonable quickness of city men, they soon arrived at Mrs. Crull's. The good lady was sitting at one of her front windows, sewing. As she looked into the street, her face was seen to have a sad and thoughtful expression. She came to the door in response to a sharp ring by Wesley Tiffles, who was tentative of bellpulls. Mrs. Crull kept two servants, but she could never get over the impulse to answer the door, when she was near it.

Overtop explained that they were desirous of seeing Miss Minford on important business.

"The poor, dear child!" exclaimed Mrs. Crull, in a broken voice. "She is not here."

"Not here!" cried Overtop. "Where is she, then?"

"I don't know, sir; and that's what troubles me so." Here the good Mrs. Crull began to twitch about the mouth. But she did not cry. She had too much of the masculine element for that. Her whole life was a struggle between the weakness of her feminine body and the strong self-control of her manly soul, in which the latter, after an effort, always came out victor.

Mrs. Crull then proceeded to explain, a little incoherently, that she had taken Miss Minford to her house, the day after the murder, and had asked the poor child to live with her, to be her adopted daughter. Miss Minford had gladly accepted the offer, and had stayed there until yesterday. During the last two or three days, she had noticed that Miss Minford, or Pet, as she always called her, was worried about something. She would not tell Mrs. Crull what was the matter, but Mrs. Crull somehow guessed that it was a love affair. She remembered the handsome, dissipated young man at the inquest, and she had seen him standing at the corner below her house, only two days before Miss Minford left.

"Left!" exclaimed Overtop, jumping at a conclusion. "Then that villain has abducted and ruined her."

"It's bad enough, I fear," continued Mrs. Crull; "but perhaps not so bad as that 'ere. Anyhow, I hopes not. I spoke to Pet about that young man, and she looked as innocent as a spring lamb at me, though she kind o' blushed when she denied having met him since the trial. And, to do her justice, I don't think she had met him then, though I sort o' suspeck she seen him from the window two or three times—she had a habit of looking out o' the window—and that he contrived to have a talk with her somewhere and somehow, the day before she went away. And I think he must have had the cheek to come into this very room" (Mrs. Crull had shown her visitors into her front parlor), "because one o' my servants says that she heerd a strange voice in the entry, and the door shut as if somebody had gone out. When she come into the entry to see who it was, she saw Pet hurrying into the parlor, and heerd her humming a tune. Pet wasn't in the habit of humming tunes; and the servant thought that rather 'spicious. So do I—not of any wrong, mind you. I wouldn't believe that till it was proved. But, to make a long story short, here is the note that poor Pet left on my dressin' table. Read it. I—I haven't got my spectacles."

The truth was, that Mrs. Crull's eyes were filling with tears, and she could not have read the now familiar lines on that little piece of paper even with the powerful aid of her spectacles.

"Monday Evening.

"Dear Mrs. Crull:

"Please pardon me for what I have done. I knew you would not consent to it, and so I did not tell you. I was afraid I should become a burden to you; though you are too good-hearted to say so. I have a nice place, and am earning my own living honestly. Do not try to find me, but believe I will always be good, and worthy of your love, and, some day, will repay you for all your kindness.

"With love and respect,

"Patty Minford."

"A very strange note!" murmured Overtop. "Young girls are not apt to complain of being burdens, or to take such misanthropic views of life. There is a man's hand in this. That wretch, Van Quintem, jr., without a doubt. Did you never warn Miss Minford against him?"

"Once," said Mrs. Crull, with a faint choke in her voice. "I had noticed his glances toward her at the inquest, and I told her he was a bad young man, and she must not allow him to speak to her in the street, and that, if he should come to my house to see her, I should shut the door in his face."

"And what did she say to that?"

"She said all she knew about him was, that he had saved her life once. She couldn't forget that. Then I showed her how improper it was in him to hide his own name from her, and what horrid holes these gambling dens was which he goes to. I also p'inted out how unfeelin' his conduct was to his poor old father."

"And what did she say to all that?"

"She nodded her head, and said, 'Yes, so it was;' but I see, now, that all my talk didn't make no impression on her."

"The sum of it is," said Overtop, "that she loves this worthless vagabond, and knew that you would not permit his visits to your house. Therefore she has left you."

Mrs. Crull was a woman of firmness as well as affection. She regretted that her opposition to this young man should have been the means of driving Pet away. But she knew that she had done what any prudent mother would have done for her own child.

"I'm sorry it has come to this," said she; "but I did it all for the best, Heaven knows. Gen'lemen, we must find this child. But how?"

Tiffles, being a man of infinite expedients, and accustomed to solve problems for himself, and everybody else, at the shortest notice, answered at once:

"*Not* by advertising for her, or putting the police on her track. Young Van Quintem would take the alarm, and move her out of town. She will go anywhere with him, if I mistake not, until she finds him out better. Have you no clue to her whereabouts; or can you think of any one that could give us any information?"

Mrs. Crull reflected. "Unless I am much mistaken," said she, "I saw that tall, clean-looking boy, Bog, I believe they call him—you remember him at the inquest—walking on t'other side o' the street, two or three times since Pet come to live with me. He looked sideways and kind o' sheepish at the house as he passed. I've a notion that he was a lover of Pet's, too."

"He's the man, or boy, for us!" cried Tiffles. "Is in the bill-posting business, and knows the town better than I do, if anything. A shrewd fellow, judging from his looks; and, if he's in love with Miss Minford, then he's sure never to tire of hunting her up. He must disguise himself, and find young Van Quintem, and follow him day and night, till he brings up at Miss Minford. That's the shortest road. When Miss Min ford has been found, then we will consider what is to be done next."

Mrs. Crull and Overtop at once approved of this plan, and no time was lost in putting it into execution.

CHAPTER V.

BOG'S OPEN SESAME.

Bog was easily found, and gladly consented to do the work allotted to him. It was agreed that he should conduct the search alone, and in his own way; but that, after he had succeeded in tracing Miss Minford to her place of concealment, he should send word, without delay, to Mrs. Crull, and also to old Van Quintem, whose advice upon the subject had been obtained. It was thought that the reasoning and entreaties of the two together would win back the poor girl from the path of danger which she was unconsciously treading.

Bog disguised himself by putting on his old, discarded working clothes; and, as he looked at his reflection in the glass, thought how much truth there was in the maxim, that "fine feathers make fine birds."

"Go, my good boy," old Van Quintem had said to him, in faltering accents; "go among the gambling houses, and other dens of infamy, and you will surely hear of my son."

Acting on this advice—which confirmed his own opinion—Bog proceeded to visit the gambling houses on Broadway. Child of the city as he was, he knew the locations of them all. His constant travels about town, day and night, had made him a master of all this knowledge, and much more of the sort, which is only useful when, as in the case of this poor orphan boy, it serves to show where evil must be avoided, not sought. Thus the pilot, taking his vessel through Hellgate, profits by his knowledge of the rocks and the shallows, to steer clear of all dangers, and come safely into port.

Bog, before leaving his shop, had been provided with this decoy note, written by the ingenious Wesley Tiffles in cunning imitation of Miss Minford's handwriting. The long, elegant curves, and all the delicate peculiarities of her chirography, taught by Miss Pillbody, had been copied from the sample furnished by her note to Mrs. Crull. It ran as follows:

"MR. VAN QUINTEM:

"DEAR SIR: Come to me at once, for I am in trouble.

"PET."

The plan (Bog's contrivance all this) was to inquire at the gambling houses where Mr. Van Quintem, jr., was most likely to be, and, when he was found, to send this note in to him by a servant. Bog, having delivered the note, was to withdraw to the sidewalk, lie in ambush, till young Van Quintem came out, and then follow him to Miss Minford's retreat. There he was to wait, and send a swift messenger to Mrs. Crull and old Van Quintem. It was not known that young Van Quintem had ever seen Miss Minford's handwriting; but, to make the game sure, the note had been written with a skill worthy of a counterfeiter, or that most dexterous of penmen, young Van Quintem himself.

Bog commenced operations about three o'clock in the afternoon—the hour when the gambler and debauchee, who have been up all the previous night, are ready to begin their feverish life again.

He first visited a snug establishment near the lower end of Broadway. It was situated in the second story, over a nominal exchange office, and was the favorite resort of down-town brokers, who, having gambled on Wall street till the close of business hours, dropped in to flirt with Fortune an hour or two before going home to dinner. Sometimes their hour or two was protracted to six o'clock next morning, when they staggered home to breakfast and a curtain lecture together. This Temple of Faro was never impertinently molested by the police; and it was a subject of remark, among people who thought they had been robbed there, that there was never a policeman within sight of the door.

In the hallway of the second story occupied by this gambling saloon, were a number of doors, which the experienced eye of the boy at once decided to be blinds, or, in other words, no doors at all, but only imitations. The appearance of the second story was that of a suite of unoccupied offices. Whoever rapped at these blind doors, could obtain no admission.

At the end of the hallway, Bog came upon a long window, which was painted white on the inside. He saw, by a glance at the grooves of the lower sash, that it was often raised. There was a boot-worn hollow on the floor beneath the window. The unusual length of the lower sash, and the nearness of the sill to the floor, would permit persons to step into the room easily when the window was raised.

Bog rapped thrice at this window. He had a vague idea—derived from reading, perhaps—that three raps were an open sesame to mysterious rooms the world over. The last rap had not ceased to vibrate on the pane of glass, when the window was suddenly shoved up, as if by somebody waiting on the other side.

A negro of intense blackness stood revealed. He took a hasty inventory of Bog's old clothes, and then said, "Clare out, now!" He commenced to close the window.

"I was told to give you a half dollar," said Bog, bethinking himself of a powerful expedient, "if you would find out whether Mr. Van Quintem was here, and hand him a letter."

The negro's eyes dilated, and his thick lips wreathed into a grin.

"Mr. Fan Squintem—a little feller with a big black mustache? I knows him. Dunno wether he's in. 'L see fur ye." The negro paused. The interrogatory, "Where's your half dollar?" could be plainly seen in his great eyes.

"Here it is," said Bog.

The negro grinned his satisfaction, pocketed the coin, disappeared through another door from which there exhaled an odor of cigars and mint juleps, and returned, in a minute, with the intelligence, "He a'n't in, Mister. P'a'ps you want to leave some word for him?"

Bog had no time to lose. He said, "Nothing partickler," and hurried off, leaving the negro to puzzle over his half dollar.

At the next gambling saloon, near the junction of Broadway and Park Row, Bog simplified his method of operations. Before making any inquiry of the servant who answered his triple rap, he thrust a half dollar at him, and then put his question. This plan saved surly looks and explanations. Mr. Van Quintem was a well-known patron of the establishment, but had not been there for a week: which was rather strange, the man politely added.

Bog continued his search, walking as fast as he could. In second stories, in third stories, in fourth stories, in the rear of ground floors, in one or two basements, among all the more fashionable gambling dens, which, at that period, lay between Fulton and Tenth streets, he picked his way. His new system had drawn heavily upon his stock of loose silver, and he had but two half dollars left. The question now was, how to spend them?—for Bog knew of no more resorts of gamblers on Broadway; and there were none on any of the side streets which a man of young Van Quintem's style would be likely to frequent. It was the edge of evening.

The boy walked up and down between Tenth and Fourteenth streets, thinking what it would be best to do next. He kept a sharp lookout at the passers by, hoping to see the object of his search. He paused to rest himself a few minutes in the doorway of a photographic gallery; and, while there, observed two young men, with sickly complexions and bloodshot eyes, coming up the street. He recognized them as young men whom he had often seen issuing from gambling places in the small hours of the morning. They were talking briskly, and Bog pricked up his ears.

"The very d—l's in the cards lately," said the whitest-faced of the two.

"Luck must have a turn," said the other. "By ——" (with a horrid oath), "suppose we try Van's?"

"Van's? Where's that?"

"Why, the concern just opened on the corner above. The biggest kind of suppers there, they say."

"All right," said the other, wearily. "We'll try Van's."

Van is a common prefix of names in New York; but Bog needed no further assurance that this Van belonged to Quintem. The opening of a new gambling saloon under his name (with some wealthy backer furnishing the capital, as is usually the case) would explain why young Van Quintem had not been seen at any of his old haunts on Broadway for a fortnight past.

Bog followed his guides at a short distance. After proceeding two squares, they stopped in front of a stylish old mansion, and, after a furtive look up and down and across the street, ascended the steps, and opened the door. As they did so, Bog swiftly passed the house, and saw that a muscular servant stood within the entry, for the obvious purpose of preventing the intrusion of persons not wanted there. The large diamond breastpins and depraved faces of the two young men were their passports, and were *viséd* without hesitation by the diplomatic attendant.

Bog took a half dollar in his hand, advanced to the door, which was now closed, and boldly opened it.

The athletic guardian of the place, being confronted with this audacious youth in old clothes, put on a commanding look, and said:

"Well, sir, and what the d—l do you want here?"

"Only to give you half a dollar, as I was told to," said

Bog, "and to ask if Mr. Van Quintem was in. Note from a lady, sir; that's all." Bog winked.

The servant smiled, and took the coin.

"He's in," was the reply.

"Then please hand this to him, and say as how it's 'mportant. No arnser wanted."

The servant received the note, and sententiously remarked, "Consider it done;" whereon the boy Bog hurriedly retreated, and hid himself in a doorway nearly opposite. He had hardly done this, before the door of the house opened again, and disclosed the man whom he longed to see. The letter was crumpled in his hand, and his pale face betrayed agitation. He cast wary looks in all directions, and then descended to the sidewalk, and walked fast down Broadway. Bog emerged from his seclusion, and followed him at a distance, always keeping somebody between him and the object of his pursuit.

At the corner of Astor Place, young Van Quintem stopped; and Bog came to a halt also, half a block behind.

The next minute, the Eighth-street stage, going up, approached the corner at a rapid rate, as if the driver were hurrying home to his supper. There were but few persons in the stage.

Young Van Quintem hailed the conveyance, jumped in before it could stop, and the driver whipped up his horses to an increased speed. Bog was tired, and he knew not how far he might have to follow the stage at a full trot. He resolved upon his course instantly. Turning the corner of Clinton Place, he ran up that side of the triangular block, and met the stage. He pulled his old cap farther over his eyes, to prevent the possibility of recognition by young Van Quintem, and, gliding swiftly behind the stage, when he was sure that the driver was not looking, hooked on to the step behind, just as he had done a thousand times when he was a smaller boy.

CHAPTER VI.

TRACKED.

YOUNG Van Quintem sat at the farther end of the stage, absorbed in his own thoughts. His thin lips moved restlessly at times, as if he were arguing to himself. In his hand he still held the crumpled note. Twice he unfolded it, and read the contents carefully; then crushed it in his hand again. Bog watched him through the window of the stage door—not looking straight at him, but with that side vision with which we trace the outline of faint comets. He was aware that young Van Quintem looked at him twice suspiciously, and then settled back into his own meditations. Bog felt safe in his disguise—or rather his original and native dress.

When the stage stopped to take in or let out passengers, Bog slipped from his perch, and hid himself from the driver's sight. Long experience had taught him how to render himself invisible to that vindictive personage.

The stage rolled on to the Greenpoint ferry, dropping all its passengers by the way, excepting the pursued and the pursuer. It was now evident that young Van Quintem was going to Greenpoint.

The ferry boat was not in, and would not be in, and ready to leave again, for ten minutes. Bog, having seen his game enter the ferry house, thereby conclusively proving his intention to cross the river, slipped into a boiler yard near the ferry. There, against a post, he scrawled with a stump of pencil, on the back of two playbills (which he had brought with him for stationery), two notes, as follows:

"Tuesday Evening, about 8 o'clock.

"Please come to the ferry house on the Greenpoint side, and wait there till I send for you. BOG."

These notes he addressed to Mr. Van Quintem, sen., and

Mrs. Crull, at their residences. The next step was to find a boy to deliver them. Bog did not have to wait long for that. Boys of the ragged and city-wise variety may be picked up at any corner of New York at any hour of the day or night.

Another Eighth-street stage, which came rattling toward the ferry, brought a fine specimen of the juvenile vagrant and dare-devil, seated on the step. Bog looked out of the boiler yard, and hailed him with a shrill whistle, formed by thrusting two fingers in the mouth, and blowing fiercely. The boy recognized the signal of his ragged tribe, slid off the seat, and came running to where Bog was standing. As he drew near, Bog recognized him as a trusty lad whom he had employed as file leader in a walking advertisement procession, several weeks before.

"Wot yer want, hey?" asked this youth.

"Know me?" asked Bog.

"Know ye? No. Yer a'n't one of our fellers."

"Look again." Bog raised his ragged cap, and smoothed his hair back.

"Why, it's Mr. Bogert. Cuss me if it a'n't!"

"Just so, Bill. I'm trying to catch a chap that owes me something, you see. He's in the ferry house there, waiting for the boat. I'm going to follow him to Greenpoint, and find out where he lives. Then I'll have him arrested. Now, there are two people I would like to have as witnesses, when I track him to his house. The names are written here; and what I want of you is, to deliver these notes to them as soon as you can, and tell them to come right away. Will you do it, Bill?"

"Won't I, Mr. Bogert? Jest tell me the names, streets, and numbers, cos I can't read handwritin' very well, yer know."

Bog read the addresses, and, at the same time, produced a quarter from his fast-diminishing stock of silver. "Take that,' said he.

"No yer don't!" said the eccentric youth. "You've

done some good turns to me. Bill Fish don't forget his friends, I can tell yer. Here goes, now."

Bill Fish snatched the notes from Bog's hand, and ran down the street after a stage which had just left the ferry house on its down trip. Bog saw him seat himself on the step, with his head well hid from the driver, and sent a parting whistle after him, to which Bill Fish responded with an enormous grin and a jerk of thumb over shoulder at his natural enemy on the box.

"I'll give Bill Fish a good job, some day," mused Bog. "Now for the scoundrel."

The boat had come in. Bog watched from his hiding place until he saw young Van Quintem step on board, and disappear in the ladies' cabin. Then he hastened to the ferry house, paid his fare, and entered. To avoid being seen by young Van Quintem, he took a seat in that repository of stale tobacco-smoke called the "Gentlemen's Cabin."

At the Greenpoint landing, Bog watched young Van Quintem's departure from the boat, and stole out, taking the opposite side of the street. It was then quite dark, and, with reasonable precaution, there was no fear that the pursued would see him.

The young profligate walked up the street several blocks, and turned into a side street, occupied by residences, with small shops and groceries at the corners, and occasionally at intervals between them. Suddenly, Bog observed him looking around, as if to be sure that he was not watched. Bog slipped behind a large tree. Having apparently come to the conclusion that nobody was observing him, young Van Quintem strode on rapidly a few rods farther, and then made a sharp turn into a neat little millinery shop, which stood quite remote from all other places of business.

When the young man's form had disappeared, Bog ran at the top of his speed to a point opposite the shop, where he could readily see what was going on within.

The door was open, and a strong light from the interior

shone across the street. There was no tree or awning post, or other object, on the sidewalk, behind which he could conceal himself. Exactly opposite to the shop, and in the full blaze of its light, was a high door shutting on a small alley way. Bog tried the latch, and found the door locked. With instant decision, he caught the top of the door, and vaulted over it, trusting to fortune not to be caught on the inside. Applying his eye to the keyhole, he observed the following condition of things:

The shop was a milliner's, beyond all question. It was filled with articles of ladies' wear, whose names and uses were all unknown to Bog; while outside, in the air, dangled various patterns of skirts which had just then come into fashion; and the public and obtrusive exhibition of which is one of the singularities of our rapid civilization.

Behind the counter stood one of those thin ladies who have dedicated themselves to the millinery and a single life. At that distance, she looked to Bog like a perfectly respectable woman, with a sharp eye to business. Farther on, toward the end of the same counter, was the angel of his heart, Patty Minford. Her appearance, pale, and therefore more touchingly beautiful than ever, threw his senses into that sweet flutter which is the proof and mystery of love. He repeated the vow which he had made to himself, and dreamed of fulfilling a thousand times, to save her from harm at the risk of his life. She was folding up articles on the counter, and packing them into little boxes, and did not look toward young Van Quintem. Bog thought this a good sign.

The young man leaned over the counter, and addressed some words to her, to which her lips moved as if in reply, while her eyes were still downcast on her work. He then smoothed out the crumpled note which he had carried in his hand, and placed it before her. She started in amazement, as she remarked the close imitation of her handwriting; and, having read it, shook her head with a wondering air. Young Van Quintem's inexpressive face assumed a look of astonishment, and he instantly walked to the door, and peered up and down the street, and opposite. Then he nodded to Miss Minford, as if to excuse himself for a moment, and, darting out of the shop, walked rapidly to the street below, and then to the one above, passing Bog's hiding place on that side of the street, and causing that youth to remove his eye from the keyhole for fear of detection. When he had made this reconnoissance, and satisfied himself that there was no spy about, he returned to the shop. In the mean time, some pantomime had been going on between Miss Minford and the shopwoman, which Bog interpreted to mean that Miss Minford appealed to her for protection, and that the shopwoman promised it. This was followed by the retiring of the young lady through a door in the rear of the shop, and the locking of the door by her female friend, who put the key in her pocket.

Young Van Quintem came in, and was surprised not to see Patty. The shopwoman explained, with a gesture, that she had gone up stairs, whereon he consulted his watch, and then sat down in an armchair in front of the counter, as if with the determination of waiting for her.

Bog judged, from all the circumstances, that Miss Minford would not again show herself for some time; that young Van Quintem would wait, in the hope of seeing her; and that the shopwoman could be depended on as her friend to the last. He therefore concluded that he might safely spend time to go to the ferry house, and procure the company of old Van Quintem and Mrs. Crull, who had probably reached the rendezvous. Watching for an opportunity when the young man's back was turned, Bog lightly vaulted from his hiding place, and noiselessly ran down the street.

CHAPTER VII.

FOUND AND LOST.

When he arrived at the ferry house, the boat was coming in, with his venerable accomplices on board. Upon receiving her cue from the faithful Bill Fish, Mrs. Crull entered her carriage (which had been in readiness for her since Bog started out on his search), and was driven to Mr. Van Quintem's. The old gentleman, who was sitting in his study, with his light overcoat and hat on, prepared for any journey, took the spare seat in the carriage, and, in less than twenty-five minutes, by fast driving and the timely coöperation of the ferry boat, they were at the appointed spot.

"Have you found her, you dear Bog?" asked Mrs. Crull, breathless.

Bog answered "Yes," and that Mrs. Crull should see her in five minutes. That lady then assisted him into the carriage, and kissed him on the forehead in a motherly way, which would have astonished the sedate family coachman, if he had not been entirely used to Mrs. Crull's eccentricities.

"My good boy," said old Van Quintem, in a trembling voice, "are you sure we are not too late—quite sure?"

"Sure!" said Bog.

"Thank God! thank God!" murmured the old gentleman. Then he looked with a strange interest upon the honest and intelligent face of the lad. He was contrasting the history of the poor boy, which he had learned from Mrs. Crull, with that of his abandoned son.

The carriage was stopped, by the order of Bog (who calmly took charge of the whole proceedings), at the corner of the street below the shop; and the party (excepting the driver) walked slowly toward the scene of interest. Old Van Quintem's increasing infirmities compelled him to lean for support on the arm of Mrs. Crull, and also with greater and more confiding weight, on that of Bog.

As the party entered the shop, young Van Quintem was sitting with his head turned toward the door by which Miss Minford had vanished, savagely biting his finger nails. He wheeled in his chair, and confronted the intruders.

"What the —— are you doing here?" he cried to his father.

"We are here to save a young girl from ruin, and you from another crime," said the old gentleman, greatly agitated, and leaning with his whole weight, now, on Bog's arm.

"The —— you are! And you have brought along an old woman, and a boy that looks like a pickpocket, to help you."

The phrase "old woman" stirred up Mrs. Crull. She left the old gentleman's side, and advanced to within a yard of the profligate. "Old as I am," said she, "I'm strong enough to spank such a white-livered, broken-down puppy as you are. But I'll leave you to the hands of the law. It's a long lane that hasn't any turning, remember; and you'll pull up at the gallows at last. That's some comfort!"

Mrs. Crull here became conscious that it was highly impolite to lose her temper, and she fell back to the support of her old friend. Young Van Quintem laughed at her, showing his white teeth unpleasantly.

"Ah, I recognize you now," he continued, looking maliciously at the boy Bog. "You are the young thief that tracked me here, are you? I'll settle with you now."

He sprang from his chair, and strode toward the lad. He was met halfway by Bog, whom the insulting epithet had stung to the quick.

A foe met halfway is half vanquished. A single glance at Bog's clear, courageous eye, and his sinewy proportions, assured young Van Quintem that he had more than his match.

"This—this is no place for a row," he faltered. "I'll attend to you, some time, in the street."

"I shall always be ready for you," said Bog, smiling at this pusillanimous postponement—which is a mild way of making a clear backout.

Here the attention of all was called off by the appearance of Miss Minford. The quick ear of the milliner had caught her footstep on the stairs, coming down. She unlocked the door, and the beautiful object of their search stood before them. She was very pale, and tears dimmed her eyes. Mrs. Crull flew toward her, and the poor girl fell on her breast, and cried as if her heart would break.

Good Mrs. Crull helped her to a sofa, and sat down, and strained her young friend closely to her bosom. "Be calm," said she, "dear child!"

Old Van Quintem and Bog looked on with sad interest. The young villain stood in a corner, gnawing his finger nails, and revolving schemes of vengeance. All waited for Miss Minford to become calm before any explanation was sought.

Under the soothing caresses of Mrs. Crull, the young girl soon became comparatively tranquil. With her head still pillowed on the broad bosom of her protectress, she made a broken statement to the following effect, in response to the tender questionings of that lady:

She said that she had no thought of leaving the house of her dear friend, until he had told her how much better it would be to earn her own living at some easy and pleasant trade, than to be dependent on one who was not a relative. He had also told her that, one day, when he was passing the house, he heard Mr. Crull scolding because Mrs. Crull had brought a girl home to be her companion.

At this point, Mrs. Crull turned furiously toward the pale offender. "You miserable wretch!" said she. "I only wish my dear old man was here, to thrash you soundly. Why, he loved this little darling almost as much as I did. Besides, I'm the mistress of our house; and he never meddles with my affairs. Go on, dear Pet."

Pet then stated that he (she never called him by his name) had promised to get a place for her, and that she, supposing he was a true friend, had accepted the offer of his aid. One day, when they had met by appointment (which was very wrong, she admitted, with a fresh torrent of tears), he told her that he had found a nice situation for her in a milliner's shop in Greenpoint, and that she must come right away, or she would lose the chance. She went home, and packed up her few things in a handkerchief, and came with him here in a carriage.

She came directly here, and had not been out of Mrs. Wopping's sight since then. Mrs. Wopping had treated her very, very kindly.

Mrs. Wopping, who had been lying in wait for her opportunity, here spoke up. She was a respectable woman, she said, thank God! and had been in the business for fifteen years, in New York. They could inquire about her in Canal street, where she had served her apprenticeship; in Division street, where she had been a forewoman; and in Grand street, where she had kept a shop. In an evil hour, she had been persuaded to start a millinery establishment in Greenpoint; and a very bad time she had had of it. All she knew about this unfortunate affair, was this: The young man, there, had called on her, a few days ago, and said that he wanted to do a favor for an orphan girl, who was a distant relative of his. She was poor, he said, but proud—no strange thing, Mrs. Wopping believed—and would not accept anything directly from him.

"Therefore," said Mrs. Wopping, "he wanted to arrange with me to give her some easy work to do, enough to make her think she was earning her own living, and he would pay me her board, and give me twenty shillings a week to hand to her as her wages. By this plan, I could get a boarder at a fair price, and the services of a young lady to wait on the shop for nothing. Very imprudently, I consented, but not before I had made the young man there swear to Heaven that his intentions were honorable. This he did in the most solemn manner. I loved the dear girl at first sight, and determined to watch over her, and keep her from harm. I had a little sister once—long since dead—that much resembled her. I should add, that, though Miss Minford seemed to think very well of the young man there, when he brought her here, she became quite suspicious of him yesterday—he was here all yesterday afternoon—and refused to ride out with him, though he had brought a handsome carriage for her. I advised her not to go."

"Thank you, good Mrs. Wopping!" said Mrs. Crull, shaking that lady by the hand, "you have been a true friend to our dear child; and I'll order my bonnets from you for the futer. Virtue shouldn't always be its own reward.

"You see, now, my darling," continued Mrs. Crull, "what a scoundrel you have escaped from. Will you be my adopted child forever? Speak, my precious!"

Poor Pet threw her soft white arms around the thick neck of her protectress, and cried for joy. "Dear, dear mother!" she murmured.

There was a pause, during which everybody but young Van Quintem had occasion to wipe their eyes. He paced up and down, his brow wrinkled, and inextinguishable hate flashing from his eyes.

"Well, sir," said his father, calmly, "what atonement have you to make for this outrage?"

"You're a —— old fool, and that's all I've got to say."

"Heaven be praised that his poor mother was not spared for this sorrow!" was the tranquil reply.

"Curse you—and the old woman's memory. You're always making a fuss about her."

The benignant expression of old Van Quintem's face vanished instantly, and a just rage gleamed on every feature. "Unnatural son! monster! fiend!" he cried, raising his hands aloft; "at last you have gone too far. Leave my presence, sir, and never—never—let me see your face again. I say to you, and before these witnesses, that I disown and disinherit you forever—forever—forever!"

The coward son could not endure that terrible visitation of parental wrath, and fled, without another word, from the shop.

Old Van Quintem fell exhausted upon the strong shoulder of the boy Bog.

"Henceforth," said he, "you—you—shall be my son."

FATHER AND SON.

BOOK TWELFTH.

SPECULATIONS—PECUNIARY AND MATRIMONIAL.

CHAPTER I.

THE "COSMOPOLITAN WINDOW FASTENER."

The "Cosmopolitan Window Fastener" was a veritable success. For the first time in his life, Mr. Wesley Tiffles's theories had been demonstrated by results. Had the "Cosmopolitan Window Fastener" been his own invention, and disposed of for his own behoof, he would have abandoned it long before its merits had been fairly tested, and tried some other of the myriad schemes that floated through his brain. But the profits of the "Cosmopolitan Window Fastener" went to another; and this was the secret of Wesley Tiffles's persistent (and therefore successful) exertions.

This was his plan of operations: In the first place, from the funds supplied by Marcus Wilkeson, he procured a patent for the invention. In the second place, he put an advertisement a column long in every daily paper—six insertions paid in advance—and handed a highly polished brass model of the invention to the editor, with a request to notice, if perfectly agreeable. The just and logical result followed. Instead of the ten-line paragraph with which patent churns and washing machines are ordinarily turned loose on society, the "Cosmopolitan Window Fastener" received notices so long and ornate, that it was quite impossible to derive from them a correct idea of the matchless simplicity of the invention.

Having thus roused public curiosity, Tiffles, in the third place, took an office on Broadway, and put up a large sign inscribed in gilt capitals, "The Cosmopolitan Window Fastener Manufacturing Co." From this *pou sto*, Archimedes-like, he commenced to move the world of house owners. This he accomplished by the following manœuvre: He caused double-leaded advertisements, under the head of special notices, to be inserted in all the papers, informing the public that it would be utterly impossible to supply the demand for the "Cosmopolitan Window Fastener," and that, therefore, it would be useless to send in orders. The Company were employing all the resources of two large manufacturing establishments; but it was evident that these would fail to meet the extraordinary and totally unexpected demand for this indispensable protection against burglars—this moral safeguard, as it might not inappropriately be called, of civilized homes. The Company had made every effort, but without success, to secure a force of skilled workmen equal to the emergency. Justice to their customers in all parts of the country, compelled the Company to announce that no orders received after that date could be filled under two months. Under these remarkable—they might say, in some respects, disagreeable—circumstances, they begged leave to throw themselves on the indulgence of a generous public.

These notices were put forth not only in the form of newspaper advertisements, but as placards and handbills, which were stuck all over the city, and thrown into all the stages, falling like autumn leaves into the laps of passengers. This was the coöperative work of the boy Bog, who, though adopted by old Van Quintem as his son and heir, had not yet given up the bill-sticking business, but, on the contrary, had increased it, and now had a practical monopoly of it in the city, with branches in the suburbs. Bog would not eat the bread of idleness—and so he had modestly told Mr. Van Quintem—and that fine old gentleman had patted him on the back, and told him that there was genuine Dutch blood in him.

Bogert & Co. now employed a hundred lads; and Bog's department of labor was the general planning of operations, and the receiving and disbursement of the money—and a very nice and agreeable department it was. It enabled Bog to dress neatly, and keep his hands clean—two points upon which he was now extremely fastidious. Bog was growing tall, manly, and handsome. He was also showing a great improvement in his grammar and pronunciation—the fruit of diligent attendance at the evening school.

The public, being thus continually informed that orders for the "Cosmopolitan Window Fastener" could not possibly be filled under two months, very naturally began to send in orders for the invaluable invention, to be filled after that period. Every mail brought hundreds of them from all parts of the country. The Company—that is, Wesley Tiffles—sat at their desk in the Broadway office from nine to three o'clock, exhibiting the window fastener to hundreds of visitors, and receiving orders rather as a matter of favor to the customer than to the Company.

At the end of a month, when orders to the amount of nearly seventy-five thousand dollars had been received—every Northern and Western State being extensively represented on the books—the Company issued another advertisement, to the effect that, owing to the overwhelming pressure of business, they were willing to dispose of patent rights for two of the States.

There was a rush of applicants, to all of whom the Company could truthfully exhibit large and genuine orders from all the States. The rights for two States were readily sold, and the Company then found that they could spare one more for a fair compensation; and so on, until every State in the Union had been disposed of, and the Company had not an inch of

United States territory left. Not only this, but liberal purchasers were found for Cuba, Canada, South America, England, France, Germany, Russia, and all the countries of the Continent.

In three months, the Company had disposed of their entire interest, and realized about one hundred thousand dollars cash. This sum Tiffles had faithfully paid over, as fast as received, to Fayette Overtop, who not only represented Marcus Wilkeson (unknown to Pet), but was Pet's own attorney and agent. By Fayette Overtop it was placed in bank, credited to Miss Patty Minford, and subject to her order alone.

Thus it happened that the poor inventor had not toiled in vain for the child that he loved.

Tiffles—with that strange unselfishness sometimes found in men of his class—had not thought of or desired any compensation for his services, other than the payment of all the bills incurred in the operation. The pleasure which he took in manipulating the public, and seeing his labors crowned with success, was the only reward that he wished for.

Marcus Wilkeson, however, as soon as he saw that Tiffles was actually about to perform the amazing feat of raising money, determined, as an act of common justice, to insist upon his receiving twenty per cent. of the total. Tiffles flatly refused, at first, saying (which was true) that he could work a great deal better if he had no personal interest in the scheme; but yielded, at length, to the earnest solicitations of Marcus, backed by the emphatic declaration of Miss Minford (through her attorney), that she would not touch a penny of the money unless he consented. So, when the affairs of the Company were wound up, Tiffles found himself the possessor of twenty thousand dollars—a sum whose existence in a concrete form he had always secretly disbelieved. And Tiffles's first act was to settle up all his outstanding debts.

The unexpected acquisition of this immense sum imparted a charm to every object in life except Miss Philomela Wilkeson.

Poor Miss Wilkeson was quick to discern the change in Tiffles's manner toward her. His calls were as frequent as ever, but were exclusively on her half-brother, and had no side bearing in her direction. He no longer lingered in the entry to converse with her; and flatly refused her invitation to take a glass of wine in the dining room. Most ominous of signs, he did not press her hand in the least, when he took it in his own. His voice was no longer winning, but harsh and neglectful. Indifference brooded in the heart of the monster. The worst of it was, that he had been so cautious and non-committal in his declarations, that she could not upbraid him for his perfidy. With a cold calculation worthy of a demon, he had made love in the pantomimic way, and eschewed written or verbal communications of an erotic nature. No jury could have mulcted him one cent for damages in a breach-of-promise case, and he knew it.

While Wesley Tiffles slipped off Miss Wilkeson like a loose glove, she might as well have tried to divest herself of her natural cuticle as to banish all thoughts of him. Miss Wilkeson was accustomed to allude mysteriously to certain sentimental affairs of her youth. In confidential moments, her friends had been favored with shadowy reminiscences of a romantic past. But truth compels us to state that Miss Wilkeson had never been the recipient of that delicate and awkward thing known as a proposal, and that she had never been kissed by man or boy since she wore long dresses. Hence the magnified importance which she attached to that kiss which, in a moment of reckless but cheap gallantry, Wesley Tiffles, on one fatal evening, had impressed upon her withered hand. She loved the destroyer of her peace with the pent-up energies of forty years.

CHAPTER II.

MIDDLE-AGED CUPID.

Being in ignorance of Tiffles's sudden fortune, she was at a loss how to explain his defection. She conjectured all things, and finally settled down to the conclusion that he was a coy young man, and had not been sufficiently encouraged by her. She remembered instances where he had exhibited signs of ardor—in one case so far as beginning to slip a hand around her waist—and she had repelled him. He was evidently waiting for some marked encouragement. How foolishly prudish she had been!

One evening, as Wesley Tiffles was passing through the hall to the door, after a rattling hour with the three bachelors, he was confronted by Miss Wilkeson, who chanced to leave the front parlor on a journey up stairs at that moment. She was dressed in a light silk, and her hair was carefully braided, and her face had a pink color in some parts, which contrasted well with the pallor in other parts; and her glass had told her that she was looking uncommonly youthful and charming. She had carefully studied her part, which was to be a bold one, throwing off all reserve.

"Good evening, Mr. Tiffles," said she, promptly offering her hand.

He took it with unsqueezing indifference. She had expected that.

"Mr. Tiffles," said she, with an air of youthful raillery, "you are a naughty man, and I had an idea of not speaking to you again."

"Naughty!" said Tiffles, astonished. "How?"

"Why, you have hardly been civil to me, of late. I do believe you wouldn't speak, or shake hands with me, if I didn't always set the example." This in a half-complaining, half-laughing way.

It suddenly flashed upon Tiffles that he had been, for some

time, rather neglectful of the lady. It also forcibly occurred to him that it was wise policy to be on good terms, at all times, with the mistress of the house; and such was Miss Wilkeson's present position. He therefore clutched her hand again, gave it a faint squeeze, and said that he apologized a million times for his rudeness; but the fact was, he had so much business on hand, that he had been turned into a perfect bear, he supposed. He playfully challenged Miss Wilkeson to step into the parlor and take a glass of wine, and he would show her that he was not the brute she fancied.

Miss Wilkeson laughingly accepted the challenge. "But I do believe," she added, "that it is only the glass of wine you care for. Now tell me, Mr. Tiffles, aren't you a woman hater?"

When a man is asked that question, categorically, by a woman, his most effective answer is to make love to her out of hand. Tiffles was not prepared to do this in the present case, but he was willing to pay compliments to any extent.

"Ah, Miss Wilkeson, there you do me great injustice," said he, with his pleasantest of laughs. "I drink this glass of wine to 'lovely woman,'" with a nod at Miss Wilkeson.

Miss Wilkeson giggled, and took a fly's sip from the brim of her glass.

Tiffles heaved a sigh. "We bachelors are poor, unhappy fellows, really to be pitied."

"You are horrid creatures—you know you are—and deserve no pity from us!" Miss Wilkeson played her frisky, juvenile part admirably.

"So charming, and yet so cruel!" said Tiffles, uttering the first preposterous compliment that he thought of.

"You flatterer!" said Miss Wilkeson, beating a breeze toward him with her fan.

Tiffles, observing that matters were coming to a crisis, paused. Miss Wilkeson interpreted his silence as another attack of timidity. Time was valuable to her, and this kind of conversation might be kept up all night, and amount to nothing. She resolved upon her final *coup*.

"Oh! oh! Mr. Tiffles, what—what is the matter?" She looked wildly about her.

"The matter! What matter?" exclaimed that gentleman, little suspecting what was to happen.

"The wine—the warm weather—something—oh! oh!"

With these inexplicable remarks, Miss Wilkeson dropped her fan, uttered a slight but sharp scream, and fell back in her chair, like a withered flower on a broken stalk.

"By thunder, she has fainted!" said the excited Tiffles. He had never been in a similar dilemma, and did not know what to do. He had heard tickling of the feet highly recommended in such cases; but that was obviously impracticable. A dash of cold water in the face was also said to afford instant relief; but there was no water at hand. "I must call for help," said he.

This remark appeared to arouse Miss Wilkeson. "Support me," she murmured. "I shall be better soon."

Tiffles, all accommodation, clasped her fragile waist with an arm, and gently inclined her head upon his shoulder. She heaved a sigh, and gave other tokens of returning animation. Tiffles here noticed that her face had not the prevailing paleness which always accompanies fainting. He instantly suspected the true nature of Miss Wilkeson's complaint.

The noise of quick footsteps resounded in the entry. Marcus, Overtop, and Maltboy had heard the sharp scream, and were rushing to the rescue.

"Good heavens! what will they say?" exclaimed Tiffles. "Don't be silly, Miss Wilkeson, at your time of life." This cutting remark was wrung from him by the annoyance and confusion of the moment.

It served as a wonderful anodyne; for Miss Wilkeson jerked herself into an erect position, and said, "You're a fool!"

At this juncture, before Tiffles had quite uncoiled his serpentine arms from her, and while she was looking fiery indignation at him, the door was pushed open, and the three bachelors rushed in.

"I really beg pardon," said Marcus. "No occasion for my services, I see—ahem!"

"Heard a scream—thought it was here—no intention to intrude," added Overtop.

The tableau reminded Maltboy of his own innumerable little affairs, and he laughed. "It's a lovers' quarrel," said he, "and not to be interrupted, of course."

The three bachelors hastily evacuated the room, and their merry laughs rang in the entry.

"Miss Wilkeson," said Tiffles, consulting his watch—he carried a gold one, with an enormous gold chain—"you must really excuse me. Important business engagement at nine. Good evening." So saying, Tiffles precipitately retired, with the determination not to enter the house again until he knew that Miss Wilkeson was out of it.

A week from that memorable day, Tiffles met Marcus Wilkeson on Broadway.

"Why haven't you been to see us?" said Marcus.

"Not been very smart, of late," explained Tiffles.

"Fainting fits, perhaps. Maybe they are catching, eh?"

Tiffles smiled, for he saw that Marcus knew the truth. "How is Miss Wilkeson?" he asked, respectfully.

"She has gone into the country for her health, and will probably stay away a number of years. In short, I have engaged for her the position of first preceptress of a female seminary in the middle of the State. She said she was quite sick of the hollow and heartless life of New York."

Marcus spoke truly. Miss Wilkeson had retired to the country with a thorough feeling of disgust for town existence. She has taught for several years, and is still teaching in the ——— Young Ladies' Seminary, with eminent success, though her fair pupils complain, with much pretty pouting, of her savage restrictions upon all walks and talks with the eligible young beaux of the village. They say that she hates the men; and they call her a cross old maid, and a great number of other hard epithets.

But, sometimes, a tear is observed in the corner of her eye, which she hastily wipes away. That tear is an oblation upon the memory of a lost love. That lost love was, and is, and always will be, Wesley Tiffles.

CHAPTER III.

SLAPMAN *vs.* SLAPMAN.

The case of Slapman *vs.* Slapman occupied the attention of the referee, Samuel Goldfinch, Esq., over two months. That gentleman was corpulent, fond of good dinners, and had a highly cultivated taste for scandal. It had been his custom to give this interesting case a hearing one or two hours every afternoon, daily, after court. It was a relief from the heavy business of the day; for Goldfinch had heavy business, which came to him because he was a fat and pleasant fellow, with a large head, and a great circle of miscellaneous acquaintance. The real work of the office was done by a modest, unappreciated man named Mixer. On the occasion of these anti-matrimonial audiences, Mixer sat in the back room, grubbing among his dusty papers; while Samuel Goldfinch, Esq., in the front room, with shut doors, leaned back in his easy chair and surrendered himself to enjoyment.

In the case of Slapman *vs.* Slapman, a great number of witnesses had been examined on each side. Affidavits, amounting to hundreds of pages, had been obtained in distant States—some as far away as California. The lawyers had spared neither their own time nor the money of their clients in raking together testimony which would bear in the slightest degree upon the interests which they represented. All the relatives of Mr. Slapman had testified that he was a gentleman uniformly kind and courteous, possessing a singular placidity of temper, and indulgent to his wife to a degree where indulgence became a fault. Those relatives, and they were numerous—particularly in the country branch—who had passed anniversary weeks at Mr. Slapman's house, were very severe on Mrs. Slapman. She was a proud, disagreeable woman. She was continually snubbing her husband before people. She had a great many male friends, whose acquaintance she had retained in defiance of his wishes. She was known to have received letters from men, and when her husband had desired to peruse them, had laughed at him. It is true that she pretended to be a patroness of literature, science, and the arts; but anybody could see that those things were only the cover of the grossest improprieties. She had been heard to listen without remonstrance, to declarations of love from several young men. It turned out, upon cross-examination, that these irregularities took place in charades and plays, of which Mr. Slapman's relatives had been shocked spectators. With regard to Mr. Overtop's transactions in the family, they could say nothing; for they had long since ceased to visit Mrs. Slapman, on account of her disgraceful conduct—and also (they might have added, but they did not add) because Mrs. Slapman latterly had her house full of Jigbees, and put her husband's relatives into obscure rooms in the third story, and quite forgot their existence afterward.

Per contra, all the Jigbees—and they were a prolific race—swore that their distinguished relative was a pattern of artlessness and innocence. That she was remarkable from early childhood for a charming frankness and transparent candor. That when this bright ornament of the Jigbee stock was sought in marriage by the defendant, the whole family, with one mind and voice, opposed the match. They had felt that a being of her exalted intellectual tastes was too good for a sordid money-getting creature like Slapman. But that man, by his ingenious artifices, had succeeded in winning the hand of their gifted kinswoman, and married her against their unanimous protests. There was but one consolation for this family misfortune. Mr. Slapman was reported to be wealthy, and could afford to indulge his wife in the exercise of her noble longings for TRUTH. They were willing to say that Mr. Slapman had not been illiberal, so far as vulgar money was concerned. He had given to his wife the house and lot which she occupied, and had never stinted her in respect of allowances. But what was money to a woman of Mrs. Slapman's soul, when her husband withheld from her his confidence and trust, regarded her innocent labors in behalf of Art, Literature, and the Drama, with a cold, unsympathizing eye, and finally descended so low as to feel a brutal jealousy of those gentlemen of talent, of whom she was the revered patroness?

"Money" (we are quoting here from the remarks of Mrs. Slapman's eminent counsel) "is very desirable in its way, but is it not the vilest dross, your Honor, when compared with the pure gold of connubial trust and sympathy?" Mr. Goldfinch nodded his head, as if to say that he rather thought it was.

The testimony of two servant girls established the fact that Mr. Slapman had several times been overheard to tell his wife that she would regret it; and that the time was fast coming when forbearance would cease to be a virtue; also that the worm, when trodden on repeatedly, might at last turn and sting, and many other enigmatical sayings of that character. The very vagueness of these threats, implying unknown horrors, had inspired his wife with a mortal dread of him. She did not know at what moment this jealous and revengeful man might strike her dead. She had been living in the fear of her life for six years, and, during all this time, had never complained, or expressed that fear to one of her relatives or friends.

"Such is the noble, uncomplaining nature," said the eminent counsel, in reference to this fact, "of the woman that Fate has thrown into the arms of a fiend."

But the most striking proof of Mr. Slapman's murderous designs upon his wife, was his conduct at the last dramatic *soirée*. Twenty witnesses swore that it was his evident intention to spring on her and strangle her, and that he was only thwarted in this horrid purpose by the noble courage of Fayette Overtop, Esq. Mr. Overtop briefly and modestly testified to this effect also; and, furthermore, narrated all the particulars of his acquaintance with Mrs. Slapman, holding before her a shield, from which the arrows of calumny, aimed by her husband, fell harmless.

Mr. Slapman had not shown himself in the referee's office since the investigation began. He had become convinced that he had lost the case into which his mad jealousy and his lawyer's advice had plunged him. Mrs. Slapman, according to the testimony of the two servants and several others, was immured in her house, and brooding over this saddest episode in her unhappy history.

"Nothing but that instinct of self-preservation," said the eminent counsel, "which bids the dove to fly from the hawk, and the rabbit to evade the pursuing hounds, could have induced that delicate, shrinking lady to lay bare the horrors of her prison house to the world, and to ask, in the name of common humanity, a release from the tyrant, and a liberal alimony."

The eminent counsel repeated this flight of fancy in the ear of Mrs. Slapman, at the opera that evening, whither she was accompanied by a few of the Jigbees, and she smiled, and said that it was really beautiful.

The protracted case—of which we have given a mere sketch—was decided by Samuel Goldfinch, Esq., in favor of the lady, a separation was decreed, and alimony fixed at six thousand dollars a year, that being only a wife's fair proportion of Mr. Slapman's income. Mrs. Slapman, with a well-assumed appearance of levity, gave a *grande soirée musicale et dramatique* at her house, in honor of the event, at which Overtop was a favored guest. Mr. Slapman went direct to Slapmanville, and raised the rent on all his tenants, turned a superannuated non-paying couple into the street, and took a general account of his property, to see how much he could sell out for, preparatory to leaving for Europe, and so dodging the payment of the alimony.

The illustrated papers published two portraits—one of an angel, the other of a demon. The angel was Mrs. Slapman: the demon was her husband. The comic papers served him up in puns, conundrums, and acrostics, of the most satirical import. The daily papers, always on the look out for subjects to write about, improved the occasion to overhaul the question of divorce, in its statistical, moral, social, and religious bearings. Two editors, in pursuance of a previous agreement, continued to discuss the question with great warmth in their respective journals, until they had written about two hundred octavo pages, when the debate was published in book form, with paper covers, and sold for their joint benefit.

CHAPTER IV.

HOW OVERTOP SEALED A CONTRACT IN A WAY UNKNOWN TO CHITTY.

THE notoriety which Fayette Overtop had derived from his questionable connection with the Slapman Divorce case, had (as has been already stated) materially contributed to his professional income. By the time the case was decided, the firm of Overtop & Maltboy ranked among the most successful of the Junior Bar.

Now that Overtop had his hands full of business, his thoughts reverted to matrimony more strongly than ever. It is a singular fact, that business men find more time to think of marriage, than men of leisure.

Thoughts of matrimony invariably brought Miss Pillbody into Overtop's head. He would project mental photographs of her at the top of a table, beaming sweetly upon him, opposite, with her dim, lovely eyes, and pouring out the tea from a small silver pot. Overtop never could explain it; but this imaginary picture realized all his desires of domestic happiness.

Overtop not only thought of Miss Pillbody, but, what was

more to the purpose, he visited her. For this, pretexts were not wanting. They never are. At first, he professed to have been requested, by a friend in the country, to find a suitable private school for two young daughters. This justified several visits, until Miss Pillbody could decide positively that it would be impossible for her to take them—an announcement which greatly relieved Overtop, though it temporarily put an end to his calls. Then he hit upon the expedient of pretending to write an essay on Popular Education, for a monthly magazine, and desired to obtain hints from her upon the subject. Miss Pillbody, not displeased with the compliment, though declaring that she had not an idea to give him, gave him a great many good ideas, to which he appeared to listen, while he was contemplating her trim figure, and the animated expression of her face, and thinking how very well she would look at the head of that poetical table behind that phantom teapot. At last the topic of Popular Education ran out; and Overtop felt that this kind of imposition could not be practised much longer.

One day, while Overtop sat at his desk, with a mass of law papers before him, thinking not of them but of his dilemma with respect of Miss Pillbody, a small boy brought him a beautifully written little note from that lady, asking him to call that evening on business. Overtop sent a reply, written with extraordinary care (this is a sign of love), saying that he would be happy to call, as requested. At the same time, he felt a pang of apprehension that she had found places in her school for the two young daughters of his supposititious country friend.

Overtop dressed with unusual care that evening, and presented himself at Miss Pillbody's house, punctually at the appointed hour. The young teacher was hard at work in the back parlor, setting copy for the illiterate wife of a rich city contractor to try her brawny fist on next day. Miss Pillbody's bewitching eyeglasses bestrided her nose; and the narrow collar, wristbands, and dainty apron with the red-bound pockets, looked whiter than ever.

The teacher blushed slightly as Overtop entered, and put

away the copy book on a high shelf, thereby intimating that she should not work more that night, and Overtop could stay as long as he would. Thus, at least, that sagacious student of men, women, and things, interpreted it. Without a particle of those preliminary commonplaces for which Overtop had a cherished aversion, Miss Pillbody broke into business at once.

She said that a Mrs. Cudgeon, the wife of a citizen who had made a large fortune in butter and eggs, had been taking lessons in all the English branches, and French (here Miss Pillbody smiled), for six months, but had postponed payment on one pretext and another, and had finally withdrawn from the school, leaving unpaid tuition to the amount of one hundred and fifty dollars. Miss Pillbody had written several dunning letters to Mrs. Cudgeon, and received no answer. The soft grass of epistolary entreaty having failed, Miss P. now proposed to try what virtue there was in the hard stones of the law. She had sent to Mr. Overtop for advice.

Overtop listened to the statement of the case with professional attentiveness. He was sub-thinking, all the time, what an extremely sensible woman Miss Pillbody was, not to allow herself to be cheated, but to go to law in defence of her rights. He assured his interesting client that she could count on his best services, and that she might consider the one hundred and fifty dollars as good as recovered. From this point the conversation glided off into a wilderness of general topics. Overtop had a habit (a bad one, it must be confessed) of sounding people's mental depths. He found that Miss Pillbody was no shallow thinker. He left the house at eleven o'clock, supposing it was ten, and had a delightful vision, that night, of the little round table and the teapot, and the presiding angel.

Next day, Overtop wrote the following letter:

"New York, ——.

"Mr. J. Cudgeon:

"Sir: Enclosed is a bill of items, amounting to one hundred and fifty dollars, for your wife's tuition at Miss Pillbody's private school. Be good enough to look it over, and inform me, to-morrow, what you will do about it. I will tell you candidly, that it is for our interest, as a young law firm, to sue you for the debt; but my client will not consent to this, until all other efforts fail, out of regard to the feelings of Mrs. C.

"Your obedient servant,

"OVERTOP & MALTBOY,

"No — ——— Building.

"J. CUDGEON, Esq."

Overtop remembered that one J. Cudgeon had run for the Assembly at the previous fall election, and he surmised that, being a politician and a public character, J. Cudgeon would not like to see the bill of items in print. Overtop reasoned correctly; for, at ten A. M. the following day, that gentleman called at the office and paid the one hundred and fifty dollars, and said that he was very much obliged to Overtop & Maltboy for their gentlemanly conduct in the affair. Mr. Cudgeon had not been aware of his wife's pupilage at Miss Pillbody's private school, though he had observed (he added, confidentially), for some months past, a slight improvement in her grammar. "I am not ashamed to say that we were poor once," said Mr. Cudgeon, with a glow of pride.

When Overtop placed the one hundred and fifty dollars in the white hand of the schoolmistress, she looked at him with gratitude and admiration, which more than repaid him. Not only this, but she asked him, with not a particle of hesitation, how much his fee was.

"Fee!" exclaimed Overtop, a little nettled at the implied insult. (Young lawyers are apt to be.) "Nothing, Miss Pillbody; decidedly nothing."

"But I prefer to pay you, Mr. Overtop. Why should you work for me for nothing, when I am not willing to do the same thing for Mrs. Cudgeon? 'The laborer is worthy of his hire,'" she added, laughing. "I set that adage in a copy book to-night."

"But I won't take anything," said Overtop, no longer nettled, but charmed to perceive this exhibition of sound good sense in a young lady.

"But I insist that you shall," continued Miss Pillbody, pleasantly. "Tell me, now, how much it is."

Overtop was standing within two feet of the schoolmistress, and her soft, dim eyes were beaming right into his. We leave psychologists to settle the phenomenon as they will; but the fact was, that each saw love in the eyes of the other. Overtop, in his bachelor musings, had thought over a hundred odd methods of putting *the* question. At this critical moment in the history of two hearts, a new form of the proposition occurred to him, so original and eccentric, that he determined to propound it at once.

He took Miss Pillbody's hand in his, before she knew it. She blushed, and would have withdrawn it; but he retained the hand with a gentle pressure.

"My dear Miss Pillbody," said Overtop, "I will take five dollars from you on one condition, and no other. Will you grant it?"

The schoolmistress, not knowing what she was saying, said "Yes."

"The condition is, that I shall buy an engagement ring, and put it on this dear hand."

Miss Pillbody blushed, and cast down her gentle eyes. The sagacious young lawyer, interpreting these signs as a full consent, stole his arm around her waist, and sealed the contract in a way all unknown to Chitty.

CHAPTER V.

A RETURNED CALIFORNIAN.

At last, Matthew Maltboy was engaged. He had, since twenty, been dallying on the edge of a betrothal. Now he had taken the momentous step into that anomalous region which lies between celibacy and married life, where a man is not exactly a bachelor, nor yet, by any means, a husband. It is the land in which the dim enchantments of romance begin to assume the plain outlines of reality. It is the land in which the pledge of undying affection, breathed, at some rapturous moment, into a delicate, inclining ear, becomes invested with awful meaning, and has a value in the legal market like a bond and mortgage. It is the land where the excitement of pursuit is over, and the game is securely cornered, but not yet in hand. It is the spot where the ardent huntsman of Love pauses to look back, and ceases to bend his longing gaze into the distance beyond.

How it came to pass that the unreliable Matthew Maltboy had become the affianced one of the pleasant widow Frump, it is not the purpose of this history to record. Let it suffice to say, that the mutual aversion which they felt, some months before, at Mr. Whedell's house, on New Year's day, was the starting point in their course of true love. Such an aversion, subsequently smoothed away, is often the most promising beginning of a courtship.

Mrs. Frump had frequently met Matthew on the street, and been gratified with his deferential bow. His bulk, to which, as a rotund lady, she had taken an antipathy, seemed to dwindle down as it was looked at. Matthew, whose ideal was a delicate woman with observable shoulder blades, had also, by repeated sights of Mrs. Frump, become reconciled to her ample proportions. Meantime, they had heard much, incidentally, of each other through Marcus Wilkeson. Matthew had come to esteem Mrs. Frump for her affectionate devotion to old Van Quintem; and Mrs. Frump had secretly admired the powerful though silent legal ability displayed by Mr. Maltboy in the inquisition before Coroner Bullfast.

One night, Matthew accompanied Marcus to his old friend's house; and, on the second night following, this couple were engaged—a happy event, which was brought about no less by the widow's experience, and conviction that there was no time to lose, than by Matthew's impulsive ardor.

He had been engaged ten days; and so entirely had he talked out the time to the widow, that it seemed six months.

"Why is it," thought Matthew, stretching himself in his chair, and looking critically at the widow, who was knitting crotchet work, "why is it that I no longer adore her? She is just as pretty, just as amiable, just as affectionate as ever. Now, why don't I care a button for her at this moment?" Matthew was not a transcendental philosopher; and the true answers to these questions did not come to him.

Old Van Quintem, pale and beautiful in his declining years, sat by the window that opened on the green leaves of the back yard, calmly smoking his pipe, and thinking, with a holy sadness, of his dead wife and his worse-than-dead son. The old gentleman, and the two quiet affianced ones, who sat near him, made up a well-dressed and handsome group; the pictorial effect of which was suddenly marred by the apparition of a stranger in the doorway.

He was tall, muscular, and what little could be seen of his face through a heavy growth of whiskers was mild and prepossessing, in spite of two large scars just visible below the broad brim of a rough hat. His dress was faded and dirty.

The stranger stood in the doorway, and surveyed the occupants of the room.

Old Van Quintem looked at the intruder a moment, and then said, as if remembering something, "Are you the man sent by Crumley to mend my piazza railing?"

There was the least hesitation in the man's voice, as he answered, "Yes, sir. I'm here to do that job." His voice was a deep growl, as of a grizzly bear half tamed.

"Where are your tools?" asked old Van Quintem.

The stranger communed with himself, and then replied, in the most natural manner, "I s'pose I only want a saw, a hammer, and a few nails. You have 'em, haven't yer?"

"You're a funny sort of carpenter, to travel without your

tools. Do you know, now, that you look more like a California miner than a carpenter ? "

"That's not very 'markable," returned the stranger, in profound guttural accents, "considerin' as how I come from California this week."

"You have brought home tons of gold, I dare say," said old Van Quintem, playfully.

"A little," growled the stranger. "The diggins was poor in Calaveras County when I fust went there, but latterly they improved."

At the mention of Calaveras County, the widow suddenly fixed her eyes upon the stranger, and then dropped them on her crotchet work.

Matthew Maltboy here conceived a happy thought, namely, to ask this stranger if he ever knew Amos Frump (the deceased husband of Mrs. Frump), who was killed in that very county in an affray growing out of a disputed claim, five years before. Mrs. Frump, after her engagement to Matthew, had furnished him with slips from three California papers, giving full particulars of the sanguinary affair. Before he was engaged, he had never felt the slightest curiosity to know the history of his predecessor; but, since then, he had entertained a strong secret desire to learn more of him, and especially of the reasons which induced him to abandon a young and lovely wife, and make a Californian exile of himself. Upon this subject the widow had never volunteered any satisfactory information, and he had been politely reluctant to ask her about it.

Old Van Quintem, who was too sleepy at that time to talk much, procured the necessary tools from a cupboard in the kitchen, and showed the stranger what work was to be done. The old gentleman then returned to his easy chair by the window, threw a handkerchief over his head, and settled himself for a nap.

Before the carpenter had struck the first blow, Matthew Maltboy rose, remarked to the widow that he wanted to stretch himself a little, and walked out upon the piazza.

The carpenter stood near the door, with the saw in one hand and the hammer in the other, very much in the attitude of listening. At Matthew's approach, he commenced feeling the teeth of the saw, as if to test their sharpness.

"I would like to speak a word with you, sir," said Matthew, in a low voice, motioning the carpenter to accompany him to a corner of the piazza, out of the widow's possible hearing.

Having attained that safe position, Matthew opened the great subject.

"You remarked that you had dug gold in Calaveras County," said he. "Did you ever happen to know a man by the name of Frump—Amos Frump—who was a miner there?"

"Frump!" replied the carpenter. "He was an intimate friend of mine."

"Now that's lucky," said Matthew, "for I want to find out something about the man."

"Then you've come to the right shop," answered the carpenter; "for his own brother—if he ever had one—couldn't tell you more about him than I."

"I am indeed fortunate. In the first place, then, this man Frump is really—dead?"

The carpenter pulled his rough hat farther over his forehead, and replied:

"As dead as two big splits in the skull could make him. But 'xcuse me, sir; he was my bosom friend, and I can't bear to talk of his death."

"He *is* dead, then, and no mistake," said Matthew, soliloquizing. "Yet I am not exactly glad to know it."

The carpenter's face expressed surprise at this remark.

"I beg your pardon," said Matthew. "Of course I am not glad to hear of your friend's death. But, to tell the truth," he continued (inventing an excuse), "I had always heard that this Frump was a wild fellow; that he didn't treat his wife decently, and at last ran away from her. You see I am acquainted with the family. In fact, I know Mrs. Frump quite well."

"And did she tell you all this about her dead husband?" asked the carpenter.

"Oh, no!" returned Matthew, who began to fear that he had gone too far. "She never says anything about his personal character. I only spoke from common report."

"Then common report is a common liar; for I know there never was a steadier chap than this same Amos Frump; and his wife can't say that he ever struck her, or said a cross word to her. Amos told me all about himself; and I'd believe him through thick and thin." The carpenter spoke in his dismal chest voice, without the least indication of excitement.

"Then why did he leave his wife? and why did she never hear of him until the time of his death? You will confess that *that* was odd."

"I give you the reasons," answered the carpenter, "as Amos give 'em to me. It seems that *he* was a poor, uneducated feller. *She* had a few thousand dollars from her grandfather's property, and was sent by her parents to the best o' schools. Though he and she were so much unlike, they got up a kind o' fondness for each other from the time when Amos saved her from bein' run over by a horse. They used to meet each other secretly, because, you see, her folks didn't like Amos. They thought that a girl with three or four thousand dollars in her own name, ought to set her eyes rather above a feller like him. Well, arter no end o' trouble, they was married. Her folks pretended to treat Amos all right, but was allers talkin' agin him; and finally they pizened her mind with the idee that he had married her only for her money, and that all the while he loved another gal. She began to treat him very cold like, and, one day, when she was in a little bit of temper——"

"Has Mrs. Frump any temper?" asked Matthew, anxiously. "I never saw it."

"But you a'n't her husband," replied the carpenter. "Amos told me that she did show a leetle temper now and then. However, he allers said she was a pooty good gal in the main,

Well, one day, when her dander was up about somethin', she told him that she b'lieved he married her for her money, and she'd die before he should have a cent. Amos was a proud feller, if he *was* poor; and, when he heerd this, he left the house right off, walked to New York, and shipped as a sailor to San Francisco. I met him when he fust come to the mines, and, as he was a spry, tough chap, I let him work a claim with me on shares. We ate and slept together, and many a time, in the dark night, has he spoke to me about his wife, and how much he thought of her; but he said he never should go back till he had money enough to buy out her and her hull family. We was very unlucky, and Amos got down-hearted, and took to drink. By and by he moved off to another claim, and worked on his own hook. He did better there; but all the gold he dug out he used to spend in gamblin' and rum; and at last a drunken quarrel put an end to Amos Frump."

"Poor fellow!" said Matthew. "And do you think the widow ever grieved for him?"

"No, I guess not; for Amos allers said that she was not a very lovin', affectionate woman; though, if he had been as rich as her, or if her family had let her alone, she would have made him a tol'able wife."

"Not loving! Not affectionate!" thought Matthew. "And I am about to marry her!" A cold shudder crept over him.

Hiding his emotions with an effort, he again interrogated the affable carpenter:

"And do you really think that Mr. Frump would have returned, and lived again with his wife, if he had become rich?"

"To be sure he would. He couldn't marry anybody else, yer know, without committin' bigamy. He allers said he didn't care much whether his wife loved him, so long as she treated him civilly."

"Mr. Frump had practical views of married life," suggested Matthew.

"Amos was sensible in some things," said the carpenter. "But he was a queer feller, too. He allers had a notion of comin' home kind o' disguised, so that his wife shouldn't know him. I used to tell him that a few more years in Californy would make him so thin, yaller, and grizzly, that he wouldn't need no disguise."

CHAPTER VI.

REVELATIONS OF A LAUGH.

THE carpenter here burst out with an extraordinary peal of laughter. It was so very peculiar, that, once heard, it would always be identified with the person making it. This singular laugh consisted of a brilliant stacatto passage on a high key, interrupted by occasional snorts, and terminating with a slur which covered the whole descending octave. It was also very loud and very long.

It had the effect of bringing Mrs. Frump to the door. She thrust out her head, unseen by either the carpenter or Matthew, and looked at the former with a wondering air.

"It was an odd idea," said Matthew, laughing slightly out of compliment to the carpenter, though he could not understand what there was to laugh at.

"And now," continued he, when the carpenter's cachinations had subsided, "I will explain to you my motive in asking all these questions. I am engaged to Mrs. Frump, and she is now——"

The carpenter immediately broke into another of his remarkable laughs, louder and longer than before.

"Well, sir," said Matthew, sarcastically, "when you get through, perhaps you will be good enough to tell me what you are laughing about?"

"The idee—ha! ha!—of your—ha! ha!—marrying Mrs. —ha! ha! ha!" and the remainder of the sentence was lost in that monstrous laugh.

Matthew, irritated by this most aggravating species of ridicule, took the carpenter's measure for a kick—but judiciously refrained from fitting him with one.

The second of the carpenter's laughs had made the widow (still stealthily looking out of the door) turn pale. The third had inspired her with a painful curiosity, which she had determined to gratify, at any risk. Before the last laugh, she had, therefore, crept up, unobserved, near where Matthew and the carpenter were standing, with their backs toward her. Coming around suddenly in front of them, she saw the carpenter's mouth wide open, still in the act of laughing, and observed that one of his front teeth was out. The widow screamed, and fell—into Matthew's arms, nearly flooring him.

"Hold on to her," said the carpenter. "She will come to in a minute."

"Who, sir—who on earth *are* you?" shouted Matthew, struggling under the burdensome widow and a sense of mental bewilderment.

"I am Amos Frump," he replied, in a voice which had suddenly risen five notes.

"The widow's husband! The dead come to life!" exclaimed Matthew, starting back, and nearly dropping the inanimate form.

Astounded as he was, he did not forget the marital rights of the man before him; and he said, with a trembling voice, politely, "I beg your pardon; but, as you are this lady's husband, perhaps you had better hold her."

"She appears to be doing very well where she is," replied the singularly calm Amos Frump. "A moment more, and she will be out of her fainting spell. I've seed her very often this way before."

Mr. Frump's prediction was verified; for his lips had scarcely closed on the words, when Mrs. Frump opened her eyes, and feebly said, "Is it a dream?"

"No, Gusty," replied the composed Amos; "it is a husband come back from Californy, with fifty thousand dollars."

"It is—it is my own husband's voice!" cried Mrs. Frump, throwing herself impulsively out of Matthew's arms upon the patched and faded coat of her restored consort.

"I thought you would know the voice," said Amos, "and that's the reason I changed it into a growl. This 'ere old Californy suit was a pooty good disguise, too. But my confounded laugh betrayed me. I didn't think to change that."

The third laugh had roused old Van Quintem from a nice nap, and he came out on the piazza.

"Hallo, Mr. Carpenter! what are you doing there?" said he, good-naturedly.

A few words from the supposed carpenter defined his position, and threw old Van Quintem into the appropriate state of amazement. Looking at the shaggy face by a variety of lights, he soon came to recognize it as that of his niece's husband, whom he had seen a few times on his yearly visits to the country, before his farming brother, Nicholas Van Quintem, father of Mrs. Frump, had died.

"From the way Gusty hangs to you, I judge you are no ghost," said old Van Quintem, when he had partly recovered his senses.

"No more than I am a carpenter," was the dry response.

"But how does it happen that you are no ghost?" asked old Van Quintem, with fearful interest.

This was what everybody wanted to know; and so Mr. Frump, supporting his wife by the waist, while she, apparently half stupefied, reposed her head on his shoulder, explained the mystery of his appearance. He had been severely injured in a drunken quarrel about a claim—he would not deny *that;* and, taking off his broad-brimmed hat, he showed the two deep scars extending from his eyebrows to the roots of his hair. He was left on the ground for dead, and his assailants ran away. The enterprising correspondent of three San Francisco papers saw him when he was first found, and, learning that he would undoubtedly die, the enterprising correspondent regarded him as already sufficiently dead for newspaper purposes, and sent three thrilling accounts of his butchery, written up with ingenious variations, to the three journals of which he was the indefatigable "special." In a few days, the nearly murdered man was out of danger. On learning that the news of his death had already been sent to the papers, the singular idea came into his mind to let the report go uncontradicted, change his name, give up drinking, move away to some place where he was not known, and begin his miner's life over again. The special correspondent, on being consulted by him, assured Mr. Frump that he could depend on his (the correspondent's) silence, since it was his invariable practice never to take back or qualify any statement made by him—such a course being obviously fatal to his hard-earned reputation for accuracy. The correspondent also very obligingly supplied him with copies of the papers containing the circumstantial accounts of his death, which he directed in a disguised hand, and sent through the mail to his wife. He had then assumed another name, gone into Benicia County, was successful in gold digging, and, after making about two thousand dollars, had taken up his residence in the nearest village (undesignated), and had invested his money in speculations (kind not particularized). Fortune followed him, but he found it convenient, for certain reasons (not given), to move away to another village, in a few months. In fact, he had, within four years, made the entire circuit of California, never staying in one place more than a quarter of a year.

"I don't want to brag," said Mr. Frump, "but it is well enough to have it understood that I made my pile."

Mr. Frump nodded his head quietly, as one who does not lie.

Old Van Quintem had hitherto hesitated to congratulate Mrs. Frump upon the reacquisition of her husband. He now advanced, and shook her warmly by the hand.

"I wish you joy," said he. "And you too, Mr. Frump. I never had the pleasure of meeting you often, though I had frequently heard of you. With regard to those unpleasant family difficulties in which you became involved, they are now at an end; for Gusty's parents are both dead, and the old house and farm are sold. Let bygones be bygones."

"So say I, Mr. Van Quintem," said Mr. Frump, grasping the extended hand. "As for my wife's relatives, I'm sure I allers forgave 'em. As for the old house and farm, if you like, Gusty, we'll buy it back agin."

Mrs. Frump, still resting on her husband's shoulder, sobbed a little, and clung closer about him.

"Here is one friend of the family," continued Amos, in his pleasantest manner, pointing to Matthew, "whom I don't know by name, though we've scraped an offhand 'quaintance."

"Mr. Frump—Matthew Maltboy, Esq.," said old Van Quintem.

Matthew, like Mrs. Frump, had fully appreciated the awkwardness of his situation, and had kept a rigid silence since the returned Californian resumed possession of his wife. The minute after Mr. Frump's identity had been established, Matthew could have hugged him with ecstasy. But, having lost the widow, his fickle mind straightway began to discover in her a great many excellencies that he had never seen before. Therefore, when he submitted his hand to the grip of Mr. Frump, his face expressed a strangely mingled joy and regret.

"I like you," said Mr. Frump, "and, as soon as wifey and I commence housekeepin' agin, I'll expect lots o' visits from you. Whenever I'm not at home, wifey 'll make everything comfortable. Won't you, dear?"

"If you wish it," replied Mrs. Frump, looking up into his face, which was not a repulsive one, "for your word shall always be my law."

"I must say," said Matthew, his face exhibiting unqualified admiration for Mr. Frump, "that you are the most generous man I ever met. And, if Mrs. Frump will promise to introduce me to some nice young woman, that she could recommend for a wife, perhaps I'll accept your invitation."

"I'll get you a wife in less than a week," said Mrs. F., who was rejoiced that the interview between her recovered husband and late suitor had ended peacefully.

"But one thing you haven't yet explained, Amos," said old Van Quintem. "How did you get into Crumley's employment?"

"Bless your innocent heart, I am not! I arrived this mornin', in the steamer ——, straight from Aspinwall, with this old scarecrow suit on, jest as you see me now. I was intendin' to take the railroad for Tioga County, and play off a leetle surprise on Gusty, and her relations up there. But, before goin', it 'curred to me to call on a Mr. Lambkin, who was raised in Tioga, and keeps a grocery store in the lower part of Washin'ton street. I found Mr. Lambkin in, and he told me as how, accordin' to last accounts, Gusty was stayin' with her uncle Van Quintem. I knowed your address, and come up here short metre. I was goin' to pretend that I was a man in search of work, and trust to luck to get a sight of Gusty. I found your front door open, and walked through the entry to the back parlor, where you fust see me standin'. Afore I could ask you for any work, you wanted to know if I hadn't been sent to mend your piazza railing. It was easy to say 'Yes,' and I said it."

"And very well you carried out the joke, Amos," said old Van Quintem. "You wouldn't make a bad actor."

"Rather better actor than carpenter, I guess," said Mr. Frump.

"Perhaps so," said old Van Quintem; "but a financier of your talent needn't act, or mend railings, for a living. I should like to know, now, how you made your money in California. Nine out of ten who go there, come back poorer than they went."

"'Tisn't best to ask too many questions of a returned Californian," answered Amos, in perfect good humor.

"Nor of anybody else, about business matters. You are right," added old Van Quintem.

"I say to wifey, and to all my friends, 'Let bygones be bygones. Take me as you find me, and I'll take you as I find you; and we'll ax no questions on either side.'"

"Dear Amos, you are the best of husbands!" said Mrs. Frump, looking fondly in his face. Mr. Frump improved as he was looked at.

"'Let bygones be bygones' is a very good rule," said old Van Quintem.

"Mr. Frump," said Matthew, unable longer to repress the compliment, "you have a wonderful amount of good sense!"

"I told you," was the laughing reply, "that 'Amos was sensible in some things.'"

BOOK THIRTEENTH.

THE STRANGE LADY.

CHAPTER I.

A STORY OF THE PAST.

ANOTHER year slipped away, and wrought many changes among the inhabitants of the block. Some of them had passed from stately mansions to those narrow houses which are appointed for all the living. Others had wedded, and moved to other blocks which were to be their future homes—till the 1st of the following May. Some of them had grown rich by quick speculations, and got into the choicest society by the simple manœuvre of taking a four-story brownstone front in the avenue which formed the eastern boundary of the block. Others had attained to poverty by the same process, and had migrated to cheaper lodgings in blocks remote, expecting that a lucky turn of Fortune's wheel would bring them back to fashionable life next year, as it most likely would. The principal personages of this history had been radically affected by this lapse of time—as will hereafter be shown—with the single exception of Marcus Wilkeson.

For one year, life had passed tranquilly, uneventfully. He had sought, and found, in his dear books, a panacea for that sickness of the heart which sometimes attacked him in his lonelier hours. At such times, he would repeat to himself these expressive lines of an old poet:

"This books can do; nor this alone; they give
New views of life, and teach us how to live;
The grieved they soothe, the stubborn they chastise;
Fools they admonish, and confirm the wise.
Their aid they yield to all; they never shun
The man of sorrow, or the wretch undone.
Unlike the hard, the selfish, and the proud,
They fly not sullen from the suppliant crowd,
Nor tell to various people various things,
But show to subjects what they show to kings."

The end of the quiet, sad (but not unpleasantly sad) twelve months found Marcus, on a bright morning in the month of August, sitting at his window, with a favorite book on his knees, looking—where he should not have looked so much—at that window in the old house where the only tragedy of his life had been wrought. As he gazed, like one fascinated by a spell, his features lengthened, and the habitually melancholy expression of his face became deepened and confirmed.

So wrapt was he in these unhappy self-communings, that he did not hear a vigorous "rat-tat-tat" on the door of the little back parlor. A repetition of the performance aroused him, and to his call, "Come in," Mash, the cook, presented herself.

"A woman at the door wishes to speak to you, sir, on important business, she says. Shall I show her in, sir?" Mash laid stress on the word "woman," in retaliation for the somewhat peremptory way in which the person in question had accosted her at the door. The "Buttery and the Boudoir—a Tale of Real Life," afforded her a precedent on this point.

"Show in the lady," said Marcus, wondering who she could be.

A tall, shapely person, dressed in deep black, and wearing a thick veil, was ushered into the room. She bowed slightly, and took a seat which Marcus offered her, near the window, and then looked significantly at Mash, who lingered in an uncertain way about the door.

"You may shut the door, Mash," said Marcus; and Mash did so with a little slam, intended to pierce the heart of the mysterious woman in black, for whom that domestic had, in one minute, conceived a mortal dislike.

The strange woman drew back her veil, and revealed a thin, pale face, which might have been handsome twenty years back. "Do you remember having seen me before?"

Marcus looked into the thin face with polite scrutiny. "Yes, madam," said he, at length. "I think I saw you on a railway train in New Jersey, over a year ago; and also in the town of ——, in that State, on the evening of a certain unfortunate exhibition. But you are changed, in some respects, since then."

"You would say that I am paler and thinner; and I am here to tell you why I am, and also to make all the atonement in my power for a crime that I have committed."

Marcus Wilkeson's first thought was of the unfathomed murder. His startled face expressed what was passing through his mind.

The strange woman read his thoughts. "The crime to which I refer is not the murder of Mr. Minford; of which, I may here say, I believed, from the first, that you were entirely innocent. Crimes—of that character, at least—have never been known in your family."

"All that you say, taken in connection with some curious circumstances which occurred on that railway ride, and that memorable night in New Jersey," said Marcus, "make me intensely anxious to hear what you have to tell. Please impart the information at once, and fully. I call Heaven to witness, that your name, your history, the secret which you are to reveal, shall pass with me to the grave, if you desire it."

"I accept your offer," said she, with emotion, "though my crime is so flagrant that no publicity, no punishment would be too great for it. Still, as full justice can be done, and reparation made, without this public disgrace, I prefer that my identity should be unknown except to you. I think that I have but few months to live." The woman expelled a hacking cough.

"My story must be short," said she, "and suited to my strength and this cough. You probably remember Lucy Anserhoff, who was a little playmate of yours in your native village? I see, by your nod, that you do. I am—she. You may well look surprised, for there is little in my haggard face and wasted form to recall that once innocent girl. You remember, I presume, my engagement to your brother Aurelius—excuse my faltering, sir, for, even at this distance of time, I cannot speak of your dead brother without emotion. It is not necessary to recall to your memory the details of your brother's conduct to me, and how he afterward married—another—and moved to this city. This early portion of my unfortunate career is well known to you, as it was to all the people of our little village."

Here the strange visitor paused, and coughed. The cough was dry and hollow.

She continued: "I think I may say that I was amiable and good enough, as a child. But your brother's desertion changed my whole nature. I dwelt upon one thought—revenge. I shudder as I confess it, but, for months, I meditated taking the life of the man who had wronged me. I came to this city twice, and lay in wait for him; but my heart faltered, and, thank God! I did not commit that crime. Soon, Heaven interposed—so it seemed to me at that wicked time—to help on my work of vengeance. Your brother's wife died, giving birth to a female child. I used to ride into the city twice a week regularly after this, and watch for him near his place of business, that I might gloat on his pale, unhappy face. I see the look of horror with which you receive this part of my confession; but you will bear in mind, sir, that I am here to tell the truth, concealing nothing. You remember, sir, the old lines about a woman scorned? I, sir, can bear witness to their awful truth."

Another fit of coughing here interrupted her. At length she resumed, in a feebler voice: "I must hasten while I can talk at all. One day, while I was watching near your brother's house for his appearance, the door opened, and a servant appeared, with a child in her arms—his child. The servant walked down the street, and I followed her, unobserved, until she came to Washington Parade Ground. She entered the park, and took a seat near the fountain. I sat down on a bench near her. It was not long before I made the girl's acquaintance, and had the child in my arms, caressing it with well-counterfeited kindness. Suddenly, the girl recollected that she had left the street door of the house unlocked, and was afraid that the house, having not a soul in it, would be robbed during her absence. She was so much troubled about it, that she asked me to hold the child—then about a year old—until she could go and lock up the house, and return. A horrible suggestion came into my mind, and I took the child in my arms. The servant was no sooner out of my sight, than I rose, and, clasping the child tightly, walked rapidly in the opposite direction. When I had got out of the park, among the side streets near North River, I ran until I was tired, turning at every corner, to avoid pursuit. My plan was clear from the moment that the child was left in my charge. It was, to give her into the keeping of some stranger, and so rob the widowed father of his only child. It was a scheme worthy of the lost and wretched woman that I then was."

A fit of coughing here set in, interrupting the narrative for several minutes. Marcus offered his strange guest a glass of water. She sipped it, until her cough was checked.

"I wished to make a full and minute statement, sir; but this cough again warns me to be very brief. In a word, then, I had not gone far, before I saw a German woman—a neat, elderly person—sitting on the stoop of her house. An impulse moved me to leave the child with her. I accosted her, but she answered me in German, saying that she could not speak English. Hardly knowing what I did, I mounted the steps, and placed the child in her arms, first kissing it. Then I tossed my pocket book, containing about twenty dollars, into her lap, and, without another word or act, ran off again. As I drew near the next corner, I turned, and saw the German woman still sitting on the stoop, looking at the child, and then at the money, and then at my flying form, in perfect amazement.

"Well, I returned to my country home in safety. Next day, I saw in the New York papers a reward of five hundred dollars for the recovery of the child, and the same amount for the arrest of the woman who stole it. My person was described, according to the recollection of the servant, but so imperfectly that I could not be identified. In two weeks I visited the city again, found the house where I had left the child—for I had remembered, even in my haste, the street and the number. The poor little thing was well, and had learned to love its new mother, who, in turn, seemed to love it as well as her own two children. I kissed the child, left more money with the German woman, and fled again to my home. These visits I repeated from week to week for six months, without detection. The German woman supposed that I was the mother of the child, but knew there was a secret, and did not seek to disturb it. At the end of the six months, your—your—brother died." (There was here a slight quaver in her voice, almost instantly passing away.) "Soon after this, my mother died, and the last of our family estate was spent on her burial." (Another tremor in the voice, but brief. The woman seemed to have perfect control of her feelings.)

"Fortunately, I was qualified to earn my living as a seamstress. I went to the city, advertised for such a place, and obtained it. I visited the child secretly, sometimes, and left money for its support and clothing. But the idea of detection and exposure troubled me greatly. One day, I read an advertisement from a married couple who had no children, offering to adopt a girl under two years of age. I answered the advertisement, and thus became acquainted with——"

"I anticipate the disclosure," said Marcus. "Mr. Minford! And the poor, dear child is my niece. Heaven be praised, she is found at last!"

CHAPTER II.

POSSIBLE LOVE.

"You have guessed rightly. Miss Minford is your niece. The proofs will be found in this packet. They are articles of clothing, taken from the child as fast as new ones were supplied, to prevent its identification, bearing the initials of Helen Wilkeson. I preserved them, with the vague idea of benefiting her by them, some day. I have seen the child by stealth a few times since I gave her to Mr. and Mrs. Minford, but never called at their house. It was agreed between us that I should never make myself known as the child's mother, and that they should never seek to learn my name and history. I acted as seamstress in several families in this city, until, about five years ago, I obtained an engagement in a family in New Jersey, living in the very town where that unlucky panorama was exhibited. It happened, as you know, that you and I rode in the same car from New York, where I had been on a shopping excursion. I recognized and was profoundly impressed with your resemblance to your brother. Learning that you were connected with the panorama, I attended the exhibition, that I might observe you more closely. There you were arrested on the charge of murdering Mr. Minford—of which, I again say, I always believed that you were totally innocent. You may remember that a woman fainted away. I was she. The sudden recollection of those two names—Wilkeson and Minford—in such a connection, was too much even for my nerves. I read the trial with fearful interest, and rejoiced in your release from the accusation. Providence at last seemed to point out the way to make all the reparation for my crime. I should have done it immediately after your acquittal, had I not seen by the papers that a wealthy lady—Mrs. Crull—had given your niece a home in her family. I postponed this act of justice from one week to another, until my failing health warned me that it could not be put off with safety longer. I thank Heaven that I have had strength and resolution to do it at last."

"This act of atonement, madam," said Marcus, "entitles you to my respect and sympathy. If you ever need a friend, I trust you will do me the favor of calling on me."

"I thank you," she replied; "but I have means enough to support me for the remainder of my days, which are numbered. The family in which I live, little knowing my true history, are very kind to me."

The protracted conversation had not been closed too soon. A violent cough seized upon the poor woman's frame, and shook it like a leaf. When it had ceased, Marcus observed that her lips were streaked with blood.

He begged to send for a doctor, but she would not have one, and rose to take her leave.

Marcus insisted, however, upon ordering a carriage for her conveyance to the New Jersey Railroad Depot, and she at length consented to receive that kindness from him.

To the driver he whispered words of caution, and instructed him to take the lady to a physician, in case she was ill on the journey; and, if so, to report, immediately thereafter, to him. He then shook her hand frankly, and begged her again to remember that he should always be her friend,

She smiled sadly, as she replied: "Again and again I thank you, sir; but it is useless to accept your kind offers, for we are meeting for the last time."

The carriage was driven slowly away.

The poor woman's words were true; and Marcus never saw her more.

CHAPTER III.

UNCLE AND NIECE.

Marcus Wilkeson had seen Pet but twice since the inquest—once in Mrs. Crull's carriage, and once afoot, on the opposite side of the street. He was delicately conscious that she regarded him with distrust or aversion; and, raising his hat politely to her, bowed, and passed on. He had expressly enjoined upon Tiffles and Overtop, in the communications which they had with her relative to the "Cosmopolitan Window Fastener," not to mention his name. He shrank from appearing to force himself on her notice.

The discovery of her real parentage had modified Marcus's sensitiveness somewhat. He was now no longer in the ridiculous position of a middle-aged, hopeless lover, but was an uncle, with a charming niece whom he could honorably love like a father. His first impulse, after the departure of the mysterious woman, was to hurry around to Mrs. Crull's house, unpack his bundle of proofs, and embrace the dear child with avuncular affection.

Upon him, glowing with this impulse, came the calm, deep Overtop, to whom Marcus told the strange story. Overtop listened with lawyer-like composure, and, when Marcus had finished, asked for the bundle. "The story is likely enough," said he, "but a lawyer wants to know all the proofs."

So saying, he removed from the parcel the string which bound it, and which, with the wrapping cloth, had become yellow with age, and brought to view a baby's long frock, and a cap made of the finest materials, and heavily fringed with lace, and a pair of tarnished golden morocco shoes of fairy dimensions. Upon an edge of the dress were daintily wrought, in needle work, the initials, H. W. A separate package contained extracts from three daily papers, giving accounts of the "Mysterious Disappearance of a Child," and an advertisement, signed Aurelius Wilkeson, offering five hundred dollars for the recovery of his daughter Helen, and describing the circumstances of the abduction so far as they were known, and the articles of dress which the infant wore at the time.

"So far, so good," said Overtop; "but it now remains to identify the original owner of these baby clothes with Miss Minford. We must find some old friends or acquaintances of the late inventor, who can testify that he adopted a child during the year 18—."

Marcus, whose memory was tenacious of names, recollected that Mr. Minford, in his few confidential moments, had told him of several persons whom he had known in more prosperous days.

With these memoranda to guide him, Overtop went resolutely to work, and, in two days, found four old friends of Mr. and Mrs. Minford, who remembered the very year when they adopted an infant child. It was the same year that the daughter of Aurelius Wilkeson had disappeared. Overtop, being a Notary Public, took the affidavits of these persons as he went along.

Here Overtop would have stopped, and left Marcus to break the important news of his new-found relationship to the young lady. But Marcus, who had a perfect horror of scenes, begged his friend to do this troublesome piece of diplomacy for him, but promised, when it was done, to appear at Mrs. Crull's in his new character of uncle.

Overtop performed the difficult task with success. He found Pet not altogether unprepared for the discovery. She recalled to mind several conversations and significant glances between Mr. and Mrs. Minford (the latter died in Pet's twelfth year), in which there was an evident allusion to the mystery of her birth. She remembered how often persons had expressed surprise that she did not resemble her supposed father or mother in the least. She remembered that, on those occasions, Mrs. Minford had been much disconcerted; and Mr. Minford, remarking that it was a freak of nature, he presumed, had always seemed desirous of changing the subject

She remembered that this strange want of resemblance to either of her reputed parents had often been a puzzle to her before Mrs. Minford's death.

With regard to Lucy Anserhoff, and the causes which prompted her to the abduction of the child, Overtop said nothing; because, among other reasons, Marcus, true to his solemn pledge, had told him nothing. He explained that the crime had been committed by a person who had formerly been a servant in her father's family; and that she had made full confession to her uncle, only on condition that her name should never be mentioned to any human being.

Mrs. Crull, who to a practical mind united a love of the romantic and marvellous, accepted Overtop's proofs even more readily than Pet. She said she had observed, at the inquest, a wonderful resemblance between Mr. Wilkeson and her darling, especially in the nose and eyes. Overtop, being appealed to to mark the likeness, took an oracular three-quarters view of the young lady, and said that the word "niece" was written on her face.

"He's your uncle, my dear," said Mrs. Crull. "There a'n't no doubt o' that. But don't forget that I'm your mother, now."

Pet kissed Mrs. Crull, and placed her little hand confidingly in the large, ineradicably red hand of her protectress.

"Now that Marcus Wilkeson stands in the relation of uncle to you," said Overtop, "there is no harm in telling you something." He then broke to her the secret of her uncle's important aid in the affair of the "Cosmopolitan Window Fastener"—the sole credit of which had always been attributed by Pet and Mrs. Crull to Wesley Tiffles and Overtop, agreeably to the wish of Marcus.

"What a fool I've been," said Mrs. Crull, "to feel the least doubt about this excellent man! It was very weak of me, I s'pose, Mr. Overtop; but I don't mind tellin' you, that, after what had 'curred, I thought that Mr. Wilkeson's 'quaintance with Pet had better be stopped. I take all the 'sponsibility of it. We must make it up, by thinkin' all the more of him now."

At the suggestion of Overtop, a servant, with Mrs. Crull's carriage, was now sent for Marcus, and soon returned with him.

When he entered the room, Pet rose, and walked toward him, half hesitating. Her face was very pale, and her lips quivered. "My dear uncle!" she said, and turned her sweet face up to be kissed.

Marcus, to whom the probable character of his reception had been a distressing subject of conjecture, was delighted at this frank, affectionate greeting, and stooped and imprinted an uncle's kiss on the young girl's brow. It was a pleasant way out of an embarrassment.

The conflicting emotions of the hour were too much for Pet; and she tottered to Mrs. Crull's arms, and wept for a few moments.

"You are her uncle, Mr. Wilkeson," said Mrs. Crull, extending her red right hand, while, with her left, she smoothed Pet's thick brown hair, "but I am her mother." Mrs. Crull seized upon this early opportunity to give notice that her rights as adopted parent were not to be abridged.

"And happy she is in having such a mother, my dear Mrs. Crull," said Marcus.

A quick ring, as of a familiar visitor, was heard at the door. The servant ushered in Bog. He was much changed since his last presentation to the reader. Six months of worldly polish, of private tutoring, and of a strong desire to appear well in the eyes of one he loved, had turned the clumsy boy into the quiet but stylish young gentleman. He had given up the bill-posting business, not because he was sick of it, or ashamed of it, but because old Van Quintem loved his adopted son so well, that he could not spare him from his side. Bog passed the greater portion of every day with him, rambling through the streets, or riding to the suburbs in the old family carriage, or reading the dear old books to him. Bog read well now, and had learned to love those repositories of wit and wisdom with almost as keen a relish as the venerable white-headed listener. This was another bond of affection between the old gentleman and himself.

At Bog's entrance, Pet looked up, and showed the sparkling tears in her eyes. A deep shade of anxiety passed over the young man's face, and he looked around for an explanation.

The prompt Overtop was ready to give it; and, in a few moments, Bog was enlightened with the great discovery.

"And Pet has been crying a little because she is so happy—that's all," added Mrs. Crull. "Sit down here, Bog."

Mrs. Crull made room for him on the other end of the sofa where she was sitting—her left hand still smoothing the soft brown hair of her adopted child.

Bog took the seat, and smiled across the good lady's broad figure to Pet, who smiled back at him again.

This expressive exchange of glances was not lost on Marcus. He instantly saw, what he had not divined before, that the devotion, the self-sacrifice, the constant, unswerving love of the boy, had at last sounded its echo in the bosom of the maiden. As he swiftly contrasted the manly, athletic figure of the young man, with the delicate beauty of his niece, he thought how well they were adapted to each other; and wondered that he could ever have been so blind and conceited as to suppose that a nervous old bachelor like himself could win the heart of that fresh and youthful image of loveliness. And how thankful he then was that he had never, by a single word, hinted at the mad love which he once felt for her.

He had no cause to blush now!

BOOK FOURTEENTH.

HAPPY DAYS.

CHAPTER I.

OWNERS OF THE BEAUTIFUL.

THE world and all its inhabitants had rolled round to another fragrant spring. The buds were bursting in city parks and gardens, and birds twittered in the dusty air. Every happy heart said to itself, "This green, and these opening roses, this music of the birds, this shining day, this temperate breeze, are all mine, and made for me."

There were two young persons, one sweet morning in May, who experienced a delightful sense of that universal proprietorship of the Beautiful. They were a couple who appeared to be expressly made for each other; for the young man was tall and broad chested, the young woman short, and delicately formed; his eyes were black, hers blue; he was calm, resolute, deliberate in every movement, she quick and impulsive. There never was a clearer case of mutual fitness by virtue of entire dissimilarity.

Any one could see that they loved each other, and that, if they were not married, they were engaged—for her little hand was entwined most trustingly about his muscular arm, and she leaned toward him with that gentle inclination which seems to be a magnetism of the heart.

"Are you happy, my own Pet?" asked the young man, looking proudly down at the beautiful face beside him.

"Happy! dear Bog—for I *will* always call you Bog. You know I am!" Her blue eyes filled with tears.

If excess of happiness had not choked her voice, she would have asked Bog if he thought she could be other than perfectly happy in the love of her adopted mother, in the love of her dear uncle—who was at once a father and brother in his tender solicitudes—in the love of that darling old gentleman, Myndert Van Quintem, and in one other love, which it was not necessary to mention.

But Bog knew that she was supremely happy, and he needed no such elaborate answer. He also knew that he possessed the first, fresh, and only love that she had ever cherished. All the events in connection with her Greenpoint adventure, both before and after it, proved that she had never loved young Van Quintem, and that her sentiments toward him were only those of gratitude for his supposed saving of her life, and an innocent, childlike confidence in his good intentions.

The lovers sauntered down the street slowly, as if they would protract the walk. Not another word was said. Passing a garden full of roses, Bog reached through the fence, and plucked a full-blown white one, and handed it to Pet. She eagerly took it, and pinned it to the bosom of her dress.

"Here we are, dearest; and I am almost ashamed to show myself to uncle, for I am such a stranger," said Bog, breaking the silence, as they stood at the foot of the memorable bell tower. "Hallo, Uncle Ith!" he shouted, looking upward.

The old gentleman thrust his white head out of an open window at the top, and said, "All right. Come up."

The door at the foot of the tower was open, and the young couple proceeded to comply with the invitation. Bog led the way, and gently dragged Pet from step to step, with much laughter on his part, and many charming little feminine screams on her part, until the trap door was reached. Uncle Ith had combed his hair with his five fingers, retied his old black cravat, and put on his coat, to receive them. He smiled through the trap door, as they came in sight, and said, "Be very careful of the young lady, Bog. Mind, now, how the young lady steps."

Bog jumped through the trap door into the cupola. Then he lowered a hand to Pet, and Uncle Ith lent her the same assistance, and the two raised the precious burden to a place of safety. Uncle Ith, after he had been introduced to Pet, proudly, by his nephew, looked at her for a moment in silent admiration. He had never seen her before, but he knew her well from Bog's descriptions (hurriedly communicated by Bog when they had met in the street), and said to himself that the boy had done no more than justice to her rare beauty.

Then Uncle Ith looked at his nephew. "Ah, Bog," said he, shaking his head at him, "what changes Time does make! It seems only a few days ago that you was a little scrub of a chap, runnin' 'round town and pickin' up your livin'. And a very good and honest livin' you picked up, too. Now, here you are, a nicely dressed, tall, handsome young man, with a snug little fortun' all of your own earnin', not to mention your bein' the adopted son of that splendid old gentleman, Myndert Van Quintem. And, last and best, you are goin' to be married to this dear young lady to-morrer."

Pet blushed; and Bog said, "That is why we are here to-day, dear uncle. We must have you at the wedding."

Uncle Ith faltered. "Me at Mr. Van Quintem's! I should feel like a fish out o' water." He said nothing about the antiquated blue coat with brass buttons, the short, black trousers, and the figured satin vest, hanging up in a closet at home; but he thought of them, and what a stiff figure he would cut in them.

"But you must come, Uncle Ith!" said Pet, with her sweetest smile. "I ask it as a particular favor."

"You are my only living relative, you know, uncle," added Bog.

"We should not be happy, if you were away," said Pet, placing her hand confidingly on the old man's shoulder. Young persons always took to the good old man in this spontaneous way.

The entreaties of the couple, and the continual iteration of that name by which he loved to be called—"Uncle Ith"—finally overcame his objections. He reconciled himself to the prospect of the blue coat, short trousers, and gaudy vest, and solemnly promised to attend the wedding.

This important matter having been settled, Uncle Ith pointed out to Pet all the interesting objects to be seen from the tower, and adjusted the spyglass for her, and gave her near views of Governor's Island, the Palisades, and other remote objects. He also explained to her the process of striking the bell by means of the long iron lever, and told her that, if she would wait there long enough, she could hear how the big chap sounded ten feet away. Pet put her hands to her ears, in anticipation of the stunning noise, and laughingly said that she didn't think she would wait long.

CHAPTER II.

THE LAST OF A MYSTERY.

After Pet had looked at all the objects of interest visible from the bell tower—Uncle Ith pointing them out with the pride of an owner—Bog called Pet aside, and said, "Now, Uncle Ith, I have something to show her that I used to think most interesting of all."

Pet rested her hand upon his arm, and gazed through the southeastern window, in the direction indicated by Bog's forefinger.

"Right there," said he, "midway between those two tall chimneys, and a trifle south of the line of that steeple—the last two windows in the upper story of that old house—do you see them?"

Pet looked along his outstretched arm, to get the precise direction, and then said, hurriedly, "It is my old home."

The sight of those familiar windows, in which the calico curtains still hung, recalled the horrid vision of that dreadful night. Pet turned pale, and shuddered. "Let us look elsewhere, Bog," said she.

"I beg your pardon, dearest; but I wanted to tell you how many hours I had spent in this cupola, day and night, gazing at those two windows, and feeling, oh, so happy! if I could but catch a glimpse of you or your shadow. But I never told Uncle Ith about it."

Uncle Ith had not overheard this conversation, but he had followed with his eyes the direction pointed out by Bog. As the young couple stepped back from the window, he said:

"I see some strange sights occasionally, my children" (he was fond of calling young people his children), "I can tell you. There are a couple of windows, in the upper story of that old brick house, between the two big chimneys, that used to interest me some."

"We see them," said Bog and Pet.

"About five years back, I began to notice lights burnin' in that room, long after all other lights, except the street lamps, was put out. Of course, this attracted my attention, and I used to feel a queer kind of pleasure in looking into the room with my spyglass, and wonderin' what was goin' on there. The curtains were usually drawn over the lower sashes; but, this tower bein' fifty or sixty feet higher than the house, I could look over the top of the curtains, and see somethin'. An old man, tall and slim, and a young girl, 'peared to be the only folks that lived there. Are you sick, young lady?" said he, observing that Pet looked pale.

"Oh, no; I am not sick—only a little fatigued."

"What a brute I was, not to offer you a chair! Now do sit down, young lady."

Pet did so, and Uncle Ith resumed:

"The old gentleman was a machinist, I s'pose, for I used

to see his shadow on the wall, goin' through the motions of filin', sawin', and hammerin', though I could never guess what he was workin' on. I have known him sometimes to be at this queer business till daylight. For three years the strange old gentleman never missed a night at his work. I fear you are not quite well, young lady. Take a glass of water."

Pet sipped from the proffered glass, and declared that she was much better now.

"One night, about two years ago, I took a look into this room with my spyglass. I generally didn't do it until three or four o'clock in the mornin', when all the other lights in the neighborhood was out. But, on that partickler night, about eleven o'clock, I happened to observe that one of the window curtains which covered the lower sash was left partly undrawn. This had never occurred before, and so I brought my glass to bear on the room at once. A tall gentleman, whose face I had often seen movin' in the room over the top o' the curtain, was just in the act of takin' his departure, which he did without shakin' hands. The old man then went to his place at the other window, and tackled to his work again. He had been at it about twenty minutes, when a bar, or rod, which stuck up above the curtain, and was somehow connected with his work, fell forward with a quick motion, as if it was jerked away. The old man stooped, picked it up, and fixed it in its place again. His face, as well as I could see through my glass in the night time, at that distance, showed a wonderful amount of surprise and astonishment—at the fall of this rod or bar, I s'pose. He then seemed to be filin' on somethin', and afterward stooped down, as if to put it into some part of the machine, or whatever it was. Jest at that minute the Post Office struck, and I put down my glass, and turned my head toward the sound, to catch the district. It struck seven. I jumped to the lever, and started the old bell for seven, too. As I was strikin' the first round, my eyes happened to rest on the strange window again. The old man was not standin' there. The bar, or rod, had fallen out of its place again, I s'posed, and I expected every minute to see the old man appear at the window, and fix it again. But he didn't show himself any more that night—and (which is the curious part of my story) I've never seen him since. Whether he dropped dead from heart disease, I can't guess; but certain I am that he is dead, for——"

Poor Pet here exhibited such signs of faintness, that Bog, who had been leaning against the edge of the window, gazing at the well-known window with a strange fascination, sprang to her side, and instantly bathed her brow with water from Uncle Ith's old pitcher, near at hand. This restored her. "Be calm, dearest," said Bog.

"What—what is the matter with the young lady?" asked Uncle Ith, in great trepidation. "Shall I run for a doctor?"

"No, Uncle Ith; no doctor. But we won't talk any more about this strange room at present. It affects Miss Wilkeson's nerves."

"The shock is past, dear Bog," said she, "and I can bear to hear everything."

"But you must promise to control yoursell, darling," said Bog, tenderly.

"One question, Uncle Ith," said he. "How long a time were your eyes off the room, after the first stroke for the Seventh District?"

"Not more than three seconds."

"And you are sure that there was nobody in the room?"

"Certain; for I must have seen him enter, or go out."

"Then, Uncle Ith, you have cleared up a great mystery."

"What! What mystery?"

"The death of Mr. Minford, the inventor, my old friend, and the protector and guardian of Miss Wilkeson. He lived in that very room! He was at work on a perpetual-motion machine! It was operated, somehow, by weights! It started suddenly, when you saw that rod, or lever, fall to the floor! Mr. Minford put the rod in its place, and made some little improvement in the works! The machine started again at a moment when your eyes were turned away! The rod fell with greater violence, struck the inventor on the head, and killed him! That is the whole story; and stupid we have all been not to have guessed it before."

Nature furnished her own sweet relief to Pet's pent-up emotions. She burst into tears. "Thank Heaven," said she, "it is all plain now!"

Pet had not whispered it to Mrs. Crull, or Bog, or her uncle, or to any other living soul, but the mystery of that awful night had hung over her young mind like a pall, which in vain she had tried to lift.

"What a blockhead I am," cried Uncle Ith, "not to take the papers! If I had only taken the papers, now, I should ha' read all about that affair, and might ha' guessed that the man who was s'posed to be murdered was the man I had seen workin' in that room for three years. Then I should ha' offered myself as a witness, and might ha' thrown some light on the business. I'll 'scribe for a paper to-day, instead of trustin' to hearsay for the news."

"And a very neglectful fellow was I," said Bog, "not to have called here and seen you, after that sad affair. But the truth was, that Pet went to live with her best of friends, Mrs. Crull, and I had no longer a desire to look at the room from your bell tower. In fact," Bog added, with a smile, "the tower has not been quite as interesting for two years past as it used to be. If I had come up here at any time since Mr. Minford's death, I should probably have told you of the supposed murder, and pointed out those windows to you. But——"

"But you forgot all about your old uncle. Ha! I understand. Well, I forgive you, seein' what there was to 'sturb your recollections." Uncle Ith looked affectionately at Pet, who smiled and blushed through her tears.

The old man continued: "I 'member once when we met in the street, about two years ago——"

"I used to come around this way, you must know, Uncle Ith, in order to meet you, two or three times a week."

"I give you credit for that, Bog. You never disowned your poor old uncle. But, as I was sayin', I 'member one time when we met, that you told me somethin' about the murder of somebody of your 'quaintance. But I didn't take no partickler interest in it, because I didn't know any of the parties concerned. And, of course, I didn't dream that poor Mr. Minford was the man I had seen workin' away there for three years. But the main fault is mine, because I don't take the papers. I see, now, that every man ought to take the papers—if only as a duty to his feller man." Uncle Ith coughed, as one who utters a maxim of great moral depth.

It was then agreed, at Bog's suggestion, that Uncle Ith, accompanied by him, should call at Overtop's office, at early business hours (when Uncle Ith was off duty), next day, and consult upon the best course to be adopted to make his testimony public, and set the mystery of Mr. Minford's death forever at rest.

This having been done, Bog and Pet withdrew, and had hardly reached the foot of the tower, when the musical thunder of the great bell announced the constantly reiterated story of a fire in the Seventh—that most combustible of all the city districts.

CHAPTER III.

LOVE CROWNED.

LATE on a fair afternoon of May, wedding guests began to assemble at old Van Quintem's house. The old gentleman had been out of society many years; and he improved this happy occasion to bring together his few surviving relatives, and friends of his former business days.

Heavy antique carriages rolled up to the door, with retired merchants and their wives. The retired merchants were of a pattern not altogether extinct in New York, who, at the ages of sixty years and upward, had cleared their skirts of business, and settled down to a calm retrospect of the past, and serene anticipations of the future. They were evidently destined for a good old age, and had fat pocket books to help them through. The proper place to look for this class of retired merchants is on the tax books, and not in public assemblies, or among the Directing Boards of benevolent institutions. They are good, charitable souls; but, having got out of business, they desire to keep out of it literally, leaving to a younger generation the task of managing men and affairs.

A more stylish vehicle deposited at the door a bachelor Bank President, who was not only the old personal friend of the host, but his trusted adviser in business affairs. The parlor of the ——— Bank was one of the few places that old Van Quintem still visited in the bustling haunts of the city; and to old Van Quintem's house the bachelor Bank President made monthly pilgrimages of friendship. He was a handsome man of fifty, with long white hair, which matched beautifully with his yet ruddy cheeks, and a figure portly and full of strength. Nobody but himself knew why so eligible a man remained a bachelor.

In a humpbacked chaise drawn by an exemplary horse, there rode a fat and pleasant old gentleman, who was uncomfortably swathed about the neck with a white cravat. He crawled from his narrow coop with the nimbleness of one who is on professional business. He was followed by his wife, a little woman, who was the mother of ten children from two to twenty years of age—just two years apart, and all strongly resembling their father. This fat, pleasant old gentleman was the old-fashioned minister of the old-fashioned church to which Mr. Van Quintem had belonged for forty years. The little woman was his second wife; and there was a first crop of children, who had been safely launched on the world for many years, and were doing extremely well.

The sole surviving relatives of old Van Quintem were three elderly ladies, who, by some contagious fatality, remained unmarried. After pining romantically over their doom for some time, they had settled down to the conviction that they were much happier single than wedded, and that they had escaped a great many dangers and disappointments—which was unquestionably true. It was really pleasant for them to reflect that the snug property which their father left them had not been squandered upon designing husbands, but had been kept, improved, and added to, until it was one of the prettiest estates on Staten Island. These ladies were first cousins of old Van Quintem, and had an odd habit of staying at home. They came to New York always on important business, which could not be transacted by any one else, four times a year; and, on those occasions, paid state visits to old Van Quintem, who reciprocated the civility by calling on them, in a ceremonial way, twice every summer.

Uncle Ith came on foot; and wore his old blue coat with brass buttons, his flowered vest, and shining trousers so awkwardly, that people who did not know him stared at him as at a strange spectacle. People—and they were many—who did know him, stared at him with a still greater surprise, wondering what extraordinary event in his history was about to occur. Uncle Ith felt the additional embarrassment of fame, or notoriety; for an affidavit, prepared by Overtop, giving the full particulars of his observations from the bell tower, had been published in all the city papers that morning. Before noon, Uncle Ith had been waited on by six newspaper reporters, to whom he had furnished particulars of his early life; and had promised to sit for his photograph, for the use of an illustrated weekly, on the following day. For all these reasons, added to his natural modesty, he pulled the door bell with a feeling of profound regret, which was followed by a strange desire to run around the corner. Before this desire could have been gratified, the door was opened by a servant, and Uncle Ith was ushered in.

The anticipated awkwardness of an introduction to old Van Quintem, was prevented by the approach of that gentleman before his name was announced.

"Welcome! welcome!" said he, shaking him by the hand

with Dutch fervor. "I know you from Bog's description, you see. Your statement in the morning papers has lifted a load from several hearts, I can tell you. Bog will be delighted to see you. He was beginning to be afraid you would not come. Hallo, Bog!" said the good old gentleman, shouting up the stairs; "here is Uncle Ith."

The bridegroom bounded down the stairs with boyish impetuosity, looking so fine that Uncle Ith hardly knew him. It was difficult to realize that the ungainly, ignorant boy of a few years back, had become this nice-looking, graceful young gentleman. Thus readily does the rough diamond of a good heart and brain, under the guiding hands of Ambition and Love, take its polish from contact with the world and with society!

"Dear Uncle Ith!" said the bridegroom.

"Happy to see you, Uncle Ith!" exclaimed Fayette Overtop, who, with Marcus Wilkeson and Matthew Maltboy, had been drawn from the second floor at the mention of his name.

Marcus had not before seen Uncle Ith, though he had been thinking of him all day. The publication of the old man's affidavit was an entire surprise to Marcus—Overtop and Maltboy having said nothing to him about it. Other people read the document with interest, because it solved a mystery. But to Marcus it wore the profounder, vastly greater importance of clearing the last shadow of foul suspicion from his name. It may be unnecessary to say, that it also gave rise to learned and interesting, but profitless discussions, in several of the papers, upon the possibilities of perpetual motion—which lasted until the explosion of a steam boiler under the pavement turned every editor to the consideration of steam boilers, their nature and habits, the rights of owners and of the public, and the necessity of stringent legislation for the better management of those subterranean powers of good and evil.

Upon being introduced to Uncle Ith, Marcus gave the old man's hand a warm pressure, but said nothing. But Uncle Ith saw in his eyes an expression of the deepest gratitude, and he knew what it meant; for he had read the report of the inquest at Overtop's office, and there learned, for the first time, the unhappy connection of Marcus Wilkeson with the Minford affair.

Maltboy, who, being one of the appointed groomsmen of the day, was in extraordinary spirits, was profuse in his congratulations to Uncle Ith, and insisted, rather unnecessarily, upon introducing him to the retired merchants and the bachelor Bank President. They had all read his affidavit, and regarded him with undisguised interest.

For a man who has always been a lamb in his shyness and self-depreciation, to find himself suddenly transformed into a lion, is a cause of no little embarrassment. Uncle Ith was so much flustered by all these tokens of popularity, that he could not utter an articulate word, but only mumble, and wipe his heated brow. He wished that the usages of society would permit him to take off his coat, as he did in the bell tower, and be comfortable.

A few more guests arrived, mostly of the ancient order, and a little too much of one sort to please a lover of variety. The advent of Mr. Frump, with all his impulsive occidental peculiarities of character fresh upon him, was a decided relief to the decorous company already assembled in the parlors. In less than ten minutes, he was on terms of offhand friendship with everybody, and was telling strange stories of Western adventure to a group of eager listeners.

Old Van Quintem received all his guests with that simple cordiality which leaves no doubt of a sincere welcome. The common remark was, "How well you are looking, Mr. Van Quintem!" And it was very true. Few men at seventy could show a figure so straight, cheeks so smooth, and an eye so bright. The unavailing sorrow which tenanted his heart two years before, had gradually disappeared. From the hour that his son fled abashed from his presence, he had not seen or heard of him, and had at last come to regard him as dead —though the old gentleman could not have given a good reason for that singular belief, except that his son had been a constant cause of sorrow and trouble to him when alive. He preferred to think of the lost son not as the ripened villain, but as the innocent child prattling upon its mother's knee. This mental picture filled a select chamber of the old man's memory. But the affection and reverential duty of a son had been supplied by the boy Bog; and, in the virtuous character and filial love of that young man, he saw what the innocent child might have grown to, had all his prayers and tears been answered.

When old Van Quintem's wishes were consulted with regard to the wedding, he had but one favor to ask; and that was, that the ceremony might take place at his house. It was a whimsical idea, he said, but he would like to see his old home gay once more, as it used to be years ago. "Besides," said he, "I am rheumatic, and might not be able to attend the wedding, if held elsewhere."

Mrs. Crull, when she first heard, from the lips of the blushing Pet, that Bog had proposed and been accepted, immediately outlined the plan of a wedding at her house, which should be something unprecedented in point of magnificence. The plan took shape as she thought of it, and she had already settled upon the number of invitations, and the other principal arrangements, when old Van Quintem's wish was mentioned to her. The sacrifice was a great one; and Mrs. Crull would make it only on condition that she should superintend the preparations with the same freedom as at her own house. Old Van Quintem consented to this, only stipulating that he should pay all the bills; and, for over a week before the wedding, Mrs. Crull, assisted by that most buxom and busy of women, Mrs. Frump, had taken tyrannical possession of the dwelling, and made such extraordinary transpositions of the carpets and pictures, and other movable property, that old Van Quintem, on surveying the work of renovation, hardly recognized the house as his own. The only apartment that was not inwardly transformed by these female magicians was the library. To that he clung, conscious that both his services and his advice were of no value.

The house was soon filled with guests—or rather appeared to be filled, for the whole number invited and present was only forty. But forty people, moving about uneasily, and expecting something, look like a hundred or more. Among them were many whose only claim to an invitation was their friendship for the host, or Mrs. Crull, or the bride, and not any mental, moral, or physical excellence which entitles them to mention in this history.

There were two rooms on the second floor, upon which the interest of loungers, male and female, was concentrated.

In one waited the bridegroom, his groomsmen Overtop and Maltboy, Marcus Wilkeson and Wesley Tiffles. They were a happy party, and not at all frightened at the approaching nuptials. Bog—for such his friends always did, should, and will call him—could not have been happier—far from it! —if he had held a sceptre in each hand. Overtop was happy in the contemplation of his marriage with that most sensible of girls, Miss Pillbody, which was set down for the week following. The affair would have come off six months before, but for Miss Pillbody's illness, happening soon after her mother's death. In consequence of this illness, her select school had been given up—never to be revived. Poor Overtop did not know how much he loved her, until he saw how near he came to losing her. She had completely recovered, was ruddy and pretty with new health, and was Pet's first bridesmaid. Overtop thought pleasantly of her, and combed back his intractable cowlick. Matthew Maltboy was happy because he had taken a serious fancy to Miss Trapper, the second bridesmaid, a charming but peculiar girl, and the particular juvenile friend of Mrs. Frump. Matthew had met this young lady two or three times, and had suffered sweetly from her black eyes. Marcus Wilkeson was happy in his contented bachelorhood, in the happiness of his niece and of all around him, and in the clearing up of the "Minford enigma." Wesley Tiffles was happy because happiness was his constitutional disposition, under all circumstances and in all weathers. The arrival of Uncle Ith was the only event that had drawn this good-natured party from their retreat; and those who watched for their reappearance were disappointed.

In the other room, the bride had been dressing for several hours, and was still hard at it, under the immediate supervision of the indefatigable Mrs. Crull, Mrs. Frump, and the two bridesmaids. Only the favored few were admitted to this retreat of mysteries. But they were kindly communicative. They brought back minute reports of the appearance and condition of the bride elect, in the various stages of her enrobement and ornamentation; and there was not a woman in the house who did not, every ten minutes, have the image of Helen Wilkeson stamped on her mind as accurately as the changeful phases of an eclipse on the photographer's plate.

At the soft, calm, mystic, love-making, marrying twilight hour, the bridal party took their stand near the southern end of the great double parlor. The forty guests were grouped before them, an audience without seats.

Pet was pale, and leaned for support on Bog's arm. He stood firm, erect, unblenching, with that instinct of physical strength which one feels when the woman that he loves hangs confidingly on his arm. Fayette Overtop, with his well-known dislike for conventionalism, was thinking how tedious all that formality was, and how much more sensible to be married by an alderman or justice of the peace, privately, in two minutes. Miss Pillbody did not agree with her future husband on this point, and was thinking, at that very moment, what a solemn thing marriage was, and with what ceremonious deliberation it ought to be entered upon. Matthew Maltboy had had great experience as a groomsman, and he speculated with perfect composure on this important question: Whether the gentle tremor of Miss Trapper's hand was caused altogether by the fluttering novelty of her situation, or partly by the love-enkindling contact of their interlocked elbows?

As the six took their chosen positions, and gazed at a particular pattern in the carpet, selected by them at a private rehearsal in the morning, they were the subject of mental comment by the forty guests. The women, looking at the costly dress of the bride, pronounced her beautiful. The men, never noticing her dress, but observing her pale face and heavy eyes, were not vividly impressed with her loveliness. Bog was admired by all, and envied by none to whom his history was known. The old ladies took a mild maternal interest in him, because he was an orphan; and the young ladies thought extremely well of him, because he was a strong, gallant, handsome fellow. Overtop was regarded with curiosity, as the reputed hero of the Slapman scandal. Matthew Maltboy was universally condemned as too fat, and, with that brief criticism, was dismissed. Miss Pillbody was pronounced "a little proud," because she stood straight, with shoulders thrown back, which was her usual attitude. Miss Trapper was admitted to be a very modest and diffident creature, because she had a slight stoop in the back, which was chronic.

Old Van Quintem stood near the wedding party, and recalled, with fond minuteness, the hour when one, about the same age as Pet, and resembling her in the freshness of her youthful beauty, had crowned him with happiness. Mrs. Crull was close by, and looked at the bride, whom she had dressed, with the pride of an artist. Mrs. Frump stood next to her, and shared in the same sentiments. Marcus Wilkeson's appointed place was somewhere in the neighborhood of the bride; but he shrank away to the side of Uncle Ith, who also obstinately clung to the other end of the room.

The venerable clergyman stepped into the centre of the small open space which had been left in front of the bridal party, and uttered a cough, at which signal the buzz of conversation ceased.

The ceremony was very brief and simple—according to

the ritual of the Dutch Church—and people were married by it before they knew it. The minister had received, in advance, a fee of unprecedented size, which was, at that moment, lying at the bottom of his wife's pocket, and which that good woman had already spent, in imagination, on a new bonnet for herself, a new hat for the minister, dresses for the girls, books for the boys, and playthings for the baby. If the dimensions of the fee had any effect whatever on the mind of the excellent minister, that effect was to hurry up the ceremony, and make the two one with the least possible delay.

At last the magical, binding words were spoken; and the husband, stooping proudly to the not-averted face of his blushing wife, gave her the first kiss. And at the same instant a little band of musicians, with chosen instruments, secretly stationed in the library, of which the door was now thrown open, struck up Mendelssohn's divine Wedding March. As its jubilant notes floated through the house, the round of congratulations commenced.

Blest Pet! What had she ever done—she thought, so far as giddy happiness would allow her to think—to merit all these kisses (of which her two shy uncles bestowed two), these benedictions, these tears, and, above all, the possession of this noble heart by her side, henceforth to be all her own? The exultant peals of the Wedding March—that highest expression of triumphal love—but faintly interpreted her joy.

The bridegroom received his full share of the universal good wishes. Everybody was pleased with his behavior; and the bachelor Bank President, and other members of the old school of gentlemen, pronounced him a glorious young fellow, a refreshing contrast to the puny, cadaverous youth of the day, and altogether worthy to have flourished thirty years ago. The bridesmaids and groomsmen were not neglected either; and both Miss Pillbody and Miss Trapper thought that the next best thing to getting married, was to assist others in the operation.

As for old Van Quintem, after kissing the bride, and calling Bog his son, and giving both of them his blessing, he had retired from the room to hide the tears of happiness which not even seventy years of this hardening world could keep from his eyes.

For the second time in five minutes, Amos Frump approached Matthew Maltboy, and shook hands with him. "Fat and jolly as ever," said he.

From the first adjective Matthew recoiled; though he tried to justify the propriety of the second by a laugh.

"And I like you—hang me if I don't!" said Mr. Frump, with Californian bluntness, "*because* you're fat and jolly. But here's wifey, and I know she wants to say somethin' to you."

"So I do," said Mrs. Frump. "My head was so full of business to-day, that I had quite forgotten it. But you must step aside with me," she added, looking significantly at Miss Trapper.

Matthew stepped aside; and she placed her lips to his ear, and whispered, "What do you think of Miss Trapper?"

"A very pretty girl," said Matthew.

"So she is; and one of the best-hearted creatures that ever lived. A little singular in one respect, perhaps."

"What is that?"

"Oh! she speaks out her mind—that's all. But then you always know where to find her."

"She has not spoken any of it to me, at all events," said Matthew. "I can't get her to talk."

"That's because she's modest. Cultivate her, and you'll find her a splendid girl. Between you and me, I have recommended you to her, and, depend upon it, she will meet you halfway."

"All right," whispered Matthew, gratefully.

Here the full voice of old Van Quintem announced dinner, for which the elderly ladies had been demurely waiting for some time. Two by two the bridal party and the guests marched to the banquet, spread in the long, broad dining room, which was one of the best features of this sturdy, old-fashioned house.

What the bill of fare was; what tunes the band played in the library; what kind things were said to the bride and bridegroom; what compliments were breathed into young female ears, and not rebuked; what vows of love were exchanged; what courteous remarks of the old school were made by the bachelor Bank President; what ancient jokes were passed off by the wits of the party as new; what abominable conundrums were then and there honestly invented; what overwhelming confusion Uncle Ith experienced, when he found himself seated next to a lady who talked loud at him, and how he wished himself at home, one hundred feet from the ground; what complete happiness was felt and expressed by everybody, but especially by old Van Quintem and Marcus Wilkeson; what improbable stories were told by Mr. Frump; what philosophical sayings uttered on the spur of the moment by Fayette Overtop; what slightly impertinent but always amiable remarks advanced by Wesley Tiffles;—all this might be imagined, with a slight mental effort; but not so Matthew Maltboy's new misfortune.

Profiting by Mrs. Frump's friendly suggestion, Matthew had exhausted all his resources of conversation in an effort to interest Miss Trapper. She had listened, and had returned faultlessly proper replies, and had conducted herself so much like all the other young women that Matthew had ever met, that he was puzzled to guess in what respect her singularity consisted. He longed to see a piece of that mind, which, according to Mrs. Frump, she was in the habit of exhibiting to people. He was soon gratified.

Miss Trapper had remarked, that, in a few days, she was going to visit her friends in Chemung County, and would probably remain there three months. It struck Matthew as the right time to make a point.

"Then I shall not see you, Miss Trapper, during all that time!" he said, with a sigh.

Miss Trapper levelled a sharp glance at him, and said, "I suppose not."

The remark was tartly made; but Matthew had noticed that she habitually spoke quick and short.

"Our acquaintance has thus far been very pleasant, Miss Trapper; at least on my side," whispered Matthew. "Must it stop here?"

To which Miss Trapper replied, "I don't know."

Though the observation was not encouraging, it was, on the other hand, not entirely forbidding.

"Since we are to be separated for three months, Miss Trapper, might I solicit the great privilege of corresponding with you occasionally?"

Miss Trapper's thin lips expelled two words, like shot out of a gun: "What for?"

"What for?" echoed the amazed Matthew. "Why—for the pleasure of exchanging our ideas, you know."

"That would be a bore," said Miss Trapper.

"I didn't understand you," said Matthew, distrusting his ears.

"I said it would be a bore—a bore!" returned Miss Trapper, with painful distinctness. "I hate letter writing."

"Oh! ah! Do you?" said Matthew, feebly. "Perhaps you would like some pickled cauliflower, Miss Trapper?"

"Thank you."

Matthew handed the pickled cauliflower to her, and held his tongue, satisfied with what he had seen of Miss Trapper's singularity, and not at all anxious to receive a larger piece of her mind.

"I am doomed to be a bachelor," thought Matthew, with a suppressed groan. But Hope, which attends upon fat and lean men alike, whispered in his mind's ear, "Why not marry a woman as fat as yourself?"

"A capital idea!" thought Matthew; "and if there's no other way to find one, I'll advertise for her."

Dinner was protracted to a length that seemed tedious to

all but the representatives of the old school. When it did come to an end, the party adjourned to the parlors, where a reasonable time was devoted to conversation and flirtation. At length the musicians, having taken their wedding dinner in their apartment, and drank full bumpers (which, somehow, never interfere with the accuracy of musical performances) to the health of the happy pair, struck up a quadrille, which was at once interpreted by the younger people as a signal for dancing. Two sets were instantly formed, and rattled through with. The Lancers followed, and was liked so much that the musicians were called upon to repeat it three times. The sets had now increased to four, filling the two parlors, and crowding the elderly people to the wall or the hallway. Then, luckily, old Van Quintem bethought himself of the old-fashioned contra-dance, as a contrivance for bringing his contemporaries on their legs. By an extraordinary piece of good fortune, the musicians had learned it, and played it at a silver wedding the week previous.

As the familiar notes, not heard for years, saluted the ears of the bachelor Bank President, he showed the animation of an old war-horse at the sound of the trumpet. "Now is our time," said he.

Moved by common impulse, the members of a past generation rose, and took their places. Old Van Quintem, temporarily forgetting his rheumatism, led off, escorting Mrs. Crull. The bachelor Bank President took charge of a widow, in whose breast he had revived feelings that flourished twenty years before. The retired merchants brought each other's wives upon the floor. Even Uncle Ith came out from his seclusion in a corner, where he had been listening to the soound of his own fire bell, rung by other hands that night, and felt that here, at least, he should make no blunders. The tall, talkative lady, from whom there seemed to be no escape, had fastened on him as a partner. The good clergyman was the only old or middle-aged gentleman who did not take his place in the set, and he looked on and laughed.

The dance commenced, slow at first, then gradually faster The younger people, when they came to understand the simple movement, fell into the chain couple after couple, until it extended into the hallway, and through it into the parlors again. Everybody was drawn in now, old and young, married and unmarried, the minister and his wife only excepted, and they marked the measure with their heels. Round and round, and faster and faster, went the chain, with its constantly changing links. The musicians, playing the same strains over and over again, became frenzied by the repetition, and doubled the time without knowing it. Legs that had entered slow and stately upon the interminable maze, became, without the knowledge or consent of their owners, nimble and gymnastical.

It was a delightful peculiarity of this wonderful dance, that couples could withdraw without breaking up the figure. The bride and groom, acting upon this privilege, slipped out of the flying circle, and sought, unaccompanied, the solitude of the vine-covered piazza behind the house, there to commune for a moment upon their new-found happiness.

The night was calm. A faint breeze from the south stirred up secret odors in the hearts of dew-covered flowers, and musically sighed through the leaves and vines. The heavens were dark, but unclouded; and, as the lips of the lovers met in one clinging kiss, the host of stars beamed down upon them, and proclaimed an Eternity of Love.

CHAPTER IV.

FIVE YEARS.

Five years are an eventful space in the history of blocks, as of men. Within that period, they may be burnt down, blown down, or torn down to make room for grander blocks. In quick-growing American cities, the average life of blocks is less than that of the human generation that tenants them. First wood, then brick, then brownstone or marble—these are the successive forms of block life, before anything like stability is reached. Marble is the only real type of the permanent in American architecture. Nobody pulls down marble.

But five years had made little change in the exterior of our block. It was situated at a point in the city from which the ebb tide of Fashion was slowly receding, and which the flood tide of Trade had not yet touched. There was not a new house on the block, or an old one materially altered. A little paint, and a diligent application of broom and Croton water, had kept the block quite fresh and jaunty. On the south side there were some slight external modifications, in the shape of oblong black signs, fastened near basement doors, and bearing names of doctors. Ten of these signs had been added to the south side within five years. There were only two houses upon that side, now, to which you could come amiss in pursuit of medical advice.

One of these was old Van Quintem's. Five years had passed over the old house and the old man lightly (both had been made to last, and were well taken care of), and gave to them only a mellower and riper look. The old man's long white hair had not commenced falling out; and his cheeks still bloomed with a ruddiness that does not belong to second childhood. He could still read his dear old books—and carefully chosen new ones—without spectacles; though he often preferred to hear them read in a soft, sweet tone, by a dear girl whom he always called Pet, and who would sit for hours at the old man's feet, giving to the noble thoughts of poet, novelist, or philosopher, the added charm of a sympathetic voice. At such times, a fine fellow, who was still known as Bog, would look on and listen, with rapt attention, and the happiest smile on his face. Sometimes these tranquil scenes would be pleasantly broken in upon, and the meaning of the author profitably obscured, by the entrance of a certain little Helen, whom the old man would kiss, and call "Grandpop's sugarp'um," and "Sweety peety." Bog would then catch it up, and toss it aloft, all whirling with curls, laces, and blue ribbons, and would say, "Cud-je-wod-je now, cud-je-wod-je now, cud-je-wod-je now," at each tossing; and the child, with the marvellous instinct of eighteen months, would understand this mysterious dialect, and then would smile through large blue eyes that looked like its mother's.

To this house, Myndert Van Quintem, jr., had never returned; and no authentic intelligence of him had ever come. Fayette Overtop, Esq., while on a professional visit to St. Paul, Minnesota, to settle a large land claim, had heard of a notorious Van Benton, who had kept a gambling house there several years, and was finally killed by a spendthrift whom he had cleaned out of his last cent one night. The best description which he could get of this man, tallied precisely with that of Myndert Van Quintem, jr. But Overtop, with that discretion which was continually enlarging his circle of paying practice, said nothing of this to the old gentleman. Among the reports that Overtop had heard of this Van Benton, was one, that he had forged his father's signature to large amounts in New York city, and had fled to the West, and there changed his name to avoid the arrest and punishment which his father had promised him. Had the old gentleman been informed of this circumstance, he would at once have identified Van Benton as his son; for it was known to him alone, that young Myndert had repeatedly forged his name (evidences of which had been found in the desk where Marcus Wilkeson had often seen the young man busily writing—evidences which the forger had accidentally omitted to burn), and that he had been induced to leave the city through fear that his father would give him up to justice at last. On the memorable night in the milliner's shop in Greenpoint, the young profligate had seen that his father was terribly in earnest, and had quailed in the presence of that outraged and indignant soul.

The second house not ornamented by a doctor's sign, on the south side of the block, was the old tenement building of which

Mr. Minford had occupied the upper story, five years before. The tenants had all been changed two or three times; but the "Minford tragedy" was still a current legend among them. Murders, or strange homicides, are fixtures of houses where they occur. Nothing obliterates their memory but tearing down the houses, and building anew—which is the course of treatment that the proprietor was proposing to himself, in consequence of the steady depreciation of rents. Pet never passed that house, or dared to look at it even from a distance.

Bachelors' Hall, on the north side of the block, was still occupied by the three original tenants; and they liked it so well, that they had bought it, and owned it on the Tontine plan—viz., that, upon the death of one of the owners, his share shall go to the survivors.

Five years had improved Marcus Wilkeson's relish for a good book, an after-dinner pipe, and a chat with a friend. It was plain to all his friends—even to those who were happiest in their wedded lives—that Marcus was a great deal better off single than married. His was the genial monkish nature, which thrives best in celibacy.

Every afternoon Marcus visited his white-haired neighbor opposite, and never forgot to take along a toy, or some candy, for his grandniece Helen. He brought these offerings in lieu of baby talk, which he could never master. This fact pointed him out, beyond all question, as a predestined old bachelor.

The general supervision of the house was intrusted to Mrs. Overtop; and most sensibly did she manage it. Knowing that a bar of cast iron is more easily bent than the set habits of men of twenty-five and upward, she attempted no changes in the domestic regulations of the establishment. The three friends found that they had not only all of their old freedom, but a charming female voice to accompany them in their songs, and on the piano or guitar, and a capital fourth hand at whist, and a beautiful reader, and an ever-cheerful companion. "If I could find such a wife, now!" Marcus and Maltboy would say. "But you can't," Overtop would answer. "There's not another like her in this world." There was a little Fayette Overtop, jr., two years old, a great pet of the bachelors, and the far-off husband of little Helen, on the other side of the block.

Matthew Maltboy weighed two hundred and twenty pounds. As associate counsel of Overtop, he made an imposing show in court, which was not fully borne out by his legal attainments. He was always talking of matrimonial intentions—a sure sign that a man never will be married. His last rebuff from Miss Trapper (now the wife of a wealthy tanner and currier) had taught him to keep his flirtations within narrower limits; but he openly professed, and probably believed, that, when he really wanted to marry—without joking, you know—he could take his pick from the wide and varied ranges of female society. He smoked incessantly like a martyr, to reduce his flesh, but no adipose matter ever vanished in that cloud of sacrifice!

Mash, the cook, bestowed her honest hand and maiden heart upon Patching, the artist, who had first seen her at the station house, and there contracted an artistic admiration of her face and figure. She would have preferred a pirate; but Patching's enormous hat gave him a freebooterish appearance, which went far to reconcile her to him. She was really a pretty woman—much handsomer than some of the shadowy beauties Patching was wont to put on canvas—and she made him a good and faithful wife—and cooked better dinners for him, at a small expense, than he had ever eaten before—and sent him out into the world clean and tidy every morning. Patching affected to be ashamed of his wife, and snubbed her sometimes in the presence of other people. But everybody who knew the couple, saw that he had the best of the bargain. Mrs. Patching still took her favorite weekly, and cried over the stories as copiously as ever.

Mrs. Crull continued to be the dearest and best friend of Pet and Mrs. Overtop; and little Helen and little Fayette would never know the great debt of gratitude that they owed to that excellent lady. Whenever she called on Mrs.

Overtop, she always began to be extremely circumspect in her pronunciation and grammar, from force of habit; but soon relapsed into those old errors which, happily, were of the head, and not of the heart. Mrs. Crull made no mistakes in her affections. She was in mourning for Mr. Crull, and truly vowed that she would never marry again.

Mrs. Slapman had ceased to live on the block. Mr. Slapman had basely defeated the beneficent decree of the law, by turning his property into ready cash, and sailing for Europe. This deprived Mrs. S. of her alimony the second year after their separation, and compelled her to give up housekeeping, and the pursuit of TRUTH, in New York. She is now living among a small colony of Jigbees, in an obscure village of Connecticut, the pride of her family, the envy of the neighbors, and the idol of two local poets and of the professor of a High School in an adjoining town, who has learned her history, and is now patiently waiting for Slapman to die before offering her his hand in marriage.

Uncle Ith rang the great bell in the high tower for a number of years, with perfect satisfaction to himself and to the firemen. He took a paper, and he read it, and he found its political arguments so powerful, and so interesting, that he adopted them as his own—as many another man of greater pretensions has done—and he got into the bad habit of talking politics in a small way. It happened, not long after, that there was an election for mayor; and a mayor was chosen who held to a variety of politics quite the opposite of that which was so ably inculcated in Uncle Ith's favorite journal. About a month later, Uncle Ith turned to the political column of his paper, and there read that he had been turned out of office, and that one Schimmerfliming—a German politician of the ———th Ward, who had been of great service in compassing the election of the new mayor—had been appointed in his place. The fact was, that Uncle Ith was highly acceptable to all parties as a no-party man. But, when he turned politician, he made himself amenable to the harsh laws of political warfare, and became (as his paper phrased it) "the hoary-headed victim of the unprincipled tyrant who, with the cunning of the serpent and the vindictive ferocity of the hyena, weaves his spider's web of mischief in his dark corner of the City Hall." Uncle Ith retired to private life with a snug property, patiently saved up and thoughtfully invested. But, as Adam went on eating apples, notwithstanding the disaster which had come to him from that species of fruit, so Uncle Ith took his newspaper, and paid for it punctually, and devoured it daily to the last.

While Uncle Ith fell by politics, Coroner Bullfast rose by it. A judicious distribution of money and liquors, a notoriety for street fights, a singular talent for profanity, and an unstinted adulation of the basest classes of the community, won for him, in succession, some of the best prizes of the Municipal lottery. He has his small, sunken eyes now fixed on one of the highest offices of the State; and it will take a strong combination to defeat a candidate backed by such powerful agencies and interests.

Mr. and Mrs. Frump lived happily on their country property. Mr. Frump tried experiments in blackberry raising, which proved a success, and was, at last accounts, concentrating his talents on the development of a new strawberry seedling. Whenever he went to town, he made a point of carrying back Matthew Maltboy, for whom his regard was inexplicably strong; and nothing gave him greater pleasure than to see his wife, gracefully mounted on the spirited filly, and Matthew, heavily astride of the sober gray, starting off for a morning's ride, while he stayed at home to push on the seedling.

When Wesley Tiffles had spent ten thousand dollars in elegant leisure, he arrived at the noble determination to "salt down," as he called it, the remaining ten thousand dollars, in ten different savings banks. He distributed it thus, in order that the failure of one of the banks might not ruin him. The interest of this money, drawn half-yearly, furnished him with a basis for operations of a character requiring genius, pens, ink, and paper, rather than ready cash. Whenever Tiffles's resources ran short, as they did occasionally, he always borrowed, and paid on the next interest day. In this policy he was inflexible; and he flattered himself on the sternness of his self-denial.

Among the schemes which failed to receive the cordial approbation of capitalists, were the following: "A process for extracting green paint from green leaves;" ditto for "making nutritious food from the direct combination of earth, air, and water;" a plan (submitted to the unappreciating Government of Naples) to "extinguish the volcano of Vesuvius, by pumping water from the Bay into the crater, in consideration of the sum of one million florins, and a monopoly of working the extinct volcano for lava."

Wesley Tiffles, profiting, at a late day, by the lesson of the "Cosmopolitan Window Fastener," finally invented and patented a striking improvement in an apple-paring machine, and, at last accounts, was clenching a good bargain for the sale of his invention.

THE END.

Any of the above sent free by mail on receipt of price.

NEW PUBLICATIONS

OF

D. APPLETON & CO.,

443 and 445 Broadway, New York.

Evidence as to Man's Place in Nature.

By THOMAS H. HUXLEY, F. R. S., F. L. S. 1 Vol. 12mo. Cloth. Illustrated, $1.25.

CONTENTS:

I. On the Natural History of Man-like Apes.
II. On the Relation of Man to the Lower Animals.
III. On some Fossil Remains of Man.

Money.

By CHAS. MORAN. 1 Vol. 12mo. Cloth, $1.25.

"The constantly increasing division of labor daily increases the exchange of commodities and services, in which money plays so important a part. The subject of money is, therefore, supposed by the writer to be of sufficient general interest to warrant the publication of the present work. If it shall aid in dissipating any of the numerous errors and prejudices so long connected with money, and thus increase the power of this instrument to further the well-being and progress of humanity, the object of the writer will be attained and his labors amply compensated."

The Gentle Skeptic;

Or, Essays and Conversations of a Country Justice on the Authenticity and Truthfulness of the Old Testament Records. Edited by the Rev. C. WALWORTH. 1 Vol. 12mo. Cloth, $1.25.

"This is one of those books that require not only reading but *studying*, and yet it can be read with interest even by those who never study. It is a book rich in scholarly research, masterly in argument, admirable in methodical arrangement." —*The Tablet.*

The American Annual Encyclopædia,

And Register of Important Events of the year 1862. Embracing Political, Civil, Military, and Social Affairs; Public Documents; Biography, Statistics, Commerce, Finance, Literature, Science, Agriculture, and Mechanical Industry. 1 Vol. 8vo. Cloth, $3.50; Library Leather, $4.00; Half Mor., $4.50; Half Russia, $5.00.

The favorable reception given to the volume for the preceding year, has induced us to make special efforts in the preparation of this one. Its contents embrace the material and intellectual progress of the year, particularly in this country; the important civil and political measures of the Federal and State Governments; an accurate and minute history of the struggles of the great armies and their battles, illustrated with maps and plans of actions taken from official copies; the debates of the Federal and Confederate Congresses; financial measures of the Government, commerce, &c., &c.; the proceedings in the Confederate States to maintain the war and establish their government; also, the progress of foreign nation; the developments in the physical sciences; the progress of literature; mechanical inventions and improvements, embracing the results of the British Industrial Exhibition; the principles involved, and the developments in plating ships with iron; descriptions of the most useful patents; the present statistics of the religious denominations; and biographical sketches of the eminent persons deceased in 1862, &c.

The United States Bank Law:

An Act to Provide a National Currency, secured by a pledge of United States Stocks, and to provide for the circulation and Redemption thereof. Paper covers, 25 cents.

The Pentateuch and Book of Joshua,

Critically examined. By the Right Rev. John Wm. Colenso, Bishop of Natal. 2 Vols., 12mo. $1.25 each.

"Bishop Colenso's books, in which the genuineness and authenticity of the earlier portions of the Old Testament are doubted, or, as he expresses it, his 'arguments to prove the non-Mosaic and unhistorical character of the Pentateuch,' have created intense interest in England."—*Chicago Post.*

Man's Cry, and God's Gracious Answer,

A Contribution Toward the Defence of the Faith. By Rev. B. Franklin. Cloth, crimped, 50 cents.

"A thoughtful discussion of theism—or man's need of a God, and what kind of a God; and of Christianity—or God's gracious answer to that need, and how it is an answer."—*Congregationalist.*

Prof. Huxley's Lectures "On the Origin of Species."

1 Vol. 12mo. $1.25.

1. The Present Condition of Organic Nature.—2. The Past Condition of Organic Nature.—3. The Method by which the Causes of the Present and Past Conditions of Organic Nature are to be discovered. The Origination of Living Beings.—4. The Perpetuation of Living Beings, Hereditary Transmission and Variation. —5. The Condition of Existence as affecting the Perpetuation of Living Beings.—6. A Critical Examination of the Position of Mr. Darwin's Work "On the Origin of Species," in relation to the complete Theory of the Causes of the Phenomena of Organic Nature.

"Readers who cannot accept Mr. Darwin's doctrines and conclusions will still be delighted with these lectures, since they embody so much curious information and so many important principles of biological science, expressed so clearly as to render the book, even to readers possessing scarcely any previous knowledge of the subject, not only intelligible but more interesting than any romance." —*Weldon's Register*

Lectures on the Symbolic Character of the Scriptures.

By Rev. ABIEL SILVER, Minister of the New Jerusalem Church. 1 Vol., 12mo. 286 pages. $1.25.

These lectures, delivered to a mixed congregation during the past winter, are now given to the public.

"The author assures the reader, who has not looked into the spiritual sense of the Holy Word, that if he has a desire to do so, and will study the science of correspondences, and read these simple illustrations of the sacred Scriptures, with a sincere desire to become acquainted with the Word of God that he may the better know his Heavenly Father, his own soul, and the true way of life, that he may walk in it, the Lord will open to his mind a new field of thought and lead him to a fountain of heavenly wisdom which he will prize as more valuable than all things else; for he will find therein the true life of Heaven."—*Extract from Preface.*

The New and Complete Tax-payer's Manual,

Containing the Direct and Excise Taxes; with the Recent Amendments of Congress, and the Decisions of the Commissioner. Also, complete Marginal References, and an analytical index, showing all the Items of Taxation, the Mode of Proceeding, and the Duties of the Officers, with an Explanatory Preface. 1 Vol. 8vo, 184 pages. Paper covers, 50 cents; cloth, 75 cents.

An indispensable book for every citizen.

The Crisis.

1 Vol., 8vo. Paper covers, 95 pages, 50 cents.

Madge;

Or, Night and Morning. By H. G. B. 1 Vol., 12mo. $1.25.

From the Congregationalist.

"It contains the story of a young girl 'bound out,' as the custom is in the New England villages. Her Northern mistress was a harsh, selfish and unfeeling woman, and the 'bound girl's' character is pleasantly and interestingly portrayed, as it becomes moulded and hewn out by the hard circumstances of her lot, till she becomes 'purified by suffering,' a perfect woman."

The New American Cyclopædia.

Edited by George Ripley and Charles A. Dana. Now complete, in 16 vols. 8vo, double columns, 750 pages each. Cloth, $3.50; Sheep, $4; Half Mor., $4.50; Half Russia, $5 per volume.

The leading claims to public consideration which the *New American Cyclopædia* possesses may be thus briefly stated:

"1. It surpasses all other similar works in the fulness and ability of the articles relating to the United States.

"2. No other work contains so many reliable biographies of the leading men of this and other nations. In this respect it is far superior even to the more bulky Encyclopædia Britannica.

"3. The best minds of this country have been employed in enriching its pages with the latest data, and the most recent discoveries in every branch of manufactures, mechanics, and general science.

"4. It is a library in itself, where every topic is treated, and where information can be gleaned which will enable a student, if he is so disposed, to consult other authorities, thus affording him an invaluable key to knowledge.

"5. It is neatly printed with readable type on good paper, and contains a most copious index.

"6. It is the only work which gives anything approaching correct descriptions of cities and towns of America, or embraces reliable statistics showing the wonderful growth of all sections."

Two Pictures;

Or, What We Think of Ourselves, and What the World Thinks of Us. By Maria J. McIntosh, author of "Two Lives," "Charms and Countercharms," etc. 1 vol., 12mo., 476 pages. $1.50.

"The previous works of Miss McIntosh have been popular in the best sense of the word. The simple beauty of her narratives, combining pure sentiment with high principle, and noble views of life and its duties, ought to win for them a hearing at every fireside in our land. The lapse of time since we have had any work of fiction from her pen, has only served to increase her power."

A Glimpse of the World.

By Miss Sewell, author of "Amy Herbert," etc. 1 vol., 12mo. Cloth, $1.25.

"Of the authoress's style and language it would be superfluous to speak. The simplicity of a refined nature, the ease of a skilled writer, and the correctness of an industrious one, are conspicuous in every page. There is no straining at effect, no distortion of English palmed off as originality, no distrust of native vigor evinced by a recourse to artificial."—*The Press.*

The History of Civilization in England.

By HENRY THOMAS BUCKLE.—2 vols. 8vo. Cloth, $6.

Whoever misses reading this book, will miss reading what is, in various respects, to the best of our judgment and experience, the most remarkable book of the day—one, indeed, that no thoughtful, inquiring mind would miss reading for a good deal. Let the reader be as adverse as he may to the writer's philosophy, let him be as devoted to the obstructive as Mr. Buckle is to the progress party, let him be as orthodox in church creed as the other is heterodox, as dogmatic as his author is skeptical—let him, in short, find his prejudices shocked at every turn of the argument, and all his prepossessions whistled down the wind—still there is so much in this extraordinary volume to stimulate reflection, and excite to inquiry, and provoke to earnest investigation, perhaps (to this or that reader) on a track hitherto untrodden, and across the virgin soil of untilled fields, fresh woods and pastures new—that we may fairly defy the most hostile spirit, the most mistrustful and least sympathetic, to read it through without being glad of having done so, or, having begun it, or even glanced at almost any one of its 854 pages, to pass it away unread.—*New Monthly (London) Magazine*

History of the Romans under the Empire.

By CHARLES MERIVALE, B.D., late Fellow of St. John's College. 7 Vols. small 8vo. Handsomely printed on tinted paper. Price, $2 per Vol. (Nearly ready.)

CONTENTS:

Vols. I and II.—Comprising the History to the Fall of Julius Cæsar.

Vol. III.—To the Establishment of the Monarchy by Augustus.

Vols. IV. and V.—From Augustus to Claudius, B.C. 27 to A.D. 54.

Vol. VI.—From the Reign of Nero, A. D. 54, to the Fall of Jerusalem, A.D. 70.

Vol. VII.—From the Destruction of Jerusalem, A.D. 70, to the Death of M. Aurelius.

This valuable work terminates at the point where the narrative of Gibbon commences.

. . . . "When we enter on a more searching criticism of the two writers, it must be admitted that Merivale has as firm a grasp of his subject as Gibbon, and that his work is characterized by a greater freedom from prejudice, and a sounder philosophy.

. . . . "This history must always stand as a splendid monument of his learning, his candor, and his vigorous grasp of intellect. Though he is in some respects inferior to Macaulay and Grote, he must still be classed with them as one of the second great triumvirate of English historians."—*North American Review, April*, 1863.

The Iron Manufacture of Great Britain,

Theoretically and Practically considered. Including descriptive details of the Ores, Fuels, and Fluxes employed, the Preliminary Operation of Calcination, the Blast, Refining, and Puddling Furnaces, Engines and Machinery, and the various Processes in Union, &c. By W. TRURAN, C. E. Second Edition. Revised from the Manuscript of the late Mr. TRURAN. By J. ARTHUR PHILLIPS, author of "A Manual of Metallurgy; Records of Mining," etc., and WM. H. DORMAN, C. E. 1 vol., 8vo. Illustrated with 84 Plates. Price, $10.

What to Eat and How to Cook It,

Containing over One Thousand Receipts, Systematically and Practically Arranged, to enable the Housekeeper to prepare the most Difficult or Simple dishes in the best manner. By PIERRE BLOT, late Editor of the Almanach Gastronomique, of Paris, and other Gastronomical Works. 1 vol., 12mo. Cloth. $1.

"A desideratum long looked for, has been that of a Cook-Book, which, while possessing the excellencies of French cooking, will yet combine the simpler and cheaper dishes of a moderate household. The author has had opportunities of observation rarely equalled, and being a resident of the United States is familiar with the necessities of American homes."

Album for Postage and other Stamps;

American and Foreign. 1 vol., small 4to. Cloth, $. French Morocco, $. Morocco, extra, $.

"The collecting of Postage Stamps has become a matter of such general interest, that it is believed the publication of an Album, affording facilities for their arrangement and preservation, in a convenient and elegant form, will be warmly welcomed by the community. It has been sought in the volume here offered to the public, to combine instruction with amusement, and to render the collection valuable in itself, doubly valuable as the nucleus of a large amount of important geographical and statistical information."—*Extract from Preface.*

Critical History of Free Thought,

In Reference to the Christian Religion. Eight Bampton Lectures, preached before the University of Oxford, in the year 1862. By ADAM STOREY FARRAR, M. A. 1 vol., 12mo. Cloth, $2.

"The Hand-Book of German Theology, contained in this volume, should therefore be read by every clergyman, both for its own merits, and for the immense importance of the subject. There is not a more memorable chapter in modern mental history than that which records the vast, continuous, and co-operative effort of the German Schools to understand and appreciate Christianity."

A Supplement to Ure's Dictionary,

OF ARTS, MANUFACTURES, AND MINES

Containing a clear exposition of their Principles and Practice. From the last edition, edited by ROBERT HUNT, F. R. S., F. S. S., assisted by numerous contributors, eminent in Science and familiar with Manufactures. Illustrated with 700 Engravings in wood. 1 vol., 8vo. Cloth, $5. Sheep, $6.

The Complete Work, with Supplement. 3 vols., 8vo. Cloth, $12. Sheep, $15.

"This volume of URE'S DICTIONARY of Arts, Manufactures and Mines, contains the additional knowledge which has accumulated within the past ten years. Not a year has passed but that some important improvements in the Arts and Sciences have taken place, all of which form an important increase to knowledge, which cannot well be dispensed with by those who are engaged in the various pursuits in which they are employed.

Principles of Political Economy,

With some of their Applications to Social Philosophy. By JOHN STUART MILL. 2 vols., 8vo. $ (Nearly ready.)

"His varied knowledge, and his truly Catholic spirit peculiarly fitted him for the task; and the great characteristic excellency of his work is the combination, in every instance, of a simple, yet severely accurate exposition of the abstract doctrine (the pure political economy), with an inquiry into the modifications to which the doctrine is subject, when applied to any given and really existing condition of things. The absence of any such modifying explanation, in many celebrated treatises on political economy, has, in no small degree, contributed to create doubt and distrust respecting the science itself."—*Frazer's Magazine.*

The Natural Laws of Husbandry,

By JUSTUS VON LIEBIG. Edited by John Blyth, M.D., Professor of Queen's College, Cork. 1 vol., 12mo. 387 pages. $1.50.

"In the following work Baron Liebig has given to the public his mature views on agriculture, after sixteen years of experiment and reflection. The fundamental basis of the work is still the so-called mineral theory, which holds that the food of plants is of inorganic nature, and that every one of the elements of food must be present in a soil for the proper growth of a plant. The discovery of the remarkable power of absorption possessed by arable soil, has necessarily led to a modification of the views regarding the mode in which plants take up their food from the soil. As the food of plants cannot exist for any length of time in solution in soils, it is clear that there cannot be a circulation of such solution towards the roots, but the latter must go in search of food: hence the great importance of studying the ramifications, of the roots of plants, and the mode of growth of the different classes of plants cultivated by man."—*Extract from Preface.*

MADGE:

OR,

NIGHT AND MORNING.

BY

H. B. G.

1 Vol. 12mo, Cloth. Price $1.25.

OPINIONS OF THE PRESS.

From the Providence Press.

"An admirable book of its class, and an execellent class it is. The tale does not startle the reader by a succession of almost impossible events, but it is deeply interesting, and exquisitely told. The incidents are graphically described, the style is pure, and the whole effect purifying."

From the Boston Journal.

"This is an interesting domestic tale, abounding in the variety of real life rather than the startling contrasts of fiction. The incidents of the tale are graphic and picturesque, but truthful to life, and a high moral tone pervades the book."

Dr. Holland, of the Springfield Republican, says:

"The perusal of Madge has given me great pleasure. It is one of the purest books I ever read, interesting from beginning to end. I notice in it particularly, and with peculiar pleasure, the Christian element; it is full of it, and hallowed by it."

From the Manchester Mirror.

"With a well-constructed plot, it is yet a story whose interest does not depend upon an exciting denouement, but the charming simplicity of the style, the ease and naturalness with which the characters are sketched, will hold the reader's attention to the end."

From the Star in the West.

"We have been greatly pleased with this story of New England life. The plot is well conceived and natural. The impression left upon the reader is agreeable and healthful."

From the New York Times.

"A story of tender interest, pervaded by a fine moral sentiment, and taking a strong hold of the sympathy of the reader."

Chicago Christian Times.

"It is a beautiful story, touchingly and pleasantly told, coming out, as it should, all right. Unless we are much mistaken, 'H. B. G.' will be heard from again, and to advantage."

From the New York Chronicle.

"Abounding in noble sentiments, sufficiently dramatic to awaken deep interest, delving deep into the mysteries and sufferings of social life, and above all, inspiring a holy trust in a superintending Providence, this book cannot fail of a large and beneficent mission."

WORKS OF FICTION.

Miss Sewell's Works.

The Earl's Daughter. 12mo.................... ....Cloth, $1 00
Amy Herbert. A Tale. 12mo..................... Cloth, 1 00
Gertrude. A Tale. 12mo........................ Cloth, 1 00
Laneton Parsonage. A Tale. 3 vols. 12mo.......... Cloth, 3 00
Margaret Percival. 2 vols......................... Cloth, 2 00
Experience of Life. 12mo.......................... Cloth, 1 00
Walter Lorimer, and Other Tales. 12mo. Illus.......... Cloth, 1 00
Katharine Ashton. 2 vols. 12mo.................. Cloth, 2 00
Journal Kept for the Children of a Village School.... Cloth, 1 25
Ivors. A Story of English Country Life. 2 vols.... Cloth, 2 00
Ursula. A Tale of Country Life. 2 vols. 12mo.... Cloth, 2 00
Cleve Hall. A Tale. 12mo...................... ..Cloth, 1 50

Emile Souvestre's Works.

The Attic Philosopher in Paris. 12mo.................... 63
Leaves from a Family Journal. 12mo...................... 1 00

Alice B. Haven's Works.

Loss and Gain; or, Margaret's Home...... .... 1 00
The Coopers; or, Getting Under Way 1 00

Miss Yonge's Works.

Heir of Redclyffe. 2 vols. 12mo.................... Cloth, 2 00
Heartsease. 2 vols. 12mo......................... Cloth, 2 00
The Daisy Chain; or, Aspirations. 2 vols. 12mo..... Cloth, 2 00
The Castle Builders. 12mo........................ Cloth, 1 00
Richard the Fearless.............................. Cloth, 75
The Two Guardians................................ Cloth, 1 00
Kenneth; or, the Rear Guard...................... Cloth, 1 00
Lances of Lynwood. 16mo......................... Cloth, 1 00
Dynevor Terrace; or, The Clue of Life. 2 vols......... Cloth, 2 00
Beechcroft. 12mo................ .... Cloth, 1 00
Hopes and Fears. 2 vols.......................... Cloth, 2 00
" " Cheap edition...................... Paper, 50
The Young Step-Mother. 2 vols..................... Cloth, 2 00

WORKS OF FICTION.

Grace Aguilar's Works.

The Mother's Recompense. 12mo....................Cloth, $1 00
Home Influence. 12mo..............................Cloth, 1 00
Women of Israel. 12mo.............................Cloth, 2 00
Vale of Cedars. 12mo..............................Cloth, 1 00
Woman's Friendship. 12mo..........................Cloth, 1 00
The Days of Bruce. 12mo. 2 vols...................Cloth, 2 00
Home Scenes and Heart Studies. 12mo...............Cloth, 1 00

Mrs. Cowden Clarke.

The Iron Cousin. A Tale. 12mo......................... 1 50

Mrs. Ellis' Works.

Hearts and Homes; or, Social Distinctions. 1 vol. 8vo...... 2 00

Julia Kavanagh's Works.

Adele: a Tale. 1 thick vol. 12mo..................Cloth, 1 50
Women of Christianity, Exemplary for Piety and Charity. 12mo...Cloth, 1 00
Nathalie: a Tale. 12mo............................Cloth, 1 25
Madeleine. 12mo...................................Cloth, 1 00
Daisy Burns. 12mo.................................Cloth, 1 25
Grace Lee...Cloth, 1 25
Rachel Gray. 12mo.................................Cloth, 1 00

Miss Macintosh's Works.

Woman in America. 12mo............................Cloth, 62
Two Lives; or, To Seem and To Be. 12mo............Cloth, 1 00
Aunt Kitty's Tales. 12mo..........................Cloth, 1 00
Charms and Counter Charms.........................Cloth, 1 25
Evenings at Donaldson Manor. 12mo.................Cloth, 1 00
The Lofty and Lowly. 2 vols. 12mo.................Cloth, 2 00
Meta Gray; or, What Makes Home Happy..............Cloth, 1 00

MODERN BRITISH ESSAYISTS,

COMPRISING

The Critical & Miscellaneous Works

OF

ALISON,	**CARLYLE,**
JEFFREY,	**MACAULAY,**
MACKINTOSH,	**SYDNEY SMITH,**
STEPHEN,	**TALFOURD,**

And Prof. WILSON.

In 8 vols., large 8vo., uniform Cloth, $13. Sheep, $17 Half Calf Ext., $25.

Each Volume to be had separately.

Alison's Essays.
Miscellaneous Essays. By ARCHIBALD ALISON, F. R. S. Reprinted from the English originals, with the author's corrections for this edition. 1 large vol. 8vo. Portrait. Cloth, $1 75; sheep, $2 25.

Carlyle's Essays.
Critical and Miscellaneous Essays. By THOMAS CARLYLE. Complete in one volume. 1 large vol. 8vo. Portrait. Cloth, $2,50; sheep, $3.

Jeffrey's Essays.
Contributions to the Edinburgh Review. By FRANCIS JEFFREY. The four volumes complete in one. 1 very large vol. 8vo. Portrait. Cloth, $2.50; sheep, $3.

Macaulay's Essays.
Essays, Critical and Miscellaneous. By T. BABINGTON MACAULAY. New and Revised edition. 1 very large vol. 8vo. Portrait. Cloth, $2.50; sheep, $3.

Mackintosh's Essays.
The Miscellaneous Works of the Right Honorable Sir JAMES MACKINTOSH. The three volumes in one. 1 vol. large 8vo. Portrait. Cloth, $2.50; sheep, $3.

Sydney Smith's Works.
The Works of the Rev. SYDNEY SMITH. Three volumes complete in one. 1 large vol. 8vo. Portrait. Cloth, $1 75; sheep, $2 25.

Talfourd's and Stephen's Essays.
Critical and Miscellaneous Writings of T. NOON TALFOURD, author of "Ion, &c. Critical and Miscellaneous Essays of JAMES STEPHEN. In 1 vol. large 8vo. Portrait. Cloth, $1 75; sheep, $2 25.

Wilson's Essays.
The Recreations of CHRISTOPHER NORTH [Prof. JOHN WILSON.] Complete in 1 vol. large 8vo. Portrait. Cloth, $1 75; sheep, $2 25.

www.ingramcontent.com/pod-product-compliance
Lightning Source LLC
LaVergne TN
LVHW020921110826
845150LV00004B/732

* 9 7 8 1 4 2 5 5 5 4 7 2 9 *